Sherlock Holmes

THE HIDDEN YEARS

Also by Michael Kurland

Sherlock Holmes Anthologies
My Sherlock Holmes

The Professor Moriarty novels
The Infernal Device
Death by Gaslight
The Great Game

The Alexander Brass novels
Too Soon Dead
The Girls in the High-Heeled Shoes

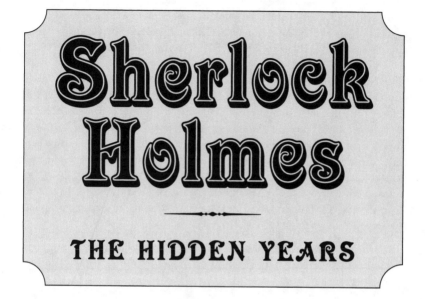

Sherlock Holmes

THE HIDDEN YEARS

Edited by

Michael Kurland

St. Martin's Minotaur

New York

"The Beast of Guangming Peak" copyright © 2004 by Michael Mallory. "Water from the Moon" copyright © 2004 by Carolyn Wheat. "Mr. Sigerson" copyright © 2004 by Peter Beagle. "The Mystery of Dr. Thorvald Sigerson" copyright © 2004 by Linda Robertson. "The Case of the Lugubrious Manservant" copyright © 2004 by Rhys Bowen. "The Bughouse Caper" copyright © 2004 by Bill Pronzini. "Reichenbach" copyright © 2004 by Michael Kurland. "The Strange Case of the Voodoo Priestess" copyright © 2004 by Carole Bugge. "The Adventure of the Missing Detective" copyright © 2004 by Gary Lovisi. "Cross of Gold" copyright © 2004 by Dennis Lynds. "God of the Naked Unicorn" (first appeared in *Fantastic* magazine, August 1976) copyright © 1976 by Richard Lupoff.

www.minotaurbooks.com

Design by Phil Mazzone

Library of Congress Cataloging-in-Publication Data

Sherlock Holmes—The hidden years / edited by Michael Kurland.
p. cm.
Contents: The case of the lugubrious manservant / by Rhys Bowen—Reichenback / by Michael Kurland—God of the naked unicorn / by Richard Lupoff—Mr. Sigerson / by Peter Beagle—The Beast of Guangming Peak / by Michael Mallory—Water from the moon / by Carolyn Wheat—The adventure of the missing detective / by Gary Lovisi—The mystery of Dr. Thorvald Sigerson / by Linda Robertson—The bughouse caper / by Bill Pronzini—The strange case of the voodoo priestess / by Carole Bugge—Cross of gold / by Michael Collins.
ISBN 0-312-31513-9
EAN 978-0312-31513-9

PR1309.H55S47 2004
813'.087208351—dc22

2004046802

First Edition: November 2004

10 9 8 7 6 5 4 3 2 1

I dedicate this book to the authors herein
and thank them for their imagination,
their wit, and their industry.

Contents

Contents

Sherlock Holmes

THE HIDDEN YEARS

Sherlock Holmes: The Hidden Years

An Introduction

Michael Kurland

I don't want to keep you from reading these wonderful stories any longer than necessary, really I don't. So just a few brief words to tell you what this book is all about.

This book is all about the world-famous consulting detective Sherlock Holmes. It chronicles, through the eyes of an assortment of different people, a series of adventures of the great detective that have not previously been presented to the public. Indeed, some of them his amanuensis Dr. John Watson knew nothing about. Holmes did so like having his little secrets.

There has been much speculation over the past century by those who speculate about such things as to what Sherlock Holmes did during the three years not chronicled by Watson; the so-called missing or hidden years. Or, as they have been termed by avid Sherlockians, the "Great Hiatus." For those of you not as familiar with the life of the famous consulting detective as you should be—and there will be a test in next week's class—let me explain.

In his memoir entitled "The Final Problem," written sometime in 1893, Dr. Watson writes:

> It is with a heavy heart that I take up my pen to write these the last words in which I shall ever record the singular

gifts by which my friend Mr. Sherlock Holmes was distinguished.

He goes on to tell us how, some two years earlier, Holmes had an encounter with his archenemy Professor James Moriarty at Reichenbach Falls in Switzerland, which resulted in the deaths of both Moriarty and Holmes, whom Watson describes as "the best and wisest man whom I have ever known."

But it turned out that the encomium was a bit premature, as was revealed in "The Adventure of the Empty House," where Holmes returns after a three-year absence, causing Watson to faint for the first time in his life when he turns and sees Holmes standing there. Holmes's excuse for keeping Watson in mourning for three years is inadequate, as is his relating of his experiences while he was gone:

> I traveled for two years in Tibet, therefore, and amused myself by visiting Lhassa and spending some days with the head Llama. You may have read of the remarkable explorations of a Norwegian named Sigerson, but I'm sure that it never occurred to you that you were receiving news of your friend. I then passed through Persia, looked in at Mecca, and paid a short but interesting visit to the Khalifa at Khartoum, the results of which I have communicated to the Foreign Office. Returning to France, I spent some months in a research into the coal-tar derivatives, which I conducted in a laboratory at Montpelier, in the south of France.

Let's look at a few of the problems. First, in "The Final Problem" Holmes describes Moriarty as "the Napoleon of crime." And yet Watson has never heard of him before. Holmes is ready to lay down his life to rid the world of this menace that he never bothered to mention to his best friend and biographer. Sure. The story begins when Holmes goes to Watson to tell him that he (Holmes) is in immediate danger of death by airgun. That Moriarty and his whole gang will be rounded up in a few days, but until that is accomplished Moriarty is gunning for him. So there is nothing for it but Holmes must flee the country and travel about Europe.

Now I ask you, if someone were trying to kill you, and you knew that he was to be arrested by the British police in a few days, would you skip over to Europe, knowing your enemy would follow, and thus put himself beyond the arrest warrants of Scotland Yard? Would you not, perhaps, spend a couple of days camped out on Lestrade's couch in his Scotland Yard office until the arrest was accomplished?

And then Holmes puts on one of his clever disguises to meet Watson on the Continental Express. Watson, of course, is not disguised, indeed could not successfully wear a disguise if his life depended on it. Are we to believe that it would never occur to Moriarty or his henchmen to follow Watson if they lost track of Holmes?

There are more problems with the story Watson relates in "The Final Problem," but we must assume that Watson believed what he was told and that any chicanery was purely Holmes's. I leave it for you to find the logical inconsistencies with the note, the stick, and the fight itself. I will now skip lightly over to "The Adventure of the Empty House," and we shall examine the holes in Holmes's explanation of where he had been for those three years.

> *I traveled for two years in Tibet, therefore, and amused myself by visiting Lhassa and spending some days with the head Llama.*

Which was a good trick, as the nearest *llamas*, head or otherwise, were some 3,000 miles away in South America. For, as Ogden Nash pointed out: "The two-l llama, he's a beast." Holmes, if he was there at all, was communing with the one-l, or priestly, version of the genus Lama.

There's also the fact that, when in 1903 a British expedition headed by Lieutenant Colonel Younghusband forced its way into Lhassa, there was no mention of a Norwegian named Sigerson or any other European ever having been in the holy city before.

> *You may have read of the remarkable explorations of a Norwegian named Sigerson, but I'm sure that it never occurred to you that you were receiving news of your friend.*

And why should it have? Nowhere in the chronicles of Holmes's adventures except at this one damned spot is there any indication that Holmes spoke Norwegian.

> *I then passed through Persia, looked in at Mecca, and paid a short
> but interesting visit to the Khalifa at Khartoum, the results of which
> I have communicated to the Foreign Office.*

It must have been an interesting visit indeed, for Khartoum had
been captured and destroyed by Mahdists (a religious sect who believed that their leader, one Muhammad Ahmad, was the Mahdi
[Messiah], but had no sense of humor about it) back in 1885. Six
months after the sack of Khartoum the Mahdi died of typhus and,
after a short tussle among various interest groups, Abdallahi ibn
Muhammad, called the Khalifa (successor), took control of the
Mahdists, ruling from the town of Omdurman. On September 2,
1898, Herbert (later Lord) Kitchener overthrew the Khalifa, in a
pitched battle before Omdurman, and the Khalifa was killed in another battle at Umm Diwaykarat in November of 1899.

> *Returning to France, I spent some months in a research into the
> coal-tar derivatives, which I conducted in a laboratory at Montpe-
> lier, in the south of France.*

Montpelier is the capital of Vermont. Montpellier is a city in
the south of France.

"It is an old maxim of mine that when you have excluded the impossible, whatever remains, however improbable, must be the truth,"
Holmes says in "The Beryl Coronet." And again, in "The Boscombe
Valley Mystery," he tells Watson, "You know my method. It is
founded upon the observance of trifles."

So what can we glean from these, admittedly trifling, mistakes
in Watson's, or Holmes's, narrative? Merely that Holmes told Watson a fanciful tale, designed to assuage Watson's curiosity, but bearing scant relation to the truth.

"What is truth?" asked Pontius Pilate. We'll try not to get so
metaphysical here. The truth of where Holmes spent those missing
years may lie within this book; or perhaps it's just a collection of rol-
licking good tales, no more or less truthful than the story Holmes
told Watson.

Einstein showed us* that what we perceive as the passage of time is determined by our frame of reference. So if some of these stories seem to have happened both before and after each other, it's merely because each author had a different frame of reference. The stories put Holmes in the Himalayas, in Thailand, in the Duchy of Bornitz, in New York, San Francisco, New Orleans, above the Arctic Circle, and some even less likely places. They are worthy additions to the Holmes universe, and I am proud to present them to you here.

Read and enjoy!
Michael Kurland
Somewhere near Reichenbach Falls,
January 2004

---

* You have to admit that this is the first time you've seen the names Einstein and Pontius Pilate within one paragraph of each other. Pretty impressive, eh?

The Beast of Guangming Peak

Michael Mallory

"Wake up, Colonel Mackay, it's time for dinner," the nurse said, gently shaking the elderly, wheelchair-bound man out of a snoring sleep. The man's sunken eyes opened, and he looked up at her. *A right cutey*, was the first thought that passed through his mind, *almost an angel—and she fancies me to boot*. Mentally, Colin Mackay reckoned himself to be about thirty-eight. Physically, however, he was seventy-seven years old, and felt every day of it. *At least I still have my dreams*, he thought. Even a wheelchair could not slow down his dreams. He smiled at her, revealing his ten remaining teeth, and she gave him a dimpled smile back. "What did I miss, Cynthia?" he asked.

"Nothing, Colonel, but it's time for dinner, though I'm afraid we don't have meat today."

"No matter," Mackay muttered, straightening himself up in his wheelchair and wincing from the pain in his right hip, which he had broken two years earlier. "I've been through worse."

Cynthia stepped around behind the chair and pushed him into the dining room of the retirement home, where the table was already set. Nine other military pensioners were seated there, all from various wars, though none of them went as far back as the Boer conflict, which was Mackay's first taste of gunpowder. As usual, some of the men were grumbling over the failings of the menu.

"Damnable war's been over for seven years and still no meat," said Glendower, an army man, who was always complaining about something. "I just hope I live long enough to see the end of these shortages."

Rooney, late of the Royal Air Force, said, "Ah, there could be an entire corned beef in front of you, and you'd still spend so much time complaining that you'd miss it entirely!"

Some of the men laughed, one uttered, "hear, hear," and Glendower simply snorted and turned away. But the banter at the table ceased when Mackay settled behind the head of the table. "Good evening, Colonel," they each said, in recognition of the fact that he was the highest-ranking man among them.

"Good evening, lads," Mackay returned, and dinner commenced.

After the meal was finished, Mackay was the first to be moved away from the table, as always. Cynthia pushed him back into the sitting room, close to the crackling fire. It was December, and the staff of the home had begun to hang up Christmas decorations.

December 1951, the old man mused . . . King George VI, the great-grandson of the sovereign who had ruled during Mackay's first twenty-eight years and who had lent her name to an age, and in whose name Mackay had first picked up a rifle and bayonet, now sat on the throne. Her *great-grandson*. Mackay could hardly believe it. He had been through three different wars and had escaped more bullets than any man ever had a right to. He had been in and out of more scrapes in his life than most men would have thought possible, and still he had managed to last into the start of the second half of the twentieth century. Certainly it was a bother and a burden to have lost the ability to walk, but the fact that he was here at all, when so many of his compatriots had fallen, was little short of astounding.

"Would you like the newspaper, Colonel?" Cynthia asked, handing him a copy of that day's London *Times*. Mackay always got first crack at the paper, which was not an elaborate courtesy, since only two or three of the other pensioners ever bothered to read it. The old man pulled out a pair of glasses from his sweater pocket and flipped through the pages, finding it hard to develop interest in what the Bank of England was forecasting for the new year economically, or what Winston Churchill had to say about the chances of the cease-fire talks in Korea. He was about to fold the section up when a photograph on page twelve suddenly caught his eye. Reading the text underneath it, he muttered, "Crikey."

"Did you want something, Colonel?" Cynthia asked.

"My dear, could you get me closer to the light, please?" he asked, and the young nurse complied, wheeling him closer to the table and lamp, which allowed him to see the photograph more clearly.

The photo had been taken by Eric Shipton, who was mountaineering through the Himalayas alongside a chap named Michael Ward. It showed an enormous footprint, vaguely human in shape, but the length of an ax head, one of which had been placed next to the print in the photo for comparison. What struck Mackay about the print, though, was not the size but the fact that it appeared to have only four toes. "Good God," he uttered.

He reread the accompanying article, more slowly this time, his mind barely able to contain the news that was being offered: the footprint, according to the *Times*, was the most conclusive proof yet of the existence of the *mirka*, the *metoh*, the *kang-mi*, the *yeti*, or, as it had come to be known in the Western world, the Abominable Snowman.

As he continued to stare at the photo, the room began to turn cool. The Christmas decorations faded from view and the hardwood floors turned white and powdery. His lungs began to ache, and he seemed to have to fight for every breath. He was a young man again, a mere nineteen years old, fit as a bull, and possessing a mouthful of hard, white teeth. He walked through the freezing cold with the powerful legs of an athlete.

He was on the mountain again. On the mountain. Once more facing the danger . . .

Colin Mackay could no longer feel his legs, which was not a good sign. While still a relative novice at climbing, he had nonetheless seen a number of men succumb to the suddenness of frostbite and vowed that it would not happen to him. He was not about to part with a precious limb before his twentieth birthday. But he could not deny the numbness . . . no, it was not even numbness, it was the total absence of feeling, an emptiness of sensation as pronounced as the total deprivation of color that stretched as far as he could see in every direction. White . . . nothing but white. *Keep moving*, he commanded himself, forcing his lungs consciously to measure every cold, fire-stinging breath, and keeping his mind alert by running Gilbert and Sullivan songs forward and backward in his mind. When the point came that he was no longer able to concentrate on *precisely what was meant by commissariat*, Mackay would know that the mountain had won.

But he would not succumb easily, not while there was a fragment of thought in his mind or a cubic inch of oxygen in his body.

How in blazes had he managed to lose all contact with the others? How long had he been trudging through the snow and wind without the benefit of a compass, desperately hoping to find any sign that would tell him that he was in proximity to the rest of the expedition? How far away was the camp?

Far enough for your legs to lose all feeling, he thought grimly.

"No," he spoke, expelling a precious breath. There had to be a way back. He had been no more than ten minutes away from the camp when the wind had suddenly gusted, knocking him over, whiting out his vision, and covering over any tracks that he had made with blown snow. From that moment on, Mackay was effectively lost. Why had he been the one ordered to go out and track down the source of the mysterious cry they had all heard, a howl so eerie and foreboding that he could not believe Foss's judgment that it came from a lost sled dog? Why had not Foss been sent out? He was the more experienced mountaineer, after all. But it had been he, Mackay, whom the captain had sent, and the captain was in charge.

He continued on, though his steps became more labored. Finally he knelt and packed the snow around his legs, praying that, somehow, that would allow the feeling to return. He had heard other mountaineers talk about packing a frostbitten limb in ice, and could not imagine how that would work, but it was better than doing nothing.

As he sat there, quoting *the fights historical from Marathon to Waterloo in order categorical,* Colin Mackay suddenly had the terrible feeling that he had gone mad. How else could one explain the thin stream of black smoke that appeared out of nowhere in the distance? At first he thought it had to be his imagination, or worse, a hallucination announcing the beginnings of a seizure caused by altitude sickness. But as he watched, there was no mistaking the curl of the line of smoke. Someone, somewhere, up ahead, was burning something!

Mackay began to trot toward the line of smoke, never letting it out of his sight, refusing to succumb to a whiteout again, drinking in each breath and holding it as long as he could to prevent himself from panting and wasting oxygen. He still had no feeling in his legs, but they continued to move at his command. He would make the site of the smoke or die trying, he thought, and Colin Mackay had no desire to die trying.

He was close enough now to smell the smoke—though perhaps that was an olfactory hallucination. No . . . no, it had to be real. And there was another smell now . . . God in heaven, it was coffee! He refocused his entire being on that coffee, imaging the taste, the sublime bitterness, the heat in his stomach. He imagined pouring a cup of it on his legs, if that was what it took to restore the feeling.

Closer, he saw that the smoke was coming out of what looked like a cave. *Sherpa?* he wondered. He did not know much about the tribal people who inhabited the mountainous regions of Nepal and Tibet, but he had always heard that they were village dwellers, not cave dwellers. When he was close enough to the opening, Mackay called, "Hellooooo!" and waited. Still trotting, he was about to call again, when he saw a figure emerge from the cave.

"Hello," the figure called back. A British voice; a countryman. Mackay began to run outright now, run toward the smoke, the cof- fee, the figure of the tall, lean, bearded man dressed in some kind of skin-and-fur parka. And when the man and the cave opening were close enough to touch, he fell, and all went dark.

Colin Mackay's next sensation was one of warmth—warmth and a million needles in his legs, stinging him, as though he had im- mersed the lower half of his body in a beehive. Opening his eyes, he realized he was lying inside somewhere, out of the cold and wind, next to a fire, under a pile of blankets and furs. Leaping up, he began doing a strange sort of dance, alternately appreciating and disdain- ing the pinpricks in his legs.

"You were very nearly frostbitten," a voice said, and Colin turned to see the bearded man. He was inside the cave, he realized. Shadows from the fire pit danced over the jagged walls around him.

"And I'm paying for it now," Mackay said, continuing his dance. "Crikey, that stings!"

"The tingling will go away soon, Mr. Mackay."

"How do you know my name?"

"That was quite an obvious deduction. When we brought you in here I removed your coat and saw the tag inside, on which your name was stitched. Less obvious, but still discernible, were the facts that you are left-handed and that your father has recently died. Please accept my condolences."

"My father . . . how could you possibly know that?"

"Upon removing your coat a watch fell out. It is a good watch, but rather old and worn. More to the point, it is inscribed with the initials 'P. MACK,' which differs just enough from the name in your coat—'C. MACKAY'—as to imply a relative, most likely a father. And the simple fact you possess the watch indicates that it was part of an inheritance, unless you are a thief, a possibility that I immediately discounted since a thief would be far more likely to sell or pawn the object he stole, not carry it up the side of a mountain."

Mackay's legs now felt more or less normal, though his mind was reeling. "All right, but how did you know my father died recently?"

"For the same reason as you are not a thief," the man said. "One does not carry a keepsake such as this on an expedition in the Himalayas unless one's personal attachment to it as an artifact is stronger than the probability that it will very likely be broken or lost in the snow, particularly when carried loose in a pocket. The kind of sentiment betrayed by that rather illogical act implies that you are still mourning your father and wanted to have something of his with you at all times, which implies that his passing must have happened quite recently, and again, my condolences."

"Thank you," Mackay muttered, "it happened three months ago." Then: "Just a second: a moment ago you said 'we'—'we brought you in here'—but I don't see anyone else in the cave. Who is with you?"

"My guide, Chatang. He is a Sherpa from the village near Rongbuk. I asked him to look outside to see if he could find the journal you have been keeping, which was not on you, but which might have told us more about you and where you came from."

"It is back at camp . . . hold on, how could you possibly know I keep a journal?"

A small, satisfied smile broke through the man's thick beard, which was strangely of a reddish brown hue, in contrast to his black hair. "When I removed your gloves, I noticed a trace of graphite on the tip of the middle finger of your left hand, a sign that you have been writing with a pencil—quite sensible, since ink up here would freeze. The mark is pronounced enough to indicate that you have been writing quite a lot, certainly more than simply a letter, more like daily entries in a journal. Since the smudge was on your left hand, I knew that you must be left-handed."

"Crikey," Mackay muttered. "Who are you?"

"I am called Greison," the man said, extending a hand, which looked thin and delicate, but betrayed surprising strength when Mackay shook it. "Would you care for some coffee?"

"The very thought of it is what got me here."

As Greison picked up a blackened pan filled with strong, hot liquid off the fire pit, the Sherpa Chatang returned to the cave. Greison spoke to him in what Mackay could only assume was Tibetan, and the native merely nodded and sat down by the fire. Then turning to Mackay, Greison explained, "I asked his forgiveness for sending him out into the cold needlessly, as the journal in question is back at your camp."

"You apologized to a servant?" Mackay asked, puzzled.

"I said Chatang was my guide, not my servant." Greison poured the steaming, aromatic black liquid from a battered pot into a tin cup and handed it to Mackay, who wrapped both hands around and sipped with great satisfaction.

"How is the coffee?" Greison asked.

"Absolutely terrible," Mackay answered, "and indescribably wonderful."

In the flickering light of the fire, Mackay was able to examine the man who had become his savior against the harsh, unforgiving mountain. Probably no more than forty, Greison was lean to the point of being almost skeletal, and his face showed a deep tan, not much lighter, in fact, than the Sherpa's, which implied he had been on the mountain for some time, braving the powerful sunlight that bounced off the surface of the white snow. Startlingly clear grey eyes shone out as though lit from behind.

"Are you with a party?" Mackay asked.

Greison reached a stick into the fire and used it to light a long-stemmed clay pipe. "We are on a mission to find someone," he said, "another Sherpa, who according to his family is helping to guide the expedition of a certain Sir George Lennox."

"Crikey!" Mackay cried. "Captain Lennox! That's my expedition!"

Greison eyed the young man. "Indeed? Then we are closer than I thought." Turning to Chatang, he related something in the native tongue, then turned back to Mackay. "You must know the man we are seeking, then. His name is Nimu."

"Oh, good Lord," Mackay said. "I knew Nimu, yes."

"*Knew* him?"

"Yes, I'm afraid he's dead."

Greison frowned, cast a glance toward his Sherpa companion, and said something softly to him. Chatang stiffened, then bowed his head, and Greison placed a hand on the Sherpa's shoulder. "What are the details of his death?" he asked Mackay.

The young man coughed and hesitated before answering. "Well, sir, it appears that he was killed by a yeti."

At the sound of the word, Chatang's eyes widened, and he turned to Greison with a look of alarm.

"Did you say a yeti?" Greison asked.

"That's what the captain said. About four days ago, Captain Lennox and Nimu set out on their own for Bei Peak, leaving Foss and me at the camp. Foss is the other member of our party. The captain told us that if they made it to the top, he would come back and lead the rest of us up, but until he knew that the summit could be reached, he considered it too dangerous to take the entire party. They made it to the top of the peak, all right, but on the way back down, the captain said that they heard an ungodly howl, then this creature appeared. The captain described it as close to seven feet tall and completely covered with yellowish hair. Since they had no weapons with them, all they could do was try to get away from it, but the thing caught Nimu and . . . well, he dragged the poor bugger away while the captain watched, helpless. All he was able to bring back was one of Nimu's boots. The captain was badly shaken, I can tell you, and it takes a lot to shake Sir George Lennox. In fact, that was the reason he sent me out last night following that horrible cry. He was afraid it was the yeti coming back. I got lost looking for it."

"Hearing what happened to Nimu, how fortunate that you did not find it."

"Right." Mackay then realized the full implications of what the older mountaineer had said, and added, "Crikey, I never thought about that."

"I must tell Chatang of this incident." Turning to the Sherpa, Greison began to speak in the strange language. Mackay could make out the words *Lennox, Nimu, Bei* and of course *yeti*. Whatever else the Englishman was saying, it appeared to Mackay to upset the native guide, so much so that he began to talk back, appearing, even, to argue. Mackay had never before seen a Sherpa argue with a white man, but Greison kept talking, more soothingly now, and eventually he managed to calm the native down. Chatang cast a dark glance at Mackay, then got up and moved to a far corner of the cave.

"What was all that about?" Mackay asked.

"He is naturally upset," Greison answered. "Nimu was his brother."

"His brother? Oh, I'm sorry. Why were you looking for him in the first place?"

"Family matters in the village." Then Greison raised his head, closed his eyes and tented his fingers together into a steeple, and showed all signs of going to sleep sitting up.

"Um, good night, then," Mackay said, then finished his coffee and slipped back over to the makeshift bed Greison had made for him and slid between the blankets and fur skins, exhausted by the events of the day.

When Mackay awoke the next morning, he felt surprisingly refreshed. Greison and Chatang were already up and appeared to be preparing to venture out onto the mountain. Mackay was startled at how little gear they had between them. Crawling out from under the blankets, he walked to the mouth of the cave and saw bright sunshine and no trace of the storm that had gotten him lost.

"In one sense it was an ill wind that blew you to us, Mr. Mackay," Greison said, tapping out the bowl of his pipe, "but in another sense, it was our great fortune. When you are ready, we will set out to find your party."

"Right," Mackay said, venturing out into the cold just enough to get a handful of snow, which he rubbed onto his face, chasing away any lingering sleep that was left on him. Rushing back in to get his coat, he saw that Greison was writing something in chalk on the wall of the cave. *S. Greison-Rimpoche Chatang, May 1892*, it read. Mackay studied the name, then the truth dawned upon him. "Crikey, I've just realized who you are!" he cried.

The older man turned to him. "Have you indeed?"

Stepping up to the cave wall, Mackay took the chalk. "That night's sleep must have cleared my head," he said. "Look: if you rearrange the letters of *S. Greison*, you get this." He wrote *Sigerson* on the stone wall. "You're Sigerson! You're the one everybody's been talking about. They say you rescued a party of six men after they'd been trapped by an avalanche."

"If they had listened to me beforehand and taken a different route, they never would have gotten trapped in the first place," Greison answered.

"Hey, you're supposed to be Norwegian. How come you speak without an accent?"

"My dear Mackay," Greison replied, with a whisper of a smile, "when I speak with Chatang I do so without an accent as well. With the proper attention and study, any language can be mastered without an accent. As for my name, now that you have discovered it, I hope you will keep it to yourself. As you have pointed out, everyone is talking about Sigerson, and that fact infinitely complicates one's passing through camps inconspicuously." Using the sleeve of his coat, Greison rubbed the chalk word *Sigerson* from the cave wall.

"You're a rare one, if you don't mind my saying so," Mackay said. "Every other mountaineer is up here because we *want* to do something that will make the rest of the world talk about us. You sound like you're trying to avoid it."

"My dear Mackay, I am not so much trying to avoid it as ignoring it. Might I suggest that you visit one of the several lamaseries in this region. They are quite open to Western visitors. It is, in fact, my opinion that all men who wish to conquer the Himalayas should do so. It does wonders for the outlook. Now, then, are you coming with us or not?"

"Coming, coming," Mackay said, buttoning his coat and following the two out into the cold.

The view from the mouth of cave was one of unending white. Greison pulled a collapsible telescope from his pocket and scanned the wide horizon. "How long had you been walking before you came upon the cave?" he asked. "An hour? More than an hour?"

"About an hour," Mackay answered, shielding his eyes from the blinding sun, "though it was hard to tell."

"Pity you didn't use your pocket watch. During the trek, did it seem like you were going uphill or downhill?"

"It was all pretty straight and level, at least until I got close to the cave."

"Straight and level," he muttered, surveying the ocean of snow and white. "Ah! That way, if I'm not mistaken." Chatang took the lead as the three of them headed off for what to Mackay looked like an infinity of white.

Within an hour, however, the tents were sighted. "I'll be damned," Mackay said, "that's the camp, all right!"

When they had gotten within hailing distance, a Sherpa guide from the camp approached, and when he saw Mackay, he ran into the largest of the tents, emerging moments later with a large man with a thick thatch of dark blond hair that tumbled over his weathered brow and an unruly beard beginning to grey. "By God, Mackay," George Lennox's voice echoed across the glacier. "We'd given you up for lost! Get over here!"

They made their way to the tent, where Lennox greeted Mackay like a stern father. "What the devil happened to you, boy?" he demanded. "I should have sent Foss, he has a better sense of direction."

A small, rugged, bulldoggish man emerged from another tent, and when he spotted Mackay, he grinned broadly, and cried, "Well, the prodigal has returned!" He rushed up to welcome him, though not as expansively.

Eyeing Greison, Lennox said, "I imagine you are the one who found him?"

"Actually, Mr. Mackay found us. My name is Greison."

"Sir George Lennox, Mr. Greison, and this is Patrick Foss," he said, gesturing to the smaller mountaineer. Then he glanced at Chatang, standing behind. "You've brought your own pack mule, I see."

"I presume you are speaking about my traveling companion?"

"Call them what you like, they're still the best pack mules you can find. Damn things seem to produce their own oxygen from the inside"

"Speaking of inside, might we avail ourselves of a tent?" Greison asked.

"By all means, come in and have a drink. Foss, have you checked the supplies yet?"

"Not yet, Captain," Foss said. "I was about to do it."

"Be about it, then. Greison, your Sherpa can help out my mules."

"As you wish," Greison said. Then, turning to Chatang, he uttered a few words in Tibetan and watched as the man went off toward the other guides, who were presently inspecting the climbing ropes. Lennox, meanwhile, opened the heavy canvas tent flap and ushered Greison and Mackay inside. In the center of the tent was a folding table, piled with maps and papers, which were held in place by a severed and preserved red bear's paw. "Sit down," Lennox said, gesturing to the three folding stools set around the table. He picked up a small duffel from the corner and pulled from it a bottle of brandy and a ram's horn filled with cigarettes. Finding three small jars, he poured the drinks and offered the two cigarettes. "I'm eager to hear about Mackay's adventure getting lost on the mountain."

Mackay told as much of the tale as he could, explaining how he had used Gilbert and Sullivan songs to focus his concentration. When he had finished, Greison supplied the details of how he and Chatang had pulled the unconscious young man into the cave.

"By God," Lennox said, with a hearty laugh, "that is probably the only time anyone was ever saved by the *Pirates of Penzance*. I'll have to remember that and bone up on the scores. I was never much for theater in my youth, certainly not operettas, though I used to play a little bugle. I don't suppose that counts for much, though." He refilled Greison's and Mackay's jars and poured a third for himself, then raised it in a toast. "Here's to you, boy, the one who fought off frostbite with Gilbert and bloody Sullivan."

"Now that we have heard the boy's story," Greison said, "there is one I would very much like to hear from you, Sir George. I understand you lost a man on the mountain."

Lennox gulped his brandy. "Well, not man, exactly, just one of the blasted Sherpas. But yes, I lost him to a yeti. Now, you might say that yetis are nothing but the stuff of legend, but George Lennox will put you right, because I saw it with my own eyes. Christ, I'll never forget its cry . . . a sound so terrible that you can't imagine that a flesh-and-blood creature could make it. It was like it wasn't an animal at all, but some sort of spawn of Hell. I promise you, Greison, you've never heard anything like that cry."

"Actually, I may have, once. It turned out to be a very large hound."

"This was no dog. It was a beast. I saw the hate in its yellow eyes. I saw what it did to the Sherpa. I suppose the boy here told you I sent him out when I heard the sound again last night."

"He did," Greison said, sipping the brandy. "And it was the same cry?"

"The same cry," Lennox replied. "I hope you're not going to try and convince me it was one of my sled dogs, like Foss attempted to do."

"Not at all. I understand that the incident happened on Bei Peak."

Lennox nodded and poured himself another drink. "Coming back down from the peak."

"On the north side? You did take the north route, I presume?"

"Of course. And yes, the attack happened on the north side."

"It is quite a distance from here to Bei Peak," Greison mused. "Could the creature really have come all that way?"

"Crikey, if the thing is stalking us," Mackay said, "maybe we should pack up and move somewhere else?"

"No, we'll stay here, at least for the time being," Lennox said. "We'll just keep a good watch. Besides, as close as you came to frostbite, you should probably rest a bit before your next long trek. Give your legs the chance to recover fully."

"Thank you, sir. I was quite worried for a while, when my legs lost all feeling."

"I know how that is," Lennox responded, and began unlacing his boot. As his two guests watched, he removed both the boot and his heavy wool sock, and lifted his bare left foot up for them to see. The second toe, the one nearest the big toe, was missing.

"It happened five years ago, while I was in the Arctic Circle," Lennox told them. "I came down with frostbite and didn't even know it. It's not like you're normally conscious of your tall toe, so when the feeling goes away, you don't even notice it. But then the feeling in my entire foot started to go away." George Lennox wiggled his remaining four toes and grinned conspiratorially. "Now I'll show you something I've rarely shown to anyone." He lowered his foot, reached into the pocket of his jacket, and pulled something out, which he set on the table.

"Crikey," Mackay muttered.

"A good luck charm?" Greison asked.

"More of a reminder," Lennox said, picking up the black, desiccated human toe and studying it. "It's a reminder to know my limits and never do anything foolish while on a mountain." Then he picked up the bear's paw paperweight from the table. "At least I fared better than this fellow," he said, laughing. "I shot the owner of this some years back and kept his paw as another reminder."

"Of what?" Greison asked.

"To hold steadfast and keep courage."

The wind suddenly came up again, buffeting the tent walls as Lennox put his sock and boot back on. Chatang appeared in the doorway and motioned for Greison, who got up and quietly conversed with him for a moment, then returned to the table, as the Sherpa disappeared as quickly as he had arrived.

"In light of the wind, would it be too much of an imposition if we were to stay here for the evening?" Greison asked. "Chatang tells me that there is space in the Sherpa tent, and I am certain I could make do somewhere."

"By all means, stay here," Lennox said. "I would hate to have turned a man away during a storm, never to see him again. Perhaps you could bunk in Mackay's tent, since you're old friends now."

"Excellent," Greison said.

Mackay finished his drink, and said, "Poor Chatang seems to be taking the news of his brother's death well at any rate."

Lennox crushed the butt of his cigarette. "His brother? You mean your Sherpa is the brother of Nimu?"

"I am afraid so," Greison said. "It's a small world, isn't it?"

"Hmm. Were they close?"

"They were brothers. There is always a bond between brothers, no matter how aloof they might appear to those around them. The reason we are here on the mountain was to track down Nimu and bring him back to the village."

"Why? What did he do?"

"He did nothing," Greison said. "But I am afraid his mother has died. We were coming to get him because of that, Chatang and I."

"Crikey," Mackay said. "I know what it's like to lose a parent. But to lose your mother and your brother just like that . . ."

"It is a tragedy," Greison agreed.

"How did you even know where to look for Nimu?" Lennox asked.

"Oh, that was no problem. We already knew that Nimu had signed on with your expedition. He told his brother as much before leaving. Then it became a question of discovering your whereabouts on the mountain. Even though we were not far away, it was fortuitous that Mackay stumbled into the cave we had been using as shelter."

Lennox lit another cigarette and took in as much smoke as his lungs would accept in the high altitude. "Did Nimu tell his brother anything else about me?"

"I have no idea," Greison replied. "What should he have told him?"

"Oh, maybe that I pay more for guides than anyone else on the mountain. I offer five rupees a day, which is twice what these Tibetan dogs will get from anyone else. I would hate for that to become common knowledge among the pack mules, because then I would be swarmed by them, all begging for guide jobs, no matter what their proficiency on a climb."

"You seem to take a dim view of the native people here, Sir George."

"They are what they are," he replied. "They have a certain amount of knowledge about climbing, and they have whatever odd mutancy it is that allows them to thrive on little oxygen, but they have neither the inclination nor the intelligence to give orders to others. You do not see a Sherpa leading an expedition, do you? No, because they cannot. They are followers. Pack mules. But I will give you this: if I can find the right one to support me, George Lennox will go down in history as the first man to stand atop Everest."

The wind was picking up, and Lennox stood. "I'd better make certain that the dogs are properly kenneled," he said. "I hope my camp will prove comfortable for you, Greison. It's not Buckingham Palace, but it's better than freezing to death."

"I am certain it will be more than sufficient."

"I have work to do," Lennox said. "Feel free to remain in here for a while if you like, but leave some of the brandy. Oh, and there's one other rule here, and that is that this is my camp and my expedition, and in my expeditions, the Sherpas don't come into the men's tents. I'll thank you to abide by that, Greison."

"I will remember."

"Right," Sir George Lennox said, and putting his fur-lined hood up over his head, he slipped through the door flap.

"Just imagine, Everest!" Mackay was saying. "I'd like to be in that party."

"I think it is highly unlikely that any man will stand atop the world's highest peak," Greison said, "at least not in my lifetime."

"Oh, I'd put my money on the captain to do it. They said Guangming Peak couldn't be conquered either, but he did it, just last year. The Queen was so impressed she knighted him for it."

"But Guangming is not Everest. Besides, there are the mountain gods to contend with. I daresay they would not like to be disturbed."

"Now you're having a go at me because I'm just an apprentice mountaineer," Mackay charged, "but I don't spook easily. And I don't believe in the local superstitions."

"My dear young friend, to paraphrase a playwright even more insightful than Gilbert and Sullivan, there are more things in heaven and earth than are dreamt of in your philosophy."

"Well, I'll stick with my philosophy for the time being."

"As you wish," Greison said, rising from the table. "As long as we are here, let us see if there is some way in which we can help out in the camp."

Throughout the day the two helped to prepare the camp against the likelihood of another powerful storm, and on several occasions, Mackay saw Greison slip over to where Chatang was and engage him in brief conversations. Shortly before the evening meal, Greison spoke with all three of the Sherpas. Mackay said nothing at the time, but later, inside their tent, after the sun had gone down, taking a break from penciling notes in his journal, he broached the subject to Greison. "You're not planning something, are you?" he asked.

The inside of the tent was illuminated only by the red glow of Greison's cigarette. "Whatever do you mean?"

"You've spent a good part of the day talking with the Sherpas. I'm not the only one who noticed. I saw the captain watching you like a bird of prey. You're not planning on . . . I don't know . . . inciting a revolt, or anything like that, are you?"

"Sherpas are not of a revolutionary nature, my friend. Even if I wanted to, I doubt I could spark something so dramatic as that."

"Then what are you doing?"

"I merely asked them to keep watch."

"Watch over what?"

"Over the reappearance of the yeti, of course."

"I hope I never have to face a thing like that," Mackay declared. "Hearing it was bad enough."

Greison suddenly sat up on his cot. "Since you have brought the matter up, how would you describe the sound that you heard last night, before you ventured out into the storm?"

"It was just like the captain described: eerie, almost unearthly."

"Was it something like this?" Placing one hand over his mouth, Greison began to make a startling, high-pitched cry, which echoed through the tent, prompting Mackay to leap up from his cot as though given an electric jolt. "That's it! That's it exactly! You've heard it too!"

"I have heard it, all right, but it is not a yeti. I was imitating a snow leopard. Under the right circumstances, their howl can indeed sound unearthly."

"It was nothing but a snow leopard we heard then?"

"There is no reason to sound disappointed, Mackay. A snow leopard is still a formidable threat."

"It's not that, it's just—"

His words were interrupted suddenly by the sound of a wail coming from somewhere outside. Mackay started to speak but Greison hushed him. The sound came again, the bone-chilling, pitiful howl of a beast somewhere near the camp. Another sound then rent the night: the collective panicked shouts of a half dozen men. That was followed by a scream.

Immediately, Greison and Mackay were up and threw on their coats and boots, and ran outside. Foss was already there, lighting a torch, though it was nearly too cold for fire. Then George Lennox appeared, crying, "What happened!"

"We don't know yet," said Foss.

"Check the Sherpas' tent," Greison called, and the men ran there, only to find a large, jagged rip in the canvas wall.

"Crikey!"

"Look at this, Captain!" Foss lowered his torch to the snow, revealing a trail of blood. Following it, they quickly came upon one of the Sherpas, lying facedown in the snow. "Don't touch him, he might still be alive!" Lennox said, kneeling to examine the prone figure. After a few moments, though, he looked to the others and shook his head. Then he rolled the body over. The sight of the Sherpa's face seemed to shock George Lennox. "Good God, it's Ang!"

"Aye, and look at him," Foss said, wincing.

The Sherpa's face had been slashed as though by the claws of an enormous animal.

"Is anyone else missing?" Greison asked.

Foss quickly surveyed the party and said, "The other two Sherpas are here."

"But I don't see Chatang anywhere," Mackay said.

"Maybe the blasted thing got him, too," Foss said.

"Are there any more torches here?" Greison asked.

"Aye, over there." Foss led the rest to a supply box and pulled out and lit two more torches.

"Are we to look for Chatang, then?" Mackay asked.

"Yes, but also look for footprints," Greison said.

"What kind of footprints?"

"Any that you can find. Mackay, Foss, you check over there. I will look in this direction."

The three of them set off in different directions from the camp, their torches burning holes of light in the dark frigid night. Lennox, meanwhile, was instructing the two remaining Sherpas to pull the body of Ang out and away from the camp. But they refused to touch it, which angered the expedition leader.

"Ang can't hurt you!" Lennox barked. "Move him the hell out of here, or else that thing will come back into the camp to get it, and maybe you, too!" Still they refused to touch it. "I know you dogs speak the Queen's English well enough to know what I'm saying, so what's wrong with you? Move! Move now, or I'll . . ." Lennox raised his hand to strike the closest one, but at that moment Greison appeared behind him and grabbed his arm, restraining it. Lennox growled, "What the hell do you think you're doing? Let go of me!"

"Hitting them will do no good," Greison said.

"I will not have my authority challenged on this expedition, not by them, and not by you!"

"The reason they are disobeying you is because they want to say a *mani* over the body before moving it."

"A what?"

Greison let go of Lennox's arm. "A prayer."

"A prayer," Lennox repeated, "like they've got a soul? Ha! They're two-legged yaks, nothing more."

"If you want the body moved, I'm afraid you will have to let them have their way."

Casting a cold gaze from Greison to the guides and back, Lennox spat, "Be quick about it, then."

The two Sherpas nodded to Greison and began to chant something over the remains of their friend.

"What about that coolie of yours?" Lennox demanded of Greison. "Has he been found yet?"

"Not yet, though I am certain we shall see him again."

"Not if the snowman gets him first."

"It is my opinion that the snowman would be foolish to try."

"What the hell is that supposed to mean?"

Just then Mackay ran up, panting precious spouts of breath and holding his blazing torch high. "No sign of footprints," he gasped.

"Never run in this altitude, boy," Lennox said. "Haven't you learned anything from me?"

Foss appeared a moment later, with the same report. There were no fresh footprints to be found anywhere around the camp, other than those the mountaineers had made.

"That is most interesting," Greison said, tenting his gloved hands in front of his mouth.

"What's all this footprint rubbish about anyway?" Lennox asked.

"We all heard the cry of the yeti, did we not? And we have seen the effect of its presence on poor Ang?"

"We did and we have," Lennox said. "What are you getting at?"

"How strange, then, that there are no footprints," Greison said. "There should be a trail of rather sizable marks coming from some direction into the camp, and yet there appear to be none. Likewise, there are no footprints leaving the camp. Surely it did not fly in, kill its victim, then fly out again."

"Crikey, he's right!" Mackay exclaimed.

"So that means . . ." Foss began.

"It means that the killer of Ang never journeyed to the camp and never left the camp. He is, and always has been, right here."

In the flickering torchlight, the men looked from one to the other.

"Are you trying to say that there is no yeti at all?" Lennox asked. "That one of us killed Ang?"

"That seems to be the most likely conclusion," Greison replied.

"Bollocks!" Lennox shouted. "I saw the thing, man! All of us heard it! What more do you want?"

Foss's expression was one of a man trying to work out a puzzle in his mind. "We still haven't found the Sherpa that you brought with you, Greison," he said. "Maybe he killed Ang, then fled."

"Then he would have had to fly as well, since there is no trail of footprints leading away from the camp," Greison said.

"*Pah!*" Lennox spat. "I've taken as much of this as I'm going to. I have another guide dead, and you're worried about footprints. Greison, I'm willing to attribute your ridiculous allegations to dementia from lack of oxygen to the brain and leave it at that. Once the sun comes up, I'm sure you'll be able to find all the footprints you like. But if you want to keep looking for them in the dark, armed with nothing but torches, go right ahead. I'm going to go to my tent. Good night."

"Sleep well, Sir George," Greison said, as the man walked toward his tent. "Oh, by the way, I would not be overly concerned about Chatang's disappearance, I am certain he will turn up. He is most likely off grieving his brother's death in solitude. It turns out that he and Nimu were quite close. In fact, he told me that Nimu confided in him often, and told him all about the various expeditions he guided, including the last one of yours."

Lennox stopped and turned. "Did he offer any details?"

"Some pertinent ones, yes, but that is neither here nor there. I only bring this up to demonstrate how close the brothers were. You had asked me about that earlier, if you recall."

"I recall." Then Lennox turned around again and trudged to his tent.

Once Lennox was inside the tent Mackay said, "Did you see the look on the captain's face when he saw it was Ang? I thought he was shaken by Nimu's death, but this one's really rattled him."

"Aye," said Foss, whose face bore a troubled look. "We should turn in, too."

"I agree," Greison said. Then, in an unusually loud voice, he added, "I suggest that the two of you sleep in the same tent tonight. Foss, why don't you relocate to the tent I had been sharing with Mackay. I will take this one."

Foss was about to protest, but Greison was already dousing his torch outside the tent in question. Lifting the flap, he disappeared inside.

"That's one queer duck you brought back with you," Foss told the young man. "Who is he, anyway?"

"I don't know if I should be telling you this," Mackay said, "but you've heard of Sigerson, right?"

"Sigerson? You mean *he's* Sigerson?"

"For some reason he doesn't want people to know. Crikey, my lungs are burning. I need to get inside."

As Mackay and Foss retired to their tent for the evening, the Sherpa guides finished carrying the body of Ang beyond the edge of the camp, far enough away that if an animal—or beast—were to return for it, it would not venture into the tent area. Then they made their way back to their tent.

Within an hour, all was dark and silent, the only sounds being the steady whine of the wind and an occasional yip from one of the sled dogs, which were huddled together against the cold inside a lean-to. The only light came from the moon, which cast cold blue rays over the snowy mountain plateau. Nobody saw the shadow move through the camp. Nobody heard anything, not even the slow ripping of tent canvas.

It moved through the open wall of the tent and groped its way to the cot inside. Then it began slashing at the figure in the cot, striking it again and again.

It was the cry that awoke Foss and Mackay, a terrible banshee-like wail that seemed to exist only to announce a death. Leaping up, the two jumped into their coats and boots and raced out of the tent. Lennox and the Sherpa guides were already there. "Did you hear it?" Lennox cried.

"Aye," Foss answered. Then: "Where's Greison?"

"Crikey, you don't think it got him, do you?"

Just then, as though in reply, the cry sounded again, startling Lennox so much that he nearly lost his balance and fell down. "What in God's—" he shouted.

"It came from over there," Foss said.

"It's coming from your tent, Captain!" Mackay said.

As the three of them watched, a dim light appeared from inside the tent, and they could make out the silhouettes of two figures inside. Mackay and Foss started toward it, but Lennox said, "No, men, don't go in there. Don't!"

The flap of the tent opened, and Greison stepped out, a lit candle in his hand.

"No!" Lennox cried. "How could—"

"Come in before you freeze, gentlemen," Greison said.

"Who's in there with you?" Foss called.

"Only my friend, Rampoche Chatang." The previously missing Sherpa appeared in the opening of the tent.

"Rampoche?" Foss said. "Isn't that the title for a lama?"

"For the High Lama," Greison replied.

"Crikey."

Foss and Mackay entered the tent, but Sir George Lennox stayed where he was.

"Sir George, your presence is required here as well, if you don't mind."

"I bloody well do mind," the explorer declared. "Get that damned Sherpa dog out of my tent!"

Greison sighed. "I was hoping this would not be necessary. Sangwa, Passang . . ." In an instant, the two Sherpas from the expedition grabbed Lennox's arms and held him fast, while pushing him into the crowded tent. "Let me go, you mountain niggers!" he cried, but he was unable to break free of them.

"What the hell's going on here, Sigerson?" Foss demanded.

"Sigerson?" Lennox repeated, glaring at the man.

"I see Mackay has let that particular secret out of its box," Greison said. "No matter now: what is going on, my dear Foss, is murder at it's most cold-blooded—specifically, the murders of Ang and Nimu, by the hand of Sir George Lennox."

"Crikey!"

Lennox smiled thinly. "You're insane," he said.

"There is no question that you killed them, Sir George," Greison said. "And do not bother trying to break free. Passang and Sangwa now obey Rimpoche Chatang, not you."

"That's a hell of an accusation, man," Foss said. "I don't suppose you have anything in the way of proof, do you?"

"In the pocket of Lennox's coat, I believe you will find the severed paw of a bear."

"The captain's paperweight?" Mackay said.

Lennox made another attempt to break free of the Sherpas, but it was impossible. He cursed and spat as Foss walked over to him and thrust a hand in his coat pockets, pulling out his ram's horn cigarette holder and, ultimately, the bear's paw. "I'll be damned," Foss muttered.

Taking the paw from him, Greison held the candle close to it and examined the claws. "You see? A bit of Ang's blood is still visible."

"So that paw was used to kill Ang?" Foss asked.

"Oh, I doubt it. Were Ang's body to be carefully examined, I am certain that a knife wound would reveal itself. But there is no question that this paw was used to simulate the attack of a wild beast, which Sir George was hoping would be accepted as a yeti. I have no doubt whatsoever that the claws will match the slashes on his face perfectly."

"God almighty," Foss uttered. "Are you some kind of detective, Mr. Greison, or Sigerson, or whatever your name is?"

Greison's eyes remained riveted on the tense figure of Sir George Lennox. "Up until a fortnight ago, I was nothing more than a traveler in this land, like yourselves, enjoying the hospitality at Rongbuk Monastery, as I have done on several previous occasions. With the Lama's help, I have all but conquered my dreaded intolerance of boredom, as well as a few other personal problems . . . but that is immaterial at present. After some time, the serenity of the place was shattered by the news that Lhamu, the mother of Nimu and Chatang, had died suddenly. The family, knowing that Nimu was away on an expedition, desired to get word of the passing to him and bring him back to the village, if possible. Chatang himself decided to go since, prior to achieving the status of *rimpoche*, he journeyed extensively across the mountains and knew the terrain quite well. He did, however, ask me to accompany him, feeling that I might have more success convincing Sir George to let Nimu leave the expedition, being a fellow European. At the time I thought it quite unnecessary, given Rimpoche Chatang's standing. However, having witnessed for myself the man's utter arrogance and delusion of superiority, I now understand his concern."

"To hell with you!" Lennox spat, still held fast by the Sherpas.

"What I don't understand is why?" Mackay said. "Why would someone like the captain kill those Sherpas in cold blood?"

"To protect his secret," Greison replied, setting both the paw and the candle down on the table. "You see, gentlemen, in addition to being a murderer, the famed and much heralded Sir George Lennox is also a fraud and a liar." He paused to let that sink in, then spoke again: "His expedition to Guangming Peak last year earned him a knighthood, did it not? It also made his reputation as the premiere

British mountaineer of our time, and no doubt helped to secure funding not only for this expedition, but future ones as well. How distressing it would be if the world were to learn that it is predicated upon a falsehood—George Lennox never set foot on Guangming Peak. He never came close."

"*Liar!*" Lennox shouted.

"How do you know?" Foss asked.

"Exactly the way Lennox feared I knew it: Nimu, who accompanied Lennox on the climb, and who actually *did* reach the summit, told the truth of the situation to his brother, Rimpoche Chatang, who in turn told me. Sir George had actually become weak and incapacitated from the altitude and had to stop climbing, while Nimu, proceeding onward, reached the top. For a man so convinced of his own superiority as Sir George Lennox, the fact that a native had reached the summit, accomplishing what he himself had proven unable to do, was intolerable. So he drew every bit of information about the climb from Nimu, even questioning him about the view from the summit, and set about spreading the lie that he had, in fact, conquered the mountain. He received a knighthood and an unearned reputation, and no one was the wiser—no one, except, of course, Nimu. All this I knew even before I ever set foot in this camp, but at the time it had no particular bearing on my reason for being here, which was to find Nimu and bring him back to the village. Sir George's moral lapses were of no concern to me."

Lennox had ceased struggling and now stared madly at Greison, his face actually moist with sweat, despite the frigid temperature.

"All that changed, however, when I learned of Nimu's death and the circumstances surrounding it," Greison went on. "I asked Sir George questions about the route he had taken to Bei Peak, and his answers only confirmed the suspicions that were growing in my mind."

"I remember that," Mackay said. "You asked if he took the north route, and he said yes."

"Precisely. That, however, proved to me that he had never been on Bei Peak at all, because there is no north route to it. It is completely inaccessible from that direction. I have scaled the peak myself, so I was testing him on his knowledge of the mountain, and he failed, miserably. This time, however, his lie was not born of a desire to preserve his reputation, but rather to cover his true activities. You see, at first Sir George believed he had nothing to fear from Nimu, the only person on earth who could put lie to his claim. But after receiving his knighthood, and the notoriety that came with it, he realized that the stakes of the game had been raised considerably. If the knowledge Nimu carried were ever to get out, it would invalidate his knighthood and destroy him. So he had to get rid of Nimu. Sir George specifically sought him out for this expedition, all the while plotting his death. He took Nimu with him on the presumed climb to Bei Peak, making the excuse that it was too dangerous for the entire party to go. He went out far enough not to be seen, killed Nimu, hid the body, then returned to camp with the story of having survived an encounter with a yeti. And that, he thought, was the end of it. But then he learned that Nimu had a brother, and began to fear—correctly, as it turned out—that Nimu had confided in his brother the secret of the Guangming expedition."

"Why kill Ang then?" Foss interrupted. "Why not kill the Lama?"

Greison's face darkened. "That was a tragic mistake. In his haste—for he only had the most fleeing of moments to execute his attack—he killed the wrong man. It is a tragedy for which I must carry a share of the blame, and I do so heavily. I had warned Rimpoche Chatang of my suspicions and had prepared him for what might happen, but I did not properly inform the expedition guides. Had I done so, Ang might be alive today. When Lennox realized his mistake, however, he became quite agitated, as you, Mackay, mentioned at the time. I instructed Chatang to hide, and he managed to sequester himself with the sled dogs. Having fully realized how dangerous Sir George Lennox was, I knew that I had to be the one to stop him, before another innocent man—and hear me, Lennox, I said *man*, not *yak*, not *dog*, not *mule*—died. I intimated to Sir George that I, too, knew the secret that he was willing to kill to protect. Do you remember earlier this evening, I made a special point of suggesting the two of you share a tent, while I take one of my own? I did so loudly enough that Sir George would be able to hear me as well. That was my way of announcing to him where I would be sleeping, so he could come and attack me, if he were so inclined, as I believed him to be. And he did attack me—or so he thought."

Mackay rattled his head. "Or so he thought?"

"If you examine the tent that I had chosen, you will find one wall slashed through and a roll of blankets and skins ripped to shreds on the cot. I positioned those blankets in such a manner as to give a fair facsimile of a sleeping man in the darkness. Thinking they were I, fast asleep, Sir George attacked them with the bear's paw, then rushed back out before he had a chance to realize the deception. His shocked reaction upon seeing me emerge from his tent, whole and alive, moments later, I believe, spoke for itself."

"What about that cry we heard?" Foss asked.

"Hand me that ram's horn," Greison said. "Granted, I am not the experienced bugler that Sir George claims to be, however . . ." Greison put the horn to his lips and blew a convincing imitation of the cry that the men had heard earlier that night.

Mackay now looked confused. "But what about that last cry we heard?" he protested. "The captain was with us that time, and I never saw him take out a horn and blow it. So how do you explain that?"

Greison smiled slightly and handed the candle and horn to Mackay. "Really, my boy, what a short memory you have. Don't you remember our conversation about a snow leopard?" Then he cupped his hands over his mouth, uttering a high, piercing cry that sounded remarkably like the ram's horn. "That is the closest I can come, but it served the purpose."

"Aye, it was close enough to fool me," Foss acknowledged. "So what's going to happen to the captain now?"

"That is not up to me," Greison said. Then he turned to Chatang and began speaking in Tibetan, after which he sank down on the cot.

Looking at the *rimpoche*, Sir George Lennox began to laugh. "After the load of balls I've just had to endure, you're now going to turn me over to the *Sherpa?*" he said. "You might as well let me go right now, because these dogs aren't going to do anything to me. It's against their nature."

Chatang waved his hands, and the two Sherpas holding Lennox released their grips. The mountaineer shook his arms, then brushed his coat sleeves as if trying to remove a bad stain from them. Rising to his full height, which was considerable, he regarded Greison with a withering stare. "There is nothing you can do to me," he said icily. "There is nothing anyone can do to me. And there is nothing you can prove. You could have stolen that bear's paw and clawed up Ang yourself, Greison, then had one of these dogs slip it in my pocket when they were forcing me in here. You, or your friend, the High bloody Lama. You've already proven that you can howl like a yeti, so why couldn't you have done the rest, eh? So be damned, the whole lot of you!" He turned to Chatang with hatred in his eyes. "Especially you."

Rimpoche Chatang looked back, his gaze steady, but his expression was not one of anger. Instead, it was a look of pity. He spoke one word in Tibetan, then turned away.

"What did he say?" Lennox asked.

Greison stood up. "He said, 'leave.' That is your judgment."

"Leave? That's all?"

"That is all."

Sir George Lennox smiled defiantly. "Tell the red-skinned bastard to sod off," he said. "This is my bloody expedition, and I'll leave it only when I'm ready to leave it."

"You could, of course, defy his judgment and stay," Greison said, "but if you do, I will have no compunction about binding you with rope and leaving you in that condition until I can get you back down the mountain and to the British consulate, to whose officials I will tell the entire story."

Lennox looked from man to man, and seemed to realize for the first time that he no longer had a friend in the camp. "Flee or be turned in, eh?" he said. "All right, I'll go, and I'll get to the consulate first, and I'll tell them my side of the story. Who do you think they would be more likely to believe?"

Rimpoche Chatang spoke again, softly, and Greison translated: "He said, 'You will never escape the mountains.'"

"Is that so? Mackay, help me get a pack together. I'll leave right now and be down in two days."

Mackay stood where he was.

"Mackay, snap to it, boy! Give me a hand with my pack."

"No," Mackay said.

Lennox approached Mackay and for a moment it looked like he would strike the young man, but Mackay did not flinch. "So," Lennox sneered, "I suppose you feel like a man now, eh, *boy*? Defying your captain? Mutiny? Is that what you think it takes to put hair down below?"

Mackay returned Lennox's gaze. "I feel like a better man than you, Sir George."

"Aye," Foss said, "and that goes for me, too. Put your own damn pack together."

"All right, I will," Lennox said. "I'll leave here, and I'll make it back to civilization and see all of you exposed as slanderous liars. But here's the question, lads: will any of you make it back to civilization at all?"

"Is that a threat, Sir George?" Greison asked, tensely.

"A threat? No. It's a statement of fact. Without me to lead you, do you really think you'll get off of this mountain? Think about that, and once you have, bugger off, the stinking lot of you!" Sir George Lennox bolted through the tent flap and spent the next quarter hour tearing through the camp, putting together the provisions he would need for the descent, including taking down one of the tents and rolling it up to carry, and grasping a pickax to use as a walking stick. Then, defying the darkness and bitter cold, he started down the mountain.

Inside the tent, no one spoke. Then Mackay broke the silence. "You know he'll die out there."

"Aye," Foss said. "If we let him face the mountain at night, we're killing him as surely as he killed Ang and Nimu."

"No," Rimpoche Chatang said in English, surprising the mountaineers. "Not die. Never die. Gods of mountains will have, will have . . ." The last word he spoke in Tibetan, leaving Greison to translate it as *vengeance*. Then Chatang and the other Sherpas solemnly filed out of the tent.

After the last one had gone, Mackay asked, "What did he mean, vengeance?"

"It means the mountain will claim him as another victim," Foss said.

Greison seated himself on a stool. "I daresay you are right, though perhaps not in the way you are thinking," he said. "Have you ever heard the legend behind the yeti?"

Foss and Mackay shook their heads.

"According to the legend, there was once a prince of this region who believed himself to be the ruler of the entire Himalayan range. He was proud and arrogant, and he defied the gods who are believed to inhabit these mountains. Angered by his arrogance, those gods cursed him to roam the mountains forever, not as a man, but rather as a lowly beast, feared and hated by all who encountered him. As a result, the man . . . who had now become the yeti . . . hid from the eyes of other men, living out his eternal existence in misery and solitude. Well, that is the story, anyway. Mackay, is that watch of yours still working?"

Pulling the battered timepiece from his pocket, he opened the lid, and announced, "It's half past ten."

"The sun will be up before you know it. Chatang and I will set off for the monastery in the morning. We should all attempt to get some sleep. And for our safety, gentlemen, I suggest that we remain together, in one tent."

"Aye," said Foss.

"Right," muttered Mackay, putting his watch back in his pocket, and pulling out instead his battered journal and a stubby pencil.

"Crikey," muttered Mackay, shaking himself out of the memory. So long ago . . . a lifetime ago . . . had it really happened?

"Are you all right, Colonel?" Cynthia the nurse was asking.

"Hmmm? Oh, yes, quite."

"For a moment there you looked a bit . . . I don't know . . . lost."

"I am fine now," he said, working up a smile. Then he stared at the newspaper photograph again.

When Sir George Lennox left camp that night in May 1892, it was the last time anyone ever saw him. His disappearance was treated as death on the mountain, and he was hailed as a hero. Mackay, Foss, the man who called himself Greison, and the Sherpas, of course, made it back to the village without incident, and in the years that followed, Mackay never attempted to contradict the heroic legend surrounding Sir George Lennox, and sensed that no one would have believed him had he tried. Neither, to his knowledge, had Foss, with whom he had remained in contact until the bulldoggish mountaineer perished while on another expedition, not long after the turn of the century.

Outside of the Sherpas, whom Mackay never saw again, only one other man knew the truth.

Quite some time after the expedition, he had learned the true identity of the man who traveled under the names Sigerson and Greison. At the time of their meeting, of course, he had assumed, like the rest of the world, that Sherlock Holmes was dead. It was not until after the First World War that he had screwed up the courage to write a letter to him, addressing it simply to "S. Holmes, Sussex." In the letter he reintroduced himself and happened to mention that, while he never achieved the rank of major general, he at least could tell the difference between a Mauser rifle and a javelin.

It was nearly a year before the reply came, a brief note that read:

My *dear Mackay:*

I am delighted to hear you are well. And now that it is no longer a matter of life and death, let me confess that I have always detested Gilbert and Sullivan.

Yrs.
SH

Mackay still had the note somewhere, along with his old journal. But for now, his full attention was on the newspaper photograph. *Could it be true? Could it really be true?*

Of course not, it's absurd, said his rational mind, his military mind. *Still . . .*

With shaky, aged fingers, Colin Mackay folded the newspaper around the photograph and carefully tore along the creases until he had removed the photograph from the page. He would hang on to this one. For the first time in quite some time, he actually was looking forward to waking up the next day, just so he could spend the day contemplating the mystery of the picture, this alleged yeti photograph of Shipton's that showed the monstrous print of a left foot with the second toe missing . . .

Just like the foot of Sir George Lennox.

Water from the Moon

Carolyn Wheat

To be or not to be—Sigerson. That was the question. The tall Englishman with the hawk nose pondered a case of identity as his mount lumbered through the dense forests of northern Siam, swaying the howdah on its back from side to side with a rhythmic regularity that had most British stomachs crying for mercy.

He had received a telegram in Katmandu: GO TO CHIANG MAI AT ONCE STOP CONTACT AGENT BORNEO COMPANY STOP POLLUX.

Pollux was, of course, his brother Mycroft. He was supposed to find the agent for the Borneo Company and introduce the word "castor" into the conversation. In return, he would be given intelligence to be sent via several safe addresses back to Whitehall. Thus was the Great Game played in the East; a Norwegian explorer made the chance acquaintance of a British teak *wallah* who passed along information gathered from a Siamese crown prince, a Kachin opium smuggler, a Karen elephant trainer, and a Chinese merchant. In this way did Whitehall extend its tentacles into the farthest reaches of its empire and beyond.

Had anyone seen him receive the telegram? Did anyone suspect that the man who'd made news by penetrating the secret Tibetan capital of Lhasa and meeting with the high lama was now entering Siam on a mission for the British government?

If anyone on earth suspected, then he must not retain the name Sigerson.

He could not resume his own name, for that name belonged to a dead man.

He hadn't realized dying would be so inconvenient.

The mahout grunted an order and the elephant stopped its surprisingly quick progress through the thick foliage. "Come to boat soon, Missa Sigson," the brown man said. A smile quirked at the corners of the Englishman's mouth. Why did a three-syllable name like Sigerson seem unpronounceable to a people whose king was called Chulalongkorn?

The shot startled the elephant, which raised its huge head and trumpeted its distress. The slow, lumbering gait gave way to a gallop that could have challenged the Derby winner. Holmes clung to the howdah with both hands, then realized there was nothing to be gained in remaining with the beast. He slipped out of the box, grabbed the elephant's rope with one hand, and swung himself to the ground. He hit the bracken at speed, bruising his hip and twisting his ankle, while the elephant brayed and ran, knocking over small trees in its panic. Holmes rolled over and hid himself in the dense undergrowth as three men armed with rifles raced past him, chasing the beast.

The mahout was dead. Holmes found his body near the place where he'd heard that first shot. Holmes laid several branches over the body, but not until after he'd taken the dead man's food stores. He'd need to keep up his strength—and he'd need to shed his latest identity. It was clear that Sigerson was no longer a safe name under which to travel.

Louis Leonowens was worried. He'd been expecting Castor for almost three weeks. He sat in his office at the Borneo Company in Chiang Mai and looked out at the familiar sight of elephants dragging teak logs toward the river, where they would float toward Bangkok. Even after all his years in Siam, the beasts continued to fascinate him. Though they possessed sufficient strength to lay waste to the entire plantation, they allowed themselves to be put through their paces by the tiny mahouts and their well-placed hooks.

The hooks looked more vicious than they really were. Long sticks with a metal hook on the end, they were used to prod the elephants' legs or to tickle that sensitive spot behind the flapping ears. As one mahout explained it, the prodding wasn't painful, thanks to the pachyderm's thick hide, but served to remind the beast that its trainer was near and expected obedience. Herd animals, the elephants expected to obey a leader, and the mahout's job was to be his charge's leader. Both trained together from a young age, and a mahout and his elephant were as married—in some cases, far more married—than that same mahout and his wife. Indeed, the Siamese had a saying that a marriage was like an elephant: the husband was the front legs and chose the direction, but the wife was the back legs, which provided the power.

A man would come, Louis reminded himself. A man had always come. He would receive a mysterious message telling him to expect someone who would say a certain word, and when he heard that word, he was to turn over the dispatches. In this way the Crown kept abreast of the ever-changing situation in the Shan States to the north, where the more militant hill tribes fought British rule in Burma. The Crown kept abreast, and the Siamese king, the Borneo Company, and Louis Leonowens all maintained the appearance of neutrality.

If a man did not come—but Louis didn't want to dwell upon that possibility.

The gaunt, feverish half skeleton who stumbled out of the jungle into the clearing bore but a passing resemblance to the healthy, hawk-nosed Englishman who had escaped the attack three weeks earlier. Hobbled by an injured leg, alternately sweating and shivering with fever, racked by an infection that weakened him, and in dire need of food and drink, this pitiful wreck lay twitching and moaning in the clearing until a kindly rice farmer tossed him onto the back of an oxcart and brought him to the missionaries at the McCormick Hospital.

He lay in bed for the better part of a week, tossing and moaning in the throes of fever, making little progress in spite of heavy doses of quinine.

"The elephant did nothing in the nighttime," the delirious Englishman muttered. "That was the curious incident." He tossed and turned in his sweat-soaked sheets, rambling through random memories in his malaria-addled brain.

Nurse Martha Stubbins paid him no mind. Who knew what people would say when the fever was upon them? She'd heard far worse in the Indian Army hospital where she'd trained. She motioned to Lucy to slide a bedpan under the moaning creature, just in case.

Her assistant, Lucy Pritchard, was the daughter of an American missionary, determined to learn the profession of nursing despite her youth and newness in the country. She was a willing girl, eager to learn, but she was still awed, bewildered, and occasionally frankly terrified by the foreignness of her surroundings. Now she jumped as a heavily tattooed Shan entered the room and inquired about a fellow countryman in the native ward.

"Who was that?" Lucy asked as the burly man made his way in the direction Martha had indicated. "He looks so fierce. He's not Siamese, is he?"

Martha harrumphed. On the one hand, she disapproved of gently bred young ladies playing at Lady Bountiful in her hospital; on the other, she grudgingly acknowledged that, so far, Lucy had done all that she'd been asked to do, without complaint. It wasn't her fault that she was from a faraway place called Kansas and had never seen a Shan tribesman before.

"He's Colonel Prothero's manservant. He comes from the Shan States to the north," Martha explained. "It's a part of Siam that extends into Burma as well. It's been a thorn in the side of the empire ever since Mandalay fell. The men scar themselves and put blue dye into the scars. It's a way of warding off evil. Sometimes," she went on, warming to her theme, "they put precious stones inside the cuts. It's supposed to make them immune to bullet wounds."

Lucy's face lit up with a smile that showed her uneven teeth and her good nature. "There are Indians in America like that, Ghost Dancers. They think dancing a certain way and wearing certain clothes will keep them from dying, too. Of course," she said, her smile dimming, "the poor creatures are wrong and get slaughtered at once if they meet the cavalry."

"Oranges, bring me oranges," the patient begged in a pathetically thin voice. "The five orange pips, all redheaded. All redheaded, and all in the league." The gaunt man sat bolt upright in bed, his eyes bulging, his expression one of stark terror. "Beware the Red-Headed League!" he cried in a terrible voice.

"Now, now," Martha said in her most soothing tone, as she gripped the man's bony shoulders and tried to force him down onto the bed. "No redheaded men here."

Despite his weakness, the unknown patient was too strong for Martha and Lucy combined. "Go fetch Khun Seng," Martha said between gasps as she rested her full weight on the man's legs.

"Who?" Lucy asked.

"The man with the blue scars," Martha explained. "He's in the native ward."

When Khun Seng arrived, he took charge of the situation at once. Years of service to Colonel Prothero in Burma had taught him Army discipline and Army dispatch. He grabbed the patient around the chest, lifted him out of bed as if he were no more than a rag doll, and waited while Lucy changed the sweat-soaked sheets. Martha Stubbins shoved a spoonful of laudanum into the man's mouth, and Khun Seng placed the patient onto the bed with surprising tenderness.

As he subsided into his drugged sleep, the man murmured, "The blue carbuncle. I must have the blue carbuncle."

"Strange notions these fever patients get," Martha said. She didn't notice that Khun Seng gazed sharply at the man in the bed, as if seeing him clearly for the first time.

The next morning, the fever broke, and the sick man knew reason again. He no longer muttered about redheaded elephants in the nighttime or called out for a Dr. Watson to come to him. He was weak as a kitten and could barely swallow the thin rice gruel given to him, but he was awake and aware at last. He knew his name.

"Sigerson," he said in a rasping voice. "Arne Sigerson."

As soon as Louis Leonowens learned that Sigerson, the famous explorer, was lying in the McCormick Missionary Hospital recovering from fever, he breathed a sigh of relief. While Chiang Mai attracted many visitors, most had official business too obviously connected to the teak plantations to qualify them as Foreign Office spies. But Sigerson, a man traveling under a non-British passport, a man apparently out to tour the world, was the perfect spy. Sigerson must, therefore, be his expected visitor.

With a light heart, he set out for the hospital. In short order, he secured the man's release with the promise of caring for him at his own house.

He half expected his guest to breathe the word "castor" as soon as the two left the hospital, but Sigerson did no such thing. As they walked with the slow gait of the sick toward the row of *samlors* outside the hospital—rickshaw affairs with bicycles propelling three-wheeled carts—the Norwegian grasped Louis's arm and said in a low voice, "Never take the first *samlor*."

Louis nodded gravely; he'd known the dispatches carried news of the latest outbreak of war among the *sawbwas*, petty chieftains of the Shan tribes in British Burma, but he hadn't considered that there might be treachery right here in Chiang Mai.

Once inside the carriage, Sigerson sat, blanket over his shoulders, and stared out at the Old City of Chiang Mai with its elaborate teak mansions, white domed pagodas, and open marketplaces. Eager as he was to complete his part of the business, Louis approved of the man's caution. There would be time enough at home to discuss their deep affairs.

He was annoyed to discover that he wasn't to be alone with his guest. Colonel Prothero, late of the British Army, sat on the open teak verandah with a gin and tonic in his hand.

"Leonowens," he said in his booming parade-ground voice, "I took the liberty of stopping in to meet your distinguished guest. I'm sure you know that Sigerson here is the man who penetrated the secrets of Tibet."

Louis allowed himself to be introduced to his own guest, giving himself only a moment to wonder how the colonel knew Sigerson would be there. The colonel, as he knew to his cost, had a way of finding things out, and was always on the cutting edge of happenings in Chiang Mai. The colonel also had a way of assuming command no matter where he was—or in whose house he found himself. Louis suggested, rather pointedly, that the explorer needed rest, but Sigerson said he felt up to sitting on the verandah and drinking some fruit juice, so Louis rang for a servant.

"So, Leonowens," the colonel boomed, "our little village and your house will boast two famous men while Sigerson is here." He punctuated his words with a bark that Louis had come to recognize as a particularly mirthless laugh.

The explorer raised a single eyebrow. It was clear he had no idea why Louis could lay claim to fame. Louis sighed and embarked upon his tale.

"The colonel will have his little joke," Louis said affably, although he privately wished the colonel's humor were not quite so heavy-handed. "It is not, properly speaking, my fame, but my mother's. She wrote a book many years ago in which she told the story of our coming to Siam."

"Ah, of course," the thin Norwegian replied. "Your mother was the royal tutor. I remember now. She wrote a most fascinating account of her experiences with the present king's father."

"My mother's account was rather too highly colored for my taste. Those who encouraged her to write her story were fascinated by tales of Oriental barbarity, and I'm afraid she obliged them rather too thoroughly." He smiled, but the smile held a hint of pain. "One cannot always separate fact from fiction when a Boswell puts your life in print."

The mention of Boswell triggered something in the back of the explorer's mind. A Boswell who added rather too much romance to what ought to be tales of the scientific—but what did that mean? What had he to do with science? He brushed the thought aside; surely it came from the fog and mist of illness.

Two days later, when Sigerson had begun to exhibit signs of increasing strength, the colonel held a dinner party in his honor. Louis had by that time begun to wonder if Sigerson was, in fact, Castor. Frustrated by his guest's reticence, he had himself introduced the subject of castor beans, which were grown in the area, into the conversation with no visible results. The man's entire conversation had been castor-free even when they were alone.

Could it be that Sigerson wasn't Castor, and that his true contact was still at large?

What, then, would he do with the information he'd gathered—information that had to be in Whitehall's hands at the earliest opportunity? He dared not go through more open channels; the king of Siam, his boyhood friend, held on to the independence of his country only because he'd learned to walk a very fine line. Louis did not want to be the one to blur that line and cause trouble for his onetime schoolmate. Louis pondered the question so intently that he scarcely listened to the polite talk going on around him.

The colonel sat at the head of his elaborately set table, his wife at the foot. "We usually serve English food," she said in her high, fluting voice, "but in honor of our distinguished guest, I thought it would be amusing to make a meal of Siamese dishes. My cooks have been preparing this feast for two days."

Small, slender brown women wearing long, colorful skirts tiptoed into the bungalow's dining room carrying trays with many small plates. These they set in the center of the table instead of at the place of any single diner. Apparently one took samples of each dish and added condiments in the form of chopped green herbs, hot-looking orange chilis, and other, less identifiable, substances in a riot of colors ranging from saffron yellow to deep purple to flaming red.

"It is said," Sigerson remarked in his light, ironic voice, "that Siamese curries sting like a serpent, stimulate like strychnine, and are as subtle and sensual as a Chinese courtesan."

The colonel managed to laugh heartily while at the same time conveying a "not in front of the ladies" disapproval.

"Of the last praise," the explorer continued blandly, "I can be no judge."

The shocked but secretly pleased expression of the colonel's wife's face was priceless. To a man with a love of the theatrical, playing a part offered a rich banquet of pleasures. Unfortunately, this particular actor had forgotten he was playing a role.

He was Sigerson, who vaguely remembered having heard the name Sherlock Holmes, but couldn't quite place it.

After dinner, the ladies withdrew, and the colonel poured brandy into snifters and handed it around, offering soda as well. By this time, Sigerson was well enough to accept a proper drink.

"A native meal requires a native smoke," Colonel Prothero said with a wink. Into the room stepped the prettiest of the female servants, bearing a large silver bowl. Long white tubes wrapped with red foil bands stuck out of the bowl; the girl picked one and handed it to Sigerson.

"Ever had a genuine cheroot?" The colonel beamed approval as the explorer examined the cigar intently. "These are the best cheroots in Burma, came from the king's own stores in Mandalay. Took 'em from the palace myself as a little souvenir."

"The colonel," Louis felt constrained to point out, "was present when King Thebaw was exiled to India in 1885."

The lithe brown-skinned servant girl pulled out a matchbox and lit each man's cigar with an expert hand, then retreated, leaving the bowl on the table.

Sigerson puffed several times, his face knotted in concentration. He blew a smoke ring, looked up at the elaborately carved teak ceiling, and said, "Thanat leaves, dried, a touch of wood seasoned with tamarind, crushed tobacco leaves, wrapped in a betel nut palm frond. Excellent. Mild enough for a lady—and I am told the ladies of Burma enjoy their cigars as much as any man."

"That they do, sir, that they do." The colonel's smile was wide; he was a man who loved showing off, and he loved it even more when his gestures were properly appreciated.

"I have written a monograph," the explorer continued, "on the 140 varieties of ash I have encountered in my studies. I believe the Indian *lunkha* was number 135 and the Burmese cheroot was 136. Of course," he went on, "this is, as you say, the highest form of the art; the peasants smoke a vile green weed."

"Why," the colonel wondered aloud, "would anyone write a monograph on ash?"

For the life of him, Arne Sigerson had no answer to that question. He had no idea why those words had escaped his lips.

Louis Leonowens was beginning to believe, not only that his visitor was not the much-anticipated Castor, but also that he was quite mad.

The evening's entertainment did not end with the smoking of the cheroots. The colonel had arranged another local treat for his distinguished visitor—an exhibition of Siamese fighting fish.

"*Betta splendens*," he said as he gestured toward the two small bowls on the teak table.

"Splendid indeed," the explorer remarked. The fish were gorgeous, one deepest indigo and the other flaming orange. Each boasted long feathery fins and tails, and each swam with a delicate grace.

The colonel scooped the indigo fish up with his hand and thrust it into the bowl occupied by the orange betta. The two lunged at one another, struggling in the water like wrestlers, colors flashing and water churning.

Within seconds, it was over. The water ran pink with blood, and the flame-colored fish lay on top, dead, while its victorious blue rival swam in swift, agitated circles around the bowl.

As he watched the two creatures locked in mortal combat, Sigerson had the strangest sensation. It felt as if he were falling. He heard the sound of rushing water, swift and deadly, and felt himself plunging to his doom, arms clasped around the body of another man. As with the fish, one must die, the other must live.

But which was he?

He gripped the side of the table, but it was not enough. He slid to the floor in a dead faint.

When he awoke, there was one word on his lips. "Watson," he said weakly. "Fetch Dr. Watson."

"There's no one here by that name," Louis said uncertainly. The man was either mad or relapsing into his fever. Since he was calling for a doctor, the latter seemed more likely. But when the doctor who had attended Sigerson at McCormick's Hospital came to see him, he pronounced the explorer fever-free and said he was on the mend.

Louis was not the only person in the room to doubt the explorer's sanity. Sigerson himself, sitting quietly in the *samlor* on the way back to his host's house, had come to a similar conclusion. The colonel had been most inquisitive about his journey to Lhasa, and these questions he had answered with ease—but when the conversation turned to his life before Tibet, he had turned silent and awkward.

He remembered Tibet. He remembered nothing before Tibet.

He might as well have been born in the temple where he sat at the feet of the head lama.

And why *would* anyone write a monograph on ash?

The next day, Louis offered his guest a tour of Chiang Mai, an invitation gratefully accepted. As they strolled past the Foreign Cemetery, dominated by a life-sized statue of Queen Victoria, they noticed that one of the graves was open and two Siamese were lifting a coffin from its burial place.

"Taking him home for a proper burial, no doubt," Louis remarked. "Some families dislike the idea of their relatives being buried so far away."

Just then, one of the workmen's hands slipped on his rope and the coffin rolled over onto the emerald green lawn. It fell open and out tumbled, not an embalmed body wrapped in a winding sheet, but a pile of brown-stained bones that looked more like dried firewood than the remains of anything human.

The native screamed and ran away. His fellow stayed only a second longer, but left with even more speed.

"Bad luck," Louis explained. "No doubt they think evil spirits are at work. They will make an offering at a spirit house to placate the demons."

Sigerson stepped quickly toward the open coffin. He knelt on the smooth lawn and examined the bones, turning them in his hand and peering at them as if trying to read a message in their fissures and cracks. He turned his head and gazed up at Louis with a serious expression on his thin face. "If there is such a thing as a policeman in this city," he said, "we had better summon him."

"Why?" Louis demanded. "I can see that the body did not receive proper preparation for burial, but surely that's no crime."

"This body," the explorer replied, "is not that of a European. What's more," he continued, "it was female. Finally, it was murdered."

The police station in Lampang was a long building on stilts with rooms at either end and an open space in the center in the Siamese fashion. It was painted white above and black below, and its garden plot brimmed with brightly colored blooms. Behind his teak desk Sergeant Taed Chutima sighed as he read over the reports from his six officers. Several drunken mahouts had driven their elephants through a farmer's rice paddies, a Chinese merchant had been robbed of three freshly caught fish, and one sampan had been reported stolen only to turn up in the river outside the house of the owner's brother-in-law.

Taed sometimes wondered why he'd become a policeman. He'd learned English and a bit of French from the missionaries and loved reading stories of crime in those languages. He'd admired Vidocq, and he'd considered C. Auguste Dupin the world's greatest detective—until he'd found an old copy of the *Strand Magazine* in a bookstall in Bangkok. There he'd read with fascinated interest the story of a detective far more brilliant than all the rest: Sherlock Holmes.

But the crimes the great Holmes solved in the city of London were real crimes committed by real criminals, not the petty day-to-day wrangles of country people who'd had too much to drink or who borrowed things without permission. He longed for a murder, a mystery, a *case*.

The bones in the Foreign Cemetery in Chiang Mai held promise, he told himself as he boarded the steam launch that would take him upriver. At least it would be a respite from the ordinary, a chance to go into the field and interrogate witnesses. He smiled contentedly as he savored the familiar sharp taste of betel on his tongue and watched the rice barges making their way downriver toward Bangkok.

The witnesses who awaited him at the burial grounds were three *farangs:* one tall and lean with a hawk nose, who introduced himself as Sigerson; one mustached and balding, who said he was Louis Leonowens of the Borneo Teak Company; and the third a white-haired, ramrod-straight man with a red face who demanded to know the meaning of this outrage.

"Colonel Prothero," Taed said with a tight smile. "How good of you to come and take charge of this unfortunate situation." Politeness was integral to the Siamese way of life; it would never have occurred to Taed to tell the old buzzard to go away and let him investigate in peace, even though every fiber of his being longed to do just that. The former Army officer seemed incapable of realizing that Siam was not a British colony.

"The coffin and the gravestone belong to a British Army veteran. Of course I must take responsibility. It is the least I can do for the poor boy's family."

"Wherever your 'poor boy' is," Sigerson pointed out gently, "he is not in his assigned grave."

"How can you be so sure?" the colonel asked. "All we have here are bones. Who's to say whether they're male or female, European or Asian?"

"As to the sex," the explorer replied calmly, "look at the pelvis. It's wider than a man's, for obvious reasons. By measuring the shinbone, we can see that she was only five feet tall. Add to that the fact that her cheekbones are more prominent than a European's and she has a shovel-shaped indentation behind her upper front teeth, and I say she is of Asian ancestry. And look at her tibia, there."

"What about it?" The colonel had never been a patient man, and Taed was interested to see that he treated his fellow Europeans with the same disregard for feelings that he used toward those he referred to as "natives."

"See those lumps at the end of the bone nearest the ankle?" Taed followed the explorer's finger as it pointed toward the long leg bone. In a flash he understood what the *farang* meant and his eyes lit with recognition and admiration. He ought to have seen it himself.

"What of it? Are you saying she was deformed?"

"Look at that man squatting beside the food stall," Sigerson commanded, pointing a bony finger. A broad-faced beggar hunkered down on his heels, chewing betel and gazing at the passersby with a contented expression. "See how he squats with his knees in the air and his buttocks on his heels? That squatting creates facets of bone on the lower tibia. Have you," he challenged the colonel, "ever seen a European who could squat like that?"

Taed suppressed a smile. The vision of the colonel, or any other red-faced *farang* for that matter, squatting on his heels and rolling betel leaf was too precious not to be savored.

"All right," the colonel conceded crossly, "she's a native. But what is she doing in Robinson's grave and why do you say she was murdered?"

Taed could have answered that question himself, but he'd learned to keep himself in the background as much as possible when dealing with the European community. He would take over the case when they'd tired of their game. Once the novelty had worn off, he knew they would have little interest in the murder of a native woman.

In this he was wrong. Leonowens, the teak *wallah*, pleaded the press of business and returned to his office, but the tall lean man and the colonel remained at the site. The colonel's Shan servant, Khun Seng, fetched baskets and sieves, brushes and small metal tools. Taed accepted the role of assistant, helping Sigerson lay the bones in proper order, large ones first, small ones as they were retrieved, using the sieves to sift dirt and collect even the smallest fingers and toes. Sigerson and Taed used the brushes and instruments to clear away the dirt after the bones were removed from the basket. In all his years as a policeman, Taed had never seen a body handled so deftly, and with such scientific precision. He wasn't sure even the great Holmes would have taken such care.

At one point, Sigerson plunged his tweezers into the dirt and pulled something out. "Sergeant," he called, "come look at this if you will be so good. I don't know exactly what it is, but it may be significant."

Taed hurried toward the gravesite. He took the tweezers from the European's hand and examined its contents.

"Elephant tail hair," he said. "Twisted to make a ring. It's a custom among some of the hill tribes." With a sudden smile that lit his nut brown face, he called out, "Khun Seng, have you seen a ring like this before?"

"How dare you address my servant without my permission," the colonel said. "I won't have insubordination from a native."

But he was too late. Khun Seng stood over the diminutive Taed, his eyes fixed upon the braided ring with a look of horror in their dark depths. His cocoa-colored face had paled, making his blue scartattoos stand out like lines on a map.

"These rings are quite common in the Shan States," the colonel said, taking it from the tweezers and tossing it onto the ground. "It's just an amulet for good luck, that's all."

"This poor creature had little of that," Sigerson remarked. "Look at the scars on these bones. She was beaten to death."

Khun Seng gave an animal cry and ran from the graveyard as if all the demons of hell were after him.

"Superstitious," the colonel said with a snort, "like all these Orientals."

Two days later, Khun Seng appeared at the Leonowens bungalow to announce that the colonel was ill and could not attend that day's racing at the Turf Club. The Shan had an amiable smile on his tattooed face as he repeated the colonel's self-diagnosis: "Prothero *thakin* say it is dengue fever, the curse of the tropics."

"He'll be all right in a day or two, then," Louis replied. He explained to his guest, "The colonel picked up all sorts of foreign bugs in his Army days; he doses himself and comes out right as rain in a few days."

But the next day Colonel Prothero was dead.

Siam was not England, and Chiang Mai was not Bangkok, let alone London. There was no Inspector Lestrade to stand over the body and proclaim the death a natural one, daring the world's first consulting detective to pronounce otherwise. The man called Sigerson accompanied his host to the colonel's house to pay respects to the widow without any thought other than that the military man must have succumbed to his tropical illness.

The visitors were met at the door, not by Khun Seng, but by Sergeant Chutima. "Please to come in, gentlemen," the small brown man said with a bow. "I am conducting an investigation into the colonel's death and would be very glad of your assistance."

"Investigation?" Louis was visibly shocked. "What is there to investigate?"

"As to that, sirs both, I am not yet certain. It is the lady of the house who called me here. She is of the firm belief that her husband did not die a natural death."

"What were the colonel's symptoms?" Sigerson asked with every appearance of keen interest. Taed replied that the colonel had shown all the signs of an acute gastric attack, along with fever and sweats— in short, his symptoms matched those of malaria and dengue fever, as well as those of several poisons. It was no wonder that the household had no suspicion that the death was not natural.

"What caused the lady of the house to change her mind?" Sigerson inquired. He sat at what appeared to be an excessively languid ease upon the settee, yet his deep-set gray eyes sparkled with interest.

"A single word, Mr. Sigerson," the Siamese replied. "A single word in the Burmese language. The word *padamya*."

"What does it mean?" Leonowens cried. "Does it mean revenge or murder?"

"Ruby," Taed replied. "It means ruby. The rubies of the Mogok valley in Burma are well-known for their beauty. I do not know why the colonel should leave such a dying message, or what it means, but I do know that the former king of Burma had a fortune in rubies in his palace in Mandalay."

"A palace the colonel admitted he looted during the conquest of the capital," Sigerson reminded Louis.

"I say, isn't 'looted' going a bit far? The man admitted to taking a few cheroots from the royal palace, that's all."

"A man in uniform who will steal cheroots might well steal precious stones as well, given the opportunity," Sigerson replied. "Gems of great value are the devil's pet baits; they are the nucleus and focus of crime all over the world. I once knew a blue carbuncle to appear in the unlikeliest of places, the crop of a Christmas goose."

Louis Leonowens's face wore an expression of polite disbelief, but his expression paled in comparison to Sigerson's own. For the hair stood up on the back of his neck as he remembered, as vividly as if it were yesterday, the excited man who had brought that goose, purchased from the Alpha Inn, into his rooms in Baker Street.

He who had begun to suspect he was not Sigerson at last knew his true identity. He was Sherlock Holmes, he was supposed to be dead, he was halfway around the world from his home, and he was once again staring into the face of a baffled policeman who needed his help.

"In my experience," he began, then swiftly corrected himself, "I have heard that some criminal investigators keep records of unusual crimes and refer to those records when something similar takes place. Have you," he asked Taed, "ever known of a death with symptoms like this that was not caused by illness?"

Inspired by the great Holmes and his commonplace book, Taed *had* kept such records, written in his meticulous hand in the beautiful flowing Siamese language. The records were mainly of robberies, seldom of murder, but he had managed to solve a crime in which all the members of the household were drugged by a poison root thrown into the fireplace while their house was looted by bandits thanks to an article clipped from the *Irrawaddy Gazette*. It was this brilliant solution to a puzzle considered insoluble that had won him his promotion to sergeant.

He mentally reviewed the few murders he had in his files. Nothing came close to this; he'd seen few poisonings. Most of his murders were committed in the heat of drunken anger by family members.

Death by what appeared to be illness but turned out to be poison instead—suddenly his eyes lit up and he cried, "Benja."

"What does that mean?" Louis asked.

"He was a boy, the fifth child of his family, which is why he was called Benja," Taed explained. "He died of what seemed to be a fever, just like the colonel. But when I went to his room, I found beans of *lahung*. The boy had eaten them and died."

With a strange look on his face, Leonowens explained, "Castor beans. They are quite poisonous, you know."

Castor—that meant something else. Something he was supposed to do for a man called Pollux. Castor and Pollux. He was supposed to contact the agent for the Borneo Company.

But Leonowens was the agent for the Borneo Company. He gazed at his host with a question in his eyes, a question he dared not ask and hoped would be understood.

Louis, seeing a quick flash of intelligence, sighed with relief. He gave a brief nod, and went on, "Five hundred times stronger than cobra venom."

"We know how," Holmes said in a firm voice. "Ricin poisoning. The question now is who did this."

"Do you think this death is related to the bones in the graveyard?" Louis asked.

Holmes opened his mouth to reply, then turned to the Siamese policeman. "What do you think about that, Sergeant?"

Taed found it difficult to answer at first. He was used to deferring to Europeans, and it was not the Siamese way to push oneself forward. It was the utmost in bad manners to contradict another person, and stating your own opinion too clearly and forcefully could lead to open disagreement, which would cause all to lose face. But this *farang* was different from all the others he'd met; unlike the colonel, he did not seem to consider himself superior to everyone who wasn't English. He seemed genuinely to want Taed's opinion.

"The colonel seemed most insistent that the elephant hair ring meant little," Taed began slowly. "He threw it down as if it were nothing, but Khun Seng thought it was something. Remember how he behaved when he saw that ring?"

"Superstition," Leonowens said dismissively. "Just like the men who ran when they first saw the bones."

Under the steady, approving gaze of the hawk-faced *farang*, Taed did the unthinkable. He looked an Englishman straight in the eyes and bluntly disagreed with him. "But Khun Seng did not run when he first saw the bones. If he feared evil spirits, why would he not have run when he first came? No," he continued, "it was the ring that caused him to flee. He knew that ring. He knew that woman."

"Excellent," Holmes pronounced, rubbing his hands together. "You have the makings of a fine detective, Sergeant. The fact that you have no superiors telling you that thinking is conduct unbecoming a policeman has allowed you to develop your faculties admirably."

To his dying day, Sergeant—later Captain—Taed Chutima of the Royal Siamese Police Force maintained that while Sherlock Holmes had the reputation of being the world's greatest detective, he was outshone by an obscure Norwegian named Sigerson, with whom he had once had the honor of working.

"We must talk to Khun Seng," Taed said, willing himself not to blush at the European's praise. "We must question him about the woman."

When Leonowens rang for a servant, the girl who had served the cheroots at the dinner party informed them that Khun Seng was in his little hut behind the house. He had not been seen all morning, and it was assumed he was mourning his master.

There was a strong odor of incense outside the hut occupied by the Shan. Incense mingled with something else, something more elemental. Blood.

Khun Seng was alive, but barely so. The blue scars that crisscrossed his body had been sliced open, and blood oozed from wounds freshly made. He had carved his own body, mutilated himself with an ornamental *kriss* that lay on a small teak table next to a cheap statue of Buddha.

In a bowl on the same table lay fourteen gleaming gems, as red as the blood that stained the sheets.

The three foreigners gazed at the man in the bed without a word. The mutilation was a confession of sorts—but a confession of what? Why had he harmed himself, and what did he know about the dead woman in the graveyard?

Taed began the questioning. He knew how he ought to proceed: he ought to scream at Khun Seng that all was known and that he had better confess or he would face a beating like none he'd ever endured in his life. That was how he'd been taught to deal with a man he suspected of murder.

But he looked at the suppurating wounds in the Shan's body and the pain in his face, and instead he said gently, "You loved her, didn't you? You made the ring for her."

"Her name was Kyi Nanda, which means Clear River in the language of our people. She was beautiful, and I loved her very much." Khun Seng's eyes misted, and he shook his head as if to clear away the cobwebs of memory. "She was brought to the Royal Palace in Mandalay as a child and trained as a servant to Queen Supayalat."

"The queen would never let her marry a man of your rank," Louis pointed out. He'd seen a similar situation in the Siamese royal palace when he was a child; a slavegirl brought from the hinterlands who wanted only to love and be loved by a young man of her village was beaten to near death for secretly meeting her lover.

"That is why I agreed to Prothero *thakin*'s plan," Khun Seng replied, clearly eager to be understood. "It was the only way Kyi Nanda and I could be together. The soldiers allowed the royal servants to go into the palace and take away some of the precious things. Kyi Nanda opened the royal coffers and took out rubies, but not for the queen, for us. For our future. The colonel was to take some and leave some for us to start a new life."

"But the colonel took it all, leaving you destitute," Louis guessed.

"Worse than that," Holmes corrected, shaking his head.

"It was worse, Sigerson *thakin*," the Shan agreed, giving his interrogator the honor of the Burmese equivalent of *Sahib*. "The colonel told me Kyi Nanda took her portion of the rubies and ran off with an Englishman, a sergeant in the Army. I knew that sergeant. I knew he had eyes for her, and I knew he liked native women. I believed the colonel, and I left Burma to come here with him because my heart was broken. I didn't care where I went once I'd lost Kyi Nanda."

"But when you saw the ring with the bones in the European graveyard, you realized Kyi Nanda had come looking for you," Holmes said, his own voice as gentle as Taed's. "You suspected the colonel had lied to you about her defection. You realized Colonel Prothero had killed her rather than risk exposure."

"Yes," Khun Seng said, his eyes blazing with anything but regret and remorse. "I knew my happiness had been destroyed, not by the woman I loved, but by a greedy *farang* with a lust for rubies so strong he must steal even from a poor man. He killed her; I killed him. I say it with pride, for what man worthy of the name would not have done the same?"

"I suppose the colonel's ready access to the Foreign Cemetery made it easy for him to arrange a burial for a nonexistent soldier and put the woman's corpse into a coffin," Louis remarked.

"He did not even grant her a proper funeral," Khun Seng said in a sleepy-sounding voice. "He did not burn her as we Buddhists burn our dead. Even in death he used her as he used all his servants."

"Are these the stolen gems?" Louis turned to Sigerson for enlightenment. Why a man noted as an explorer and mountain climber should be able to answer his query he did not know, but that he could answer it was beyond doubt. "How did Khun Seng get them? Wouldn't the colonel have hidden them somewhere safe?"

Holmes reached out and grasped Khun Seng's tattooed arm. Louis saw the truth at once. Khun Seng confirmed it with a nod of his head. "My people consider rubies the luckiest of gems," he said. "We tattoo ourselves with sacred runes to keep the demons away, and we sometimes embed rubies or sapphires into the knife cuts to protect us from harm. A man with a ruby under the skin cannot be killed by knife or spear, everyone in the Shan States knows this."

"How many rubies were in your flesh?" Louis shuddered as he gazed at the man's mutilated arms and legs, realizing that he'd carried his master's booty under his very skin—carried the reason his lover had died.

"I had fourteen. My fellow Shan servants had the same number. The colonel knew our tradition, and he also knew that he might be suspected of stealing gems from the palace. When he needed money, he cut the flesh of one of us and took the ruby into Bangkok to sell. He is not suspected if he sells one ruby at a time to different dealers."

"You will have to come with me to jail in Lampang," Taed said with a shake of his head. He privately thought that Khun Seng had good reason to kill the colonel, but he had his duty and he would do it.

"He won't live to make the trip," Holmes said.

"His wounds will heal." Taed spoke curtly to hide the pity in his eyes.

"His wounds won't kill him. The ricin will."

Taed nodded. It was justice, of a sort.

"He wanted water from the moon," he said sadly. "This is what we Siamese say when a man wants what he cannot have. Water from the moon."

It was assumed by all who read of the event in the Bangkok *Times* that the Order of the White Elephant was awarded to Arne Sigerson of Norway for his brilliant adventures in Tibet. Taed knew otherwise; surely the great honor was given because Sigerson solved the murder of Colonel Prothero but did not reveal the truth about the colonel's theft. He knew enough about the British to realize that stealing from a deposed Asian king would mean little to them, but once the palace became the property of the empire, the colonel would have been thought a man who stole from his own queen. It was for this reason that he had concealed his theft by murdering Kyi Nanda.

The rubies were quietly removed from the other Shan servants and sent to the British Museum in London, and the colonel was buried in the Foreign Cemetery with full honors. Only Louis Leonowens knew the complete truth: that the Order of the White Elephant was also awarded for saving Siam from a bloody clash with British Army troops in Burma, a clash fomented by Shan leaders trying yet again to break away from Burma.

Holmes sat at his ease on the verandah of the Oriental Hotel, the finest hostelry in Bangkok. He could have chosen to write his letter inside at a desk, but he enjoyed watching the incessant river traffic, and the evening was a sultry one. Outdoors was far more comfortable than the stuffy writing room.

The cool evening breeze wafted the musky scent of the Chao Phraya into his nose. He could hear the calls of boatmen and see twinkling lanterns on the prows of their tiny sampans. The Oriental Hotel boasted electricity, but all around him lay a city flickering with gaslight, cooking fires, and oil lamps. Just for a moment, its bustle and river smells reminded him of the London of twenty-five years earlier, when he had been a boy newly come from university to make his fortune in the capital.

Thoughts of London led inexorably to thoughts of his past life. He sipped his brandy, picked up a pen, dipped it in India ink, and began to write on the hotel's embossed vellum paper.

     My dear Dr. Watson,

     I wish you to know from the deepest part of my soul, how much I regret the fact that I was obliged to deceive you. My brother Mycroft convinced me that Her Majesty's government requires my continued state of "death," which means that this letter will never be sent. I shall do the bidding of the Foreign Office in places where the empire's future is uncertain and I shall play the role I have long trained for, that of objective observer of truth, in places where truth is anything but expected or respected.

Perhaps someday you will read this unposted correspondence and you will know how much your absence means to me. I may solve a crime or two, unravel a puzzle put before me, but I am only half the man I was in England since I am without the friend whose mind I use as a whetstone for my own.

I shall never mail this letter. My brother Mycroft and his gang of Whitehall thugs have seen to that. I am bound by a hundred oaths of secrecy, a convoluted web of obligations that collectively mean little to me, but the bond of blood outweighs that of desire. Besides, I am quite certain that even if I were to post one of these missives, it would be efficiently intercepted and destroyed before it reached the Siamese border.

I long for your good British common sense, my friend, as much as I long for a dinner of good British beef at the Savoy, a concert at Covent Garden, and a snifter of brandy before a roaring fire at Baker Street. It may be years before we meet face-to-face . . .

Holmes put down the pen and rubbed his tired eyes. What was the point of completing a letter that would never be read? Come to think of it, what was the point of thinking about Baker Street and the rooms that awaited his return?

He might as well ask for water from the moon.

Mr. Sigerson

Peter Beagle

My name is Floresh Takesti. I am concertmaster of the Greater Bornitz Municipal Orchestra in the town of St. Radomir, in the Duchy of Bornitz, in the country of Selmira. I state this only because, firstly, there is a centuries-old dispute between our ducal family and the neighboring principality of Gradja over boundaries, bribed surveyors, and exactly who some people think they are; and, secondly, because Bornitz, greater or lesser, is quite a small holding, and has very little that can honestly be said to be its own. Our national language is a kind of untidy low German, cluttered further by Romanian irregular verbs; our history appears to be largely accidental, and our literature consists primarily of drinking songs (some of them quite energetic). Our farmers grow barley and turnips, and a peculiarly nasty green thing that we tell strangers is kale. Our currency is anything that does not crumble when bitten; our fare is depressingly Slovakian, and our native dress, in all candor, vaguely suggests Swiss bell ringers costumed by gleefully maniacal Turks. However, our folk music, as I can testify better than most, is entirely indigenous, since no other people would ever claim it. We are the property of the Austro-Hungarian Empire, or else we belong to the Ottomans; opinions vary, and no one on either side seems really to be interested. As I say, I tell you all this so that you will be under no possible misapprehension concerning our significance in this great turbulence of Europe. We have none.

Even my own standing as concertmaster here poses a peculiar but legitimate question. Traditionally, as elsewhere, an orchestra's first violinist is named concertmaster, and serves the conductor as assistant and counselor, and, when necessary, as a sort of intermediary between him and the other musicians. We did have a conductor once, many years ago, but he left us following a particularly upsetting incident, involving a policeman and a goat—and the Town Council has never been able since to locate a suitable replacement. Consequently, for good or ill, I have been conductor *de facto* for some dozen years, and our orchestra seems none the worse for it, on the whole. Granted, we have always lacked the proper—shall I say *crispness?*—to do justice to the Baroque composers, and we generally know far better than to attempt Beethoven at all; but I will assert that we perform Lizst, Saint-Saëns, and some Mendelssohn quite passably, not to mention lighter works by assorted Strausses and even Rossini. And our Gilbert and Sullivan closing medley almost never fails to provoke a standing ovation, when our audience is sober enough to rise. We may not be the Vienna *Schausspielthaus*, but we do our best. We have our pride.

It was on a spring evening of 1894 that he appeared at my door: the tall, irritating man we knew as Herr Sigerson, the Norwegian. You tell me now that he had other names, which I can well believe—I can tell you in turn that I always suspected he was surely not Norwegian. Norwegians have *manners*, if they have no cuisine; no Norwegian I ever knew was remotely as arrogant, implicitly superior, and generally impossible as this "Sigerson" person. And no, before you ask, it would be almost impossible for me to explain exactly what made him so impossible. His voice? his carriage? his regard, that way of studying one as though one were a canal on Mars, or a bacterium hitherto unknown to mankind? Whatever the immediate cause, I disliked him on sight; and should I learn from you today that he was in reality a prince of your England, this would not change my opinion by a hair. Strengthen it, in fact, I should think.

Nevertheless. Nevertheless, he was, beyond any debate or cavil, a better violinist than I. His tone was richer, his attack at once smoother and yet more vivid; his phrasing far more adventurous than I would ever have dared—or could have brought off, had I dared.

I can be as jealous, and even spiteful, as the next man, but I am not a fool. He deserved to sit in the first violinist's chair—my chair for nineteen years. It was merely justice, nothing more.

When he first came to my house—as I recall, he was literally just off the mail coach that sometimes picks up a passenger or two from the weekly Bucharest train—he asked my name, gave his own, and handed me a letter of introduction written by a former schoolmate of mine long since gone on to better things. The letter informed me that the bearer was "a first-rate musician, well schooled and knowledgeable, who has elected, for personal reasons, to seek a situation with a small provincial orchestra, one preferably located as far off the conventional routes of trade and travel as possible. Naturally, old friend, I thought of you . . ."

Naturally. Sigerson—he gave no other name then—watched in silence from under dark, slightly arched brows as I perused the letter. He was a tall man, as I have said, appearing to be somewhere in his early forties, with a bold, high-bridged nose—a tenor's nose—in a lean face. I remember clearly a thin scar, looking to be fairly recent, cutting sharply across his prominent left cheekbone. The mouth was a near twin to that scar, easily as taut and pale, and with no more humor that I could see. His eyes were a flat gray, without any hint of blue, as such eyes most often have, and he had a habit of closing them and pressing his right- and left-hand fingertips against each other when he was at his most attentive. I found this particularly irksome, as I did his voice, which was slightly high and slightly strident, to my ear at least. Another might not have noticed it.

I must be honest and admit to you that if the dislike at our first encounter was immediate, it was also entirely on my side. I do not imagine that Herr Sigerson concerned himself in the least over my good opinion, nor that he was even momentarily offended by not having it. He accepted the insulting wage St. Radomir could offer him as indifferently as he accepted my awe—yes, also admitted—when, by way of audition, he performed the Chevalier St-Georges's horrendously difficult *Etude in A Major* at my kitchen table, following it with something appropriately diabolical by Paganini. I told him that there was an attic room available at the Widow Ridnak's for next to nothing, upon which he thanked me courteously enough and rose to leave without another word, only turning at the door when I spoke his name.

"Herr Sigerson? Do you suppose that you might one day reveal to me your personal reasons for burying your considerable gifts in this particular corner of nowhere? I ask, not out of vulgar inquisitiveness, but simply as one musician to another."

He smiled then—I can quite exactly count the times when I ever saw him do such a thing. It was a very odd entity, that smile of his: not without mirth (there was wit and irony in the man, if not what I would call humor), but just below the slow amusement of his lips I felt—rather than saw—a small scornful twist, almost a grimace of contempt. Your Herr Sigerson does not really like human beings very much, does he? Music, yes.

"Herr Takesti," he replied, graciously enough, "please understand that such reasons as I may have for my presence here need in no way trouble St. Radomir. I have no mission, no ill purpose—no purpose at all, in fact, but only a deep desire for tranquility, along with a rather sentimental curiosity concerning the truest wellsprings of music, which do not lie in Vienna or Paris, but in just such backwaters and in such underschooled orchestras as yours." I was deciding whether to rise indignantly to the defense of my town, even though his acid estimate was entirely accurate, when he went on, the smile slightly warmer, "And, if you will permit me to say so, while I may have displaced the first violin—" for I had already so informed him; why delay the plainly unavoidable?— "the conductor will find me loyal and conscientious while I remain in St. Radomir." Whereupon he took his leave, and I stood in my doorway and watched his tall figure casting its gaunt shadow ahead of him as he made his way down the path to the dirt road that leads to the Widow Ridnak's farm. He carried a suitcase in one hand, his violin case in the other, and he was whistling a melody that sounded like Sarasate. Yes, I believe it *was* Sarasate.

I had mentioned a rehearsal that night, but neither asked nor expected him to attend, only a few hours off the train. I cannot even remember telling him how to find the local beer hall where we have always rehearsed; yet there he was, indifferently polite as ever, tuning up with the rest of the strings. I gave a short, awkward speech, introducing our new first violin to the orchestra (at my prompting, he offered the transparently false Christian name of Oscar), and adding that, from what I had heard at my kitchen table, we could only gain from his accession to my former chair. Most of them were plainly disgruntled by the announcement—a flute and a trombone even wept briefly—which I found flattering, I must confess. But I reassured them that I had every intention of continuing as their devoted guide and leader, and they did seem to take at least some solace from that pledge. No orchestra is ever one big, happy family, but we were all old comrades, which is decidedly better for the music. They would quickly adapt to the changed situation.

In fact, they adapted perhaps a trifle too quickly for my entire comfort. Within an hour they were exclaiming over Sigerson's tone and his rhythmic sense, praising his dynamics as they never had mine—no, this is *not* jealousy, simply a fact—and already beginning to chatter about the possibility of expanding our increasingly stale repertoire, of a single fresh and innovative voice changing the entire character of the orchestra. Sigerson was modest under their admiration, even diffident, waving all applause away; for myself, I spoke not at all, except to bring the rehearsal back into order when necessary. We dispersed full of visions—anyway, they did. I recall that a couple of the woodwinds were proposing the Mozart Violin Concerto, which was at least conceivable; and that same trombone even left whispering, "*Symphonie Fantastique*," which was simply silly. He had them thinking like that, you see, in one rehearsal, without trying.

And we did make changes. Of course we did. You exploit the talent you have available, and Sigerson's presence made it possible for me to consider attempting works a good bit more demanding than the Greater Bornitz Orchestra had performed in its entire career. No, I should have said, "existence." Other orchestras have *careers*. We are merely happy still to be here.

Berlioz, no. They cannot play what he wrote in Paris, London, Vienna—how then in St. Radomir? Beethoven, no, not even with an entire string section of Sigersons. But Handel . . . Haydn . . . Mozart . . . Telemann . . . yes, *yes*, the more I thought of it, there was never any real reason why we could not cope decently with such works; it was never anything but my foolish anxiety—and, to be fair to myself, our national inferiority complex, if we are even a nation at all. Who are we, in darkest Selmira, operetta Selmira, joke Selmira, comically backward Selmira, Selmira the laughingstock of bleakly backward Eastern Europe—or so we would be, if anyone knew exactly where we were—to imagine ourselves remotely capable of producing real music? Well, by God, we *were* going to imagine it, and if we made fools of ourselves in the attempt, what was new in that? At least we would be a different sort of fools than we had been. St. Radomir, Bornitz, Selmira . . . they would never have seen such fools.

That was the effect he had on us, your Mr. Sigerson, and whatever I think of him, for that I will always be grateful. True to his word, he made absolutely no effort to supplant my musical judgment with his own, or to subvert my leadership in any way. There were certainly those who sought him out for advice on everything from interpretation to fingering to modern bowing technique, but for all but the most technical matters he always referred them back to me. I think that this may have been less an issue of loyalty than of complete lack of interest in any sort of authority or influence—as I knew the man, that simply was not in him. He seemed primarily to wish to play music, and to be let alone. And which desire had priority, I could not have told you, then or now.

Very well. You were asking me about the incident which, in my undoubtedly perverse humor, I choose to remember as The Matter of the Uxorious Cellist. Sigerson and I were allies—ill-matched ones, undoubtedly, but allies nonetheless—in this unlikely affair, and if we had not been, who's to say how it might have come out? On the other hand, if we had left it entirely alone . . . well, judge for yourself. Judge for yourself.

The Greater Bornitz Municipal Orchestra has always been weak in the lower strings, for some reason—it is very nearly a tradition with us. That year we boasted, remarkably, four cellists, two of them rather wispy young women who peeped around their instruments with an anxious and diffident air. The third, however, was a burly Russo-Bulgarian named Volodya Andrichev: blue-eyed, blue-chinned, wild-haired, the approximate size of a church door (and I mean an Orthodox church here), possessed of—or by—an attack that should by rights have set fire to his score. He *ate* music, if you understand me; he approached all composition as consumption, from Liszt and Rossini, at which he was splendid, to Schumann, whom he invariably left in shreds, no matter how I attempted to minimize his presence or conceal it outright. Nevertheless, I honored his passion and vivacity; and besides, I liked the man. He had the snuffling, shambling charm of the black bears that still wander our oak forests as though not entirely sure what they are doing there, but content enough nonetheless. I quite miss him, as much time as it's been.

His wife, Lyudmilla Plaschka, had been one of our better woodwinds, but retired on the day of their wedding, that being considered the only proper behavior for a married woman in those times. She was of Bohemian extraction, I believe: a round, blond little person, distinctly appealing to a particular taste. I remember her singing (alto) with her church choir, eyes closed, hands clasped at her breast—a godly picture of innocent rapture. Yet every now and then, in the middle of a Bach cantata or some Requiem Mass, I would see those wide blue eyes come open, very briefly, regarding the tenor section with the slightest pagan glint in their corners. Basses, too, but especially the tenors. Odd, the detail with which these things come back to you.

He adored her, that big, clumsy, surly Andrichev, even more than he loved his superb Fabregas cello, and much in the same manner, since he plainly felt that both of them were vastly too good for him. Absolute adoration—I haven't encountered much of that in my life, not the real thing, the heart never meant for show that can't help showing itself. It was a touching thing to see, but annoying as well on occasion: during rehearsal, or even performance, I could always tell when his mind was wandering off home to his fluffy golden goddess. Played the devil with his vibrato every time, I can tell you.

To do her justice—very reluctantly—she had the decency, or the plain good sense, to avoid involvements with any of her husband's colleagues. As I have implied, she preferred fellow singers to instrumentalists anyway; and as Andrichev could not abide any sort of vocal recital ("Better cats on a back fence," he used to roar, "better a field full of donkeys in heat"), her inclinations and his rarely came into direct conflict. Thus, if we should chance to be performing in, say, Krasnogor, whose distance necessitates an overnight stay, while she was making merry music at home with Vlad, the clownish basso, or it might be Ruska, that nasal, off-key lyric tenor (*there* was a vibrato you could have driven a *droshky* through) . . . well, whatever the rest of us knew or thought, we kept our mouths shut. We played our Smetana and our Gilbert and Sullivan medley, and we kept our mouths shut.

I don't know when Andrichev found out, nor how. I cannot even say how we all suddenly knew that he knew, for his shy, growling, but essentially kindly manner seemed not to change at all with the discovery. The music told us, I think—it became even fiercer, more passionate—angrier, in short, even during what were meant to be singing *legato* passages. I refuse to believe, even now, that any member of the Greater Bornitz Orchestra would have informed him. We were all fond of him, in our different ways; and in this part of the world we tend not to view the truth as an absolute, ultimate good, but as something best measured out in a judiciously controlled fashion. It could very well have been one of his wife's friends who betrayed her—even one of her playmates with a drink too many inside him. I don't suppose it matters now. I am not sure that I would want to know, now.

In any event, this part of the world offers certain traditional options in such a case. A deceived husband has the unquestioned right—the divine right, if you like—to beat his unfaithful wife as brutally as his pride demands, but he may not cut her nose or ears off, except perhaps in one barbarous southern province where we almost never perform. He may banish her back to her family—who will not, as a rule, be at all happy to see her—or, as one violist of my acquaintance did, allow her to stay in his home, but on such terms . . . Let it go. We may play their music, but we are not altogether a Western people.

But Andrichev did none of these things. I doubt seriously that he ever confronted Lyudmilla with her infidelity, and I know that he never sought out any of her lovers, all of whom he could have pounded until the dust flew, like carpets on a clothesline. More and more withdrawn, drinking as he never used to, he spent most of his time at practice and rehearsal, clearly taking shelter in Brahms and Tschaikovsky and Grieg, and increasingly reluctant to go home. Often he wound up staying the night with one Grigori Progorny— our fourth cellist, a competent enough technician and the nearest he had to an intimate—or with me, or even sprawled across three chairs in that cold, empty beer hall, always clutching his cello fiercely against him as he must have been used to holding his wife. None of us ever expressed the least compassion or fellow feeling for his misery. He would not have liked it.

Sigerson was perfectly aware of the situation—for all his air of being concerned solely with tone and tempo and accuracy of phrasing, I came to realize that he missed very little of what was going on around him—but he never commented on it; not until after a performance in the nearby town of Ilyagi. Our gradually expanding repertoire was winning us both ovations and new bookings, but I was troubled even so. Andrichev's playing that evening had been, while undeniably vigorous, totally out of balance and sympathy with the requirements of Schubert and Scriabin, and even the least critical among us could not have helped but notice. On our way home, bumping and lurching over cowpaths and forest trails in the two wagons we still travel in, Sigerson said quietly, "I think you may have to speak with Mr. Andrichev."

Most of the others were asleep, and I needed to confide in someone, even the chilly Herr Sigerson. I said, "He suffers. He has no outlet for his suffering but the music. I do not know what to do, or what to say to him. And I will not discharge him."

Surprisingly, Sigerson smiled at me in the near darkness of the wagon. A shadowy, stiff smile, it was, but a smile nevertheless. "I never imagined that you would, Herr Takesti. I am saying only"—and there he hesitated for a moment— "I am saying that if you do *not* speak to him, something perhaps tragic is quite likely to happen. What you may say is not nearly as important as the fact that he knows you are concerned for him. You are rather a forbidding person, concertmaster."

"*I?*" I demanded. I was absolutely stunned. "*I* am forbidding? There is no one, *no one*, in this orchestra who cannot come to me—who *has* not come to me—under any circumstances to discuss anything at all at any time. You know this yourself, Herr Sigerson." Oh, how well I remember how furious I was. Forbidding, indeed—this from *him!*

The smile only widened; it even warmed slightly. "Herr Takesti, this is perfectly true, and I would never deny it. Anyone may come to you, and welcome—but you do not yourself go out to them. Do you understand the difference?" After another momentary pause, while I was still taking this in, he added, "We are more alike than you may think, Herr Takesti."

The appalling notion that there might be some small truth in what he said kept me quiet for a time. Finally, I mumbled, "I will speak to him. But it will be no help. Believe me, I know."

"I believe you." Sigerson's voice was almost gentle—totally unnatural for that querulous rasp of his. "I have known men like Andrichev, in other places, and I fear that the music will not always be outlet enough for what is happening to him. That is all I have to say."

And so it was. He began humming tunelessly to himself, which was another annoying habit of his, and he was snoring away like the rest by the time our horses clumped to a stop in front of their stable. Everyone dispersed, grumbling sleepily, except Andrichev, who insisted on sleeping in the wagon, and grew quite excited about it. He would have frozen to death, of course, which I think now was what he wanted, and perhaps a mercy, but I could not allow it. Progorny eventually persuaded him to come home with him, where he drank mutely for the rest of the night and slept on the floor all through the next day. But he was waiting for me at rehearsal that evening.

What are you expecting? I must ask you that at this point. Are you waiting for poor Herr Andrichev to kill his wife—to stab or shoot or strangle the equally pitiable Lyudmilla Plaschka—or for her to have him knocked on the head by one of her lovers and to run off with *that* poor fool to Prague or Sofia? My apologies, but none of that happened. *This* is what happened.

It begins with the cello: Andrichev's Fabregas, made in Lisbon in 1802, not by Joao, the old man, but by his second son Antonio, who was better. One thinks of a Fabregas as a violin or a guitar, but they made a handful of cellos, too, and there are none better anywhere, and few as good; the rich, proud, tender sound is surely unmistakable in this world. And what in God's own name Volodya Andrichev was doing with a genuine Fabregas I have no more idea than you, to this day. Nor can I say why I never asked him how he came by such a thing—perhaps I feared that he might tell me. In any event, it was his, and he loved it second only to Lyudmilla Plaschka, as I have said. And that cello, at least, truly returned his love. You would have to have heard him, merely practicing scales in his little house on a winter morning, to understand.

So, then—the cello. Now, next—early that fall, Lyudmilla fell ill. Suddenly, importantly, desperately ill, according to Progorny; Andrichev himself said next to nothing about it to the rest of us, except that it was some sort of respiratory matter. Either that, or a crippling, excruciating intestinal aliment; at this remove, such details are hard to recall, though I am sure I would be able to provide

them had I liked Lyudmilla better. As it was, I felt concern only—
forgive an old man's unpleasant frankness—for Andrichev's concern
for her, which seemed in a likely way to destroy his career. He could
not concentrate at rehearsal; the instinctive sense of cadence, of
pulse, which was his great strength, fell to ruin; his bowing went to
pieces, and his phrasing—always as impulsive as a fifteen-year-old in
June—became utterly erratic, which, believe me, is the very kindest
word I can think of. On top of all that, he would instantly abandon
a rehearsal—or, once, in God's name, a performance!—because
word had been brought to him that Lyudmilla's illness had taken
some awful turn. I could have slaughtered him without a qualm and
slept soundly afterward; so you may well imagine what I thought of
Lyudmilla Plaschka. Murderous fancies or not, of course I favored
him. Not because he suffered more than she—who ever knows?—
but because he was one of *us*. Like that—like *us*. It comes down to
that, at the last.

    He sold the cello. To his friend Progorny. No fuss, no sentimen-
tal self-indulgence—his wife needed extensive (and expensive)
medical care, and that was the end of that. Any one of us would
have done the same; what was all the to-do about? At least, the Fabregas would stay in the family, just to his left, every night, while he
himself made cheerful do on a secondhand DeLuca found pawned
in Gradja. There are worse cellos than DeLucas. I am not saying
there aren't.

    But the bloody thing threw off the balance of the strings com-
pletely. How am I to explain this to you, who declare yourself no
musician? We have always been weak in the lower registers, as I
have admitted: Andrichev and that instrument of his had become,
in a real sense, our saviors, giving us depth, solidity, a taproot, a
place to come home to. Conductor and concertmaster, I can tell you
that none of the Greater Bornitz Municipal Orchestra—and in this
I include Herr Sigerson himself—actually took their time from me.
Oh, they looked toward me dutifully enough, but the corners of
their eyes were focused on the cello section at all times. As well they
should have been. Rhythm was never my strong suit, and I am not a
fool—I have told you that as well.

    But there are cellos and cellos, and the absence of the Fabregas
made all the difference in the world to us. That poor pawnshop
DeLuca meant well, and it held its pitch and played the notes asked

of it as well as anyone could have asked. Anyone who wasn't used—no, *attuned*—to the soft roar of the Fabregas, as our entire orchestra was attuned to it. It wasn't a fair judgment, but how could it have been? The *sound* wasn't the same; and, finally, the sound is everything. Everything. All else—balance, tempo, interpretation—you can do something about, if you choose; but the *sound* is there or it isn't, and that bloody ancient Fabregas was our sound and our soul. Yes, I know it must strike you as absurd. I should hope so.

Progorny gave it his best—no one ever doubted that. It was touching, poignant, in a way: he seemed so earnestly to believe that the mere possession of that peerless instrument would make him—had already made him—a musician equal to such a responsibility. Indeed, to my ear, his timbre was notably improved, his rhythm somewhat firmer, his melodic line at once more shapely and more sensible. But what of it? However kindly one listened, it wasn't the *sound*. The cello did not feel for him what it felt for Andrichev, and everyone knew it, and that is the long and the short of it. Musical instruments have neither pity nor any notion of justice, as I have reason to know. Especially the strings.

Whatever Progorny had paid him for the cello, it could not have been anything near its real value. And Lyudmilla grew steadily worse. Not that I ever visited her in her sickbed, you understand, but you may believe that I received daily—hourly—dispatches and bulletins from Andrichev. It very nearly broke my peevish, cynical old heart to see him so distraught, so frantically disorganized, constantly racing back and forth between the rehearsal hall, the doctor's office, and his own house, doing the best he could to attend simultaneously to the well-being of his wife and that of his music. For an artist, this is, of course, impossible. Work or loved ones, passions or responsibilities . . . when it comes down to that, as it always does, someone goes over the side. Right, wrong, it is how things are. It is how we are.

Yes, of course, I know perfectly well that it was remiss of me not to go to Lyudmilla at the earliest news of her illness. But in the first place, we were told almost immediately that her physician—a Romanian named Nastase—had placed her in quarantine; and if that word has some resonance for your educated ears, try to imagine how it must have reverberated in a near hamlet on the farthest splintery edge of Eastern Europe, where folk still truly believe that a baby can be born with the evil eye. Even within the choir, she had few friends in St. Radomir, and had been seen there less and less since her marriage. Now a slab-faced cook (plainly employed by Dr. Nastase; Andrichev could never have afforded a servant of any sort) drove her trap into town, did her shopping in the fewest words required, and left as shut-mouthed as she had arrived. So there was probably more talk and speculation about Lyudmilla Plaschka than ever before, but no real knowledge—and certainly no social calls.

In the second place, I didn't *like* the woman, you see—what a sour old person I must seem to you, so easily to detest both her and your hero Mr. Sigerson—and I was not hypocrite enough, in those days, to look into those ingenuous blue eyes and say that I prayed for the light of health swiftly to return to them once more. Yes, I wanted her to recover, almost as much as I wanted her to leave her husband alone to do what he was meant to do—very well, what I needed him to do. Let her have her lovers, by all means; let her sing duets with them all until she burst her pouter-pigeon breast; but let *me* have my best cellist back in the heart of my string section—and let *him* have his beautiful Fabregas under his thick, grubby, peasant hands again. Where it belonged.

Mind you, I had no idea how I would ransom it back, and reimburse Progorny (sad usurper, cuckolded by his own instrument) the money that had gone so straight to Dr. Nastase. And kept going to him, apparently, for Lyudmilla's condition somehow never seemed to improve. Andrichev was soon enough selling or pawning other belongings—books to bedding, old clothes to old flowerpots, a warped and stringless *bouzouki,* a cracked and chipped set of dishes—anything for which anyone would give him even a few more coins for his wife's care. Many of us bought worthless articles from him out of a pity that not long before, he would have rejected out of hand. I wonder whether Sigerson still has that cracked leather traveling bag with the broken lock—I think the moth-eaten fur cloak is somewhere in my attic. I *think* so.

So, though none of us ever saw Lyudmilla Plaschka at all, we read her worsening condition, and the wasteful uselessness of each new treatment, in Andrichev's face. He shrank before our eyes, that bear, that ox, call him what you like; he hollowed and hunched until there seemed to be nothing more to him than could be found inside his cello. Less, because the Fabregas, and even the DeLuca, made music of their emptiness, and Andrichev's sound—there it is again, always the *sound*—grew thinner, dryer, more distant, like the cry of a lone cricket in a desert. I still squirm with bitter shame to recall how hard it became for me to look at him, as though his despair were somehow my doing. My only defense is that we were all like that with him then, all except his comrade Progorny. And Sigerson, remote and secretive as ever, who, nevertheless, made a point of complimenting his playing after each performance. I should have done that, honesty be damned—I know I should have. Perhaps that is why the memory of that man still irritates me, even now.

Oh—Dr. Nastase himself? Yes, he had other patients, certainly, but by every account he offered them no confidences, and very gradually dismissed them, one after another, either assuring them that they were quite cured or politely passing them on to other physicians, apparently in order to concentrate his skills fully on Frau Andrichev's critical illness. They were all gone by the late-summer afternoon when, with Sigerson's comment, "We are more alike than you may think, Herr Takesti," continuing to plague me, I determined to pay a call on Lyudmilla Plaschka myself. I even brought flowers, not out of sympathy, but because flowers (especially a damp, slightly wilted fistful) generally get you admitted everywhere. I must say, I do enjoy not lying to you.

Andrichev's house, which looked much as he had in the good days—disheveled but sturdy—was located in the general direction of the Widow Ridnak's farm, but set some eight miles back into the barley fields, where the dark hills hang over everything like thunderheads ripe with rain. I arrived just in time to see Dr. Nastase—a youngish, strongly built man, a bit of a dandy, with a marked Varna accent—escorting a tattered, odorous beggar off the property, announcing vigorously, "My man, I've told you before, we're not having your sort here. Shift yourself smartly, or I'll set the dogs on you!" A curious sort of threat, I remember thinking at the time, since the entire dog population of the place consisted only of Lyudmilla's fat, flop-eared spaniel, who could barely be coaxed to harass a cat, let alone a largish beggar. The man mumbled indistinct threats, but the doctor was implacable, shoving him through the gate, latching and locking it, and warning him, "No more of this, sir, do you understand me? Show your face here again, and you'll find the police taking an interest in your habits. Do you understand?" The beggar indicated that he did, and meandered off, swearing vague, foggy oaths, as Dr. Nastase turned to me, all welcoming smiles now.

"Herr Takesti, it must be? I am so happy and honored to meet you, I can hardly find the words. Frau Lyudmilla speaks *so* highly of you—and as for Herr Andrichev . . ." And here he literally kissed his fingertips, may I be struck dead by lightning this minute if I lie. The last person I saw do such a thing was a Bosnian chef praising his own veal cutlets.

"I came to see Frau Lyudmilla," I began, but the doctor anticipated me, cutting me off like a diseased appendix. "Alas, *maestro,* I cannot permit sickroom visits at the present time. You must understand, her illness is of a kind that can so very, very easily be tipped over into"—here he shrugged delicately—"by the slightest disturbance, the least suggestion of disorder. With diseases of this nature, a physician walks a fine line—like a musician, if you will allow me— between caution and laxity, overprotectiveness and plain careless negligence. I choose to err on the side of vigilance, as I am sure you can appreciate."

There was a good deal more in this vein. I finally interrupted him myself, saying, "In other words, Frau Lyudmilla is to receive no visitors but her husband. And perhaps not even he?" Dr. Nastase blushed—very slightly, but he had the sort of glassy skin that renders all emotions lucid—and I knew what I knew. And so, I had no doubt, did Volodya Andrichev, and his business was his business, as always. I handed over my flowers, left an earnest message, then left myself, hurrying through the fields to catch up with that beggar. There was something about his bleary yellowish eyes . . .

Oh, but he was positively furious! It remains the only time I ever saw him overtaken by any strong emotion, most particularly anger. "How did you *know?*" he kept demanding. "I must insist that you tell me—it is more important than you can imagine. How did you recognize me?"

I put him off as well as I could. "It is hard to say, Herr Sigerson. Just a guess, really—call it an old man's fancy, if you like. I could as easily have been wrong."

He shook his head impatiently. "No, no, that won't do at all. Herr Takesti, for a variety of reasons, which need not concern us, I have spent a great deal of time perfecting the arts of concealment. Camouflage lies not nearly so much in costumes, cosmetics—such as the drops in my eyes that make them appear rheumy and degenerate—but in the smallest knacks of stance, bearing, movement, the way one speaks or carries oneself. I can stride like a Russian prince, if I must, or shuffle as humbly as his ostler—" and he promptly demonstrated both gaits to me, there in the muddy barley fields. "Or whine like a drunken old beggar, so that that scoundrel of a doctor never took me for anything but what he saw. Yet *you* . . ." and here he simply shook his head, which told me quite clearly his opinion of my perceptiveness. "I must know, Herr Takesti."

"Well," I said. I took my time over it. "No matter what concoction you may put in your eyes, there is no way to disguise their arrogance, their air—no, their *knowledge*—of knowing more than other people. It's as well that you surely never came near Lyudmilla Plaschka, looking like that. That doctor may be a fool, but she is none." It was cruel of me, but I was unable to keep from adding, "And even a woodwind would have noticed those fingernails. Properly filthy, yes—but so perfectly trimmed and shaped? Perhaps not." It was definitely cruel, and I enjoyed it very much.

The headshake was somewhat different this time. "You humble me, Herr Takesti," which I did not believe for a minute. Then the head came up with a positive flirt of triumph. "But I did indeed see our invalid Lyudmilla Plaschka. That much I can claim."

It was my turn to gape in chagrin. "You *did?* Did she see *you?*" He laughed outright, as well he should have: a short single cough. "She did, but only for a moment—not nearly long enough for my arrogant eyes to betray me. As you must know, there is a cook, especially hired by Dr. Nastase to prepare nutritious messes for his declining patient. A kindlier woman than her somewhat grim appearance might suggest, she let me into the kitchen and prepared me a small but warming meal—decidedly unhealthy, bless her fat red hands. When her attention was elsewhere, I took the opportunity to explore that area of the house, and was making a number of interesting discoveries when Lyudmilla Plaschka came tripping brightly along the corridor—not wrapped in a nightgown, mind you, nor in a snug, padded bed jacket, but dressed like any hearty country housewife on her way to requisition a snack between meals. She screamed quite rightly when she noticed me, and I was rather hurriedly removing myself from the premises when I ran into the good doctor." He made the laugh sound again. "The rest, obviously, you know."

I was still back at the moment of the encounter. "Tripping? Brightly?"

"Frau Plaschka," Sigerson said quietly, "is no more ill than you or I." He paused, deliberately theatrical, savoring my astonishment, and went on, "It is plain that with her lover, Dr. Nastase, she has conceived a plan to milk Volodya Andrichev of every penny he has, to cure her of her nonexistent affliction. Perhaps she will induce him to sell the house—if he has sold his cello for her sake, anything is possible. You would understand that better than I."

A sop to my own vanity, that last, but I paid it no heed. "I cannot believe that she . . . that *anyone* could do such a thing. I *will* not believe it."

Sigerson sighed and, curiously enough, the sound was not in the least contemptuous. "I envy you, Herr Takesti. I truly envy all those who can set limits to their observation, who can choose what they will believe. For me, this is not possible. I have no choice but to see what is before me. I have no choice." He meant it, too—I never doubted that—and yet I never doubted either that he would ever have chosen differently.

"But why?" I felt abysmally stupid merely asking the question. I knew why well enough, and still I had to say it. "Andrichev is the most devoted husband I have ever seen in my life. Lyudmilla Plaschka will never find anyone to love her as he does. Can she not see that?"

Sigerson did not reply, but only looked steadily at me. I think that was actually a compliment. I said slowly, "Yes. I know. Some people cannot bear to be loved so. I know that, Herr Sigerson."

We became allies in that moment; the nearest thing to friends we ever could have become. Sigerson still said nothing, watching me. I said, "This is unjust. This is worse than a crime. They must be stopped, and they should be punished. What shall we do?"

"Wait," Sigerson said, simply and quietly. "We wait on circumstance and proper evidence. If we two—and perhaps one or two others—set ourselves to watch over that precious pair at all times, there is little chance of their making the slightest move without our knowledge. A little patience, Herr Takesti, patience and vigilance." He touched my shoulder lightly with his fingertips, the first time I can recall even so small a gesture of intimacy from him. "We will have them. A sad triumph, I grant you, but we will have them yet. Patience, patience, concertmaster."

And so we did wait, well into the fall, and we did trap them, inevitably: not like Aphrodite and Ares, in a golden net of a celestial cuckold's designing, but in the tangled, sweated sheets of their own foolishness. Lyudmilla Plaschka and her doctor never once suspected that they were under constant observation, if not by Sigerson and myself, what time we could spare from music, then by a gaggle of grimy urchins, children of local transients. Sigerson said that he had often employed such unbuttoned, foul-mouthed waifs in a similar capacity in other situations. I never doubted him. These proved, not only punctual and loyal, but small fiends for detail. Dr. Nastase's preferred hour for visiting his mistress (married himself, there were certain constraints on his mobility); Frau Andrichev's regular bedtime routine, which involved a Belgian liqueur and a platter of marzipan; even Volodya's customary practice schedule, and the remarks that he grumbled to himself as he tuned his cello— they had it all, not merely the gestures and the words, but the expression with which the words were pronounced. They could have gathered evidence for the Recording Angel, those revolting brats.

"I have discovered the time and destination of their flight," Sigerson told me one morning when I relieved him as sentinel—as spy, rather; I dislike euphemism. He had gained entrance into the house on several occasions since the first, knowing the occupants' habits so well by then that he was never surprised again. "They are interesting conspirators—I discovered the trunks and valises stored in a vacant, crumbling outbuilding easily enough, but it took me longer than I had expected to find the two first-class railway tickets from Bucharest through to Naples, and the boat vouchers for New York City. Do you know where those were hidden?" I shook my head blankly. "At the very bottom of the woodpile, wrapped quite tidily in oilcloth. Obviously, our friends will be taking their leave within the next two or three weeks, before the nights turn cold enough for a fire to be necessary."

"Impressive logic," I said. Sigerson allowed himself one of his distant smiles. I asked, "What about the money they've swindled out of poor Andrichev? They'll have hidden it in some bank account, surely—in Italy, perhaps, or Switzerland, or even America. How will we ever recover it for him?"

If only Sigerson could have seen his own eyes at that moment, he might have understood what I meant by the impossibility of masking their natural lofty expression. "I think we need have no concern on that score," he replied. "Those two are hardly the sort to trust such liquid assets to a bank, and I would venture that Lyudmilla Plaschka knows men too well ever to allow her spoils out of her sight. No, the money will be where she can quickly put her hands on it at any moment. I would expect to find it in her bedroom, most probably in a small leather traveling case under the far window. Though, to be candid"—here he rubbed his nose meditatively—"there are one or two other possible locations, unfortunately beyond my angle of vision. We shall learn the truth soon."

We learned it a bit sooner than either of us expected; not from our unwashed sentries, but from the owner of the livery stable from which we always hired our traveling wagons. He and I were haggling amiably enough over feed costs for our customary autumn tour of the provinces when he mentioned that his good humor arose from a recent arrangement personally to deliver two passengers to the Bucharest railway station in his one *caleche*, behind his best team. It took remarkably few Serbian dinars to buy the names of his new clients from him, along with the time—eleven o'clock, tomorrow night!—and only a few more to get him to agree to take us with him when he went to collect them. Treachery is, I fear, the Selmiri national sport. It requires fewer people than football and no uniforms at all.

I wanted to bring the whole matter before the police at this point, but Sigerson assured me that there would be no need for this. "From what I have seen of the St. Radomir constabulary, they are even more thick-witted than those of"—did he stumble momentarily?—"the gendarmes of Oslo, which I never thought possible. Trust me, our quarry will not slip the net now." He did preen himself slightly then. "Should Dr. Nastase offer physical resistance, I happen to be a practitioner of the ancient art of *baritsu*—and you should be well able to cope with any skirmish with Frau Andrichev." I honestly *think* that was not meant as condescension, though with Sigerson it was hard to tell. A month of surveillance had made it clear to us both that Lyudmilla Plaschka, when not on her deathbed, was certainly a spirited woman.

A full rehearsal was scheduled for the following night; I elected to cancel it entirely rather than abridge it, musicians being easily distressed by interruptions in routine. There were some questions,

some grumbling, but nothing I could not fob off with partial explanations. Sigerson and I were at the livery stable by ten o'clock, and
it was still some minutes before eleven when the *caleche* drew up before the Andrichev house and the coachman blew his horn to announce our arrival.

The luggage was already on the threshold, as was an impatient
Lyudmilla Plaschka, clad in sensible gray traveling skirt and shirtwaist, cleverly choosing no hat but a peasant's rough shawl to hide
her hair and shadow her features. She had, however, been unable to
resist wearing what must have been her best traveling cloak, furred
richly enough for a Siberian winter; it must have cost Volodya Andrichev six months' pay. She looked as eager as a child bound for a
birthday party, but I truly felt my heart harden, watching her.

I stepped down from the *caleche* on the near side, Sigerson on
the other, as Dr. Nastase came through the door. He was dressed
even more nattily than usual, from his shoes—which even I could
recognize as London-made—to his lamb's-wool Russian-style hat.
When he saw us—and the coachman on his box, leaning forward as
though waiting like any theatergoer for the curtain to rise—he
arched his eyebrows, but only said mildly, "I understood that this
was to be a private carriage."

"And so it is indeed," Sigerson answered him, his own voice
light and amused. "But the destination may not be entirely to your
liking, Doctor." He came around the coach, moving very deliberately, as though trying not to startle a wild animal. He went on, "I
am advised that the cuisine of the St. Radomir jail is considered"—
he paused to ponder the *mot juste*—"questionable."

Dr. Nastase blinked at him, showing neither guilt nor fear, but
only the beginning of irritation. "I do not understand you." Lyudmilla
Plaschka put him aside, smoothly enough, but quite firmly, and came
forward to demand, "Just what is your business here? We have no time
for you." To the coachman she snapped, "The price we agreed on does
not include other passengers. Take up our baggage and let them walk
home."

The coachman spat tobacco juice and stayed where he was.
Sigerson said, speaking pointedly to her and ignoring the doctor,
"Madam, you know why we are here. The hospice is closed; the masquerade is over. You would be well-advised to accompany us peace-
ably to the police station."

I have known people whose consciences were almost unnaturally clean look guiltier than they. Lyudmilla Plaschka faltered, "Police station? Are you the police? But what have we done?"

My confidence wavered somewhat itself at those words—she might have been a schoolgirl wrongfully accused of cribbing the answers to an examination—but Sigerson remained perfectly self-assured. "You are accused of defrauding your husband of a large sum of money by feigning chronic, incurable illness, and of attempting further to flee the country with your ill-gotten gains and your lover. Whatever you have to say to this charge, you may say to the authorities." And he stepped up to take her arm, for all the world as though he were an authority himself.

Dr. Nastase rallied then, indignantly striking Sigerson's hand away before it had ever closed on Lyudmilla Plaschka's elbow. "You will not touch her!" he barked. "It is true that we have long been planning to elope, to begin our new life together in a warmer, more open land"—the elbow found his ribs at that point, but he pressed on—"but at no time did we ever consider cheating Volodya Andrichev out of a single dinar, zloty, ruble, or any other coin. We are leaving tonight with nothing but what is in my purse at this moment, and supported by nothing but my medical talents, such as they are, and Frau Andrichev's vocal gifts. By these we will survive, and discover our happiness."

Yes, yes, I know—he was not only an adulterer and a betrayer, but a very bad orator as well. And all the same, I could not help admiring him, at least at the time. Even bad orators can be sincere, and I could not avoid the troubling sense that this man meant what he was saying. It did not seem to trouble Sigerson, who responded coolly, "I will not contradict you, Dr. Nastase. I will merely ask you to open the small traveling case next to Lyudmilla Plaschka's valise—that one there, yes. If you will? Thank you."

I may or may not be a forbidding personality; he could certainly, when he chose, be a far more commanding one than I had ever imagined. I would have opened any kit of mine to his inspection at that point. Dr. Nastase hesitated only a moment before he silently requested the key from Lyudmilla Plaschka and turned it in the dainty silver lock of the traveling case. I remember that he stepped back then, to allow her to open the lid herself. Love grants some men manners, and I still choose to believe that Dr. Nastase loved Volodya Andrichev's wife, rightly or wrongly.

There was no money in the traveling case. I looked, I was there. Nothing except a vast array of creams, lotions, salves, ointments, unguents, decoctions . . . all the sort of things, my doddering brain finally deduced, that an anxious Juliet, some years the senior of her Romeo, might bring along on an elopement to retain the illicit magic of the relationship. I had only to glance at Lyudmilla Plaschka's shamed face for the truth of that.

To do Sigerson justice, his resolve never abated for an instant. He simply said, "By your leave," and began going through Dr. Nastase and Lyudmilla Plaschka's belongings just as though he had a legal right to do so. They stood silently watching him, somehow become bedraggled and forlorn, clinging together without touching or looking at each other. And I watched them all, as detached as the coachman: half-hoping that Sigerson would find the evidence that Volodya Andrichev had been viciously swindled by the person he loved most; with the rest of myself hoping . . . I don't know. I don't know what I finally hoped.

He found the money. A slab of notes the size of a brick; a small but tightly packed bag of coins; both tucked snugly into the false lid of a shabby steamer trunk, as were the tickets he had discovered earlier. The faithless wife and the devious doctor gaped in such theatrically incredulous shock that it seemed to make their culpability more transparent. They offered no resistance when Sigerson took them by the arm, gently enough, and ordered the coachman to take us back to town.

At the police station they made formal protest of their innocence, insisting that they had never seen the money, nor ever demanded any from Volodya Andrichev; but they seemed so dazed with disbelief that I could see it registering as guilt and shame with the constables on duty. They were placed in a cell—together, yes, how many cells do you think we have in St. Radomir?—and remanded for trial pending the arrival of the traveling magistrate, who was due any day. The doctor, ankles manacled, hobbled off with his warder without a backward glance; but Lyudmilla Plaschka—herself unchained—turned to cast Sigerson and me a look at once proud and pitiful. She said aloud, "*You* know what we have done, and what we did not do. You cannot evade your knowledge." And she walked away from us, following Dr. Nastase.

Sigerson and I went home. When we parted in front of my house, I said, "A wretched, sorry business. I grieve for everyone involved. Including ourselves." Sigerson nodded without replying. I stood looking after him as he started on toward the Widow Ridnak's. His hands were clasped behind him, his high, lean shoulders stooped, and he was staring intently at the ground.

Our tour began the next day—we did well in Gradja, very well in Plint, decently in Srikeldt, Djindji, Gavric, and Bachacni, and dreadfully in Boskvila, as always. I cannot tell you why I still insist on scheduling us to perform in Boskvila every year, knowing so much better, but it should tell you at least something about me.

But even in foul Boskvila, Volodya Andrichev played better than I had ever heard him. I detest people who are forever prattling about art in terms of human emotions, but there was certainly a new—not power, not exactly warmth, but a kind of deep, majestic heartbeat, if you will—to his music, and so to all of ours as well. He said nothing to anyone about his wife's arrest with her lover, nor did anyone—including Sigerson and his friend Progorny—ask him any questions, nor speak to him at all, except in praise. We did not see St. Radomir again for a week and a half, and the moment we arrived Andrichev tried to commit suicide.

No, no, not the precise moment, of course not, nor did it occur just as the wagons rolled past the town limits. Nor did anyone recognize his action for what it was, except Sigerson. As though he had been waiting for exactly this to happen, he leaned swiftly forward almost before Andrichev toppled over the side in a fall that would have landed him directly under our team's hooves and our wagon's ironbound wheels. A one-armed scoop, a single grunt, and Andrichev was sprawling at our feet before the rest of the company had drawn breath to cry out. Sigerson looked down at him and remarked placidly, "Come now, Herr Andrichev, we did not play *that* poorly in Boskvila." The incipient screams were overtaken by laughter, quickly dissolving any suggestion of anything more sinister than an accident. At the livery stable, before shambling away, Andrichev thanked Sigerson gruffly, apologizing several times for his clumsiness. It was early in the evening, and I remember that a few snowflakes were beginning to fall, a very few, twinkling for an instant in his mustache.

This night, for some unspoken reason, I passed up my own house and walked on silently with Sigerson, all the way to the Ridnak farm. The widow and her sons were already asleep. Sigerson invited me into the back kitchen, poured us each a glass of the widow's home-brewed *kvass*, and we toasted each other at the kitchen table, all without speaking. Sigerson finally said, "A sorry business indeed, Herr Takesti. I could wish us well out of it."

"But surely we are," I answered him, "out and finished, and at least some kind of justice done. The magistrate has already passed sentence—three years in prison for the woman, five for the man, as the natural instigator of the plot—and the money will be restored to Volodya Andrichev within a few days. A miserable matter, beyond doubt—but not without a righteous conclusion, surely."

Sigerson shook his head, oddly reluctantly, it seemed to me. "Nothing would please me better than to agree with you, concert-master. Yet something about this affair still disturbs me, and I cannot bring it forward from the back of my mind, into the light. The evidence is almost absurdly incontrovertible—the culprits are patently guilty—everything is properly tied up . . . and still, and still, *something* . . ." He fell silent again, and we drank our *kvass* and I watched him as he sat with his eyes closed and his fingertips pressed tightly against each other. For the first time in some while—for there is nothing to which one cannot become accustomed—I remembered to be irritated by that habit of his, and all the solitary self-importance that it implied. And even so, I understood also that this strange man had not been placed on earth solely to puzzle and provoke me; that he had a soul and a struggle like the rest of us. That may not seem, to you, like a revelation, but it was one to me, and it continues so.

How long we might have remained in that farm kitchen, motionless, unspeaking, sharing nothing but that vile bathtub brandy, it is impossible to say. The spell was broken when Sigerson, with no warning, was suddenly on his feet, and to one side, in the same motion, flattening his back against the near wall. I opened my mouth, but Sigerson hushed me with a single fierce gesture. Moving as slowly as a lizard stalking a moth, he eased himself soundlessly along the wall, until he was close enough to the back door to whip it open with one hand, and with the other seize the bulky figure on the threshold by the collar and drag it inside, protesting, but not really resisting. Sigerson snatched off the man's battered cap and stepped back, for all the world like an artist unveiling his latest portrait. It was Volodya Andrichev.

"Yes," Sigerson said. "I thought perhaps it might be you." For a moment Andrichev stood there, breathing harshly, his blue eyes gone almost black in his pale, desperate face. Then with dramatic abruptness he thrust his hands towards Sigerson, crossing them at the wrists and whispering, "Arrest me. You must arrest me now."

"Alas, all my manacles are old and rusted shut," Sigerson replied mildly. "However, there is some drink here which should certainly serve the same purpose. Sit down with us, Herr Andrichev."

A commanding person, as I have said, but one who did not seem to command. Andrichev fell into a kitchen chair as limply as he had rolled out of the wagon, only an hour or two before. He was sweating in great, thick drops, and he looked like a madman, but his eyes were clear. He said, "They should not be in prison. I am the one. You *must* arrest me. I have done a terrible, terrible thing."

I said firmly, "Andrichev, calm yourself this instant. I have known you for a long time. I do not believe you capable of any evil. Drunkenness, yes, and occasional vulgarity of attack when we play Schubert. Spite, vindictiveness, cruelty—never."

"No, no one ever believes that of me," he cried out distractedly. "I know how I am seen: good old Volodya—a bit brusque, perhaps, a bit rough, but a fine fellow when you really get to know him. A heart of gold, and a devil of a cellist, but all he ever thinks of is music, music and vodka. The man couldn't plan a picnic—let alone a revenge."

Sigerson had the presence of mind to press a drink into his hand, while I sat just as slack-jawed as Lyudmilla Plaschka and Dr. Nastase themselves at the sight of the money they were accused of swindling from Lyudmilla's besotted husband. Andrichev peered around the glass at us in an odd, coy way, his eyes now glinting with a sly pride that I had never seen there before.

"Yes, revenge," he said again, clearly savoring the taste and smell and texture of the word. "Revenge, not for all the men, all the deceptions, all the silly little ruses, the childish lies—they are simply what she is. As well condemn a butterfly to live on yogurt as her to share the same bed forever. Her doctor will learn that soon enough." And he smiled, tasting the thought.

The words, the reasoning, the *sound*—they were all so vastly removed from the Volodya Andrichev I was sure I knew that I still could not close my mouth. Sigerson appeared much cooler, nodding eagerly as Andrichev spoke, as though he were receiving confirmation of the success of some great gamble, instead of receiving proof positive that he and I had been thoroughly hoodwinked. He said, "The doctor made it different."

Andrichev's face changed strikingly then, all the strong features seeming to crowd closer together, even the forehead drawing down. He repeated the word *different* as he had the word *revenge*, but the taste puckered his mouth. "That fool, that wicked, wicked fool! He thinks he loves her, and he has made her think so herself. For that one, she would have left me, gone away forever. I *had* to stop her." But he sounded now as though he were reassuring himself that he had had no choice.

"The money," Sigerson prompted him gently. "That was indeed your money that I found in the steamer trunk?"

The furtively smug look returned to Andrichev's face, and he took a swig of his drink. "Oh, yes, every bit of it. Everything I could raise, no matter what I had to sell, or pawn, or beg, no matter how I had to live. The cello—that was hard for me, but not as hard as all of you thought. One can get another cello, but another Lyudmilla . . ." He fell silent for a moment, looking at the floor, then raised his eyes to us defiantly. "Not in this life. Not in my life. It had to be done."

Nor will we find another such cellist, I thought bitterly and selfishly. Sigerson said, "It was you alone who spread the tale of Frau Andrichev's chronic mortal illness. She and Dr. Nastase knew nothing."

"No, the doctor himself was a great help there," Andrichev said with a curious acrid humor. "He quarantined her to keep her to himself, and to give them leisure to plan their flight. We merely circulated the story rather more widely, Progorny and I, and in somewhat more detail. It was easy enough to manage; the difficulty lay in keeping it from reaching Lyudmilla's ears, or Nastase's. Progorny is a real friend"—he looked directly at me for the first time—"though he will never be a real cellist. But I am happy that he has the Fabregas."

I realized that I had been constantly shaking my head since he began speaking, unable truly to *see* this new Volodya Andrichev; trying to bring my mind into focus, if you will. I asked, lamely and foolishly, "Progorny put the money into the trunk lid, then?"

Andrichev snorted derisively. "No—when would he have the opportunity for that? The tickets under the woodpile, that was Progorny, but all the rest was my idea. The police were prepared to stop them on the road"—here his voice hesitated, and his mouth suddenly rumpled, as though he were about to cry—"just when they were thinking themselves safe and . . . and free." He took another deep swallow. "But you two made that unnecessary. I had not counted on your interference, but it was the last touch to my plan. Having two such reputable, distinguished witnesses to their crime and their attempted escape—even having one of them find the money—*that* closed the door behind them. That closed and locked the door."

"Yes," Sigerson said softly. "And then, with your plan successful, your revenge accomplished, your faithless wife and her lover in prison, you attempted to kill yourself." There was no question in his voice, and no accusation. He might have been reading a newspaper aloud.

"Oh," Andrichev said. "That." He said nothing more for some while, nor did Sigerson. The kitchen remained so quiet that I could hear the tiny rasping sound of a mouse chewing on the pantry door. Andrichev finally stood up, swaying cautiously, like someone trying to decide whether or not he is actually drunk. He was no longer sweating so dreadfully, but his face was as white and taut as a sail trying to contain a storm. He said, "I do not want to live without her. I can, but I do not want to. The *revenge* . . . it was not on her, but on myself. For loving her so. For loving her more than the music. That was the revenge." Once again he held his hands out to Sigerson for invisible manacles. "Get her out of that place," he said. "*Him*, too. Get them out, and put me in. Now. Now."

Lyudmilla Plaschka and Dr. Nastase were released from prison as soon as the magistrate who sentenced them could be located. This is a remarkable story in itself . . . but I can see that you wouldn't be interested. Lyudmilla Plaschka threatened to sue her husband, the court, the town, and the duchy of Greater Bornitz for a truly fascinating sum of money. Dr. Nastase must have prevailed, however, for she hired no lawyer, filed no claims, and shortly afterward disappeared with him in the general direction of New South Wales. I believe that a cousin of hers in Gradja received a postal card.

Volodya Andrichev was formally charged with any amount of undeniable transgressions and violations, none of which our two St. Radomir lawyers knew how to prosecute—or defend, either, if it came to that—so there was a good deal of general relief when he likewise vanished from all human sight, leaving neither a forwarding address nor any instructions as to what to do with his worldly goods. One of the lawyers attempted to take possession of his house, in payment for unpaid legal fees; but since no one could even guess what these might amount to, the house eventually became the property of the Greater Bornitz Municipal Orchestra. It is specifically intended to accommodate visiting artists, but so far, to be quite candid . . . no, you aren't interested in that, either, are you? You only want information about Herr Sigerson.

Well, I grieve to disappoint you, but he, too, is gone. Oh, some while now—perhaps two months after Volodya Andrichev's disappearance. As it happens, I walked with him to catch the mail coach on which he had arrived in St. Radomir. I even carried his violin case, as I recall. Never friends, colleagues by circumstance, we had little to say to one another, but little need as well. What we understood of each other, we understood; the rest would remain as much a mystery as on that very first evening, and we were content to leave it so.

We were silent during most of the wait for his train, until he said abruptly, "I would like you to know, Herr Takesti, that I will remember my time here with both affection and amusement—but also with a certain embarrassment." When I expressed my perplexity, he went on, "Because of the Andrichev matter. Because I was deceived."

"So was I," I replied. "So was the entire orchestra—so was everyone with any knowledge of the business." But Sigerson shook his head, saying, "No, concertmaster, it is different for me. It is just different."

"And that is exactly why I recognized you in your beggar's disguise," I responded with some little heat. "It is always somehow different for you, and that so-called *difference* will always show in your eyes, and in everything you do. How could you possibly have guessed the secret of Volodya Andrichev's revenge on his wife and her lover? What is it that you expect of yourself, Herr Oscar Sigerson? What—*who*—are you supposed to be in this world?"

We heard the train whistle, so distant yet that we could not see the smoke rising on the curve beyond the Ridnak farm. Sigerson put his hand lightly on my shoulder for a brief moment; it was the second, and last, time that he ever touched me. He said, "You know a little of my thought, Herr Takesti. I have always believed that when one eliminates the impossible, what remains, no matter how improbable, must be the truth, the one solution of the problem. In this case, however, it turned out the other way around. I will be considering the Andrichev matter for a long time to come."

The train pulled in, and we bowed to each other, and Sigerson swung aboard, and that is the last I ever saw of him. The mail coach runs to and from Bucharest; beyond that, I have no idea where he was bound. I am not sure that I would tell you if I did know. You ask a few too many questions, and there is something wrong with your accent. Sigerson noticed such things.

The Mystery of Dr. Thorvald Sigerson

Linda Robertson

Cape Stevenson
Alaska Territory
September 30, 1894

Editor
Illustrated Weekly News
755 Market Street
San Francisco, California

To the Editor:

I recently received several numbers of your publication from this past summer, and was surprised and saddened to learn from them of the mysterious disappearance of the explorer Thorvald Sigerson. I was distressed, too, to read that doubts have been expressed regarding the authenticity of Professor Sigerson's notebooks, the truth of the account of Mr. Henry Mayes, your reporter, of their journeys across the polar ice, and, indeed, the very existence of Professor Sigerson himself.

We at Cape Stevenson can vouch for the existence of Professor Sigerson. Several of us, indeed, spent considerable time with him and with Henry Mayes. I have evidence, also, that the logs and notebooks in Mr. Mayes's possession are genuine documents from the professor's expedition into the polar ice field, including copies I personally made of them from the professor's originals. And the same ship that brought me the back numbers of the *San Francisco Call* and the *Illustrated Weekly News* containing the accounts of Professor Sigerson's disappearance also brought me a letter from the professor himself. The letter is brief and says little about his circumstances, except that he was proceeding to France to continue some researches there. He had become aware, he wrote, of the accusations being made against Mr. Mayes, his companion on his Arctic journey, and asked me to help verify Mr. Mayes's story to the extent that I was able regarding the expedition and its accomplishments. In the account that follows, I shall attempt to do so.

My name is John Osborne, and I am the proprietor of a trading station at Cape Stevenson, near Point Barrow. The story of how I came to be here is a long one, and would be of little interest to you. Suffice it to say that I was a wayward, impractical youth, and my family thought it would "straighten me up" to send me to sea. But my physical strength was not up to the rigors of a sailor's life, and while in the Arctic, I became deathly ill and was left here in the care of a missionary couple, with every expectation that I would soon expire. That I did not, I owe to the care and kindness of the Reverend and Mrs. Strong, and to Lucy Elisaok, an orphaned Eskimo girl working for them, who helped Mrs. Strong nurse me. After a long convalescence, I recovered fully, except for some slight weakness in my lungs, and found work as clerk and bookkeeper for Mr. Gutkind, who ran the trading station, selling dry goods to the Eskimos and trappers in exchange for furs. By that time, Lucy and I had fallen in love, and as soon as I was on my feet and working, we were married by Reverend Strong. When Mr. Gutkind decided to try his luck prospecting for gold in the Yukon Territory a year later, I took over the store. That was three years ago. During that time I have learned something of the land and the natives here and gained some proficiency in the Eskimo language and have come to think of Cape Stevenson, for all its harsh remoteness, as my home, the Strongs as my mother and father, and Lucy and the people in her village as my family and friends.

Professor Sigerson arrived at Cape Stevenson in August of last year on the steamer *William Seward*, which also brought supplies for the winter for the mission, my store, and the weather research station at Point Barrow. Mr. Mayes was with him, as well as a Norwegian named Eilif Bergsson, who seemed to be the professor's assistant or servant. Their arrival had been preceded by letters of introduction for all of them to Lieutenant Edgewater at the weather station, and we were curious to meet them and learn more about their proposed expedition.

A crowd of people were at the shore when the launch came from the *William Seward*. Lieutenant Edgewater had sailed from Point Barrow in the weather station's skiff when he saw the smoke from the ship on the horizon, and he was at the landing to greet his guests. Sigerson was perhaps forty, tall and spare, with an aquiline face and deep-set eyes. Mayes, of course, you know. Bergsson was the largest and tallest of the three; blond-haired and square-jawed, he radiated quiet and strength. The lieutenant shook their hands warmly. "Professor, Mr. Mayes, a pleasure to meet you. I hope you had an easy voyage."

"As good as one could expect, surely," Professor Sigerson answered. "We encountered some rough weather past Kotzebue and some ice in the last few days, but Captain Fellowes did an excellent job of steering the ship through it." He spoke like an educated Englishman, with no trace of a Norwegian accent.

"Glad to hear all went well. But here, it is starting to snow; you've missed what passes here for summer, I'm afraid. Let us get you all indoors. We haven't much to offer visitors, in the way of comforts, but Reverend and Mrs. Strong have a room in their house until we can get you settled in the log house we use here when visiting from the weather station." He turned to Reverend Strong and me. "This is John Osborne, the manager of our general store, and Reverend Strong, our teacher and missionary to the natives."

"Ah, Mr. Osborne, Reverend Strong," Professor Sigerson said. "Along with the lieutenant, you are the men I was told to ask for here, to help me speak with the Eskimos and obtain their help in my enterprise."

Strong answered, "We'll be pleased to help in whatever way we can."

"As will my wife and I," I agreed.

I was busy every waking hour for the next few days, loading furs onto the ship and supervising the unloading and storing of my merchandise and supplies, so I didn't immediately have time to become acquainted with our visitors except for Bergsson. He went out to the ship in the *umiaks*, the skin boats, of the Eskimos hired to bring cargo from the ship, and unloaded many of the expedition's trunks from them himself, lifting them almost without effort onto the sledge we used to pull them to the village. Some he carried on his shoulders all the way to the log house where the party would be staying.

When I had finished unpacking and inventorying our goods, Lucy and I invited our visitors to dinner, along with the lieutenant and the Strongs. Over seal steaks and dried-apple pie, Sigerson explained his planned expedition, as we listened and contributed such advice as we thought might be useful.

"I intend to travel as far north across the ice as I can manage," Sigerson said, drawing a line with his finger across a map of the northern edge of the Alaska Territory and the ice field above it, "my goal being to investigate the possibility that a system of islands, like those above Canada, lies concealed in the ice above Point Barrow. Along the way, I shall take measurements that I hope will help determine the movement of the magnetic north pole. To cover as much distance as possible, we plan to use dogsleds, and our party will be a small one: myself, Mr. Bergsson, Mr. Mayes, and an Eskimo guide."

"The Eskimos here don't go far onto the ice field," I interjected. "They say there's no game there."

"If there are no islands and few leads of open water, that may well be true," Lieutenant Edgewater added. "You'll need supplies for at least three months, to be safe. When were you thinking of starting?"

"I think in February, when the light returns. That will give us time to travel fairly far north and return before the pack ice breaks up. I have brought what I hope are ample supplies for the men in the expedition. I will need sleds and dogs, though, and dried fish to feed them. And reindeer skin clothes, tents, and sleeping bags. All those I hope I can obtain here over the next several months."

I said that Lucy and I could find good skins and local women who could sew what they needed. "I know of a couple of men who might make good guides," I said, "but it will be difficult for a man to leave his family for that long without someone to hunt for them."

"Let them know I will pay very well," Sigerson replied.

Over the next few weeks we met several times for dinner and talked at length about Sigerson's plans and the news from the world below. Sigerson had journeyed through the mountains of India and Tibet, and Reverend Strong was enthralled at his descriptions of the ancient monasteries that cling to the bare rock of the mountains two and a half miles above the sea, and the strange and austere practices of the monks who inhabited them. We debated the case of Lizzie Borden, arguing for her guilt or innocence from the facts gleaned from the old newspapers that had come to us on the *William Seward*. Professor Sigerson seemed to have taken an interest in the case. He made a compelling argument for her guilt, drawing upon details in which we had seen no significance and upon what he called "the science of deduction" to show how she could have managed to hide the evidence of her crime from the police. "The case was handled very badly," he said. "Between the neighbors having the run of the house for the entire day of the murders and the well-meaning ineptness of the Fall River Police, Miss Borden could have hidden or destroyed a dozen bloodstained dresses without anyone being the wiser."

Mrs. Strong insisted on Miss Borden's innocence, saying finally, "Professor, despite your evidence, it's hard for me to believe that a gently bred woman would be capable of such a savage crime."

"I don't doubt that the jury felt much as you do," Sigerson replied. "It seems to be one of the strange notions of the modern civilized world that women of the middle and upper classes possess some superiority of spirit that disinclines them to harm another creature. True, many more women murder by stealth than by force, but I believe that has more to do with their inferior strength and skill than with any revulsion against killing."

I was a little surprised at the professor's apparent cynicism. Mrs. Strong, however, responded, in her gentle, yet firm, way. "I think you do us women a disservice, Professor. The willingness to kill is not bred into us, and most of us aren't taught it, any more than children are. If Miss Borden did kill her parents, I suspect it must have been the result of some dreadful torment or a deranged mind."

"But there is no evidence of that," Lieutenant Edgewater interjected. "By all accounts, the Bordens were an upstanding, respectable family."

The professor responded, "Ah, but such families often hide dreadful secrets behind the untroubled faces they present to the world. I have seen them, and Mr. Mayes and Reverend Strong, I imagine you must have also in your work."

"Sadly, yes," my friend answered, and his wife nodded in agreement.

"Oh, definitely," Mayes added, and proceeded to tell a story about a refined and charming woman in San Francisco who had married and killed three rich husbands, then fled with her ill-gotten gains to South America when the law began closing in on her.

Autumn and cold weather were by then definitely upon us. Storms swept across the cape, whitening the brown hills with snow and freezing the bay ever farther from the shore. The Eskimos, returning from their summer hunting and trading, repaired their winter huts of sod and whalebone and filled their caches with walrus, seal, caribou, and dried fish for the long winter ahead. A few times our little settlement was visited by whaling ships hastening south ahead of the ice. They brought business to my store and to the Eskimos who sold them fresh meat, but they also brought vice and disease. Despite the law prohibiting selling alcohol to the Eskimos, the whaling ships often trade it to them, and the men get drunk and fight and sometimes shoot one another. By our standards, too, the morals of the Eskimos are peculiarly lax, and the young women and girls flock to the ships to consort with the sailors, to the constant distress of Reverend and Mrs. Strong.

Lucy, when she was not helping Mrs. Strong in the mission school, was busy arranging for clothes and a guide for Professor Sigerson's expedition. She spoke with a woman in the village who she said was the best at sewing parkas and another who made the best reindeer skin boots—*kamiks*, as the Eskimos call them. When word got around that the white men were looking for caribou skins and dog salmon, people came to the store from villages up and down the coast, their dogsleds piled with bales of furs and dried fish. The sewing women came to the store and examined the skins, choosing one here and there. One day Lucy came to me, and said, "Johnny, I think Tungweruk may be willing to be a guide for Mr. Sigerson, but you need to talk to him."

"Of course, darling," I said, "but why?"

"Konok and Ongualuk have told him he should ask me to be his wife, and now I'm too embarrassed to speak to anyone in the village about him."

I wasn't surprised. The women in the village were always ribbing Lucy, telling her she should go with a man who could hunt. "You can't make fur clothes or do much of anything useful," they would say to her. "If this white man leaves, you won't get a good husband, only a lazy one who can't get any other woman to live with him."

While Lucy watched the store, Sigerson, Bergsson, and I walked to the village to find Tungweruk, the prospective guide. I knew him because he came occasionally to the store to trade skins and meat for lead for bullets, tea, flour, and household goods. We found him in the big house of his whaling crew, and he led us to his hut. Apparently he already had a wife, because a young woman was outside, cleaning a caribou hide. She followed us into the hut and listened as we talked, occasionally making a comment to Tungweruk in their language. They were a handsome couple, with broad, attractive faces and thick black hair. Their reindeer skin clothing was trimmed handsomely with rabbit, fox, and ermine, and their hut was orderly and well supplied with tools, cooking gear, and skins for bedding.

Tungweruk's wife made tea, tossing a handful of leaves into a pot of water heating over the seal oil lamp. As we drank, we discussed when and how long Sigerson intended to travel on the ice field. Tungweruk, too, asked how he intended to feed himself, saying, "There is no game in there; no seal, no bear, only ice." As I translated for them, they discussed obtaining dogs and supplies, the number of dogs and sleds that would be needed, and how Tungweruk would be paid for his work. Tungweruk had had a good season whaling and hunting for caribou and had stored a good supply of meat for the winter, but he wanted provisions to be made available for his wife while he would be gone, during the lean times in the early spring. He and Sigerson arrived at an agreement easily, and at the end, we celebrated their bargain with ship's biscuit and strips of dried whale blubber.

With Tungweruk's help, Sigerson soon acquired a couple of sleds and a dozen dogs, so that they could begin learning to drive them. They arranged to have four new sleds built to carry the men and their supplies and began buying dogs to pull them. Sigerson, Mayes, and Bergsson then left Cape Stevenson to stay with the lieutenant and his men at the weather station. Tungweruk, with his wife, also moved out by the weather observatory to teach the three men how to drive their dog sleds.

During the fall I saw Sigerson and his companions now and again, usually on clear days when one or two of them sledded here to pick up some of the supplies Sigerson had stored in my warehouse. Mr. Mayes seemed the keenest on visiting. From early on, he took to skating alongside the dogsled on a pair of odd snowshoes, like two sled runners. "They're a Norwegian invention," he said, when I asked, "called skis. Nansen used them when he crossed Greenland, and Sigerson wants to use them, too, and Bergsson is teaching us. They're much faster than running with the sled—look!" And with a push from his staff he sped down a small slope.

Sigerson made a study of the customs and language of the natives. He spent days at a time in the village, watching the men and women at their daily tasks and questioning the Strongs, Lucy, and me about them. He and Bergsson went with Tungweruk to hunt seal and caribou. And he worked at learning the native language, impressing us all with how quickly he mastered its intricacies.

In the middle of November, the sun dipped below the horizon, not to return until February. Once I had stacked enough driftwood for the stove and shored up the store and our house against the winter storms, I had little to do, and anyway the winter darkness makes me dull. I slept a lot, whittled dishes and cups from driftwood, and visited with the Eskimos from the village who came by to trade or just to pass the time in our sitting room, and read and traded books with Reverend Strong. Lucy helped Mrs. Strong teach at the mission school, knitted socks and hats, and made little gifts for Christmas and the big winter festival the villagers call Kivyik.

That winter, too, our little settlement was enlarged by the inhabitants of the *Myra*, a steam whaler that had left the whaling grounds above Canada a little too late and, its passage south blocked by ice, had had to turn back and winter at Cape Stevenson. She was a particularly sorry example of that enterprise: the ship rusty and poorly maintained, her captain a weak and irritable man, and her crew mostly ruffians. Even the Eskimo women soon tired of their uncouth ways and, for the most part, left the ship alone.

The father of one girl, Neakpuk, however, traded her to the first mate in return for tobacco and rum. The mate, Sanders, was a boor and a drunkard. When he was in his cups, which was often, he beat

Neakpuk and called her the vilest of names. The poor girl, who had been a cheerful, simple young woman, now scarcely raised her head and seldom smiled. Reverend Strong, who frequently visited the ship to talk with the men, spoke more than once to Sanders and the captain, Belcher, about Sanders's treatment of Neakpuk, but to no avail.

A number of the men of the crew took to coming to church on Sundays, influenced by the reverend's kind and cheerful presence, or just looking for something to fill their time in the long winter night. One was Sanders's son Tom, a lad of sixteen, as good-hearted, generous, and hardworking as Sanders was vicious and mean. Sanders seemed to resent his son's good nature and his popularity with his shipmates, and lost no opportunity to attack him with slights, biting remarks, and cuffs. Once I was near and heard him muttering, when he saw Tom outside the church. "Sunday school boy, just like your mother. Don't you have any work to do? Like to sit around, just like her, and just wait for me to bring home money, eh?" Tom said nothing, but I could see his jaw tighten as he turned his head away.

The ship's carpenter, a gruff man named Evers, seemed to take a fatherly interest in young Tom and had little use for Sanders, whom he called an "old windbag" and worse. "Don't let him get to you, kid," he would tell Tom, clapping a roughened hand on the boy's shoulder.

During the gloomiest part of the winter, on a stormy night not long after the end of the Christmas holidays, Sanders vanished. He had been playing cards with some shipmates and lost badly. He rose from the table cursing and consigning the other players to Hell, and stomped from the room. In his cabin, some of the men had heard his cursing and Neakpuk crying and pleading with him—"the usual," one said cynically. One or two heard footsteps, as if she had run to the deck with him chasing her.

Sanders wasn't at breakfast the next day, and when the captain looked into his cabin, it was empty. A search through the ship revealed no sign of him or Neakpuk, but the storm and the darkness made a wider search impossible. It was another two days before the weather calmed enough to let the ship's crew and some of us from the settlement, carrying lanterns and torches, fan out across the ice in search of Sanders's body, since it was assumed that he could not have survived the storm. Neakpuk, miraculously, turned up alive and well in the village. When questioned about Sanders's disappearance, she shook her head, saying, "I don't know, I ran away."

"Sneaky little savage," the captain growled. "She knows more than she's telling; you can see it." Others speculated that Sanders, wandering drunkenly in the dark, had probably fallen into a hole made by an Eskimo hunting for fish or seal.

The mystery of Sanders's disappearance soon took a backseat to the excitement of the sun's appearance over the horizon in February and, not long afterward, Sigerson's departure on his expedition north on the ice. By his purchases of dogs, sleds, dried fish, clothing, and other supplies, Sigerson had become a well-known benefactor to the Eskimos in the village. They laughed at the foolishness of the white men who went to so much trouble to travel where there was no game to catch, but many of them walked or sledded up to the weather station to see the party off. A number of the villagers followed the travelers for some distance on their sleds. The rest of us watched their forms, with their long shadows, shrink with distance until they were little more than dots, hardly visible in the gathering dark.

After they left, life in the settlement quickly returned to its regular routine. It was the hungriest time of the year, when game was scarce and the meat and fish stored the previous summer were running low. Tungweruk's wife, a little baby tucked in the hood of her parka, came to the store a couple of times to draw on her husband's payment in ship's biscuit, dried salmon, and tea. The men in the village hunted seals, waiting with infinite patience by holes in the ice, and the women and children spent long hours ice fishing. Lucy went out with them sometimes, so that we could have fresh fish, but there were few fish to be found, and Lucy and I subsisted mostly on canned food, dried salmon and bannock, and an occasional piece of seal we bought if someone had enough to trade. Nevertheless, we felt fortunate that we didn't have to go hungry, and our spirits lifted as the days grew longer and brighter.

A few of the men from the ship sometimes went fishing with us or spent idle hours sitting by the stove in the store, reading old magazines, swapping stories, and grumbling about getting out of "this godforsaken place" and back to catching whales. We speculated occasionally about how Sigerson and his crew were doing, especially when the weather turned bad. "I guess we're better off marooned in this here rathole than they are right now," Evers, the carpenter, growled one snowy afternoon as the wind blustered and rattled the windows of the house.

"What if they end up eating each other like those poor b——ds at Cape Sabine? Have a big inquest, we'll all get to go to Washington to testify," Guest, the third mate, added, with a sort of dire anticipation. Once in a while someone would mention Sanders, and from what the men said it was clear that he wasn't missed by them, and they seemed uninterested in speculating about his fate.

Contrary to Guest's dreadful predictions, Sigerson and his crew returned, ragged and exhausted, but unscathed, at the end of April. They had traveled to the eighty-second parallel, making observations along the way, a journey of some sixteen hundred miles, in which they had found no land or anything but a vast expanse of pack ice. "It appears," Sigerson told us at dinner a few days after their return, "that there may be no islands north of Point Barrow, such as there are above Canada. Instead, there appears to be a permanent, year-round pack of ice, possibly extending to the pole itself."

I had a nice, legible hand and little else to do at the time, so Sigerson hired me to make a fair copy of his logs and journal from the expedition. Mayes regaled us, for the weeks that followed, with dramatic tales of daring and privation—how one of the sleds slipped into a crack in the ice and would have been lost, with all its dogs, but for Bergsson's immense strength in holding it until it could be pulled to safety; how they barely escaped when their tents were buried in snow and ice after a storm; and how Sigerson's lead dog, Heda, had saved them from a polar bear by keeping it at bay until Bergsson could bring it down with a well-aimed shot. Sigerson and Bergsson smiled at his enthusiasm, but said little. Sigerson's journals confirmed Mayes's stories, but in the most matter-of-fact manner, as if such adventures were merely small obstacles overcome by intelligence and careful thought.

One spring evening I returned from a day of hunting geese to news of a grisly discovery. A man's body had been found in a collapsed snow house on the frozen bay, between the *Myra* and the village. I walked immediately over to where a small crowd of sailors from the ship and several Eskimos were gathered near the heap of dirty snow that had been the snow house. My glance fell on Tom Sanders, who was standing a little apart with Evers. His pale, stricken face made it immediately clear whose the body was. Several people greeted me and let me through to the center of the circle. There, to my surprise, I saw Sigerson, standing over the corpse, which had been dug out of its snowy grave and placed on a board on the snow. I could see little except its dark clothing and wet, crumpled hair. As I approached, Sigerson turned his head and waved me back impatiently. "How often must I tell you, this is the scene of a crime. Don't destroy the evidence by trampling over it like a bunch of London—oh, it's you, Mr. Osborne. Please stand back—thank you." He looked back at the corpse, then to me. "This is the missing Mr. Sanders," he said, "killed by this." He picked up an object from the table near the body. I recognized it as a barbed harpoon head of ivory turned almost the brown of mahogany with age.

"It's an Eskimo piece. Quite a handsome artifact." He pointed to some markings along its side, and I noticed, for the first time, how long and slender his hands were. "Note the incised carving; it's rather a distinctive artifact. The captain has gone with a posse of men to the village to arrest Neakpuk. I tried to tell him that he was wrong in thinking that she was the murderer, but he would hear none of it."

For a minute I simply stood in confusion, looking from him to Sanders's body and back again. Then Sigerson said, in his brisk manner, "May I use your storehouse for Mr. Sanders's remains until I can complete my examination?"

I nodded assent.

"Good. I'll get some of the crew to help me carry him."

I turned and started back toward the settlement, to unlock the warehouse door. As I left I stopped near Tom Sanders. "I'm terribly sorry," I said.

He looked at me with something like desperation. "They're blaming the girl," he said. "It—"

"There, now, let's not discuss it till we knows more," Evers broke in. "He's not himself, sir," he said to me, "with the shock of it and all."

At the storehouse, I helped construct a makeshift table of planks and sawhorses for Sanders's body to lie upon. Then, leaving Sigerson with the key, I walked over to Reverend Strong's house. I couldn't help hoping that someone had warned Neakpuk in time to let her escape or hide; but the captain's party had found her outside her hut and had brought her to Reverend Strong, insisting that she be locked up somewhere until Lieutenant Edgewater could be fetched to preside over an inquest of sorts.

The house was surrounded with curious Eskimos and men from the *Myra*. Reverend Strong greeted me as I entered his crowded sitting room. "Osborne, hello. Lucy is in the bedroom with Katherine and Neakpuk, and I'm trying to keep the peace out here." He was standing with two men whom I recognized as elders from the village. Another half dozen villagers sat on chairs and on the floor. Across the room, the captain sat, glowering, with a couple of men from his posse. Tom Sanders stood against a wall, shoulders hunched, looking down at his folded hands.

"It's a good thing most of the young men are off hunting walrus right now," Strong said to me, shaking his head, "or there would have been bloodshed, I suspect. We're at a bit of an impasse as it is. The elders think this should be handled by them, and Captain Belcher won't hear of it. He wants the girl to be tried by him and Edgewater and punished as they dictate."

"Sigerson tells me she didn't kill Sanders."

"I don't see how he can tell, but I hope he can prove it."

We sat for an hour or more, Strong and I making small talk while the captain and the two men with him sat in uncomfortable silence at one end of the room and the two elders, their faces impassive, stood at the other. Lieutenant Edgewater arrived with Mayes and Bergsson, who had gone to fetch him from the weather station. Martha, an Eskimo girl who helped Mrs. Strong around the house, made tea for everyone, and we gathered around the dinner table to discuss how the case of Sanders's murder should be handled.

We had scarcely gotten settled when the door opened and a boy from the village came in shyly and mumbled something to Reverend Strong. Strong stood up and made his way across the crowded room to the captain. "Professor Sigerson has asked you and Mr. Osborne to go to him at the storehouse, where the body is." We rose to our feet, pulled on our jackets and boots, and crossed to the warehouse. Sigerson greeted us at the door, and with something of a dramatic flourish motioned us inside, to the makeshift table on which Sanders's corpse lay in the light of a lantern suspended from the roof beam. The clothes had been removed from the body and a piece of canvas laid over its lower half. A long incision, in a Y-shape, started near its chest and disappeared under the canvas at its waist. A little to the left of it I could see the jagged edges of a wound, with a slender wooden dowel protruding from it.

Sigerson moved next to the body and began his explanation. "As you can see, I essayed a rough postmortem examination of the injuries. Although I am not a medical doctor, I have studied anatomy and have seen several dissections of cadavers, and I have also learned a little over the years from an old friend who was a battlefield surgeon. I wanted you, Captain Belcher, to see for yourself the injury which caused Mr. Sanders's death. As you see, the body is in an excellent state of preservation, since it was frozen and sealed under snow and ice for several months.

"On Mr. Sanders's abdomen you can see the mark of a single stab wound. When the body was found, this"—he picked up the ivory harpoon head from the table—"was protruding from that wound."

"That was Sanders's," the captain exclaimed. "I remember when he won it at dice from a sailor at Herschel Island. You mean she killed him with that?"

"That is the weapon that killed him," Sigerson replied.

"Well, it certainly points to her as the killer, wouldn't you say? She was in his room and could have gotten hold of that—whatever it is—and hidden it and waited for her chance."

Sigerson pulled the canvas sheet until it covered the body entirely. "Let us go back to the reverend's house," he said.

When we returned with Sigerson to the crowded room, I saw that Neakpuk was standing in the doorway of the bedroom, her hand in Mrs. Strong's. In her face I saw the resignation with which the Eskimos seem to accept the terrible hands Fate so often deals them, and it pierced my heart to see it in a girl so young. Tom had not moved from his place, but he watched us as we entered, studying each of our faces.

After we had sat down at the table, Captain Belcher was the first to speak. "Well, I've seen Sanders's body and heard what the professor here has to say, and it's as clear as it can be that the girl killed him—waited her chance, I suppose, until he left the ship that night, and stabbed him out there on the ice with his own knife."

A murmur of voices rose in the room, as people there reacted to the captain's accusation and translated it for their neighbors. Lucy spoke softly to the elders, who shook their heads and looked grave.

Amid the voices, one rose from the back of the room. Tom pushed his way forward, toward the table. His face was pale and exhausted, but its expression resolute. "No—please, no. It wasn't Nettie, it was me. I—I killed him."

Captain Belcher answered him with an oath. "What are you talking about, Tom? That girl's just a murdering savage, boy, let her be."

Tom turned to face the captain and answered in a stronger voice, "No. No, it's not right."

"D——it, Tom," the captain began, but was interrupted by Sigerson, who said, "Let the boy tell his story."

"Yes, tell us what happened," Mayes added.

Reverend Strong offered Tom his chair, but Tom shook his head. Holding the back of the chair with one hand to steady himself, he hesitated for a second or two. Then he raised his head and began. "He—my father—was beating her—you know how he was. He was drunk again—some of the men had made some home brew—and he was playing cards and losing. When he got up and left for the cabin, I followed after him. I knew Nettie—that's what we called her, because my father couldn't pronounce her name—I knew she was there that night, and I knew he'd take it out on her. That's how it's been all our lives when he was home, when he'd get drunk and take it out on my ma. I thought I'd try—sometimes I can—could stop him by talking to him or getting him angry at me instead. I felt so bad for her. She's just a little thing, no older than my little sister.

"But he got there, and he was like a wild man. He grabbed her as soon as he saw her, called her a lying, thieving whore, and started punching her. I ran in and tried to pull him off, and he turned on me. He accused me of being sweet on her and—you know—behind his back and all, and then he said he'd kill us both and pulled that harpoon blade of his out of his pocket.

"Nettie ran out and up the stairs to the deck, and he lit out after her. She got off the ship and was running on the snow, getting away from him, but it was windy and dark, and she tripped and fell, and he caught up with her. I yelled to him to stop, and he turned around and grabbed me. I tried to break away, but couldn't. He was like a madman. I got hold of his knife hand and was struggling to keep him from stabbing me. I kicked him, and he let go of the harpoon, and I got it away from him. But then he ran me over and just fell onto the harpoon head in my hand. It must have stabbed him in a vital spot, because he staggered and let go of me and sat down, slumped over, right there on the snow. I fell down with him.

"I tried to revive him, but he died there in a few moments. Then I sat there, and all I could think about was that I'd just killed my father." Tom stopped for a moment, overcome, then collected himself and went on. "I didn't think I could carry him back to the ship, so I looked for a place where I could leave his body until someone could help bring it back. And the wind was howling and the snow was blowing so, and I couldn't think clearly. There was this little snow house nearby that someone had built, I guess for ice fishing. I could just see it, and I thought maybe I could keep him there. So I dragged him into it. And while I was in it, the ice under me moved, and the snow house started coming down. I jumped up and barely made it out of there. I remember calling out for Nettie because it was starting to storm in earnest, and I was afraid she'd get lost out there, but she didn't come. I could just see the lights of the ship, and I was barely able to make it back there, half-frozen, and into my bunk.

"It was days before the storm cleared, and when it did, whatever blood or tracks we may have left were gone, and the snow house was so collapsed and buried in snow and ice that there was nothing I could do about his body. I'd had time to think about what I'd done and what might happen if they didn't believe me, and I was afraid to say anything. I've just waited since then, not knowing what to do. I figured that if the ship left before his body was found, I'd leave some sort of note with Reverend Strong, so Nettie wouldn't be blamed."

The captain was still incredulous. "But Tom," he said, shaking his head, "John Sanders, your own father—"

"I never meant to hurt him, sir," Tom responded. "But you know as well as anyone what he was like." As he said this, his voice choked, and he broke down in tears.

"Come, sit down," Strong said, gently, standing and putting an arm around Tom's shoulders.

"I was thinking of my poor mother," Tom said, his head in his hands. "What will she do now?"

Lieutenant Edgewater, sitting near me, said under his breath, "Sounds like she's well rid of him." To the rest of the table, he said, "I think, based on what Tom here has told us, that we should release the girl."

Captain Belcher was obdurate. "All we have is his word," he said. "No other evidence."

"I can provide some," Sigerson interjected.

We all turned to him. "All right," the captain said, "tell us what you have."

"You saw Sanders's body, captain."

"Yes."

"You did not see this, but when the body was found, it was lying on its back. It was clad in boots, two pair of stockings, long underwear, a shirt, sweater, a wool jacket, but no gloves or hat. In other words, clothing that a man might have been wearing sitting in a cold room, but he was not dressed to go outside. There was evidence of a trail of blood in the ice below the body and some blood beneath the body itself. This suggested that the body had been moved after the fatal wound, but only a short distance. From this I deduced that Mr. Sanders met his end not on the ship but outside, not far from where his body was found.

"As you saw, the single wound was obvious once the clothing was removed from the body. I made an incision into the chest cavity to determine what organs were injured. There was considerable blood and water in the chest cavity, but I was able to determine that the spearpoint had entered just below the rib cage and pierced the aorta. For the killer it was a lucky, or, as Tom described it, an unlucky blow, which caused death in a matter of minutes.

"With the dowel you saw in the wound I traced the track of the spear through the body. It entered a little to the right of his sternum and went left and virtually parallel to the ground, not much upward or down. This would fit with Tom's account that Sanders ran onto the spear as Tom was holding it in his left hand.

"Finally, there is the issue of the relative heights of Mr. Sanders and whoever stabbed him. Mr. Sanders was about five feet, ten inches tall. Mr. and Mrs. Osborne, may I use you for a moment, for a demonstration?"

Lucy gave me a puzzled look and joined me near Sigerson's chair.

"Mr. Osborne, how tall would you say you are?" Sigerson asked.

"A bit under six feet."

"And Mrs. Osborne, you are not much different in height from Neakpuk, true?"

"I think I'm a little taller," Lucy answered.

"Excellent," Sigerson answered. "Mr. Osborne, would you do me the favor of removing your parka?" I complied, and he handed Lucy the harpoon point. "Hold it at your waist and approach Mr. Osborne. There—perfect. Now thrust the blade—gently, it is still sharp—toward your husband's abdomen, as if you were going to stab him. Stop when the point of the weapon touches his body—ah, there, exactly! Look how much below his ribs the blade rests." It was true; the point of the harpoon had come to rest below my belt.

"Now, Mrs. Osborne," Sigerson continued, "please lift your arm or hand as if you were going to stab your blade into Mr. Osborne in the location where Mr. Sanders was stabbed."

Lucy did as he asked, and Sigerson pointed a long finger at the position of her hand. "Notice how unnatural the arm is," he said. "You must see that this is not a manner in which anyone would stab another person, nor one in which an assailant would have any strength behind the blow."

Lieutenant Edgewater spoke up. "Thank you, Professor. It appears to me that your postmortem effectively rules out Neakpuk as Mr. Sanders's killer." He turned to face the captain. "Captain Belcher, I truly believe we should call the incident self-defense and pursue it no further."

Captain Belcher, seeing from our faces that the weight of our general opinion was with the lieutenant, yielded, and said, with some reluctance, "I guess you've proved your case."

Lucy and Mrs. Strong gave Neakpuk the news that she was free again. The poor girl seemed scarcely to understand what had happened, but when it was made clear to her that the white men no longer believed she had killed Sanders and she was free to go, she hesitated only a moment at the door before running to a pair of girls among the people waiting outside the house. Talking animatedly, the three of them walked away together toward the village.

We buried Sanders the next day under a cairn of stones in the little Christian graveyard near the settlement. I made a cross for his grave and painted it white in the Russian style, and Mrs. Strong drew a sketch of the grave for Tom to take to his mother. Sigerson expressed an interest in buying the ivory harpoon head from Tom, but Tom insisted on giving it to him. "It wasn't mine," he said, "and I couldn't take money for it, after what I did."

As the weather continued to warm, leads of open water began appearing in the ice. The *Myra* left as soon as her captain could free her from the ice in the bay. I had hardly finished copying Professor Sigerson's notebooks and logs when the revenue cutter *Bear*, arrived with the winter's mail and news. Sigerson, Mayes, and Bergsson were to sail on the *Bear* to Anchorage, and before he left, Sigerson asked me to keep my copy of his records. He gave me the name and address of a friend of his in London. "Send him the copy," he told me, "if you don't hear from me by the summer of next year."

On the day the *Bear* left, many of us gathered to say farewell. Mr. and Mrs. Strong were there, with their two oldest children, as were Lieutenant Edgewater and Mr. Harris from the weather station and Neakpuk. Tungweruk and his wife were also in the crowd of well-wishers. Tungweruk's wife was wearing a new dress of blue-flowered calico—the best of our small stock of yard goods—over her parka, and the baby sleeping in her hood was bigger. Watching as the last of our visitors' goods were loaded onto the ship, I felt more than a little sad to see them go.

But I digress. What I wanted to tell you is that not only can a dozen or more people, including Lieutenant Edgewater, Mr. and Mrs. Strong, Tungweruk and Neakpuk, Lucy and I, vouch that Professor Sigerson was here at Cape Stevenson and that he set out from here on his expedition, but I still have the copy of Sigerson's notebooks and logs. I have written a letter to Professor Sigerson's friend in London, to go out with this one on the *Bear*, asking his permission to send you my copy of the professor's expedition records. If I get permission from him I will send them. It is unlikely that his reply will reach me before next spring, however. In the meantime, I hope that you will accept my word regarding the existence of the professor and the authenticity of his accomplishments. Please send my regards to Mr. Mayes.

Respectfully,
John L. Osborne

The Case of the Lugubrious Manservant

A Sherlock Holmes Story

Rhys Bowen

An hour's stiff walk up a wooded path will bring you to a pleasant little hostelry called The White Horse Inn (Gasthaus Zum Weissen Rossli). The inn is superbly situated on a bluff which affords an excellent outlook over the town of Interlaken and the lakes of Brienze and Thun. The food is simple but plentiful, the beds clean and decked with luxurious feather quilts, the hosts congenial and the view breathtaking. All in all a splendid retreat from the cares of the world.

—Everyman's Guide to Switzerland,
Cassels Publishers, London 1890

The man sitting at the rustic outdoor table feasted his eyes on the view below. The valley lay half-hidden in a rosy autumnal haze through which twin lakes glinted in the morning sun. The pine forest surrounding the inn was dotted with the bright yellow of an occasional beech or birch. The sun was warm on his face. He stretched out his legs and sighed with contentment. He was slim, dark-haired, with a neat beard and serious countenance. His attire was rather too somber and citified for the occasion, although the one concession he had made to his surroundings was a jaunty Tirolean hat.

"A beautiful day, don't you agree, Herr Doktor?"

The man wrenched his eyes from the view as the landlady of the inn approached, bearing a tray laden with freshly baked rolls, yellow butter, a dish of strawberry jam, and a large pot of coffee.

"It is indeed, Frau Muller," the man replied, now feasting his eyes on the food being placed before him, "and the air here is so bracing, it gives one a splendid appetite."

The landlady smiled benignly as she poured his coffee and watched him attack the first of the rolls. "You must be glad to be away from that smoky, noisy city," she said. "I only went to Lucern once in my life, but that was enough for me. Not enough room to breathe freely, if you get my meaning."

The man brushed a crumb fastidiously from his beard, then patted at the sides of his mouth with his napkin. "You are right, Frau Muller. If I had my choice, I should not live in a big city like Vienna. Unfortunately, my chosen profession dictates that I live close to one of the great centers of medical research."

"Are you still studying then?" the woman asked, readying herself for a good gossip. "You are not yet a fully qualified doctor?"

"I foresee that I will be studying for the rest of my life," he said, "as there is so much still to learn. However, I have been a practicing physician for some time now and also am about to become a professor at the university."

"Such high achievements for one so young," she said.

He smiled, and the smile did indeed make him look youthful. "I am nearer to forty than thirty," he said, "but you are correct. I have often been considered too young to be taken seriously by my colleagues. Some of my papers have been ridiculed."

"Papers? Like newspapers, you mean?"

"I have published papers in my field of specialization, which is the diseases of the mind."

"Can the mind be sick as well as the body?" she asked.

The doctor smiled. "Not all diseases have a physical origin. Diseases of the mind can affect our behavior and physical well-being to an extent that you would not believe. I have treated patients who cannot walk, but for no physical reason. Their minds have paralyzed them. My colleague, Dr. Breuer and I have been treating a young girl whose hysteria has rendered her unable to use her native German, but allows her to converse in French and English. What do you make of that, huh?"

"Amazing. Scarcely to be believed." She shook her head. "And can these diseases of the mind be cured then, with medicine?"

"This is what I hope to achieve in my lifetime, Frau Muller," the doctor said. "Breuer and I have tried hypnosis, with moderate success, but I am of the opinion that the cure lies in the understanding of the patient's past. I am currently conducting experiments in the interpretation of dreams. I believe that we dare to express in dreams those things that are too disturbing to be allowed into our conscious mind."

"Fancy that." Frau Muller tried to appear interested, but clearly this was going over her head.

She looked up as a door opened and a tall thin man crossed the yard, bearing a wood basket.

"If you were not on holiday, Herr Doktor, I would say that we have a case for you here," she said, her eyes following the tall thin fellow. "Our Fritzi over there—a poor tormented creature if ever I saw one."

"The manservant who carried in my bags last night?" the doctor inquired.

She nodded. "A poor simple half-wit, if ever I saw one."

The doctor smiled. "I'm afraid medical science can do nothing to improve the intelligence of half-wits. They are unfortunately born without the brain capacity of the rest of us."

"But this one has an interesting history," she went on, now bold enough to perch her large person on the edge of the bench opposite. "He came to us but half a year ago, at my sister's request. It was her husband who found this fellow sprawled on a rock in the middle of a rushing torrent. At first my brother-in-law thought the man was dead, and indeed he was more dead than alive. He must have had a nasty blow to the head, for when he opened his eyes, he had lost the power of speech and understanding. He stared like a vacant soul. He had no recollection of who he was or how he came to fall into the river. So bad was he, in fact, that they were all set to have him sent to the mental asylum. But my sister took pity on him, knowing that terrible place would be the end of him. She came to me and asked if we couldn't perhaps take on an extra manservant to help my husband with the chores. She begged me to give him a chance, and so we did."

The doctor was listening intently now. "You say he lost his memory following a blow to the head and a near drowning?"

"So we believe, Herr Doktor, although, of course, the fellow could have been born a simpleton and never had the brains to know his name or situation."

"And he still has recovered no memory of his past life, after several months?"

The landlady shook her head. "None at all. But his speech does improve, slowly but surely. At first he appeared hardly to understand a word we said. I wondered, between you and me, whether the blow to the head had not maybe affected his hearing. Now he understands us, but on the level of a child. One must speak slowly and gently to him. But worst of all is the terrible melancholy—the way he sits and stares with those hollow eyes. It fair breaks the heart, Herr Doktor. If there was anything you could do for him, anything at all . . ."

The doctor's gaze followed the servant returning from the woodshed, bearing a basketful of logs. "I had sworn that I was on holiday and wouldn't touch a book or a paper, but his case intrigues me. I will speak to the fellow, if you wish. Of course, I can't promise anything."

"I am most grateful, Herr Doktor." The landlady rose from the bench and dropped a half curtsy.

At that moment the sound of a hunting horn echoed through the crisp morning air. Frau Muller's face lit up. "It's them!" she exclaimed. "They're coming. Hansi, Fritzi, out here right away!"

"Another party is coming to the inn?" The young doctor's face fell. He had no wish for noisy company.

"Not to the inn—not highborn folk like that," she said in horror, "but they have to pass by on the way to the baron's hunting lodge, and they usually break their journey and rest the horses after the climb. You must have heard of Baron Vizkelety?"

"Of the Hungarian banking family? Of course I've heard of him. Fabulously wealthy and with connections throughout the civilized world."

Frau Muller nodded as if somehow taking credit for this. "He has a château on Lake Geneva, as you probably know, but less well known is that his hunting lodge is in the forest five miles from here. He comes for the occasional weekend with guests who desire to be away from prying eyes. I'll wager all of the crowned heads of Europe have been here, at one time or another. Why, I've even served beer to the Kaiser—our best beer, naturally."

As they spoke the sound of jingling harness could be heard approaching up the track, and soon the first of the party came into view—two mounted outriders, dressed in hunting green livery. Behind them the first of three fine closed carriages appeared and came to a halt right beside the inn. A footman sprang down and opened the carriage door, placing a step before it. A young man of military bearing was first to jump out, turning to assist a portly bearded gentleman in a tweed jacket, then an elegant gray-haired woman in a magnificent fur-trimmed cape, and finally a silver-haired man of fine Slavic features and noble bearing, who stood breathing deeply and looking around him with satisfaction.

Behind them a second carriage disgorged a pale and podgy middle-aged couple, who both looked as if they had perpetual smells under their noses, then a stunningly beautiful young woman, dressed in bright silks of the latest fashion. Last of all a large, red-faced man, whose waistcoat buttons seemed about to pop across his broad paunch, appeared at the door of the second carriage.

"Why are we stopping here?" the latter demanded in clipped German. "Something wrong with the horses?"

"There is never anything wrong with my horses or equipment, I assure you, Count." The gray-haired man walked toward the rustic outdoor tables. "It has become our tradition to break our journey here to let the horses catch their breath, while we feast our eyes on the view and our stomachs with a pint of good Swiss beer, if Frau Muller will oblige?"

The landlady had dropped a deep curtsy. "With the greatest of pleasure, Herr Baron. I'll tell my husband to get busy pouring. And for the ladies? Some spiced wine to take off the chill of the morning, perhaps?"

"An admirable idea." The baron smiled.

"Just coffee for me," the beautiful young woman said in German that bore a strong American accent. "I wasn't raised to drink wine in the mornings."

The doctor had risen to his feet when the party arrived. He stood watching as they moved around, admiring the view. The baron noticed him standing and went over to him.

"Please don't let us disturb your breakfast, young man." The baron gestured for him to resume his seat. "A few minutes, and we'll be on our way again. You are staying here?"

The doctor clicked his heels. "Jawohl, Herr Baron. Dr. Sigmund Freud, at your service. Visiting from Vienna."

"Baron Vizkelety, as I'm sure our garrulous Frau Muller will have told you. And if I'm not mistaken, Dr. Freud, I have heard of you. Are you not the young fellow who has written those interesting articles on the diseases of the mind? I read about your work with the young girl, whose hysteria has made her forget her own language and even how to swallow. That was you, wasn't it?"

"It was indeed, Herr Baron. And maybe you read an article that was published in the *Wiener Zeitung* last spring, on the hidden revelations of our dreams."

"I believe my wife read it. Our dreams reveal our hidden thoughts? Fascinating."

Dr. Freud bowed his head modestly. "I am only beginning to unlock the mysteries of the mind, Herr Baron."

"You must pay us a visit while we are here. My wife would be most intrigued to speak with you. She has always tried to interpret her dreams—with mixed success, I might add." He gave a wicked smile. "Come and shoot with us tomorrow, then stay for lunch."

"I'm afraid I am not much of a shot, Herr Baron," the doctor said. "There has been little opportunity for outdoor pursuits during my long years of study."

"Then we must remedy it."

Freud smiled. "I have to confess that I have never held a weapon. Were I to do so now, I fear I may be more of a danger than an asset to the shooting party, but I would very much like to accept your invitation to visit you at your convenience."

"Then come tomorrow anyway. Why not? I'm sure Frau Muller can arrange transportation if you don't wish to walk through the woods. You can keep my wife entertained while I'm out shooting, and maybe she will not notice how long we're away. Then we'll all have a splendid chat over lunch." He smiled genially, and the doctor bowed his head.

"Most kind of you, Herr Baron," he said. "I shall took forward to it."

The landlord appeared carrying a tray laden with beer steins, while his wife came behind him with steaming glasses of mulled wine for the ladies plus one cup of coffee. A stein was passed first to the bearded, portly gentleman, then to the rest of the party. Glasses were raised in a toast. The portly gentleman and the military type strolled to the railing together to admire the view.

"I say, Vizkelety, can we get moving? My wife feels the cold, you know," the large red-faced man said irritably.

The rest of the party turned to stare at him with a look of horror on their faces, which Dr. Freud couldn't explain. He heard the distinguished couple muttering something about "not done" and "protocol," before the portly man returned to the group and smiled genially at the young beauty. "Yes, of course. Mustn't let the little lady freeze." He took her hand to help her back into her carriage.

"It's being so long in South America. It thins the blood," the young military man said in English.

The crash of breaking glass made them look up. Fritzi, the inn servant, stood gaping at them, a tray of broken glasses at his feet. He began to stagger toward them when he was restrained by the innkeeper. "Get inside with you, Fritzi, and don't go disturbing the gentry," he said calmly. "You have to excuse him, your honors. Not quite right in the head, but harmless enough."

The servant continued to stare. "I know you," he shouted toward the portly gentleman who was being assisted into his carriage. "I know you. Do you know me?"

There was a titter of laughter as the carriage door closed and the party moved off.

"The fellow knows me. Isn't that priceless?" the portly man said in English, still chuckling.

"He may have seen Your Highness's picture in newspapers," the young man replied.

"Yes, but he expects me to know him!"

The occupants of the carriage laughed.

"Well, don't just stand there, Fritzi. Get this lot swept up," Frau Muller commanded as the servant stared after the departing horses.

The next day dawned bright and clear, with a hint of frost in the air. The smell of wood smoke mingled with the fresh scent of pines as Dr. Freud prepared to set out for the baron's hunting lodge.

"I should start early if it's a five-mile walk," he said to Frau Muller.

The landlady shook her head in horror. "You'll not go that distance on foot, surely, a city man like you."

"I assure you it's no problem, dear lady."

But Frau Muller shook her head even more vehemently. "It's not right and proper that I shouldn't take better care of my guests. And it's not right and proper that you should arrive among such highborn folks on foot. Fritzi will take you in the trap. We can spare him for a day, and it will give you a chance to question him at leisure."

Frued nodded a polite bow. "Most kind of you, Frau Muller. I accept your offer and look forward to speaking with your servant."

Fritzi appeared, obviously having been spruced up for the occasion by the landlady, his black hair parted and slicked down and wearing a jacket that was two sizes too big for him.

"You understand where you're going, Fritzi," Frau Muller said patiently. "Remember your place. No speaking with the gentry. You wait beside the trap until the Herr Doktor is ready to come home."

The man nodded and climbed into the driver's seat. Dr. Freud sat beside him.

"Now mind you're back before it's dark," she said. "There's no carriage lights on the wagon, and there's nothing as dark as a pine forest at night."

Behind the inn the pine forest stretched unbroken until it met the high meadows and snows of the first Alpine peaks. It was by this forest that they were now swallowed, following a dark and gloomy narrow track between tall trees. The stout pony's hooves were muffled by the carpet of pine needles as it plodded along willingly.

"They tell me you have no memory, Fritzi," the doctor began as the inn was left behind. "No recollection of home, family, friends?"

The servant shook his head. "None at all. Nothing. Sometimes I think I must always have been mad."

"What comes to your mind when you hear the word 'mother' for instance?"

The man paused, then shook his head. "Nothing, I cannot picture my mother."

Frued nodded. "Your conscious mind blocks your past because of a trauma. Tell me, do you have dreams?"

For a second the man's face lit up. "Dreams? Ja—I have one dream, again and again."

"Tell me about it."

"I am in a village—all nice houses, well built, comfortable. There are lights on inside them, but I cannot get into any of them. No doors will open to me, and I understand that they have a very modern system of locks for each house. I have a key in my hand, but it will not work on any of them. I am alone. Outside."

"Very interesting," the doctor said, "and easy to interpret, in the circumstances. Because you have lost all ties with your past, you feel shut out from normal society. You desire to find your way home, but you can't. You don't know which of these houses is your home, correct? While I am here, I will do what I can to help you."

"Thank you, Herr Doktor. I am very thankful."

"I wonder if cocaine might perhaps ease your anxiety," he said, almost to himself.

The servant reacted. "Cocaine?" he asked, his voice high and tight.

Freud looked at him with interest. "This word is familiar to you? You have heard of this substance?"

"Ja," Fritzi said.

"Interesting, I wonder how? Tell me, what is it?"

"White," Fritzi said quickly, then the blank expression came over his face again. "I'm sorry. I can tell you no more. It was but a fleeting impression, and now it's gone."

"But this is indeed a hopeful sign, Fritzi," Dr. Freud said. "It tells me that your past is there, waiting to be unlocked. All we need to do is to find the key. I regret that I have brought no cocaine with me. Perhaps I can persuade Frau Muller to have you accompany me to my clinic in Vienna."

"Leave this place, you mean?" the servant looked around wildly. "I don't know."

"You would be well taken care of, I assure you. And if your torment could be eased, how could you refuse?"

"You are right," he said at last. "I would do anything that would ease my torment."

The servant stared ahead of him, his eyes focused on the track, a look of bleak hopelessness in them again.

At last they reached tall wrought-iron gates, barring their way. Before the doctor could decide what to do about this, a green-liveried servant sprang out as he heard them approaching.

"Dr. Freud?" he asked. "My master expects you. Please proceed." The gate was opened, and they passed through. A hunting lodge came into view through the trees, not at all humble in size, but built in the rustic manner of pine wood, with carved balconies and a wooden shake roof. The party was already assembled on a well-manicured lawn, the men in hunting green standing together chatting, while the women sat on wicker armchairs around a white-clothed table, dogs and gun bearers waiting patiently beside a white gate.

Before Fritzi could dismount to help Dr. Freud, a servant observed them and came running to assist the doctor.

"This way please, Herr Doktor," he said and escorted the doctor to the group assembled on the lawn.

"Ah, there you are, Dr. Freud." The baron broke off his conversations and came to meet him. "Your arrival is well timed. We were just about to set off, as my guests are anxious to get started. I'm glad to be able to greet you in person and make the necessary introductions before we leave. Are you sure you won't change your mind and try your hand with a gun?"

"Thank you kindly, Baron, but I think I have to decline. I am more likely to bring down one of my fellow hunters than the quarry."

Baron Vizkeley laughed and motioned to his wife to join him.

The gray-haired hostess put a gloved hand on her husband's arm. "Just because you enjoy hunting does not mean that the rest of the civilized world shares your passion, Rudi. It is clear that Dr. Freud has little interest in your barbarous sport. He shall stay with me and tell me about my dreams," she said. "You will have your chance to chat with him when you return with your trophies. I am Baroness Vizkelety, Herr Doktor, and I have read about your work. Come, let me present you to my guests" She slipped her arms through the doctor's and led him to the company grouped around an outdoor table on which was assortment of cheeses lay on a rude board, together with local black beard, coffee, and schnapps.

"Your Royal Highness." She approached the portly man in tweeds, "may I be permitted to present Dr. Sigmund Freud from Vienna. The doctor is earning repute as a specialist in diseases of the mind. Dr. Freud, His Royal Highness, the Prince of Wales."

The doctor managed to overcome his surprise as he bowed. "An honor, sir," he stammered.

"May I also present Dr. Freud to their highnesses Prince Ruprecht von Saxe-Coburg and the Princess Gisela."

"Your servant, Highnesses." The doctor bowed again before the haughty middle-aged couple, who responded with the slightest of nods.

"And the Count and Countess Von Strezl."

The large red-faced man scowled at him. "Don't hold with doctors myself. Never had a day's sickness in my life. Not even when everyone came down with yellow fever."

"The count and countess have been living in Brazil, where I'm told the count has a rubber plantation the size of Switzerland," Baroness Vizkelety continued.

"Slight exaggeration," the count said, "but we are a week's canoe ride from our nearest neighbors."

"Fascinating," Dr. Freud muttered, eyeing the silent beauty who was not regarding him in the most friendly fashion.

"And our party is completed by Major Johnny Watling-Smythe, equerry to His Royal Highness." The baroness rested her hand on the handsome young officer's arm. "I believe you were also in South America at one time, weren't you, Major?"

"I was part of the Royal Geographic expedition to the Amazon two years ago." He spoke German fluently but with definitely English vowels. "It was most interesting."

"And did you meet the count and countess while you were there?" the haughty Princess Gisela asked.

"They were kind enough to invite our expedition to stay with them while some of us recuperated from fever."

"Living so far from civilization, one welcomes any visitors from the outside world," the American countess said, looking up briefly from the tapestry she was embroidering.

"And did you know you were destined to meet again here, of all places?" the princess continued.

"It was a complete surprise to both parties," the major said.

"What a small world it is," Baroness Vizkelety said. "Rudi invited Count Strezl because he knew the count was anxious to get in some shooting while he is away from Brazil, and the major has recently become His Royal Highness's equerry. Don't tell me you have unknown ties to our party, Dr. Freud?"

"I'm afraid I don't move in such exalted circles, Baroness. My time is spent among the poor and the troubled of mind."

The Prince of Wales chuckled. "He'd probably be interested in my family, given our history."

"Oh Highness, I'm sure . . ." the baroness began, but the prince cut her off.

"It's true. My great grandfather, poor old George Three. Mad as a hatter. If I gave the good doctor a chance to examine me, he'd probably tell me I'm also quite certifiable. What we call in England bats in the belfry." He spoke the words in English, still chuckling. "Isn't that right, Johnny?"

"Bats in the belfry? Not you, sir," the equerry said in English. "Sharp as a tack."

The company laughed politely. The unnoticed manservant let go of the horse's bridle and moved closer to the group, a look of intense concentration on his tormented face. As the doctor was offered coffee and schnapps, and the men prepared to leave for the hunt, he moved silently around the edge of the lawn area and made his way to the major, who was standing alone, staring out into the forest.

"Excuse me, sir," he began in hesitant English, "but I think I might have spoken this language once."

"You do speak it, and very finely too," the major said, eyeing him with interest. "You must have had an excellent tutor or a fine ear for languages."

"No, I meant that it might have once been my native tongue. I thought it was just the language of my nightmares that nobody else understood. What language might it be?"

"Why, English, my good man. The finest tongue in the world, only don't let the French hear me saying that. They still think theirs is the one tongue worth speaking."

"English." The manservant savored the word. "Then I may once have lived in . . . England?"

"You mean you don't remember?" the major asked.

"My entire past is a mystery to me. Until I heard you speaking in this tongue, I had thought myself to be mad."

"You should discuss this with the doctor. I understand he's the expert on such things." Major Watling-Smythe put a hand on the manservant's shoulder. "Most interesting, old chap. But I can see that His Highness is anxious to get going. Can't let the quarry slip away, can we?" He hurried to the prince's side as the party headed out into the forest, accompanied by gun bearers and dogs. The manservant went to follow him, then remained beside the fence, staring after the departing hunters, a puzzled frown on his face.

"English," he muttered to himself. "I speak English."

The baroness patted the empty wicker chair beside her. "Come, sit beside me, Dr. Freud, and let us discuss your fascinating profession." Dr. Freud sat, his eye moving with pleasure over the smooth green grass and the last roses of the season still blooming in well-manicured beds. This indeed was a small haven of civilization in the middle of the wilderness.

"I have read about you, Herr Doktor," the baroness said, "but maybe you should explain to the princess and the countess what it is that you do."

"I study the diseases of the mind, Highnesses," Dr. Freud said. "We are still very much at the learning stage about how the mind works and how it controls the body. The more I learn, the more amazed I become."

"You have done work with the interpretation of dreams, I believe," the baroness said. "That is what truly fascinates me."

"I am just beginning that study in earnest, but I am hopeful that dreams will truly prove to be a door to the subconscious mind."

"So tell me, Dr. Freud," the princess Gisela said, "is it true that if I dream about riding a dark horse, I'll come into some money?"

"More likely that it represents your repressed sexual desires coming to the fore," Freud said seriously.

The princess gasped and clutched at her throat. "My dear man, such things are not to be spoken of in polite company. Women of my age and station are not permitted repressed sexual desires. I've never heard such nonsense."

The American countess looked away and smiled for the first time.

"And what do you dream of, Countess?" Freud asked the young woman.

She stared out past him. "Flying," she said. "I am a moth, trying to get out of a closed room. I fly to the ceiling, the windows, looking for a way out."

"Interesting," Freud said, but gave her no explanation, "and you, dear Baroness?"

Baroness Vizkelety chuckled. "After your answer to the princess, I am rather hesitant to say. But I assure you that most of my dreams are commonplace, losing pieces of jewelry, forgetting to bring the right ball gowns, all the trivial things that occupy women's minds."

"I am sure there is nothing trivial about your thoughts at all, Baroness," Dr. Freud said graciously.

"So tell me, how is Vienna this fall?" the baroness asked him. "Are there any exciting new operas that I have missed? We have been in London and New York and quite out of touch with European society."

"New York?" The American beauty looked up wistfully, then went back to her tapestry.

"I'm afraid I can tell you little of society or operas," Freud said. "When I am in Vienna my work is my life. That is why I forced myself to take a break and breathe some good mountain air."

"Quite right too. All work and no play make Jack a dull boy, don't they?" the baroness said. Freud noticed that the princess had not said a word since his interpretation of her dream. Now she was staring around the garden. "Who is that strange fellow standing over there?" she asked. "Not one of Rudi's servants, surely, in that ill-fitting attire?"

"He is the servant at the inn where I lodge, Princess," Freud said. "He drove me here today in the trap and waits for me."

"Tell him to go and wait somewhere else then. He makes me quite nervous the way he stares so."

"The fellow is doing no harm, Gisela. He can't help his lugubrious appearance, I'm sure. Let's me send for some fresh coffee and some honey cake, maybe?"

Coffee and cake were brought, and the princess tucked in with enthusiasm. The young American beauty ate nothing but busied herself with her tapestry and only spoke when addressed.

After a while she rose to her feet. "If you'll excuse me, I need to fetch my cloak. I feel the cold terribly here."

"Sit down, my dear. One of the servants will get it for you," the baroness replied.

"Oh no, that's not necessary. Besides, I also need to match up the yarn for my tapestry. No servant can do that for me. They always manage to get it wrong. Please excuse me, Baroness." She stuffed the tapestry into her large needlework bag and hurried into the house.

"No wonder she's so cold," the princess muttered. "Those bright silks are quite unsuitable for a hunting lodge."

"I suppose she has little chance to wear her Paris finery at home," the baroness said, staring after the departing girl.

The two women looked at each other. The princess sighed. "Poor thing. Quite the fish out of water, isn't she? Her German simply isn't good enough for conversation. I wonder how she converses with the count at home in Brazil?"

"They don't converse, I'd imagine. He orders, she obeys," the baroness answered, with a smile.

"Why on earth do you think she married him?" Princess Gisela leaned closer, although no servants were within earshot, except for the manservant unnoticed at the fence.

"The title of course. Fancied herself as a countess. Discovered too late that titles are ten a penny in Europe. He married her for her proverbial American fortune, then discovered it didn't exist, so maybe they deserve each other."

"But I understood he is very rich?"

"Now he is." The baroness glanced back toward the house in case the young woman was returning. "He has made a fortune with his rubber plantations, but at what cost? Who would want to live in the wilds of Brazil? The poor girl hardly has a chance to spend those millions in Europe before she's dragged back to the jungle again."

"Why did your husband invite them here, I wonder? Hardly for their witty conversation."

"My dear, it's quite obvious, isn't it?" The baroness looked around again, a mischievous smile on her lips. "Rudi was asked to invite them. The Prince of Wales leaves his wife at home . . . he's out to make a new conquest."

"Ah yes. Dear Bertie's insatiable appetite with the women. It will be amusing to watch if she succumbs."

The women exchanged a smile. At that moment shots echoed through the forest.

"Ah good, they've found something," the baroness said. "Now Rudi will be in a good mood for the rest of the day. He always blames himself if the wretched animals don't allow themselves to be killed."

The princess rose to her feet. "It really is getting rather chilly. Maybe we should go inside to the fire."

The baroness rose, too, and motioned for the doctor to take her arm. They then crossed the smooth carpet of grass. More shots rang out from the forest, echoing back from the mountain slopes beyond.

"Either they missed the first time, or they've been exceptionally fortunate today," the baroness commented. "Let us pray for the latter, then the gentlemen will be in a good mood for the rest of their stay."

"What a wonderful garden you manage to keep here, in the wilderness," Dr. Freud exclaimed.

"I like to be surrounded by beauty, even here in the wilds," the baroness said. "If my husband disappears to shoot things, I insist on a place of tranquility to entertain my guests—and of course my husband denies me nothing. Would you like me to show you my roses before we go inside?"

"I would be honored," the doctor said.

The baroness led the way toward the nearest flower bed. "They have been magnificent this year, blooming so late into the autumn," she said. "I rather like this red one, don't you? It has a magnificent scent."

"I wonder if the countess is permitted to create a beautiful prison for herself in her jungle?" Dr. Freud said quietly, almost to himself.

"Yes, one does feel sorry for the poor child. If only she had better manners and was more used to society's ways," the baroness replied. "She shut herself away in her room last night and is taking an infernally long time to match that embroidery thread. Maybe we should go and root her out."

They had just reached the steps of the lodge when there was a shout, and a man came staggering out of the forest. It was one of the gun bearers, with sweat pouring down his face.

"Quick! Get a doctor—there's been a terrible accident," he gasped.

"An accident? To one of the party?" The baroness had turned pale.

"Yes, Highness. The gentleman from Brazil. The count has been shot."

Dr. Freud had released the baroness's arm. "I trained as a doctor of medicine," he said. "I have little experience in first aid recently, but I'll do what I can. I'll need alcohol, bandages, a sharp knife. Let's see what we can find in your kitchen, by your leave, Baroness."

"Whatever you need, Dr. Freud. Vodka, schnapps? Which do you think would be better? And we've the best cognac, of course. Ask the servants . . ."

Dr. Freud glanced at the fence and noticed that the manservant had approached the house behind them and was now standing in the middle of the lawn. "Come, Fritzi. You shall carry my supplies," he said.

Fritzi ran to join the doctor, a look of excited anticipation on his somber face. On their way into the house they encountered the young American, standing at the foot of the stairs, now wrapped in a long dark green wool cape. Her face was flushed and her eyes wide with fear "What has happened?" she demanded. "I was coming down from my room when I thought I heard shouting."

The baroness took her arm. "Come and sit down, my dear." She snapped her fingers to a waiting footman. "Brandy for the countess, Hans."

"Something bad has happened. Tell me. I need to know," the American was wailing, as the baroness led her into the drawing room.

The manservant watched them with interest. The drawing room had a polished wood floor. He stared at this floor, then back at the lawn.

"Come, Fritzi, take this." The doctor shoved a bag into his hands, then ran out the front door. Fritzi followed him. The gun bearer led them through the forest until they came to the edge of a clearing. The first thing they noticed was a magnificent stag, lying dead on the far side of the clearing, with the dogs and gun bearers standing guard around it. But it was not around the animal that the hunting party was standing. They were off to one side of the narrow path, clustered around a form lying in the undergrowth among the trees. The group parted as the doctor and servant approached, and they could see a man lying on his back on the forest floor. His green hunting jacket was open, and an ugly red wound stained his white shirt.

"You're too late, I'm afraid, Herr Doktor." The baron stepped forward to greet him. "I fear the poor fellow has already breathed his last."

Dr. Freud dropped to his knees, felt for a pulse, then ripped open the shirt. A small circular hole on the left side of his chest was still oozing blood. The doctor stood up again, shaking his head sadly. "He's dead all right. How did he come to be shot? Did he wander into your line of fire?"

"I don't see how," the baron said. "In fact I am convinced none of us could have killed him. When our tracker told us that there was a fine stag up ahead, we spread out and moved forward in a line—the major on the far left, then Count von StrezI, then his Royal Highness, Prince Ruprecht, and I took up the right flank. We spotted the stag, and, naturally, his Royal Highness was accorded the first shot."

"And I fired both barrels at the animal, hit it, but didn't manage to bring it down," the Prince of Wales said.

"It started to run off. The rest of us followed, fired, and brought it down successfully," Major Watling-Smythe said. "We ran forward to examine the animal, and saw that it was indeed a magnificent four-pointer. We talked about having the head mounted, and the baron suggested that maybe Count von Strezl might want to take it back to Brazil with him. That was when we noticed that the count wasn't with us. We called his name; the servants searched for him and found him lying here."

"So it was not possible that one of us shot him by mistake," Prince Ruprecht said. "We had approached the stag side by side, in plain view of each other."

Fritzi had dropped to his knees beside the body. "You are correct," he said. "You carry large hunting rifles. This wound was made by a small-caliber bullet, shot at close range."

The members of the party stared at him in surprise.

"For a simpleton, he seems to know what he's taking about," Prince Ruprecht muttered.

"Then it is as I feared," the major exclaimed. "Anarchists have been at work. We were warned before we came here that they had designs on the prince; in fact, Her Majesty was against his coming to Europe at this time."

"It is not the first time they have tried to assassinate me," the prince said. He didn't appear overly worried.

"The blackguards," Baron Vizkelety muttered. "How did they manage to get into my estate—that's what I'd like to know?"

"It would be easy enough to dig under the fence, or find a tree with overhanging branches, I'd imagine, Herr Baron," the major said. "These chaps are very skilled and resourceful. They fired at the prince when he was on his yacht last year, didn't they, sir?"

"So you think this bullet was intended for me, eh, Johnny?" the prince asked.

Watling-Smythe nodded. "It's obvious, sir. And this was all very well planned. They must have discovered our secret location and the identity of our famous guest. They lay in wait for us and fired when we fired, so that their shot was not heard. The count walked beside you, did he not, sir? You wear similar jackets and hats and are similar in stature. I was sent to protect you and have failed at my task."

The baron touched his arm. "You must not blame yourself, Major. Who could have expected such a daring attack in broad daylight? We must send for the police, although I fear our assassins will be far away by now, and the local constabulary will be hopelessly inept."

"We should not trample the area more than necessary." Fritzi the servant muttered to the major in English.

"What? No, of course not. Although I fear it is already well trampled by us and our servants. And you're not likely to find telltale footprints on this thick carpet of needles. I rather fear any search of the area would prove to be fruitless. Herr Baron, I must escort His Royal Highness back to the lodge immediately. I am sure this has been most upsetting for him, all the more since it appears he was the intended target."

"Don't mollycoddle me, Watling-Smythe," the prince said. "I'm perfectly all right. It is the baron who could use a stiff Scotch. His face is as white as a sheet."

Major Watling-Smythe took the baron's arm. "Come, Baron. Have your men bring a stretcher to transport the count back to the lodge. We can do nothing useful here. There is no point in waiting around any longer. The doctor will stand guard over the body."

The royal party set off down the path, the sound of their footsteps soon swallowed up into the silence of the forest. Dr. Freud remained on his knees, cleaning the ugly wound on the count's chest. Fritzi stared at the corpse then prowled the area.

"Doctor," he said at last. "Do you speak English?"

"Passably well," the doctor replied. "Why do you ask?"

"Because I thought you might be interested to learn that it is my native tongue," Fritzi said in English.

"Mein Gott—this is a surprise. You did not mention this when we talked earlier."

"I only discovered this fact when I heard the major speak with the prince. Until then I thought it was the language of my nightmares, as nobody else seemed to understand it."

"Most interesting," Freud said. "Does that mean your memory has now returned?"

"Alas no. Certain words or phrases have sparked brief flashes of memory, as happens when one awakes and tries to recall a dream, but I feel my brain growing more lucid with every minute."

"My dear man, I'm very glad for you," the doctor said.

"I am glad for myself. I had almost come to believe that I was an idiot with nothing more to hope for than hauling wood and washing dishes. Undoubtedly my brain was damaged in some kind of accident. Maybe I fell into the river where I was found. Maybe I was thrown in by assailants. I don't know. All I know is that when I was found, I had no memory and couldn't understand a word anyone said."

"That's because these people speak Swiss German, which even I have difficulty understanding. Quite unintelligible the way the peasants speak it up in the mountains," Freud said with a chuckle.

"I had no idea where I was or who I was. It's little wonder that they classified me as a madman."

Freud got to his feet. "There's nothing more I can do for this poor fellow," he said. "You were looking around the area. Did you find anything of interest?"

"Some white feathers," the manservant replied.

"Maybe a hunting party had been out duck shooting on a previous occasion?"

"It is not very likely to encounter ducks in the middle of the forest," Fritzi said. "To shoot ducks one goes to a lake, does one not?"

"Then how do you explain the feathers?"

"I'm not sure yet," Fritzi said. "There are several aspects of this that I find puzzling. For example the position of the wound. Would you say, in your medical experience, that a single bullet entering the chest in that position would kill a man outright?"

Freud studied the corpse, then glanced up at Fritzi. "You are right. It's too high. It should have avoided the heart and lungs and passed through the shoulder. The amount of bleeding indicates that it struck no major organ or artery. Maybe the poor fellow died of shock."

"Maybe not," Fritzi said. "And this small prick of blood on his neck?"

"There are plenty of brambles in the area. If he was intent on following a stag, he could easily have become entangled in them. See, he has a scratch on his hand, too." He stared hard at the servant. "What exactly are you hinting at? You don't believe that anarchists were waiting in the woods? You have another explanation?"

Fritzi turned to stare back along the trail to the hunting lodge.

"Mein Gott. You think one of the party did it? But that's impossible, man. They were in a line. Whoever shot the count was facing him—square on. If any of the members of the party had been in a position to shoot him, he would have been observed by all."

"And yet the count was shot in the chest, at close range," the manservant said. "I think another search of the area might disclose proof of my theory." He moved the body and sifted through the pine needles, then shook his head. "No, the assassin found it and retrieved it. Of course. This has been very well planned."

"You mean the count was shot on purpose? He wasn't mistaken for the Prince of Wales?"

"That is exactly what I mean. I will go even further, Doctor. I think the count was brought here to be killed."

"Good God, man. By whom? Can you prove it?"

"Probably not, but I shall try."

Dr. Freud stared at him. "This is the most remarkable transformation I have ever witnessed. You are obviously a man of fine intellectual powers, suppressed and deadened by a blow to the head and by lack of language facility. I should like to conduct further tests on you when we return to the inn. Then, by your leave, I shall write a paper on this subject when I return to Vienna."

"Let us hope these further tests may unlock the mystery of my identity," Fritzi said. "At least I can return to England now. Somebody there may be looking for me, have reported me as missing."

"Home to the bosom of wife and family, eh?" Freud raised an eyebrow.

"I don't picture myself with wife and family somehow, but there is one name that echoing inside my skull. What was the major called?"

"Watling-Smythe."

"That's the one. Something about that name is familiar to me. But we should leave my sad case until later, until we have solved this mystery. Here come the bearers with a stretcher. I will leave you to supervise their work while I hasten to the lodge to apprehend a murderer."

"I say, be careful, won't you," Freud called after him. "You have barely escaped death once in your life."

"I'll be careful." He set off down the path with long, fluid strides. "I suspect that I have faced danger more than once before."

When he reached the lodge, he found the party assembled in the drawing room, seated around a roaring fire, sipping hot toddy. They sat in silence, appearing to be in a state of shock. They didn't notice him as he stood in the doorway, and a quick assessment of the group revealed that the countess was not among them. He moved away from the door and mounted the stairs. A frightened chambermaid gasped as she saw him approaching.

"What are you doing up here?" she demanded.

"The countess—which room is hers?" he demanded.

"The one to the right of the stairs, but she is in shock and resting," the maid said. "The mistress said she was not to be disturbed."

"I must deliver an important message that she will want to hear," Fritzi said, pushing past the maid. He knocked gently on the door, then let himself in. The countess was standing at the window, her hands clutching at the heavy velvet drapes. She spun around when she heard the door opening.

"What the devil do you mean by coming in here, unbidden?" she demanded in German.

"You may speak to me in English since you are more at home in that language," Fritzi said. He closed the door gently behind him and approached the woman at the window. "I came to compliment you on your little scheme. It was very well thought out and executed. In fact it would have succeeded, had not I been here."

The countess's eyes widened, but her face remained expressionless. "What are you talking about? Now get out of my room before I call for help." She swept past him as if to open the door.

"Would you really want the others to hear what I am going to say to you?" he said quietly. "Would you want them to know how you killed your husband?"

The countess spun around. "Killed my husband? Are you mad? I was here, in the house, all the time."

The manservant shook his head. "Not all the time, Countess. When you appeared, wearing your cape, your cheeks were flushed. Usually fear turns the cheeks pale. And as the baroness led you into the drawing room, you left specks of mud on the polished floor. There was no mud on the baroness's shoes from crossing the lawn. Your cheeks were flushed because you had just run down the path and slipped into the house through a back entrance."

"What rubbish you talk," she said. "You are insinuating that I was able to run through the forest to a point in front of the hunting party, without being noticed, and then to shoot my husband as he approached? Rather an impossible theory, don't you think?"

"Quite impossible," the servant replied, "but that is not how it was done, is it? Your scheme required great cooperation and perfect timing. I'd imagine a major in the British army would know quite a lot about battle strategy."

For the first time the look of arrogant defiance faltered, and she looked wary. "You are trying to say that Major Watling-Smythe was involved in killing my husband? How could he? The baron told me that none of the party could have been responsible for my husband's death. He said they were in a line, advancing side by side, in full view of the other hunters and the bearers. And the only shots fired were at the stag as it tried to flee."

She was still staring at him with defiant confidence.

"As I said, the timing had to be perfect. I might not have figured it out had I not noticed a small puncture wound on your husband's neck. I was curious about it. A scratch from a bramble? But there were no brambles growing that high. Then I remembered that you met the major when you were both in Brazil. You see, I had lost my memory, but this encounter has brought some things back to me. The major's face was familiar to me. I recognized him when I first saw him at the inn. When he mentioned Brazil it came back to me in a flash—I was at a lecture at the Royal Geographic Society in London. The major spoke about his expedition. He explained how the natives used poisoned darts to bring down large animals. He demonstrated the use of the blow pipe. It is silent and deadly accurate. I must say he was most proficient. Curare, isn't that the poison's name? It paralyzes the nervous system instantly. The count would not even have had time to cry out."

The countess turned away and stared out of the window again.

"The major waited until the stag was sighted," Fritzi continued. "He knew that all eyes would be focused on the animal. It only took a second to raise the blowpipe to his lips, and he administered the fatal dart just as the prince fired the first shot so that the noise of your husband falling to the ground would be masked by the sound of shots and the thrashings of a wounded animal. I hunted for the dart on the ground, but he got to the body first, of course and retrieved it. As the party fired their guns and rushed toward the stricken animal, the count had already fallen unnoticed to the ground. And who had been waiting in the woods, hidden well by a long green cloak, but you, Countess?

"You stepped out, took a pillow from your needlework bag, and fired through it into your husband's chest just as the last shots were being fired at the stag. You probably didn't notice that a few feathers from the pillow were strewn around the area. I suspect there might have been feathers in the wound, too, but your Major Johnny got there first and removed them. Very efficient, Countess. Well planned. Top marks."

The countess turned and looked at him coldly. "This is all most interesting, but you have no proof, do you? No evidence, no witnesses, nothing."

"I can have the police examine the pillow through which the shot was fired, and the gun itself."

"If they are still to be found by the time the police arrive," she said, this time with a smile.

"And I did find this." He held up a fragment of green fabric. "From your cloak, madam, caught on a bramble near the body. I had wondered at the time why you chose such an unfashionable, unflattering garment when your other clothes are all at the height of fashion. It was to make you invisible as you moved through the forest, was it not?"

"I walked through the forest yesterday," she said. "My cloak must have caught on a bramble then. Enough of this. I grow tired."

"Should I summon them, then, and repeat my story to the entire party?"

"And who will listen to you?" she demanded. "You're only a servant, an idiot servant at that. We will dismiss your ramblings and have you sent to an asylum. You don't even know your own name."

"Ten minutes ago that was true, Countess," the servant said, "but as I worked on this case, I realized that this was a situation I had been in many times before. I know now that I am a detective by profession—not just a detective, madam, but maybe the greatest that ever lived. Regard your nemesis, madam. You are looking at none other than Sherlock Holmes."

The woman gasped and ran for her needlework bag. Holmes dived at her just as she produced the revolver. He grabbed her wrist, and the shot flew into the wooden ceiling. There were shouts and feet came running up the stairs. The baron and his party burst into the room.

"He's a madman. He tried to attack me. Have him arrested," the countess screamed.

Holmes stepped forward and held up his hand commandingly to halt their approach.

"I thank you, madam. You have now given me the proof I lacked," Holmes said calmly. "If you retrieve the bullet from the ceiling, Herr Baron, you will find that it matches the bullet in Count von Strezl's chest. They were fired from the same revolver. And if we analyze the poor man's blood, it will reveal curare—a native poison found only in Brazil. Am I not right, Major?"

Major Watling-Smythe looked at the countess. "It was worth a try, wasn't it?" he said. "We fell in love at her house in Brazil. When I saw how miserable she was, trapped in the jungle with that selfish brute, I'd have done anything to set her free."

"It would have worked, too," the countess screamed, "if you hadn't poked your nose in. Curse you, Sherlock Holmes."

"What did you call him?" the baron demanded.

"I am delighted to inform you that my memory has returned," Sherlock Holmes replied. "And it was you who started me on the road to recovery, Major. I heard you speaking English, and your name was somehow familiar to me. It made my brain connect to my old friend Watson. Then when you uttered those words about letting the quarry get away, it was as if veils fell from my mind. By the time I had solved the intricacies of the case, I knew at last who I was."

"You really are Sherlock Holmes?" the major asked. "But everyone in England believes you died."

"I barely escaped death. And with all respect to Dr. Freud and his analyzing, I knew my name all the time, at least in my dreams. It was staring me in the face. What did I dream about but locked homes? Not only locked homes, but they were secured with a most modern safety lock. Its name could be clearly read, if I had bothered to read it. Sure Locks."

He gave the company a triumphant smile and strode from the room.

The Bughouse Caper

Bill Pronzini

I

The house at the westward edge of Russian Hill was a dormered and turreted pile of two stories and some dozen rooms, with a wraparound porch and a good deal of gingerbread trim. It was set well back from the street and well apart from its neighbors, given seclusion by shade trees, flowering shrubs, and marble statuary. A fine home, as befitted the likes of Elmer Truesdale, senior vice president of the San Francisco Maritime Bank. A home filled with all the playthings of the wealthy.

A home built to be burglarized.

Thirty feet inside the front gate, Quincannon shifted position in the deep shadow of a lilac bush. From this vantage point he had clear views of the house, the south side yard, and the street. He could see little of the rear of the property, where the bulk of a carriage barn loomed and a gated fence gave access to a carriageway that bisected the block, but this was of no consequence. His quarry might well come onto the property from that direction, but there was no rear entrance to the house and the method of preferred entry was by door, not first- or second-story windows; this meant he would have to come around to the side door or the front door, both of which were within sight.

No light showed anywhere on the grounds. Banker Truesdale and his wife, dressed to the nines, had left two hours earlier in a private carriage, and they had no live-in servants. The only light anywhere in the immediate vicinity came from a streetlamp some fifty yards distant, a flickery glow that did not reach into the Truesdale yard. High cirrostratus clouds made thin streaks across the sky, touching but not obscuring an early moon. The heavenly body was neither a sickle nor what the yeggs called a stool-pigeon moon, but a near half that dusted the darkness with enough pale shine to see by.

A night made for burglars and footpads. And detectives on the scent.

The combination of property and conditions was one of the reasons Quincannon had stationed himself here. The other was the list of names in the pocket of his chesterfield, provided by Jackson Pollard of the Great Western Insurance Company—a list that was also in a housebreaker's pocket, obtained from an unscrupulous employee or through other nefarious means. Whatever the burglar's expense, it had rewarded him handsomely in two previous robberies. Tonight, if all went according to plan, it would be Carpenter and Quincannon, Professional Detective Services, who would reap the list's final reward.

Aye, and the sooner the better. A raw early-May wind had sprung up, thick with the salt smell of the bay, and its chill penetrated the greatcoat, cheviot, gloves, neck scarf, and cap Quincannon wore. Noiselessly, he stomped his feet and flexed his fingers to maintain circulation. His mind conjured up the image of steaming mugs of coffee and soup. Of a fire hot and crackling in his rooms on Leavenworth Street. Of the warmth of Sabina's lips on the distressingly few occasions he had tasted them, and the all-too-brief pressure of her splendid body against his, and the heat of his passion for her—

Ah, no. None of that now. Attention to the matter at hand, detective business first and foremost. Why dwell on his one frustrating failure, when another of his professional triumphs was imminent? Easier to catch a crook than to melt a stubborn woman's resistance: Quincannon's Law.

A rattling and clopping on the cobbled street drew his attention. Moments later a hack, its side lamps casting narrow funnels of light, passed without slowing. When the sound of it faded, another sound took its place—music, faint and melodic. Someone playing the violin, and rather well, too. Quincannon listened for a time, decided what was being played was passages from Mendelssohn's *Lieder*. He was hardly an expert on classical music, or even much of an aficionado, but he had allowed Sabina to draw him to enough concerts to identify individual pieces. Among his strong suits as a detective were both a photographic memory and a well-tuned ear.

More time passed at a creep and crawl. The wind died down a bit, but he was so thoroughly chilled by then he scarcely noticed. Despite the heavy gloves and the constant flexing, his fingers felt stiff; much more time out here in the cold, and he might well have difficulty drawing his Navy Colt if such became necessary.

Blast this blasted housebreaker, whoever he was! He was bound to come after the spoils tonight; Quincannon was sure of it, and his instincts seldom led him astray. So what was the scruff waiting for? It must be after nine by now. Wherever Banker Truesdale and his missus had gone for the evening, chances were they would return by eleven. This being Thursday, Truesdale's presence would surely be required tomorrow morning at his bank.

Quincannon speculated once more on the identity of his quarry. There were dozens of house burglars in San Francisco and environs, but the cleverness of method and skill of entry in this case narrowed the field to a few professionals. Of those known to him, the likeliest candidates were the Sanctimonious Kid and Dodger Brown. Both were known to be in Bay Area at present, but neither had done anything else to attract attention, such as immediately fencing stolen jewelry and other valuables. And if the man responsible was a newcomer, he was of the same professional stripe. In any case, the swag had surely been planted for the nonce, to be disposed of after the thief had gone through most or all of the five names on the target list.

Or so the yegg would believe. Quincannon relished the prospect of convincing him otherwise, almost as much as he relished the thought of collecting the fat fee from Great Western Insurance.

The violin music had ceased; the night was hushed again. He

flexed and stomped and shifted and shivered, his mood growing darker by the minute. If the burglar gave any trouble, he would rue the effort. Quincannon prided himself as a man of guile and razor-sharp wits, but he was also a brawny man of Pennsylvania Scots stock and not averse to a bit of thumping and skull dragging if the situation warranted.

Another vehicle, a small carriage this time, clattered past. A figure appeared on the sidewalk, and Quincannon tensed expectantly—but it was only a citizen walking his dog, and soon gone. Hell and damn! If by some fluke he *was* wrong about the place and time of the next burglary, and he was forced to spend another evening courting pneumonia or worse, he would demand a bonus from Jackson Pollard. And if he didn't get it, he would damned well pad the expense account whether Sabina approved or not.

But he wasn't wrong. That became evident in the next few seconds, when he turned his gaze from the street to the inner yard and house.

Someone was moving over there, not fifty yards from where Quincannon was hidden.

His senses all sharpened at once; he stood immobile, peering through the lilac's branches. The movement came again, a shadow drifting among stationary shadows, at an angle from the rear of the property toward the side porch. Once the shape reached the steps and started up, it was briefly silhouetted—a man in dark clothing and a low-pulled cap. Then it merged with the deeper black on the porch. Several seconds passed. Then there was a brief stab of light—the beam from a dark lantern such as the one in Quincannon's pocket—followed by the faintest of scraping sounds as the intruder worked with his tools.

Once again stillness closed down. He was inside now. Quincannon stayed where he was, marking time. No light showed behind the dark windows. The professional buglar worked mainly by feel and instinct, using his lantern sparingly and shielding the beam when he did.

When Quincannon judged ten minutes had passed, he left his hiding place and catfooted through shadows until he was parallel with the side porch stairs. He paused to listen, heard nothing from the house, and crossed quickly, bent low, to a tall rhododendren planted alongside the steps. There he hunkered down on one knee to wait.

The wait might be another ten minutes; it might be a half hour or more. No matter. Now that the crime was in progress, he no longer minded the cold night, the dampness of the earth where he knelt. Even if there was a locked safe, no burglar would leave premises such as these without spoils of some sort. Art objects, silverware, anything of value that could be carried off and subsequently sold to pawnbrokers or one of the many fences who operated in the city. Whatever this lad emerged with, it would be enough for Quincannon to yaffle him. Whether he turned his man over to the city police immediately or not depended on the scruff's willingness to reveal the whereabouts of the swag from his previous jobs. Stashing and roughhousing a prisoner for information was unethical, if not illegal; but Quincannon felt righteously that in the pursuit of justice, not to mention a fat fee, the end justified the means.

His wait lasted less than thirty minutes. The creaking of a floorboard pricked up his ears, creased his freebooter's beard with a smile of anticipation. Another creak, the faintest squeak of a door hinge, a footfall on the porch. Now descending the steps, into Quincannon's view—short, slender, but turned out of profile so that his face was obscured. He paused on the bottom step, and in that moment Quincannon levered up and put the grab on him.

He was much the larger man, and there should have been no trouble in the catch. But just before his arms closed around the wiry body, the yegg heard or sensed danger and reacted not by trying to run or turning to fight, but by dropping suddenly into a crouch. Quincannon's arms slid up and off as if greased, pitching him off-balance. The scruff bounced upright, swung around, blew the stench of sour wine into Quincannon's face at the same time he fetched him a stabbing kick in the shin. Quincannon let out a howl, staggered, and nearly fell. By the time he caught himself, his quarry was on the run.

He gave chase on the blind, cursing inventively and sulphurously, hobbling for the first several steps until the pain from the kick ebbed. The burglar had twenty yards on him by then, zigzagging toward the bordering yew trees, then back away from them in the direction of the carriage barn. In the moonshine he made a fine, clear target, but Quincannon did not draw his Navy Colt. Ever since the long-ago episode in Virginia City, Nevada, when one his stray bullets fired during a battle with counterfeiters had claimed an innocent woman's life and led him into a guilt-ridden two-year bout with Demon Rum, he had vowed to use his weapon only if his life was in mortal danger. He had never broken that vow. Nor touched a drop of liquor since entering into his partnership with Sabina.

Before reaching the barn, his man cut away at another angle and plowed through a gate into the carriageway beyond. Quincannon lost sight of him for a few seconds; spied him again as he reached the gate and barreled through it. A race down the alley? No. The scruff was nimble as well as slippery; he threw a look over his shoulder, saw Quincannon in close pursuit, suddenly veered sideways and flung himself up and over a six-foot board fence into one of the neighboring yards.

In six long strides Quincannon was at the fence. He caught the top boards, hoisted himself up to chin level. Some fifty yards distant was the backside of a stately home, two windows and a pair of French doors ablaze with electric light; the outspill combined with pale moonshine to limn a jungly garden, a path leading through its profusion of plants and trees to a gazebo on the left. He had a brief glimpse of a dark shape plunging into shrubbery near the gazebo.

Quincannon scrambled up the rough boards, rolled his body over the top. And had the misfortune to land awkwardly on his sore leg, which gave way and toppled him skidding to his knees in damp grass. He growled an oath under his breath, lumbered to his feet, and stood listening. Leaves rustled and branches snapped—moving away from the gazebo, toward the house.

The path was of crushed shell that gleamed with a faint, ghostly radiance; he drifted along parallel to it, keeping to the grass to cushion his footfalls. Gnarled cypress and tall thorny pyracantha bushes partially obscured the house, the shadows under and around them as black as India ink. He paused to listen again. No more sounds of movement. He started forward, eased around one of the cypress trees.

The man who came up behind him did so with such silent stealth that he had no inkling of the other's presence until a hard object poked into and stiffened his spine, and a forceful voice said, "Stand fast, if you value your life. There's a good fellow."

Quincannon stood fast.

2

The one who had the drop on him was not the man he'd been chasing. The calm, cultured, and British-accented voice, and the almost casual choice of words, told him that. He said, stifling his anger and frustration, "I'm not a prowler."

"What are you, then?"

"A detective on the trail of a thief. I chased him into this yard."

"Indeed?" His captor sounded interested, if not convinced. "What manner of thief?"

"A blasted housebreaker. He broke into the Truesdale home."

"Did he, now. Mr. Truesdale, the banker?"

"That's right. Your neighbor across the carriageway."

"A mistaken assumption. This is not my home, and I've only just met Mr. Truesdale tonight."

"Then who are you?"

"All in good time. This is hardly a proper place for introductions."

"Introductions be damned," Quincannon growled. "While we stand here gabbing, the thief is getting away."

"Has already gotten away, I should think. Perhaps."

"Perhaps?"

"If you're who you say you are and not a thief yourself." The hard object prodded his backbone. "Move along to the house, and we'll have the straight of things in no time."

"Bah," Quincannon said, but he moved along.

There was a flagstone terrace across the rear of the house, and when they reached it he could see people in evening clothes moving around a well-lighted parlor. His captor took him to a pair of French doors, ordered him to step inside. Activity in the room halted when they entered. Six pairs of eyes, three male and three female, stared at him and the man behind him. One of the couples, both plump and middle-aged, was Samuel Truesdale and his wife. The others were strangers.

The parlor was large, handsomely furnished, dominated by a massive grand piano. On the piano's bench lay a well-used violin and bow—the source of the passages from Mendelssohn he had heard earlier, no doubt. A wood fire blazed on the hearth. A combination of the fire and steam heat made the room too warm, stuffy.

Quincannon's benumbed cheeks began to tingle almost immediately.

The first to break the frozen tableau was a round-faced gent with Lincolnesque whiskers and ears as large as the handles on a pickle jar. He stepped forward and demanded of the Englishman, "Where did this man come from? Who is he?"

"On my stroll in the garden I spied him climbing the fence and apprehended him. He claims to be a detective on the trail of a pannyman. Housebreaker, that is."

"I don't claim to be a detective," Quincannon said sourly, "I *am* a detective. Quincannon's the name, John Quincannon."

"Dr. Caleb Axminster," the whiskered gent said. "What's this about a housebreaker?"

The exchange drew the others closer in a tight little group. It also brought the owner of the cultured British voice out to where Quincannon could see him for the first time. He wasn't such-a-much. Tall, excessively lean, with a thin, hawklike nose and a prominent chin. In one hand he carried a blackthorn walking stick, held midway along the shaft. Quincannon scowled. It must have been the stick, not a pistol, that had poked his spine and allowed the burglar to escape.

"I'll ask you again," Dr. Axminster said. "What's this about a housebreaker?"

"I chased him here from a neighbor's property." Quincannon switched his gaze to the plump banker. He was not a man to mince words, even at the best of times. And this was not the best of times. "Your home, Mr. Truesdale," he said bluntly.

Mrs. Truesdale and the other women gasped. Her husband's face lost its healthy color. "Mine? Good Lord, man, do you mean to say we've been robbed?"

"Unfortunately, yes. Do you keep your valuables in a safe?"

"My wife's jewelry and several stock certificates, yes."

"Cash?"

"In my desk . . . a hundred dollars or so in greenbacks . . ." Truesdale shook his head; he seemed dazed. "You were there?"

"I was. Waiting outside."

"Waiting? I don't understand."

"To catch the burglar in the act."

"But how did you know . . ."

"Detective work, suffice it to say."

The fifth man in the room had been silent to this point. He was somewhat younger than the others, forty or so, dark-eyed, clean-shaven; his most prominent feature was a misshapen knob of red-veined flesh, like a partially collapsed balloon, that seemed to hang between his eyes and a thin-lipped mouth. He aimed a brandy snifter at Quincannon and said challengingly, "If you were set up to catch the housebreaker, why didn't you? What happened?"

"An unforeseen occurrence." Quincannon glared sideways at his gaunt captor. "I would have chased him down if this man hadn't accosted me."

"Accosted?" The Englishman arched an eyebrow. "Dear me, hardly that. I had no way of knowing you weren't a prowler."

Mrs. Truesdale was tugging at her husband's arm. "Elmer, hadn't we best return home and find out what was stolen?"

"Yes, yes. Immediately."

"Margaret," Axminster said to one of the other women, a slender graying brunette with patrician features, "find James and have him drive the Truesdales."

The woman nodded and left the parlor with the banker and his wife in tow.

The doctor said then, "This is most distressing," but he didn't sound distressed. He sounded excited, as if he found the situation stimulating. He produced a paper sack from his pocket, popped a horehound drop into his mouth. "But right up your alley, eh, Mr. Holmes?"

The Englishman bowed.

"And yours, Andrew. Eh? The law and all that."

"Hardly," the dark-eyed man said. "You know I handle civil, not criminal cases. Why don't you introduce us, Caleb? Unless Quincannon already knows who I am, too."

Quincannon decided he didn't particularly like the fellow. Or Axminister, for that matter. Or the blasted Englishman. In fact, he did not like anybody tonight, not even himself very much.

"Certainly," the doctor said. "This is Andrew Costain, Mr. Quincannon, and his wife, Penelope. And this most distinguished gentleman—"

"Costain?" Quincannon interrupted. "Offices on Geary Street, residence near South Park?"

"By God," Costain said, "he *does* know me. But if we've met, I don't remember the time or place. In court, was it?"

"We haven't met anywhere. Your name happens to be on the list."

"List?" Penelope Costain said. She was a slender, gray-eyed, brown-curled woman some years younger than her husband—handsome enough, though she appeared too aloof and wore too much rouge and powder for Quincannon's taste. "What list?"

"Of potential burglary victims, all of whom own valuables insured by the Great Western Insurance Company."

"So that's it," Costain said. "Truesdale's name is also on that list, I suppose. That's what brought you to his home tonight."

"Among other things," Quincannon admitted.

Axminister sucked the horehound drop, his brow screwed up in thought. "Quincannon, John Quincannon . . . why, of course! I knew I'd heard the name before. Carpenter and Quincannon, Professional Detective Services. Yes, and your partner is a woman. Sabina Carpenter."

"A woman," the Englishman said. "How curious."

Quincannon skewered him with a sharp eye. "What's curious about it? Both she and her late husband were valued operatives attached to the Pinkerton Agency's Denver office."

"Upon my soul. In England, you know, it would be extraordinary for a woman to assume the profession of consulting detective, the more so to be taken in as a partner in a private inquiry agency."

"She wasn't 'taken in,' as you put it. Our partnership was by mutual arrangement."

"Ah."

"What do you know of private detectives, in England or anywhere?"

"He knows a great deal, as a matter of fact," Axminister said with relish. He asked the Englishman, "You have no objection if I reveal your identity to a colleague?"

"None, inasmuch as you have already revealed it to your guests."

The doctor beamed. He said as if presenting a member of the British royalty, "My honored houseguest, courtesy of a mutual acquaintance in the south of France, is none other than Mr. Sherlock Holmes of 221B Baker Street, London."

The Englishman bowed. "At your service."

"I've already had a sampling of your service," Quincannon said aggrievedly. "I prefer my own."

"*Nous verrons.*"

"Holmes, is it? I'm not familiar with the name."

"Surely you've heard it," Axminister said. "Not only has Mr. Holmes solved many baffling cases in England and Europe, but his apparent death at the hands of his archenemy, Professor Moriarity, was widely reported three years ago."

"I seldom read sensational news."

"Officially," Holmes said, "I am still dead, having been dispatched at Reichenbach Falls in Switzerland. For private reasons I've chosen to let this misapprehension stand, until recently confiding in no one but my brother Mycroft. Not even my good friend Dr. Watson knows I'm still alive."

"If he's such a good friend, why haven't you told him?"

Holmes produced an enigmatic smile and made no reply.

Axminister said, "Dr. John H. Watson is Mr. Holmes's biographer as well as his friend. The doctor has chronicled many of his cases."

"Yes?"

"'A Study in Scarlet,' 'The Red-Headed League,' 'The Sign of the Four,' the horror at Baskerville Hall, the adventure of the six orange pips . . ."

"Five," Holmes said.

"Eh? Oh, yes, five orange pips."

Quincannon said, "I've never heard of any of them." The stuffy, overheated room was making him sweat. He stripped off his gloves, unbuttoned his chesterfield, and swept the tails back. At the same time he essayed a closer look at the Englishman, which led him to somewhat revise his earlier estimate. The fellow might be gaunt, almost cadaverous in his evening clothes, but his jaw and hawklike nose bespoke intensity and determination, and his eyes were sharp, piercing, alive with a keen intelligence. It would be a mistake to dismiss him too lightly.

Holmes said with a gleam of interest, "I daresay you've had your own share of successes, Quincannon."

"More than I can count."

"Oh, yes, Mr. Quincannon is well-known locally," the doctor said. "Several of his investigations involving seemingly impossible crimes have gained notoriety. If I remember correctly, there was the rainmaker shot to death in a locked room, the strange disappearance on board the Desert Limited, the rather amazing murder of a bogus medium . . ."

Holmes leaned forward. "I would be most interested to know what methods you and your partner employ."

"Methods?"

"In solving your cases. Aside from the use of weapons, fisticuffs, and such surveillance techniques as you employed tonight."

"What happened tonight was not my fault," Quincannon said testily. "As to our methods—those you mentioned, plus guile, wit, attention to detail, and deduction."

"Capital! My methods are likewise based on observation, in particular the observation of trifles, and on deductive reasoning—the construction of a series of inferences, each dependent upon its predecessor. An exact knowledge of all facets of crime and its history is invaluable as well, as I'm sure you know."

Bumptious gent! Quincannon managed not to sneer.

"For instance," Holmes said, smiling, "I should say that you are unmarried, smoke a well-seasoned briar, prefer cable twist Virginia tobacco, spent part of today in a tonsorial parlor and another part engaged in a game of straight pool, dined on chicken croquettes before proceeding to the Truesdale property, waited for your burglar in a shrub of *Syringa persica,* and . . . oh yes, under your rather rough exterior, I perceive that you are well-read and rather sensitive and sentimental."

Quincannon gaped at him. "How the devil can you know all that?"

"There is a loose button and loose thread on your vest, and your shirt collar is slightly frayed—telltale indications of our shared state of bachelorhood. When I stood close behind you in the garden, I detected the scent of your tobacco; and once in here, I noted a small spot of ash on the sleeve of your coat which confirmed the mixture and the fact that it was smoked in a well-aged briar. It happens, you see, that I once wrote a little monograph on the ashes of 140 different types of cigar, pipe, and cigarette tobacco ash and am considered an authority on the subject. Your beard has been recently and neatly trimmed, as has your hair, which retains a faint scent of bay rum— hence your visit to the tonsorial parlor. Under the nail of your left thumb is dust from the type of chalk commonly used on the tips of pool cues, and while billiards is often played in America, straight pool has a larger following and strikes me as more to your taste. On the handkerchief you used a moment ago to mop your forehead is a small, fresh stain the color and texture of which identifies it to the trained eye as having come from a dish of chicken croquettes. Another scent that clings faintly to your coat is that of *Syringa persica*, or Persian lilac, indicating that you have recently spent time in close proximity to such a flowering shrub; and inasmuch as there are no lilac bushes in Dr. Axminster's garden, Mr. Truesdale's property is the obvious deduction. I perceive that you are well-read from the slim volume of poetry tucked into the pocket of your frock coat, and that you are both sensitive and sentimental from the identity of the volume's author. Emily Dickinson's poems, I am given to understand, are famous for those very qualities."

There was a moment of silence. Quincannon, for once in his life, was at a loss for words.

Axminster clapped his hands and exclaimed delightedly, "Amazing!"

"Elementary," Holmes said.

Penelope Costain yawned. "Mr. Holmes has been regaling us with his powers of observation and deduction all evening. Frankly, I found his prowess with the violin of greater amusement."

Her husband was likewise unimpressed. He had refilled his glass from a sideboard nearby and now emptied it again in a swallow; his face was flushed, his eyes slightly glazed. "Mental gymnastics are all well and good," he said with some asperity, "but we've strayed well away from the issue here. Which is that my name, Penelope's and mine, are on Quincannon's list of potential robbery victims."

"I wouldn't be concerned, Andrew," Axminster said. "After tonight's escapade, that fellow wouldn't dare attempt another burglary."

Quincannon said, "True enough. Particularly if he suspects that I know his identity."

"You recognized him?"

"After a fashion."

"Then why don't you go find him and have him arrested?" Costain demanded.

"All in good time. I guarantee he won't do any more breaking and entering this night."

Mrs. Costain asked, "Did you also guarantee catching him red-handed at the Truesdales' home?"

Quincannon had had enough of this company; much more of it and he might well say something even he would regret. He made a small show of consulting his stemwinder. "If you'll all excuse me," he said then, "I'll be on my way."

"To request police assistance?"

"To determine the extent of the Truesdales' loss."

Dr. Axminster showed him to the front door. The Costains remained in the parlor, but Sherlock Holmes tagged along. At the front door the Englishman said, "I must say, Quincannon, I regret my intervention in the garden, well-intentioned though it was, but I must say I found the interlude stimulating. It isn't often I have the pleasure of meeting a distinguished colleague while a game's afoot."

Quincannon reluctantly accepted the Englishman's proffered hand, clasped the doctor's just as briefly, and took his leave. Nurturing as he went the dark thought of a game involving *his* foot that he'd admire to play with Mr. Sherlock Holmes.

3

Sabina was already at her desk when Quincannon arrived at the Market Street offices of Carpenter and Quincannon, Professional Detective Services, the following morning. Poring over their financial ledger and bank records—a task he gladly left to her, since he had no head for figures. Other than hers, that was.

She was not a beautiful woman, but at thirty-one she possessed a healthy and mature comeliness that melted his hard Scot's heart. There was strength in her high-cheekboned face, intelligence in eyes the color of dark blue velvet. Her seal black hair, layered high and fastened with a jeweled comb, glistened with bluish highlights in the pale sunlight slanting in through the windows at her back. And her figure . . . ah, her figure. Fine, slim, delicately rounded and curved in a lacy white shirtwaist and a Balmoral skirt. Many men found her attractive, to be sure, and as a young widow, fair game. If any had been allowed inside her Russian Hill flat, he wasn't aware of it; she was a strict guardian of her private life. He knew she was fond of him, yet she continually spurned his advances. This not only frustrated him but left him in a state of constant apprehension. The very thought that she might accept a proposal of either dalliance or marriage from anyone but John Quincannon was maddening.

She had a sharp eye for his moods. The first thing she said was, "Well, John, from the look of you, all failed to go as planned at the Truesdale home."

"A fair assessment." Quincannon shed his chesterfield and derby, hung them on the clothes tree, and retreated to his desk. His loaded his briar with shaved cable twist from his pouch, fired the tobacco with a lucifer. As he puffed, the skin along his brow furrowed. "Unique scent," he muttered. "Monograph on 140 different types of tobacco ash. Faugh!"

"What's that you're grumbling about?"

"Gent I encountered last night, blast the luck. Damned infuriating Englishman. Not only did he cost me the burglar's capture, he did his level best to make a fool of me with a bagful of parlor tricks."

Sabina raised an eyebrow. "How did that come about? Exactly what happened last night, John?"

He told her in some detail, most of it accurate to a fault. When he was done, she said, "So this English fellow is a detective, too. His name is Holmes, you said?"

"Sherlock Holmes." Quincannon puffed furiously on his briar. "Sherlock! What kind of name is that?"

"A most respected one, I do believe."

"Eh?"

"I've heard mention of the exploits of Mr. Sherlock Holmes," Sabina said. "He has a sterling reputation. A fascinating man, by all accounts."

"Not by mine. Fascinating isn't the word I would use to describe him."

"Well, you didn't make his acquaintance under the best of circumstances."

"It wouldn't have mattered where I made his acquaintance. If he were handing me a bagful of gold sovereigns, I would still find him an arrogant show-off."

"Arrogance is the trademark of a successful detective, you know."

"Yes? I've blessed little of it in me."

Sabina laughed. "Come now, John. You mean to say you weren't even a little impressed by Holmes's powers of observation and deduction? Or his record of successes in England and Europe?"

"Not a bit's worth," Quincannon lied. "He may be a competent flycop in his own bailiwick, but his genius is suspect. A mentalist in a collar-and-elbow variety show at the Bella Union could perform the same tricks. World's greatest detective? Bah!"

"Poor John. You did have rather a difficult evening, didn't you?"

"Difficult, yes, but not wholly unproductive."

"You're convinced Dodger Brown is the man we're after?"

"Reasonably. When he slipped loose and swung around to kick me—"

"Kick you? I thought you said you slipped on the wet grass."

"Yes, yes," Quincannon lied again, "but how he got away is of no consequence. The important fact is that he was of the right size and that he reeked of cheap wine. Dodger Brown's weakness is 'foot juice.'"

"Yes, I remember."

He rummaged among the papers on his desk. "Where's that dossier on the Dodger?"

"Your left hand is resting on it."

So it was. He caught up the paper, scanned through it to refresh his memory. Dodger Brown, christened Hezekiah Gabriel Brown, had been born in Stockton twenty-nine years ago. Orphaned at an early age, ran away at thirteen, fell in with a bunch of rail-riding yeggs, and been immersed in criminal activity ever since, exclusively house burglary in recent years. Arrested numerous times and "put on the small book"—held as a suspicious character—by police in San Francisco, Oakland, and other cities. Served two terms in prison, the last at Folsom for stealing a pile of green-and-greasy from a miserly East Bay politician. Known traits: close-mouthed, willing to suffer all manner of abuse rather than give up spoils or acquaintances. Known confidants: none. Known habits: frequenter of Oriental parlor houses, cheap-jack gambling halls, and Barbary Coast wine dumps, in particular Jack Foyles's on Kearney. Current whereabouts: unknown. Damn little information, but perhaps just enough.

When he lowered the dossier, Sabina said, "If he recognized you last night, he may have already unplanted his loot and gone on the lammas."

"I don't think so. It was too dark for him to see my face any more clearly than I saw his. For all he knows, I might have been Truesdale home early, or a neighbor who spotted him skulking. A greedy lad like the Dodger isn't likely to cut and run when he's flush and onto a string of profitable marks."

"After such a narrow escape, would he be bold enough to try burgling another home on the insurance company's list?"

"Possibly. He's none too bright, foolish, and as arrogant in his fashion as that Holmes gent. It was a bughouse caper that landed him in Folsom prison two years ago. He's not above another, I'll wager."

"What will you do if you find him?"

"There's little profit in bracing him. I'll locate the place he's holed up, search his rooms for evidence or word of which fenceman he's approached."

"You intend to avoid reporting to Jackson Pollard first, I trust?"

Quincannon nodded grimly. Not only cash had been stolen from the Truesdale home but also a valuable necklace the banker's wife had neglected to lock away in their safe. Last night's urgings to the banker to wait before filing an insurance claim had fallen on deaf ears; Truesdale intended to do so immediately. Pollard would not take kindly to either the claim or word of Quincannon's failure to apprehend the thief.

"If Pollard should stop by here," he said, "tell him Mr. Sherlock Holmes is responsible for the night's fiasco, and I'm busy working to atone for his mistake."

"That's hardly tactful, John."

"Tact be damned. A fact is a fact."

He was redonning his coat when a knock sounded on the entrance door and a frog-faced youth wearing a cap and baggy trousers entered. The cap sported a sewn decal proclaiming his employer to be Citywide Messenger Service. The youth confirmed it in a scratchy voice and stated that he had a message for Mr. John Quincannon, Esquire.

"I'll have it," Quincannon accepted the envelope, signed for it, tore it open. The youth, looking hopeful, remained standing there. "Well? You've done your duty, lad. Off with you!" The command, accompanied by a fiercely menacing scowl and a step forward, sent the messenger scuttling hurriedly through the door.

Sabina said, "You might have tipped him a nickel, John."

"I did him a good turn by not tipping him. He'd only have spent it on profligate pleasures."

He finished opening the envelope, removed a sheet of bond paper that bore the letterhead and signature of Andrew Costain, Attorney-at-Law. The curt message, written in a rather ornate hand, read:

> I should like to discuss a business matter with you. If you will
> call on me today at my offices, at your convenience, I am sure you
> will find it to your professional and financial advantage.

He read the message aloud to Sabina. She said, "Regarding the burglaries, do you suppose?"

"Likely. He's the worrying type."

"You'll call on him, then, of course."

Quincannon glanced again at the paper, at the mellifluous phrase *financial advantage*. "Of course," he said.

4

Jack Foyles's was a shade less disreputable than most wine dumps, if only because it was equipped with a small lunch counter where its habitués could supplement their liquid sustenance with stale bread and a bowl of stew made from discarded vegetables, meat trimmings, bones, and chunks of tallow. Otherwise, there was little to distinguish it from its brethren. Barrels of "foot juice" and "red ink" behind a long bar, rows of rickety tables in three separate rooms lined with men and a few women of all types, ages, and backgrounds, a large open-floored area to accommodate those who had drunk themselves into a stupor. Porters who were themselves winos served the cheap and deadly drink in vessels supplied by junkmen—beer glasses, steins, pewter mugs, cracked soup bowls, tin cans. There was much loud talk, but never any laughter. Foyles's customers had long ago lost their capacity for mirth.

No one paid Quincannon the slightest attention as he moved slowly through the crowded rooms. Slurred voices rolled surflike against his ears, identifying the speakers as lawyers, sailors, poets, draymen, road bums, scholars, factory workers, petty criminals. There were no class distinctions there, nor seldom any trouble; they were all united by failure, bitterness, disillusionment, old age, disease, and unquenchable thirst for the grape. If there was anything positive to be said of wine dumps, it was that they were havens of democracy. Most customers would be there every day, or as often as they could panhandle or steal enough money to pay for their allotment of slow death, but a few, not yet far gone, were less frequent visitors—binge drinkers and slummers who found the atmosphere and the company to their liking. Many of them were crooks of one stripe or another, Dodger Brown among them.

But there was no sign of the Dodger. Quincannon questioned two of the porters; one knew him and reported that he hadn't been to Foyles's in more than a week. Did the porter know where Dodger Brown might be found? The porter did not.

Quincannon left Foyles's and made his way into the heart of the Barbary Coast. During the daylight hours, the "devil's playground" seemed quiet, almost tame—a deceit if ever there was one. Less than a third as many predators and their prey prowled the ulcerous streets as could be found there after sundown; most gamblers, pickpockets, swindlers, shanghaiers, footpads, and roaming prostitutes were creatures of the night, and it was the dark hours when the preponderence of their prey succumbed to the gaudy lure of sin and wickedness. Some of the more notorious gambling dens and parlor houses were open for business, as were the scruffier cribs and deadfalls, but they were thinly populated at that early hour. And mostly absent was the nighttime babel of pianos, hurdy-gurdies, drunken laughter, the cries of shills and barkers, and the shouts and screams of victims. Quincannon was anything but a prude, having done his fair share of carousing during his drinking days, but the Coast had never attracted him. He preferred to satisfy his vices in private.

Near Broadway there was a section of run-down hotels and lodging houses. He entered one of the latter and had words with the desk clerk, a runty chap named Galway—one of several of the Coast's underclass who were willing to sell information for cash or favors. Galway admitted to having seen Dodger Brown "a time or two" in recent weeks, and thought he might be residing at Foghorn Annie's, one of the seamen's boardinghouses on the waterfront.

Quincannon found a hack on Montgomery—he always rode in hansoms when a client was paying expenses—and was shortly delivered to the Embarcadero. The trip turned out to be wasted time. Scruffs were known to seek shelter among seafaring men now and then by pretending to be former sailors themselves or by paying extra for the protective coloration. Dodger Brown was known at Foghorn Annie's, but not a current resident. Visits to two other houses in the area produced neither the Dodger nor a clue to his whereabouts.

Hunger prodded Quincannon into a waterfront eatery, where he made short work of half a dozen oysters on the half shell and a bowl of fish stew. Another hack returned him to the Barbary Coast. He canvassed two other wine dumps, half a dozen gambling halls, and two parlor houses that specialized in "Asian specialities" without so much as a whisper of his quarry. The Dodger might have been a foolish dolt, but he was also sly enough to curtail his baser appetites and avoid his habitual haunts for the time being.

Enough of roaming the Coast, Quincannon decided. The time had come to call on Ezra Bluefield again. He had already approached the man once that week, just two days ago, seeking information on the house burglaries and possible fencing of the loot, and Bluefield grew testy when he was asked for too many favors. But if there was one lad in the devil's playground who could find out where Dodger Brown was holed up, it was Bluefield.

Quincannon walked to Terrific Street, as Pacific Avenue was called, turned into an alley, and entered a scabrous building in mid-block. A sign in bloodred letters above the entrance proclaimed the establishment to be the Scarlet Lady Saloon. A smaller sign beneath it read: EZRA BLUEFIELD, PROP.

At one time the Scarlet Lady had been an infamous crimping joint, where seamen were fed drinks laced with laudanum and chloral hydrate and then carted off by shanghaiers and sold to unscrupulous shipmasters in need of crews. The Sailor's Union of the Pacific had ended the practice and forced the saloon's closure, but only until Bluefield had promised to end his association with the shanghaiers and backed up the promise with generous bribes to city officials. The Scarlet Lady was now an "honest" deadfall in which percentage girls, bunco ploys, and rigged games of chance were used to separate seamen and other patrons from their money.

As usual, Bluefield was in his office at the rear. He was an ex-miner who had had his fill of the rough-and-tumble life in various western goldfields and vowed to give up his own rowdy ways when he moved to San Francisco and opened the Scarlet Lady. He had taken no active part in the crimping activities, and was known to remain behind his locked office door when brawls broke out, as they often did; the team of bouncers he employed were charged with stifling trouble and keeping what passed for peace. It was his stated intention to one day own a better class of saloon in a better neighborhood, and as a result he cultivated the company and goodwill of respectable citizens. Quincannon was one of them, largely because he had once prevented a rival saloon owner from puncturing Bluefield's hide with a bullet.

Bluefield was drinking beer and counting profits, two of his favorite activities, and seemed not to mind being visited again so soon. "I've nothing for you yet, John, my lad," he said. "You know I'll send word when I do."

"I'm the one with news today," Quincannon said. "The housebreaker I'm after is Dodger Brown."

"The Dodger, is it? Well, I'm not surprised. How did you tumble?"

"I came within a hair of nabbing him in the act last night. He escaped through no fault of mine."

"So he knows you're onto him?"

"I don't believe he does, as dark as it was."

"He'll still be in the vicinity, then, you're thinking," Bluefield said. He raised his mug of lager with one thick finger, drank, licked foam off his mustached upper lip. The mustache was an impressive coal black handlebar, its ends waxed to rapier points, of which he was inordinately proud. "And mayhap old Ezra can find out where he's hanging his hat."

"You'll make me a happy man if it can be done quickly."

"I'll put out the word. A favor in return, John?"

"Name it."

"There's a saloon and restaurant just up for sale in the Uptown Tenderloin. The Redemption, on Ellis Street."

"I know it. A respected establishment."

"I'm looking to buy it. It's past time I put this hellhole up for sale and leave the Coast for good. There'll never be a place better suited or better named for the likes of me to die a respectable citizen. I have the money, I've made overtures, but the owners aren't convinced my intentions are honorable. They're afraid I have plans to turn the Redemption into a fancy copy of the Scarlet Lady."

"And you've no such plans."

"None, lad, I swear it."

"Is it a letter of reference you're after, then?"

"Yes. Your name carries weight in this city."

"You'll have it tomorrow, by messenger."

Bluefield lumbered to his feet and thumped Quincannon's back with a meaty paw. "You won't regret it, John. You and your lady partner will never pay for a meal at Ezra Bluefield's Redemption."

Quincannon had never turned down a free meal in his life, and never would. "I'll settle for word of Dodger Brown's whereabouts," he lied.

"Within twenty-four hours," Bluefield said, "and that's a bloody promise. Even if it means hiring a gang of men to hunt through every rattrap from here to China Basin."

5

Andrew Costain's offices were in a brick building on Geary Street that housed a dozen attorneys and half as many other professional men. The anteroom held a secretary's desk but no secretary; the bare desktop and dusty file cabinets behind it suggested that there hadn't been one in some while. A pair of neatly lettered and somewhat contradictory signs were affixed to one of two closed doors in the inside wall. The upper one proclaimed PRIVATE, the lower invited KNOCK FOR ADMITTANCE.

Quincannon knocked. Costain's whiskey baritone called him in. The lawyer sat behind a cluttered desk set before a wall covered with law books, among them what appeared to be a full set of Blackstone. More books and papers were scattered on dusty pieces of furniture. On another wall, next to a framed law degree, was a lithograph of John L. Sullivan in a fighting pose.

Costain's person was more tidy than his office; he wore an expensive tweed suit and a fancy striped vest, and when he stood up, an elk's tooth gleamed at the end of a heavy gold watch chain. The successful image, however, was spoiled by his rum-blossom nose and a faint perfume of forty-rod whiskey that could be detected at ten paces. If Quincannon had been a prospective client, he would have thought twice about entrusting his legal business to Mr. Andrew Costain.

"Well, Quincannon, I expected you much sooner than this."

"At my convenience, your message said."

"It also offered you a financial advantage."

"So it did. For what service, Mr. Costain?"

"That's rather obvious, isn't it, after last night? Sit down, Quincannon. Cigar? Drink?"

"Neither." He moved a heavy volume of Blackstone from the single client's chair and replaced it with his backside.

Costain asked, "Have you caught the scoundrel yet?"

"If you mean the housebreaker, no, not yet."

"Identified him?"

"Yes. It's only a matter of time until he's locked away in the city jail."

"How much time?"

"A day or two."

"How do you plan to catch him? While in the act?"

"Perhaps."

"Don't be ambiguous, man. I have a right to know what you're up to."

"My client is the Great Western Insurance Company," Quincannon said. "I need answer only to them."

"My name is on that list of potential victims: you said so last night. Naturally I'm concerned. Suppose he wasn't frightened off by his near capture at the Truesdales'? Suppose he's bold enough to try burgling my home next, even this very night? I can ill afford to have my house ransacked and valuables stolen. Those damned insurance people never pay off at full value."

"A legitimate fear."

"I want you to prevent that from happening. Hire you to prevent it. Watch my home every night until the thief is arrested, beginning tonight."

Quincannon said reluctantly, "There are other alternatives, you know, that would cost you nothing."

"Yes, yes, I know. Move our valuables to a safe place and simply stay home nights until the threat is ended. But we have too many possessions to haul away willy-nilly and too little time to do so. Even if we did remove everything of value, the burglar might still break in and vandalize the premises if he found nothing worth stealing. That has been known to happen, hasn't it?"

"It has, though not very often."

"I don't like the idea of my home being invaded in any case. And it damned well could be. My wife and I have separate appointments tonight and a joint one tomorrow evening that we're loath to cancel. The house will be empty and fair game from seven until midnight or later both nights."

"You have no servants?"

"None that live in. And it would be useless to ask help from city police without certain knowledge of a crime to be committed."

"So it would."

"Well? There is no conflict of interest involved, after all."

True enough. If Costain wanted to pay him to do the same work for which he was being paid by Great Western Insurance, there was neither conflict nor a reasonable argument against it. The notion of another night or two hiding in shrubbery and risking pneumonia had no appeal, but minor hardships were part and parcel of the detective game. Besides, nothing warmed his Scot's blood like the fattening of the agency's bank account.

"You'll accept the job, then?"

"I will," Quincannon said blandly, "provided you're willing to pay an additional fee."

"What's that? For what?"

"Surveillance on your home is a job for two men."

"Why? You were alone at the Truesdales."

"The Truesdale house has front and side entrances which could be watched by one man alone. Yours has front and rear entrances, therefore requiring a second operative."

"How is it you know my house?"

"I tabbed it up, along with the others on the list, the day I was hired."

"Tabbed it up?"

"Crook's argot. Paid visits and scrutinized the properties, the same as the housebreaker would have done to size up the lay."

Costain opened a desk drawer, removed a flask and a finger-marked glass, poured the glass half-full, and sat frowning while he nipped at it. At length the frown smoothed off and he drank the rest of his whiskey at a gulp. "Very well," he said. "How much will it cost me?"

Quincannon named a per diem figure, only slightly higher than his usual for a two-man operation. He cared little for Costain, but the dislike was not enough to warrant gouging the man unduly.

The amount induced the lawyer to pour himself a second drink. "That's damned close to extortion," he muttered.

"Hardly. My fees are standard."

"And nonnegotiable, I suppose."

"Under all circumstances," Quincannon lied.

"Very well, then. How much in advance?"

"One day's fee in full."

"For services not yet rendered? No, by God! Half, and not a penny more."

Quincannon shrugged. Half in advance was more than he usually requested from his clients.

"You had better not fail me, Quincannon," Costain said as he wrote out a bank check. "If there is a repeat of your bungling at the Truesdales, you'll regret it—I promise you that."

"I did not bungle at the Truesdales. What happened last night—"

"—wasn't your fault. Yes, I know. And if anything similar happens, it won't be your fault again, no doubt."

Quincannon said, "You'll have your money's worth," tucked the check into a waistcoat pocket, and left Costain to stew in his alcoholic juices.

The Geary Street address was not far from his own offices; he traveled the distance on foot at a brisk pace. San Francisco was a fine city, the more so on balmy days such as this one. The fresh salt smell from the bay, the rumble and clang of cable cars on Market Street, the booming horn of one of the fast coastal steamers as it drew into or away from Embarcadero, the stately presence of the Perry Building in the distance . . . he had yet to tire of any of it. It had been a banner day when he had been reassigned to San Francisco during his days with the United States Secret Service. The nation's capital had not been the same for him after his father, Thomas L. Quincannon, himself a fearless rival of Allan Pinkerton, succumbed to an assassin's bullet on the Baltimore docks; he had been ready for a change. His new home suited him as Washington, D.C., had suited his father. The same was true of the business of private investigation.

When he arrived at the building that housed Carpenter and Quincannon, Professional Detective Services, he was in high spirits. He whistled tunefully under his breath as he climbed the stairs to the second floor and approached the door to his offices. But he stopped when he saw that the door stood ajar by a few inches and heard the voice that emanated from within.

"I consider that a man's brain originally is like a little empty attic," the voice was declaiming, "and you have to stock it with such furniture as you choose. A fool takes in all the lumber of every sort that he comes across, so that the knowledge that might be useful to him gets crowded out, or at best is jumbled up with a lot of other things, so that he has a difficulty in laying his hands upon it. Now the skillful workman is very careful indeed as to what he takes into his brain-attic. He will have nothing but the tools that may help him in doing his work; but of these he has a large assortment, and all in the most perfect order. It is a mistake to think that that little room has elastic walls and can distend to any extent. There comes a time when for every addition of knowledge you forget something that you knew before. It is of the highest importance, therefore, not to have useless facts elbowing out the useful ones."

Quincannon's cheerful smile turned upside down as he elbowed his way inside. The voice belonged to Sherlock Holmes.

6

The Englishman was sitting comfortably in the client's chair in front of Sabina's desk, a gray cape draped over his narrow shoulders and an odd-looking cloth cap hiding his ears. The office was blue with smoke from the long, black clay pipe he was smoking. Quincannon's nostrils twitched and pinched; the tobacco Holmes used might have been made from floor sweepings.

From the expression on Sabina's face, Holmes had had a rapt listener for his prattle about brain-attics. This annoyed Quincannon even more. He was not gentle in closing the door behind him, nor gracious in his opening remark.

"I seem to have walked in on a lecture," he said to Sabina.

Her sharp look warned him to be civil. "Mr. Holmes wasn't lecturing, he was simply answering a question. He really does have amazing powers of observation and deduction."

If it was possible to bow while sitting down, the Englishman managed it. "You're most kind, my dear Mrs. Carpenter."

Under his breath Quincannon muttered an unkindness.

"Why," Sabina said, "he wasn't here one minute before he knew about Adam."

"Adam? Who the deuce is Adam?"

"My new roommate."

"Your . . . *what?*"

"Oh, you needn't look so horrified. Adam is a cat."

"Kitten, in point of fact," Holmes said. "Three months old."

"Cat? You never told me you had a cat."

"Well, I've only had him two days," Sabina said. "Such a cute little fellow that I couldn't bring myself to turn away when a neighbor brought him by."

"Rather a curious mix of Abyssinian and long-haired Siamese," Holmes announced.

"He was able to deduce that from a few wisps of fur on the hem of my skirt. Adam's approximate age, as well. Isn't that remarkable?"

"Stultifying," Quincannon said. "Have you written a monograph on breeds of cat as well as tobacco ash, Holmes?"

"No, but perhaps one day I shall."

"Which will doubtless earn you the mantle of recognized authority. What brought you here, may I ask?"

Sabina said, "Mr. Holmes is interested in the inner workings of an American detective agency. And in the progress of our investigation into the house burglaries."

"Is he now. Why?"

"Now that I've finished my researches here," Holmes said, "I fear I've grown bored with conventional tourist activities. San Francisco is a cosmopolitan city, to be sure, but its geographical, cultural, and historical attractions have decidedly limited appeal."

"What researches?"

Holmes smiled enigmatically. "They are of an esoteric nature, of no interest to the average person."

Another bumptious statement. Quincannon shed his chesterfield, went to open the window behind his desk. The Englishman's strong, acrid tobacco was making his head swim.

"The time of my self-imposed exile has almost ended," Holmes was saying to Sabina. "Soon I shall return to London and my former life. Crime and the criminal mind challenge my intellect, give zest to my life. I've been away from the game too long."

"I can't imagine leaving it in the first place," Quincannon said.

"I daresay there were mitigating factors."

"Not for any reason, without or without mitigating factors."

Their gazes locked, struck a spark or two. Sabina said quickly, "You've been gone most of the day, John. What news?"

"Yes," Holmes said, "were you able to locate your pannyman?"

Quincannon ignored the Englishman, fixed his partner with a disapproving eye. "You've been confiding some of our business, I see."

"I confided little except Dodger Brown's name. You revealed most details about the case yourself, last night."

"If I did, it was from necessity."

"*Did* you find the Dodger?"

"Not yet, but it's only a matter of time."

Holmes puffed up a great cloud of smoke, and said through it, his eyes agleam, "Dr. Axminister provided a brief tour of the Barbary Coast shortly after my arrival, but it was superficial and hardly enlightening. I should like to see it as I've seen Limehouse in London, from the perspective of a consulting detective. Foul dives, foul deeds! My blood races at the prospect."

Blasted rattlepate, Quincannon thought. *The man's daft as a church mouse.*

"Would you permit me to join you on your next visit? Introduce me to the district's hidden intrigues, some of its more colorful denizens—the dance hall queen known as 'The Galloping Cow,' Emperor Norton, the odd fellow who allows himself to be beaten up for money?"

"Emperor Norton is dead, and Oofty Goofty soon will be if he allows one more thump on his cranium with a baseball bat. Besides, I'm a detective, not a tour guide."

"Tut, tut. It's knowledge I'm interested in, not sensation. In return, perhaps I can be of assistance in tracking down Dodger Brown and the stolen loot."

"I don't need assistance, yours or anyone else's. I have no intention—" Quincannon broke off because a pleasantly evil thought had popped into his head. He nurtured and fondled it for a few moments. Then he said to Sabina, "I stopped by Andrew Costain's law offices on my way here."

"Yes? What exactly did he want?"

"To have his home put under surveillance until Dodger Brown is caught."

"You didn't accept?"

"I did, and why not? There's no conflict of interest in taking payment from more than one client to perform the same task, as Costain himself pointed out."

"Still, it doesn't seem quite ethical . . ."

"Ethics be damned. A fee is a fee for services rendered, and that includes providing peace of mind to nervous citizens. Eh, Holmes?"

"Indubitably."

"We're to begin tonight," Quincannon told Sabina. "Costain's home is near South Park, not as large a property as banker Truesdale's but nonetheless substantial, and with both a front and rear entrance. I explained to Costain that proper surveillance will require two operatives, and he agreed to the extra fee."

"John," she said, "you're not going to suggest . . ."

Ignoring her, he said to the Englishman, "There are a number of operatives I could call upon; but I wonder, given your interest in this case and your eagerness to return to the game, if you might be willing to join me at the task?"

Another noxious cloud erupted from Holmes's pipe. "Splendid suggestion! I would be honored. As for payment for my services, I ask only that you acquaint me with the Barbary Coast as you know it."

If Holmes hadn't suggested this, Quincannon would have. Now the additional fee would fatten the agency's coffers in its entirety. He said, "Agreed. You'll see the Coast as few ever have." Or would want to.

Holmes smiled.

Quincannon smiled.

Sabina sighed and looked from one to the other as if she thought they were both daft as church mice.

7

During Quincannon's two-year attempt to drown his conscience in Demon Rum, Hoolihan's Saloon on Second Street had been his favorite watering hole. Its clientele consisted mainly of small merchants, office workers, tradesmen, drummers, and a somewhat rougher element up from the waterfront. No city leaders came there on their nightly rounds, as they did to the Palace Hotel bar, Pop Sullivan's Hoffman Cafe, and the other first-class saloons along the city's Cocktail Route; no judges, politicians, bankers—Samuel Truesdale had likely never set foot through its swinging doors—or gay young blades in their striped trousers, fine cravats, and brocaded waistcoats. Hoolihan's had no crystal chandeliers, fancy mirrors, expensive oil paintings, white-coated barmen, or elaborate free lunch. It was dark and bare by comparison, sawdust thick-scattered on the floor and the only glitter and sparkle coming from the shine of its old-style gaslights on the ranks of bottles and glasses along the back bar. Its hungry drinkers dined not on crab legs and oysters on the half shell, but on corned beef, strong cheese, rye bread, and tubs of briny pickles.

Quincannon had gravitated there because Hoolihan's was a short cable car ride from his rooms on Leavenworth and because staff and clientele both respected the solitary drinker's desire for privacy. Even after taking the pledge, he continued to patronize it because it was an honest place, made for those who sought neither bombast nor trouble. Far fewer lies were told in Hoolihan's than in the rarified atmosphere of the Palace bar, he suspected, and far fewer dark deeds were hatched.

He had arranged to meet Sherlock Holmes there at seven o'clock. He arrived a few minutes earlier, claimed a place at the bar near the entrance. Ben Joyce, the head barman, greeted him in his mildly profane fashion. "What'll it be tonight, you bloody Scotsman? Coffee or clam juice?"

"Clam juice, and leave out the arsenic this time."

"Hah. As if I'd waste good ratsbane on the likes of you."

Ben brought him a steaming mug of Hoolihan's special broth. Quincannon sipped, smoked, and listened to the ebb and flow of conversation around him. Men came in, singly and in pairs; men drifted out. The hands on the massive Seth Thomas clock over the back bar moved forward to seven o'clock. And seven-oh-five. And seven-ten . . .

Annoyance nibbled at Quincannon. Where the devil was he? He'd considered himself a sly fox for his conscription of Holmes, but mayhap he'd outsmarted himself. If the fellow was untrustworthy . . .

Someone moved in next to him, jostling his arm. A gruff Cockney voice said, "Yer standing in me way, mate."

Quincannon turned to glare at the voice's owner. Tall, thin ragamuffin dressed in patched trousers and a threadbare pea jacket, a cap pulled down low on his forehead. He opened his mouth to make a sharp retort, then closed it again and took a closer look at the man. Little surprised him anymore, but he was a bit taken aback by what he saw.

"Holmes?" he said.

"At yer service, mate."

"What's the purpose of that getup?"

"It seemed appropriate for the night's mission," Holmes said in his normal voice. His eyes, peering up from under the brim of his cap, were mischievous. "Disguise has served me well during my career, and the opportunity has not presented itself in some time. I must say I enjoy playacting. It has been said, perhaps truly, that the stage lost a consummate actor when I decided to become a detective."

Quincannon, with an effort, forebore comment. Quickly he ushered Holmes outside and into a hansom waiting nearby. The Englishman had no more to say on the subject of disguises, but as the hack rattled along the cobblestones to Mission and on toward Rincon Hill, he put forth a slew of questions on the night's venture, the history and habits of Dodger Brown, and the various methods employed by burglars in the United States. The man was obsessed with details and minutiae on every conceivable subject. Quincannon answered as best he could at first, then lapsed into monosyllabic replies in the hope that Holmes would wind down and be quiet. That was not to be. The Englishman kept up a running colloquy on a variety of esoteric topics from the remarkable explorations of a Norwegian named Sigerson to the latest advances in chemistry and other sciences to the inner workings and possible improvements of horseless carriages. He even knew (though Quincannon could not for the life of him figure how, and Holmes refused to elaborate) that an ex-burglar living in Warsaw, Illinois, manufactured burglar tools, advertised them as novelties in the *Police Gazette,* and sold them for ten dollars the set.

His monologue ceased, mercifully, when they departed the hack two blocks from Andrew Costain's home. It was another night made for prowling, restless streamers of cloud playing peekaboo games with stars and the scythe-blade moon. The neighborhood, the first of San Francisco's fashionable residential districts, had fallen into disfavor in '69, when Second Street was carved through the west edge of Rincon Hill to connect downtown with the southern waterfront. Now it was on the shabby side, though far from the "new slum, a place of solitary ancient houses and butt ends of streets," as it had been unfairly dubbed by that snooty writer fellow, R. L. Stevenson.

Many of the homes they passed showed light, but the Costain house, near South Park, was dark except for a porch globe. It was not as large as the Truesdale pile, but its front and rear yards were spacious and contained almost as many plants, trees, and shadowy hiding places.

Holmes peered intently through the row of iron pickets into the front yard as they strolled by. "Which of us will be stationed here?" he asked.

"You will. I've a spot picked out at the rear."

"Splendid. The *mucronulatum,* perhaps. Or . . . ah yes, even better. A *Juniperus chinensis Corymbosa Variegata,* I do believe."

"What are you talking about?"

"Shrubbery."

"Eh?"

"*Mucronulatum* is the species more commonly known as rhododendron. Quite a healthy specimen there by that garden bench."

"And what, pray, is Jupiter chinchin thrombosa?"

"*Juniperus chinensis Corymbosa Variegata,*" Holmes corrected sententiously. "One of the more handsome and sturdy varieties of juniper shrub. Its flowers are a variegated creamy yellow and its growth regular, without twisted branches and generally of no more than ten feet in height. I thought at first that it might be a *chenisis corymbosa,* a close cousin, but the *chinensis corymbosa* grows to a greater height, often above fifteen feet."

Quincannnon had nothing to say to that.

"I've decided the *corymbosa variegata* will afford the best concealment," Holmes said. "Without obstructing vision, of course. But

I should like to see the rear of the property as well, if you have no objection. So that I may have a more complete knowledge of the, ah, lay. That is the American term?"

"It is."

"I find your idiom fascinating," Holmes said. "One day I shall make a study of American slang."

"And write a monograph about it, no doubt."

"Or an article for one of the popular London journals."

They reached the end of the block and circled around into a deserted carriageway. When they came to the rear of the Costain property, Holmes peered in as intently as he had in front, then asked where Quincannon would station himself. "That tree there on your left," Quincannon lied. "I don't happen to know its Latin or its English name, but I expect you do."

"*Taxus brevifolia*," Holmes said promptly, "the Pacific yew."

Quincannon ground his teeth. The prospect of two or three more nights in the Englishman's company, not to mention a day trip to the low dives of the Barbary Coast, was about as appealing as having teeth pulled without benefit of nitrous oxide. Uncharitably he decided that Holmes's biographer and alleged good friend, Dr. Watson, must be either a saint or a long-suffering, hero-worshipping twit.

He said, "If you've seen enough, we'll take our positions now."

"Quite enough. A long low whistle if our man should appear, and we'll then join forces at the fountain in the side yard. Yes?"

"Your memory is as keen as your conversation."

Holmes said, "Indeed," and hurried on his way.

Quincannon returned to the gate that gave access to the Costain property. He made sure he was still alone and unobserved, then stepped through into the shadows alongside a small carriage barn. The surveillance spot he had picked out on his earlier tabbing was a shed set at an angle midway between house and barn. Not only did it provide a viewpoint of the rear yard, gate, and part of the side yard, but also some shelter from the wind and the night's chill. The thought of Sherlock Holmes shivering among the chenisis whosis in front would warm him even more.

He made his way through heavy shadow to the shed, eased the door open and himself inside. The interior was cramped with stacks of cordwood and a jumble of gardening implements. By careful feel with his hands he found that the stack nearest the door was low enough and sturdy enough to afford a seat, if he were careful not to move about too much. He lowered himself onto the wood. Even with the door wide-open, he was in such darkness that he couldn't be seen from outside. Yet his range of vision was mostly unimpeded and aided by starshine and patchy moonlight.

He judged that it was well after seven. Andrew Costain had told him that his wife was due home no later than ten-thirty, and that he himself would return by midnight. The odds were long against another break-in on the heels of the Truesdale misadventure. And three and a half hours was little enough discomfort and boredom in exchange for the double fee Carpenter and Quincannon, Professional Detective Services, would collect for the night's business.

As it turned out, he was wrong on both counts.

His wait lasted less than two hours. He was on his feet, flexing his limbs to ease them of cold and cramp, when to his startlement he spied the interloper. A shadow among shadows, moving crosswise from his left—the same silent, flitting approach he had observed on the banker's property the previous night. Dodger Brown was evidently bolder and more greedy and foolish than experience had taught him. Bully! The sooner he nabbed the scruff, the sooner Carpenter and Quincannon would collect from Great Western Insurance. And the sooner he would be rid of Mr. Sherlock Holmes.

Quincannon rubbed his gloved hands together, watching the shadow's progress toward the rear of the house. Pause, drift, pause again at the near end of the porch. Up and over the railing there, briefly silhouetted: same small figure dressed in dark cap and clothing. Across to the door, at work there for just a few seconds. The door opened, closed again behind the intruder.

He spent several seconds readying his dark lantern, just in case. When one of the wind-herded clouds blotted the moon, he emerged from the shed and went laterally to the bole of tree a dozen rods from the house. He was about to give the signal whistle when a low ululation came from the front yard. What the devil? He answered in kind, paused, and whistled again. In a matter of moments he spied movement approaching. Holmes seemed to have an uncanny sense of direction in the dark; he came in an unerring line straight to where Quincannon stood.

"Why did you whistle, man?" Quincannon demanded in a fierce whisper. "You couldn't have seen—"

"Andrew Costain is here."

"*What?*"

"Arrived not three minutes ago, alone in a trap."

"Blasted fool! He couldn't have chosen a worse time. You didn't stop him from going inside?"

"He seemed in a great hurry, and I saw no purpose in revealing myself. Dodger Brown is also here, I assume?"

"Already inside through the rear door, not four minutes ago."

"Inside with us, too, Quincannon!" Holmes said urgently. "We've not a moment to lose!"

But it was already too late. In that instant a percussive report came from the house, muffled but unmistakable.

Holmes said, "Pistol shot."

Quincannon said, "Hell and damn!"

Both men broke into a run. Quincannon had no need to order the Englishman to cover the front door; Holmes immediately veered off in that direction. The Navy Colt and his dark lantern were both at the ready when he reached the rear porch. Somewhere inside, another door slammed. He ran up the steps to the door, thumbed open the lantern's bull's-eye lens, and shouldered his way through.

The thin beam showed him a utility porch, an opening into a broad kitchen. His foot struck something as he started ahead; the light revealed it to be a wooden wedge, of the sort used to prop open doors. Quincannon shut the door and toed the wedge tightly under the sill— a safeguard against swift escape that took only a clutch of seconds.

Two or three additional sounds reached his ears as he plunged ahead, none distinguishable or close by. The beam picked out an electric switch on the kitchen wall; he turned it to flood the room with light. Empty. Likewise the adjoining dining room. His twitching nose picked up the acrid smell of burnt gunpowder, led him into a central hallway. He flooded the hall with more electric light, eased past two closed doors to a third at the end, where another hallway intersected this one. The powder smell was strongest there.

He paused to listen. Heavy, crackling silence. He moved ahead to where he could see along the intersecting hall, found it deserted, and stepped up to the third door to try the latch. Locked from within: there was no key on his side.

He rapped sharply on the panel, called out, "Costain? John Quincannon. It's safe for you to come out now."

No response. But more sounds came from the front of the house—a heavy dragging noise, as of a piece of furniture being moved.

"Costain?" Louder this time.

Silence from behind the door.

Movement at the corner of his eye swung him around and brought the Navy to bear on the intersecting hallway. Sherlock Holmes was but a short distance away, approaching as noiselessly as a cat stalking prey. Quincannon lowered his weapon, said as Holmes hurried up, "A sign of either man?"

"None."

"One or both must be on other side of this door. Locked from the inside."

"If the intruder is elsewhere and attempts to leave by way of the front door, he'll first have to move a heavy oak chair, and we'll hear him."

"I wedged the rear door shut for the same reason."

Quincannon holstered the Navy, then backed off two steps and flung the full weight of his body against the door panel. This rash action succeeded only in bruising flesh, jarring bone and teeth. Fortunately for Sherlock Holmes, he made no comment; he was standing with his head cocked in a listening attitude. Grumbling, Quincannon gathered himself and drove the flat of his foot against the wood just above the latch. Two more kicks were necessary to splinter the wood, tear the locking mechanism loose, and send the door wobbling inward.

Only a scant few inches inward, however, before it bound up against something heavy and inert on the floor.

Quincannon shoved hard against the panel until he was able to widen the opening enough to wedge his body through. The room was dark except for faint patches that marked uncurtained windows at the far end. He swept his hand along the wall, located a switch, turned it. The flood of electric light revealed what he'd expected to find on the carpeted floor just inside the door.

The body was that of Andrew Costain, sprawled facedown, both arms outflung, the one visible eye wide-open. Dead, and no mistake. Blood stained the back of his cheviot coat, the sleeve of his left forearm. Scorch marks blackened the sleeve as well.

The room, evidently Costain's study, was otherwise empty. Two drawers in a rolltop desk stood open, another had been yanked out and upended on the desktop. Papers littered the surface, the floor around the desk. Also on the floor, between the corpse and the desk, were two other items: a new-looking revolver, and a brassbound valuables case that appeared to have been pried open and was now plainly empty.

Holmes crowded in. Both men swept the room with keen gazes, after which Quincannon crossed to examine the windows. Both were of the casement type, with hook latches firmly in place; Dodger Brown hadn't gotten out that way. Still hiding somewhere in the house, or possibly gone by then through another window.

When Quincannon turned, he was confronted by the sight of Sherlock Holmes on one knee, hunched over the corpse like a strange, lank bird, peering through a large magnifying glass at the wound in Costain's back. His lean hawk's face was darkly flushed, his brows drawn into two hard black lines. A small smile appeared as he lifted his head. His eyes showed a steely glitter.

"Interesting," he said. "Quite."

"What is?"

"Andrew Costain was stabbed to death."

"Stabbed? Not shot?"

"Shot, too. Two separate and distinct wounds. The superficial one in his forearm was made by a bullet. The fatal wound was made by an instrument at least eight inches in length and quite sharp. A stiletto, I should say. The blow was struck by a right-handed person approximately five and a half feet tall, at an upward angle of perhaps fifteen degrees."

Blasted know-it-all!

Quincannon located the lead pellet that had passed through Costain's arm, in the cushion of an armchair near the desk, then picked up the revolver. It was a Forehand & Wadsworth .38 caliber, its nickel-plated finish free of marks of any kind. He sniffed the barrel to confirm that it had been recently fired, opened the breech for a squint inside. All of the chambers were empty. He was about to return the weapon to the carpet when Holmes stepped up, took it from his hand, and commenced to peer at it through his glass.

Glowering, Quincannon left the study to search the premises. Not long afterward, Holmes did the same. The results were rather astonishing. They found no sign of Dodger Brown, and yet every window, upstairs and down, was firmly latched. Furthermore, the wedge Quincannon had kicked under the back door was still in place, as was the heavy chair Holmes had dragged over to block the front door. They were the only two doors that provided an exit from the house.

"How the deuce could he have gotten out?" Quincannon said. "Even the cellar door in the kitchen is locked tight. And I doubt there was enough time for him to slip away *before* we entered."

"Dear me, no. You or I would have seen him."

"Well, he managed it somehow."

"So it would seem. A miraculous double escape, in fact."

"Double escape?"

"From a locked room, then from a sealed house." Holmes smiled one of his enigmatic smiles. "According to Dr. Axminister, you are adept at solving seemingly impossible crimes. How then did Dodger Brown manage either a single or double escape trick? Why was Andrew Costain shot as well as stabbed? Why was the pistol left in the locked study and the bloody stiletto taken away? And why was the study door locked in the first place? A pretty puzzle, eh, Quincannon? One to challenge the deductive mind."

Quincannon muttered five short, colorful words, none of them remotely of a deductive nature.

8

As much as Quincannon disliked and mistrusted the city police, the circumstances were such that notifying them was unavoidable. He telephoned the Hall of Justice on the instrument in Costain's study. After that he paced and cogitated, to no reasonable conclusion. Holmes examined the corpse again, the carpet in both the study and the hallway (crawling on his hands and knees), and any number of other things through his glass. Now and then he muttered aloud to himself: "More data! I can't make bricks without clay" and "Hallo! That's more like it!" and "Ah, plain as a pikestaff!" Neither had anything more to say to the other. If was as if a gantlet had been thrown down, a tacit challenge issued—which in fact was the case. They were two bloodhounds on the scent, no longer working in consort, but as competitors in an undeclared contest of wills.

The police arrived in less than half an hour, what for them was quick dispatch. They were half a dozen in number, along with a handful of reporters representing the *Daily Alta,* the *Call,* and San Francisco's other newspapers, who were made to wait outside—half as many of both breeds as there would have been if the murder of a prominent attorney had happened on Nob Hill or Russian Hill. The inspector in charge was a beefy, red-faced Prussian named Kleinhoffer, whom Quincannon knew slightly and condoned not in the slightest. Kleinhoffer was both stupid and corrupt, a lethal combination, and a political toady besides. His opinion of flycops was on a par with Quincannon's opinion of him.

His first comment was, "Involved in another killing, eh, Quincannon? What's your excuse this time?"

Quincannon explained, briefly, the reason he was there. He omitted mention of Dodger Brown by name, using the term "unknown burglar" instead and catching Sherlock Holmes's eye as he spoke so the Englishman would say nothing to contradict him. He was not about to chance losing a fee—small chance though it was, the police being a generally inept bunch—by providing information that might allow them to stumble across the Dodger ahead of him.

Kleinhoffer sneered, "Some fancy flycop. You're sure he's not still somewhere in the house?"

"Sure enough."

"We'll see about that." He gestured to a uniformed sergeant, who stepped forward. "Mahoney, you and your men search the premises, top to bottom."

"Yes sir."

Kleinhoffer's beady gaze settled on Holmes, ran over both his face and his "disguise." He demanded, "Who're you?"

"S. Holmes, of London, England. A temporary associate of the Carpenter and Quincannon agency."

"A limey, eh?" Kleinhoffer turned to Quincannon. "Picking your operatives off the docks these days, are you?"

"If I am, it's none of your concern."

"None of your guff. Where's the stiff?"

"In the study."

Kleinhoffer gave Andrew Costain's remains a cursory examination. "Shot and stabbed both," he said. "You didn't tell me that. What the hell happened here tonight?"

Quincannon's account, given in deliberate detail, heightened the inspector's apoplectic color, narrowed his eyes to slits. Any crime more complicated than a Barbary Coast mugging invariably confused him, and the evident facts in this case threatened to tie a permanent knot in his brain.

He shook his head, as if trying to shake loose cobwebs, and snapped, "None of that makes a damn bit of sense."

"Sense or not, that is exactly what took place."

"You there, limey. He leave anything out?"

"Tut, tut," Holmes said. "I am an Englishman, sir, a British subject—not a limey."

"I don't care if you're the president of England. Quincannon leave anything out or didn't he?"

"He did not. His re-creation of events was exact in every detail."

"So you say. I say it couldn't've happened the way you tell it."

"Nonetheless, it did, though what seems to have transpired is not necessarily what actually happened. What we are dealing with here is illusion and obfuscation."

Kleinhoffer wrapped an obscene noun in a casing of disgust. After which he stooped to pick up the Forehand & Wadsworth revolver. He sniffed the barrel and checked the chambers, as Quincannon had done, then dropped the weapon into his coat pocket. He was examining the empty valuables case when Sergeant Mahoney entered the room.

"No sign of him in the house," he reported.

"Back door still wedged shut?"

"Yes sir."

"Then he must've managed to slip out tine front door while these two flycops weren't looking."

"I beg to differ," Holmes said. He mentioned the heavy chair. "It was not moved until your arrival, Inspector, by Quincannon and myself. Even if it had been, I would surely have heard the sounds. My hearing is preternaturally acute."

Kleinhoffer said the rude word again.

Mahoney said, "Mrs. Costain is here."

"What's that?"

"The victim's wife. Mrs. Costain. She just come home."

"Why the devil didn't you say so? Bring her in here."

The sergeant did as directed. Penelope Costain was stylishly dressed in a lacy blouse, flounced skirt, and fur-trimmed cloak, her brown curls tucked under a hat adorned with an ostrich plume. She took one look at her husband's remains, and her face whitened to the shade of the feather; she shuddered violently, began to sway. Mahoney caught one arm to steady her. Quincannon took hold of the other, and they helped her to one of the chairs.

She drew several deep breaths, fanned herself with one hand. "I . . . I'm all right," she said then. Her gaze touched the body again, pulled away. "Poor Andrew. He was a brave man . . . he must have fought terribly for his life."

"We'll get the man who did it," Kleinhoffer promised foolishly.

She nodded. "Can't you . . . cover him with something?"

"Mahoney. Find a cloth."

"Yes sir."

Mrs. Costain nibbled at a broken fingernail, peering up at the faces ringed above her. "Is that you, Mr. Holmes? What are you doing here, dressed that way?"

"He was working with me," Quincannon said.

"With you? Two detectives in tandem failed to prevent this . . . this outrage?"

"None of what happened was our fault."

She said bitterly, "That is the same statement you made two nights ago. Nothing, no tragedy, is ever your fault, evidently."

Kleinhoffer was still holding the empty valuables case. He extended it to the widow, saying, "This was on the floor, Mrs. Costain."

"Yes. My husband kept it in his desk."

"What was in it?"

"Twenty-dollar gold pieces," she answered, "a dozen or so. And the more valuable among my jewelry—a diamond brooch, a pair of diamond earrings, a pearl necklace, several other pieces."

"Worth how much, would you say?"

"I don't know . . . several thousand dollars."

She looked again at Quincannon, this time with open hostility. Kleinhoffer did the same. He said, "You and Holmes were here the whole time, and still you let that yegg kill Mr. Costain, then get away with all those valuables—right under your damn noses. What've you got to say for yourselves?"

Quincannon had nothing to say. Neither did Sherlock Holmes.

9

It was well past midnight when Quincannon finally trudged wearily up the stairs to his rooms. After Kleinhoffer had finally finished with him, the newspapermen had descended—on him but not Holmes, who had managed to slip away. Quincannon had been pleased to assist the Englishman in avoiding publicity; in his comments to the reporters, he had referred to him as a "hired operative" and, with, relish, an "underling."

He donned his nightshirt and crawled into bed, but the night's jumbled events plagued his mind and refused to let him sleep. At length he lit his bedside lamp, picked up a copy of Walt Whitman's *Sea-Drift*. Reading always seemed to free his brain of clutter, to permit a settling and organizing of his thoughts. Usually Whitman or Emily Dickinson or James Lowell accomplished the task, but not tonight. He switched reading matter to *Drunkards and Curs: The Truth About Demon Rum*. He had once been hired by the True Christian Temperance Society to catch an embezzler, and this had led him to his second reading and collecting interest: temperance tracts. Not because he was a teetotaler himself, but because he found their highly inflammatory rhetoric both amusing and soothing.

Drunkards and Curs did the trick. At the end of two turgid chapters his mental processes were in proper condition for cudgeling and surmising. The result of this brainwork, after another hour so, lifted his spirits and permitted him a too-short rest.

He awoke not long past seven, permitted himself a hasty breakfast, and within an hour was at the agency offices. For once he was the first to arrive. No sooner had he unlocked the door and stepped inside than the telephone bell jangled. When he answered, a rough and unfamiliar voice said, "Duff's Curio Shop," repeated the name, and immediately disconnected.

A wolf's smile transformed Quincannon's mouth; another worry, small though it was, had now been reduced to a trifle and the fogbound morning was considerably brighter. He replaced the earpiece, went to coax steam heat from the radiator; on mornings such as this, the offices were as damp and chill as a cave. While he was thus engaged, Sabina arrived.

"Up bright and early this morning, John," she said. Then, as she removed her straw boater, she took a closer look at him. "But not bushy-tailed, I see. Another sleepless night?"

"For the most part."

"Not because of an eventful night at the Costain home?"

"Unfortunately, yes. Eventful as all get-out."

"Another attempted burglary so soon?"

"Not attempted—successful."

Sabina was not easily surprised; the high lift of her eyebrows as he unfolded the tale was as much marvelment as she ever exhibited. Her only comment was, "It all seems fantastic."

"That sums it in a nutshell."

"What does Mr. Holmes think?"

"Holmes? Why should you care what he thinks?"

"I was only—"

"Why don't you ask me what I think? I'm in charge of this case, not Sherlock Holmes. This is my bailiwick, not his. Or do you actually believe the bunkum that he is the world's greatest detective?"

"Calm yourself, John. I wasn't suggesting he's a better sleuth, or more likely than you to get to the bottom of the mystery." She fixed him with one of her analytical looks. "It sounds as though you're threatened by the man."

"Threatened? By the likes of that gasbag?"

"You've no reason to be."

"Exactly. No reason at all."

"I was merely wondering if you'd had a discussion with him, shared thoughts and ideas."

"I don't need his thoughts and ideas to unravel this puzzle."

"Does that mean you have a theory?"

"I have. A good, strong one." In fact it was still a bit on the amorphous side, but she needn't know that.

"Well?"

"I'll need a few more facts before I'm ready to discuss it, facts that you can obtain for me. Data on Andrew Costain, for one, with emphasis on his financial status. And second, whether he purchased a handgun within the past two or three days—specifically, a .38 caliber Forehand & Wadsworth revolver. If so, it was likely in a gunshop in the vicinity of his law offices."

"And what will you be doing?"

"Hunting Dodger Brown. We've a lead now, courtesy of Ezra

Bluefield by way of one of his henchmen." He told her of the telephone message.

"Ah," she said, "our old friend Luther Duff."

"One of the easier eggs to crack in the city. Dodger Brown couldn't have picked a better fenceman, for our purposes."

"Assuming Duff knows his whereabouts. The hideout must be deep, else Bluefield's contacts would have ferreted it out as well. Time is against us now, John. If the Dodger has begun to fence the loot from his burglaries, it must mean he's preparing to go on the lammas."

Quincannon said darkly, "The only place that yegg is going is to a cell in city prison."

"On your way then. With luck, you'll have Dodger Brown, and I'll have the Costain data before close of business."

He nodded and reached for his derby. With luck, he would also have the solution to the murder and disappearance before the end of the day. Yes, by Godfrey, and the great pleasure of using it to spit in the eye of Mr. Sherlock Holmes.

10

Luther Duff's Curio Shop was crowded among similar establishments in the second block of McAllister Street west of Van Ness. It contained, according to its proprietor, "bric-a-brac and curios of every type and description, from every culture and every nation— the new, the old, the mild, the exotic." In short, it was full of junk. This was Quincannon's fourth visit to the place, all on professional business, and he had yet to see a single customer. It might have been that Duff sold some of his fare now and then, but if so, it was by accident and with little or no effort on his part. Where he had procured his inventory was a mystery; all that anyone knew for sure was that he had it and seldom if ever added new items to the dusty, moldering stock.

Duff's primary profession was receiver of stolen goods. Burglars, boxmen, pickpockets, and other scruffs far and wide beat a steady path to his door. Like other fencemen, he professed to offer his fellow thieves a square deal: half of what he expected to realize on the resale of any particular item. In fact, his notion of fifty-fifty was akin to putting a lead dollar on a Salvation Army tambourine and asking for fifty cents change. He took a 75 percent cut of most spoils, an even higher percentage from the more gullible and desperate among his suppliers. Stolen weapons of all types were his specialty—often enough at an 80 or 90 percent profit. A Tenderloin hockshop might offer a thief more cash, but hockshop owners put their marks on pistols, marks that had been known to lead police agencies straight to the source. Hockshop owners were thus considered hangman's handmaidens and crooks stayed shy of them, preferring smaller but safer profits from men like Luther Duff.

Despite being well-known in the trade, Duff had somehow managed to avoid prosecution. That fact was both a strong advertisement and his Achilles heel. He had a horror of arrest and imprisonment, and was subject to intimidation as a result. Quincannon was of the opinion that Duff would sell his mother, if he had one, and his entire line of relatives rather than spend a single night at the mercy of a city prison guard.

A bell above the door jingled unmusically as Quincannon stepped into the shop. On the instant, the combined smells of dust, mildew, and slow decay pinched his nostrils. He made his way slowly through the dimly lighted interior, around and through an amazing hodgepodge of furniture that included a Chinese wardrobe festooned with fire-breathing dragons, a Tyrolean pine coffer, a Spanish refectory table, a brassbound "pirate treasure" chest from Madgascar. He passed shelves of worm-ridden books, an assortment of corpses that had once been clocks, a stuffed and molting weasel, an artillery bugle, a ship's sextant, and a broken marble tombstone with the name HORSE-SHY HALLORAN chiseled into its face.

When he neared the long counter at the rear, a set of musty damask drapes parted and Luther Duff emerged grinning. He was short, round, balding, fiftyish, and about as appetizing as a tainted oyster. He wore slyness and venality as openly as the garters on his sleeves and the moneylender's eyeshade across his forehead. The grin and the suddenness of his appearance made Quincannon think, as always, of a troll jumping out in front of an unwary traveler.

"Hello, hello, hello," the troll said. "What can I do for . . . *awk!*"

The strangled-chicken noise was the result of his having recognized Quincannon. The grin vanished in a wash of nervous fear. He stood stiffly and darted looks everywhere but across the counter into Quincannon's eyes.

"How are you, Luther?" Quincannon asked pleasantly.

"Ah . . . well and good, well and good."

"No health problems, I trust?"

"No, no, none, fit as a fiddle."

"Sound of body, pure of heart?"

"Ah, well, ah . . ."

"But it's a harsh and uncertain world we live in, eh, Luther? Illness can strike anytime. Accidents, too."

"Accidents?"

"Terrible, crippling accidents. Requiring a long stay in the hospital."

It was cold in the shop, but Duff's face was already damp. He produced a dark-flecked handkerchief, twitchily began to mop his brow.

"Of course, there are worse things even than illness and accident. Worse for some, that is. Such as those who suffer from claustrophobia."

"Claustro . . . what?"

"The terrible fear of being trapped in small enclosed spaces. A prison cell, for instance."

"Gahh," the troll said. A shudder passed through him.

"Such a man would suffer greatly under those circumstances. I would hate to see it happen, the more so when it could be easily avoided."

"Ah . . ."

Quincannon simulated a tolerant smile. "Well, no more of that, eh? We'll move along to my reason for calling this morning. I'm after a bit of information I believe you can supply."

"Ah . . ."

"It happens that I have urgent business with a lad named Dodger Brown. However, he seems to have dropped from sight."

"Dodger Brown?"

"The same. Wine dump habitué, gambler, and burglar by trade. You've had recent dealings with him, I understand."

"Recent dealings? No, you're mistaken . . ."

"Now, now, Luther. Prison cells are cold and unpleasant, remember. And very, very small."

Duff fidgeted. "What, ah, what business do you have with him?"

"Mine and none of yours. All you need do is tell me where I can find him."

"Ah . . ."

"You must have some idea of his whereabouts." Quincannon let the smile slip away, his voice harden. "It wouldn't do for you to tax my patience."

"Oh, ah, I wouldn't, I won't." Duff licked thin lips. "An idea, perhaps. A possibility. You won't say where you heard?"

"No one need know of our little talk but us."

"Well, ah . . . he has a cousin, a fisherman called Salty Jim."

"Does he now?" This was news to Quincannon; there was nothing in Dodger Brown's dossier about a living relative.

Duff said, "The Dodger has been known to bunk with him from time to time. So, ah, so I've heard on the earie."

"Where does this Salty Jim hang his cap? Fisherman's Wharf?"

"No. Across the bay . . . the Oakland City Wharf. He, ah, he's involved in the oyster trade."

"The name of his boat?"

"Something with *Oyster* in it. That's all I can tell you."

"Good enough," Quincannon said. "Now we'll move along to other matters. Did you sell the Dodger a revolver, new or old, recently?"

"Revolver? No. Absolutely not."

"That had better not be a lie."

"It's not! I swear I sold him no weapon of any kind."

"So he took only cash for whatever goods he brought you."

"I don't, ah, know what you mean. He came to see me, yes, but it was only to discuss selling certain property . . ."

Quincannon smiled again, drew his Navy Colt, and laid the weapon on the countertop between them. "You were saying?"

"Awk."

"No, that wasn't it. You were about to identify the items you purchased from Dodger Brown. In fact, in the spirit of cooperation and good fellowship between us, you were about to show me these items."

The troll swallowed in a way that was remarkably like a cow swallowing its cud. He twitched, looked at the pistol, nibbled at his lower lip like a rat nibbling cheese.

Quincannon picked up the Navy Colt and held it loosely in his hand, the barrel aimed in the general direction of Duff's right eye. "My time is valuable, Luther," he said. "And yours is fast running out."

The troll turned abruptly and stepped through the drapery. Quincannon vaulted the counter, followed him into an incredibly cluttered office lighted by an oil lamp. A farrago of items covered the surface of a battered rolltop desk; boxes and wrappings littered the floor; piles of curios teetered precariously on a pair of clawfoot tables. In one corner was a large and fairly new Mosler safe. Duff glanced back at Quincannon, noted his expression, and reluctantly proceeded to open the safe. He tried to shield the interior with his body, but Quincannon loomed up behind to watch the troll's hands as they sifted through the contents.

"If I find out you've withheld so much as a collar stay," Quincannon warned him, "I'll pay you a return visit that won't be half so pleasant as this one."

Duff sighed and brought forth a chamois pouch, which he handed over with even greater reluctance. Quincannon holstered the Navy Colt, shook the contents of the pouch into his palm. One ruby-studded brooch, two pairs of ruby earrings, and a diamond stickpin.

"This is only a small portion of the Dodger's ill-gotten gains. Where's the rest?"

"I don't know. I swear this is all he brought me!"

"When was he here?"

"Yesterday morning. He said he had more, that he'd bring them in a day or two, but I haven't seen him since."

"How much did you pay for the privilege of fencing these baubles?"

"Two hundred dollars. He, ah, seemed to think they were worth more, but he took the cash. He seemed in a hurry."

"Yes? Frightened, was he?"

"No. Eager, excited about something. All in a lather."

"Did he give you an idea of what had raised his blood pressure?"

"None. He grabbed the cash and ran out."

Quincannon nodded. He returned the items of jewelry to the pouch, tucked the pouch into his coat pocket.

"Here, now!" the troll cried. "You can't . . . that's my property!"

"No, it isn't. Not yours and not Dodger Brown's. These sparklers belong to Judge Adam Winthrop, the Dodger's first burglary victim. Don't worry, I'll make sure they're returned to the judge safe and sound, with your compliments."

Duff looked as if he were about to burst into tears.

"Gahh," he said.

11

A trolley car delivered Quincannon to the Ferry Building at the foot of Market Street. Ferries for the East Bay left every twenty to thirty minutes, and he arrived just in time to catch one of the Southern Pacific boats. A chilly half hour later, he disembarked with the other passengers and made his way up the Estuary to the Oakland City Wharf.

The place was a mixture of the colorful and the squalid: Arctic whalers, Chinese junks, Greek fishing boats, Yankee sailing ships, disreputable freighters, scows, sloops, shrimpers, oyster boats, houseboats; long rows of warehouses crowded here and there by shacks fashioned from bits and pieces of wreckage or from dismantled ships; and long, barren sandpits. He approached three men in turn to ask the whereabouts of an oysterman named Salty Jim, owner of a boat named the *Something Oyster*. The first two either didn't know or wouldn't say, but the third, a crusty old sailor with a Tam o'Shanter pulled down over his ears, who sat propped against an iron cleat with a half-mended fishnet across his lap, knew Salty Jim well enough. And clearly didn't like him. He screwed up his face and spat off the wharfside.

"Salty Jim O'Bannon," he said, "ain't no oysterman."

"No? What is he?"

"A damn oyster pirate, that's what."

Involved in the oyster trade indeed, Quincannon thought sardonically. He'd had a run-in with oyster pirates once and did not relish a repeat performance. They were a scurvy lot, the dregs of the coastal waters—worse by far than Chinese shrimp raiders or Greek salmon poachers. At the first floodtide in June, an entire fleet of them would head down the bay to Asparagus Island to set up raiding parties on the beds. And much of the harvest would be stolen despite the efforts of the Fish Patrol and private operatives such as Quincannon. The only thing that kept the pirates from taking complete control of the bay waters was their own viciousness. Regular consumption of alcohol and opium combined with meanness had led to many a cutting scrape and many a corpse in the sandpits.

"How come you're lookin' for the likes of Salty Jim O'Bannon?" the old man asked. "Not fixin' to join up with him, are you?"

"No chance of that. It's not him I'm after."

"Who then?"

"A cousin of his, Dodger Brown. Know the lad?"

"Can't say I do. Don't want to, if he's as blackhearted as Salty Jim."

"He may be, at that."

"What's his dodge? Not another pirate, is he?"

"Housebreaker."

"And what're you? You've got the look and questions of a nabber."

"Policeman?" Quincannon was mildly offended. "Manhunter on the scent is more like it. Where does Salty Jim keep his boat? Hereabouts?"

"Hell. He wouldn't dare. He anchors off Davis Wharf. Don't tie up for fear of somebody stealin' on board at night and murderin' him in his sleep."

"What's her name?"

"*Oyster Catcher*. Now ain't that a laugh?"

"He lives on her, does he?"

"He does. Might find him there now, but if you do, you better be carryin' a pistol and not shy about usin' it."

Quincannon made his way to Davis Wharf. Several sloops and schooners were anchored in the bay nearby, so many that he wasted no time in trying to pick out the *Oyster Catcher*. A ragged youth who was fishing with a hand line off the wharfside made the identification for him; the youth also agreed to rent Quincannon his own patched skiff beached in the tidal mud fifty rods distant. Unlike the old fisherman, the boy seemed impressed that Quincannon was on his way to talk to Salty Jim, the oyster pirate; the shine of hero worship was in his eyes. Quincannon repressed the urge to shake some sense into him. You couldn't hope to make everyone walk the straight and narrow. Besides, a new generation of crooks meant continued prosperity for Carpenter and Quincannon, Professional Detective Services, well into his and Sabina's dotage.

He stowed his grip in the skiff, rowed out to the *Oyster Catcher*. She was a good-sized sloop with a small cabin amidships, her mainsail furled, her hull in need of paint but otherwise in good repair. No one was on deck, but from inside the cabin he could hear the discordant strumming of a banjo. He shipped his oars until he was able to draw in next to a disreputable rowboat tied to a portside Jacob's ladder. He tied the skiff's painter to another rung, drew his Navy Colt, and climbed quickly on board.

The banjo player heard or felt his presence; the instrument twanged and went silent, and a moment laer the cabin door burst open and a bear of a man, naked to the waist, stepped out with a belaying pin clenched in one hand. Quincannon snapped, "Stand fast!" and brought the pistol to bear. The fellow pulled up short, blinking and scowling. He was thirtyish, sported a patchy beard and hair that hung in matted ropes. The cold bay wind blew the smells of Dr. Hall and body odor off him in such a ripe wave that Quincannon's nostrils pinched in self-defense.

"Who in foggy hell're you?"

"My name is of no matter to you. Drop your weapon."

"Huh?"

"The belaying pin. Drop it, Jim."

Salty Jim gawped at him, rubbing at his scraggly beard with his free hand, his mouth open at least two inches—a fair approximation of a drooling idiot. "What's the idee comin' on my boat? You ain't the gawddamn Fish Patrol."

"It's your cousin I want, not you."

"Cousin?"

"Dodger Brown. If he's here, call him out. If he's not, tell me where I can find him."

"I ain't gonna tell you nothin'."

"You will, or you'll find a lead pellet nestling in your hide."

The oyster pirate's mean little eyes narrowed to slits. He took a step forward, and said with drunken belligerence, "By gar, nobody's gonna shoot me on my own boat."

"I'm warning you, Jim. Drop your weapon and hold still, or—"

Salty Jim was too witless and too much taken with drink to be either scared or intimidated. He growled deep in his throat, hoisted the belaying pin aloft, and mounted a lumbering charge.

Quincannon had no desire to commit mayhem if it could be avoided. He took two swift steps forward, jabbed the Navy Colt's muzzle hard and straight into the pirate's sternum. Salty Jim said, "Uff!" and rounded at the middle like an archer's bow. The blow took the force out of his down-sweeping arm; the belaying pin caromed more or less harmlessly off the meaty part of Quincannon's shoulder. Another jab with the Colt, followed by a quick reverse flip of the weapon, a trick he'd learned from his father, and with the butt end a solid thump on the crown of the pirate's empty cranium. There was another satisfying "Uff!", after which Salty Jim stretched out on the scaly deck for a nap. Rather amazingly, he even commenced to make snoring noises.

Quincannon prodded him with the toe of his shoe; the nap and the snores continued unabated. He holstered the Colt and proceeded to frisk the man's never-washed trousers and shirt. This netted him nothing except a sack of Bull Durham, some papers, and a greasy French postcard of no artistic merit whatsoever.

He picked up the belaying pin, tossed it overboard. A frayed belt that held up the pirate's trousers served to tie his hands behind his back. Quincannon then stepped over the unconscious man and entered the cabin.

He had been in hobo jungles and opium dens that were tidier and less aromatic. Mouth-breathing, he searched the confines. It was evident from the first that two men had lived there recently. Verminous blankets were wadded on each of the two bunks, and there were empty bottles of the cheap and potent whiskey known as Dr. Hall, evidently Salty Jim's tipple, and empty bottles of the foot juice favored by Dodger Brown. The galley table, however, bore remants of a single meal of oyster stew and sourdough bread, one tin coffee mug, one dirty glass, and one bottle of Dr. Hall.

Under one of the bunks was a pasteboard suitcase. Quincannon drew it out, laid it on the blankets, snapped the cheap lock with the blade of his pocket knife, and sifted through the contents. Cheap John clothing of a size much too small to fit Salty Jim. An oilskin pouch that contained an array of picklocks and other burglar tools.

An old Smith & Wesson revolver wrapped in cloth, unloaded, no cartridges in evidence. And a larger, felt-lined cloth sack that rattled provocatively as he lifted it out. When he upended the sack onto the blanket, out tumbled a variety of jewelry, timepieces, small silver and gold gewgaws. Paydirt! A quick accounting told him that he was in possession of all the stolen goods from the first three robberies.

There was one other item of interest in the suitcase, which he'd missed on his first look. It lay on the bottom, facedown, caught under a torn corner. He fished it out, flipped it over. A business card, creased and thumbmarked, but not of the sort he himself carried. He had seen such discreet advertisements before; they had grown more or less common in the Uptown Tenderloin, handed out by the more enterprising businesswomen in the district. This one read:

FIDDLE DEE DEE

Miss Lettie Carew Presents
Bountiful Beauties from Exotic Lands

MAISON DE JOIE   244 O'FARRELL STREET

Well, well, Quincannon thought. *Is that why you were so eager for cash yesterday, you young scamp? And why you didn't spend last night on this scabrous tub?*

He considered. Should he wait there for the Dodger's return? Or should he chance that his quarry had not only elevated his taste in bawdy houses, but was still elevating? His instincts indicated the latter. His trust in them, and distaste at the prospect of a long vigil—perhaps a very long vigil—in the company of Salty Jim O'Bannon, made up his mind in short order.

He resacked and pocketed the swag, stepped out onto the deck with the Dodger's revolver in hand. Salty Jim was still *non compos* but starting to stir a bit. Quincannon left him bound, dropped the revolver into the bay, and further coppered his bet by untying and setting the rowboat adrift. Then, whistling "The Brewer's Big Horses Can't Run Over Me," one of his favorite temperance songs, he climbed down into his rented craft and began to row briskly back to the wharf.

12

The district known as the Uptown Tenderloin was a pocket of sin more genteel and circumspect than the Barbary Coast, catering to the more playful among the city's respectable citizens. It was located on the streets—Turk, Eddy, Ellis, O'Farrell—that slanted diagonally off Market. Some of San Francisco's better restaurants, saloons, and variety-show theaters flourished there, part of the Cocktail Route that nightly drew the begowned and silk-hatted gentry. Smartly dressed young women paraded along Market during the evening hours, not a few of them wearing violets pinned to their jackets and bright-colored feather boas around their necks that announced them to those in the know as sporting ladies. Men of all ages lounged in front of cigar stores and saloons, engaged in a pastime that Quincannon himself had followed on occasion, known as "stacking the mash": ogling and flirting with parading ladies of both easy and well-guarded virtue.

Parlor houses also flourished there, so openly that the reform element had begun to mount a serious cleanup campaign. The most notorious was the one operated by Miss Bessie Hall, the "Queen of O'Farrell Street," all of whose girls were said to be blond and possessed of rare talents in the practice of their trade. Lettie Carew and her Fiddle Dee Dee were among the second rank of Bessie's rivals, specializing in ladies of other cultures and different hues.

The evening parade had yet to begin when Quincannon alighted from a Market Street trolley at O'Farrell Street, his pockets empty now of the stolen loot; he had stopped off at Carpenter and Quincannon, Professional Detective Services, and locked it away in the office safe. Above him, as he strolled along the wooden sidewalk, sundry flounced undergarments clung to telephone wires, another form of advertisement tossed out by the inhabitants of the shuttered houses along the route. This, too, had scandalized and provoked the reformers. Midway in the third block, he paused before a plain-shuttered building that bore that numerals 244 on its front door. A small, discreet sign on the vestibule wall said FIDDLE DEE DEE in gilt letters.

A smiling colored woman opened the door in answer to his ring and escorted him into an ornately furnished parlor, where he declined the offer of refreshment and requested an audience with Miss

Lettie Carew. When he was alone he sat on a red plush chair, closed his nostrils to a mingled scent of incense and patchouli, and glanced around the room with professional interest. Patterned lace curtains and red velvet drapes at the blinded windows. Several red plush chairs and settees, rococo tables, ruby-shaded lamps, gilt-framed mirrors, oil paintings of exotically voluptuous nudes. There was also a handful of framed mottoes, one of which Quincannon could read from where he sat: "If every man was as true to his country as he is to his wife—God help the U.S.A." In all, the parlor was similar to Bessie Hall's, doubtless by design, though it was neither as lavish nor as stylish. None could match "the woman who licked John L. Sullivan" when it came to extravagance.

At the end of five minutes, Lettie Carew swept into the room. Quincannon blinked and managed not to let his jaw unhinge; Miss Lettie had been described to him on more than one occasion, but this was his first glimpse of her in the flesh. And a great deal of flesh there was. She resembled nothing so much as a giant cherub, pink and puffed and painted, dressed in pinkish white silk and trailing rose-hued feather boas and a cloud of sweet perfume that threatened to finish off what oxygen had been left undamaged by the patchouli and incense.

"Welcome, sir, welcome to Fiddle Dee Dee, home of many bountiful beauties from exotic lands. I am the proprietress, Miss Lettie Carew."

Quincannon blinked again. The madame's voice was small and shrill, not much louder than a mouse squeak. The fact that it emanated from such a mountainous woman made it all the more startling.

"What can I do for you, sir? Don't be shy—ask and ye shall receive. Every gentleman's pleasure is my command."

"How many Chinese girls are here?"

"Ah, you have a taste for the mysterious East. Only one—Ming Toy, from far-off Shanghai, and most popular she is, sir, most popular. Unfortunately, she is engaged at present."

"How long has she been engaged?"

"I beg your pardon?"

"Since yesterday, perhaps? By the same man—young, slight, black-haired, whose tipple is red wine?"

Lettie Carew said suspiciously, "How did you know that?"

"Is he still here now?"

"Suppose he is. What's your interest in him?"

So he'd been right: the Dodger *was* still elevating. He managed not to smile. "Professional," he said. "The lad's a wanted felon."

The madame's subservient pose evaporated. "Oh, Lordy, don't tell me you're a copper."

He didn't; he let her believe it from his stern expression.

"Bloody hell!" she said. "Can't you wait until he leaves before you arrest him? I have other customers upstairs. And I paid my graft this week, same as always . . ."

"Which room is Ming Toy's?"

"There won't be shooting, will there?"

"Not if it can be avoided."

"If there's any damage, the city will pay for it, or I'll sue. That includes bloodstains to the carpet, bedding, and furniture."

"What room, Lettie?"

She impaled him with a long smoky glare before she squeaked, "Nine," and flounced out of the parlor.

In the hallway outside, a long, carpeted staircase led to the second floor. Quincannon climbed it with his hand on the Navy Colt under his coat. The odd-numbered rooms were to the left of the stairs; in front of the door bearing a gilt-edged 9, he stopped to listen. No discernible sounds issued from within. He drew his revolver, depressed the latch, and stepped into a room decorated in an ostentatious Chinese dragon style, dimly lighted by rice-paper lanterns and choked with incense spiced with wine vapors.

An immediate skirmish, he was pleased to note, was unnecessary. Dodger Brown sprawled supine on the near side of the four-poster bed, dressed in a soiled union suit, flatulent snoring sounds emanating from his open mouth. The girl who sat up beside him was no more than twenty, delicate-featured, her comeliness marred by dark eyes already as old as Cain. She hopped off the bed, pulling a loose silk wrapper around her thin body, and hurried over to where Quincannon stood. If she noticed his drawn weapon, it made no apparent impression on her.

"Busy," she said in a singsong voice, "busy, busy."

"Not anymore. It's him I'm after, not you."

"So?" The young-old eyes blinked several times. "Finished?"

"Finished," he agreed. "I'm taking him to jail."

She understood the word, and it seemed to please her. She glanced over at the snoring Dodger. "Wine," she said disgustedly.

"I'm a teetotaler myself."

Ming Toy wrinkled her nose. "Phooey," she said, and vanished as swiftly and silently as a wraith.

Quincannon padded to the bedside. Four rough shakes, and Dodger Brown stopped snoring, and his eyes popped open. For several seconds he lay inert, peering up blearily at the face looming above him. Recognition came an instant before he levered himself off the bed in a single convulsive movement and lunged for the door.

On this occasion, however, Quincannon was ready for him and his sly tricks. He caught hold of the union suit by the neck, and with his free hand, spun the little burglar around, deftly avoided a shin kick, flung him backward onto the rumpled bed, knelt beside him, and poked the bore of the Navy Colt squarely between his bloodshot eyeballs. "Settle down, lad," he said. "You're yaffled this time, and you know it."

The Dodger, staring cross-eyed at the Colt, knew it for a fact. All the struggle and sand left him at once; he lay in a motionless puddle, an expression of painful self-recrimination rearranging his vulpine features.

"It's my own fault," he said in mournful tones as Quincannon handcuffed him. "After you near snagged me the other night, I knew I should've hopped a rattler in the Oakland yards straightaway. Gone on the lammas, 'stead of comin' over here."

"Aye, and let it be a lesson to you, Dodger." Quincannon grinned and added sagely, "The best-laid plans aren't always the best-planned lays."

13

The city prison, in the basement of the Hall of Justice, was a busy place that testified to the amount of crime afoot in San Francisco. And to Quincannon's practiced eye, there were just as many crooks on the outside of the foul-smelling cells as on the inside. Corrupt policemen, seedy lawyers haggling at the desk about releases for prisoners, rapacious fixers, deceitful bail bondsmen . . . more of those, in fact, than honest officers and men charged with felonies, and with vagrancy, public drunkenness, and other misdemeanors.

Quincannon delivered a sullen and uncommunicative Dodger Brown there, and spent the better part of an unpleasant hour talking to an officer he knew and a booking desk sergeant he didn't know. He signed a complaint on behalf of the Great Western Insurance Company, and before he left, made sure that the Dodger would remain locked in one of the cells until Jackson Pollard and Great Western Insurance officially formalized the charge. He knew better than to turn over any of the stolen goods; did not even mention that they were in his possession. Valuables had a curious way of disappearing from the police property room overnight.

By the time he reentered the offices of Carpenter and Quincannon, Professional Detective Services, it was late afternoon. He told Sabina of the day's events, embellishing a bit on his brief scuffles with Salty Jim and Dodger Brown.

"You take too many risks, John," she admonished him. "One of these days you'll pay dear for such recklessness. Just as your father and my husband did."

He waved that away. "I intend to die in bed at the age of ninety," he said. "And not alone, either."

"I wouldn't be surprised if either boast turned out to be true." Her mouth quirked slightly at the corners. "You had no difficulty finding your way around the Fiddle Dee Dee, I'm sure."

"Meaning what, my dear?"

"Don't tell me you've never been in a parlor house before."

"Only in the performance of my professional duty," he lied.

"If that's so, as randy as you are, I pity the fair maidens of San Francisco."

"I have no designs on the virtue of young virgins. Only on the favors of a certain young and handsome widow."

"Then you're fated to live out your years as celibate as a monk. Did Dodger Brown confess to his crimes?"

Quincannon sighed. Unrequited passion, especially when it was as pure as his for Sabina, was a sad and pitiable thing. "He had little to say after we left the Fiddle Dee Dee. A close-mouthed lad, the Dodger. But the loot from his burglaries will convict him."

"The Costain valuables weren't among the ones you recovered?"

"No," he said. "But I'll find them soon enough."

"There's still time to take the lot to Great Western and turn it over to Mr. Pollard," Sabina said. "Shall I ring him up?"

"No. Best wait until the morrow."

"Why? Pollard came by earlier, all in a dither. Two more claims have taxed his patience to the limit."

"Two more?"

"Both filed today by Penelope Costain."

"One for the amount of her missing jewelry. The other?"

"The Costains also have a joint life insurance policy with Great Western. In the sum of twenty-five thousand dollars." Sabina's smile was wry. "The widow wasted little time."

"That she did."

"I managed to smooth Pollard's feathers, but the sooner he knows Dodger Brown is in custody and the loot has been recovered, the better for us. Do you expect to find the Costain valuables tonight? Is that why you want to wait?"

"It's one of the reasons," Quincannon said, though it wasn't.

"Another wouldn't concern Sherlock Holmes, would it?"

"What makes you think that?"

"I know you, John, much better than you think I do."

"Bosh," he said, and changed the subject. "What did you learn in your investigations today?"

By the time Sabina had finished her report, his freebooter's beard was split in a crooked smile. "Bully! Just as I suspected."

"Does that mean you've solved the puzzle?"

"It does. All I lack now are a few minor details."

"Well? How was Andrew Costain murdered? How was Dodger Brown able to escape from the house?"

"Not until tomorrow morning, my lady. Meet me at Pollard's office at nine-thirty. You'll hear the full explanation then."

"You're being exasperating again, John Quincannon. Why can't you just give me the jist of it now?"

He said, "Nine-thirty, sharp," teased her further with a fiendish wink, and took his leave.

On Market Street he hailed a cab. He hadn't eaten since breakfast and his hunger was fierce, but there was an important errand that needed doing first. He gave the hack driver Dr. Caleb Axminster's Russian Hill address.

Some thirty minutes later, an owl-eyed housekeeper opened the

Axminsters' front door and informed him that the doctor had not yet returned from his surgery. From behind her, somewhere in the house, Quincannon could hear the cheerful, somewhat fantastic plucking of violin strings—no melody he had ever heard before. He said, "It's Mr. Sherlock Holmes I've come to see," and handed the housekeeper one of his business cards. She took it away with her. Soon the violin grew silent, and shortly after that, the housekeeper returned to show him to a sitting room off the main parlor.

Holmes was sprawled comfortably in an armchair, his violin on a table beside him. In his lap was a small bottle of clear liquid and a morocco case. He greeted Quincannon, asked him to wait a moment. With long, nervous fingers he then produced a hypodermic syringe from the case, filled it from the bottle, adjusted the needle, and rolled up his left shirt cuff. On the sinewy forearm and wrist Quincannon spied innumerable puncture marks. As he watched, Holmes thrust the needle into his arm, pressed the plunger, then sank back with a long sigh of satisfaction.

"What's in the bottle, Holmes?"

The Englishman smiled. "A seven-percent solution," he said, "courtesy of Dr. Axminster."

Quincannon did not have to ask the exact nature of the seven-percent solution. He shrugged and let the matter drop. Each man to his own vice.

"Well, my esteemed colleague," Holmes said, "I must say I'm glad you've come. I intended to call on you earlier, but I've had rather a busy day. You've saved me the necessity of going out again this evening."

"I've had a busy day myself. And a highly productive one."

"You've located Dodger Brown?"

"Located and arrested him. And recovered the burglary loot."

"My dear Quincannon, you surpass yourself!"

"That news is not the only reason for my visit," Quincannon said silkily. "I've also brought you an invitation."

"Invitation?"

"To a meeting in the offices of Jackson Pollard, head of the claims department for the Great Western Insurance Company, at nine-thirty tomorrow morning. If you'll consent to attend, I guarantee you'll find it edifying."

"In what regard?"

"I intend to explain the mystery surrounding the death of Andrew Costain."

"Ah! So your sleuthing has reaped additional rewards, has it?"

"It has."

"And now there is to be a public unveiling," Holmes said. "Splendid. You and I are more alike than either of us might care to admit, Quincannon. Often enough a touch of the artist wells up in me, too, and calls insistently for a well-staged performance."

"Then you'll be there?"

"Oh, by all means." Holmes's eyes were bright; he seemed not at all nonplussed to have been outdone. "I shall be most interested to hear your deductions. Most interested indeed!"

14

The San Francisco offices of Great Western Insurance were housed in the Montgomery Block, the largest of the city's buildings at Montgomery and Merchant Streets. It was just nine-thirty of another cold, gloomy morning when Quincannon entered the anteroom. He found Sabina and Sherlock Holmes already present, along with two other principals he hadn't expected to see—Penelope Costain and Dr. Caleb Axminster. Holmes had invited both of them, it turned out, because Mrs. Costain had a vested interest in the proceedings and Axminster was a "concerned party." Quincannon had no objection in either case. If he hadn't been so involved in his competition with Holmes, he would have thought of it himself.

In a body they were shown into Jackson Pollard's private sanctum. The claims adjustor was a fussy, bespectacled little man with sparse sandy hair and sideburns like miniature tumbleweeds. He demanded, frowning, "What's the meaning of this, Quincannon? Why are all these people here?"

"As witnesses, you might say."

"Witnesses to what?"

"That will soon become evident. Will you have chairs brought in to accomodate everyone?"

That was done, and all sat down except Quincannon. Holmes lit his oily clay pipe and sat in a relaxed posture, a small smile playing at the corners of his mouth. Sabina sat quietly with hands clasped in her lap; patience was one of her many virtues. Penelope Costain was less at ease, fidgeting in her chair, fingers toying with a tiger-eye and agate locket at her throat. Axminster sucked on horehound drops, wearing the bright-eyed, expectant look of a small boy on Christmas morning.

Pollard said, "Well, Quincannon? Get on with it." He had no patience at all. "And what you have to say had better be to my liking."

"It will be. First of all, Dodger Brown is in custody awaiting formal charges. I tracked him down and arrested him yesterday."

"Yesterday? Why didn't you notify me immediately?"

"I had my reasons."

"Yes? What about all the items he stole? Did you recover them?"

"I did."

Quincannon had stopped by the agency offices on his way there; he drew out the sack of valuables and, with a flourish, placed it on Pollard's desk blotter. The little man's eyes glowed pleasurably as he spread the contents out in front of him, but the glow faded a bit once he'd sifted through the lot. "All present and accounted for from the first three burglaries," he said. "But none of Mrs. Costain's losses is here."

"I haven't recovered those items as yet."

"But you do have an idea of what Brown did with them?"

"He did nothing with them. He never had them."

"Never had them, you say?"

"Dodger Brown didn't burgle the Costain home," Quincannon said. "Nor is he the murderer of Andrew Costain."

Pollard blinked owlishly behind his spectacles. "Then who did burgle it?"

"No one."

"Come, come, man, speak plainly, say what you mean."

"It was Andrew Costain who planned the theft, with the aid of an accomplice. And it was the accomplice who punctured him and made off with the contents of the valuables case."

This announcement brought forth an "Ahh!" from Dr. Axminster. Sabina arched one of her fine eyebrows. Even Sherlock Holmes sat up straight in his chair, his expression intent.

Penelope Costain said icily, "That is a ridiculous accusation. Why on earth would my husband conspire to rob his own home?"

"To defraud Great Western Insurance Company. In order to pay off his substantial gambling debts. Surely you know he was a compulsive gambler, Mrs. Costain. And that his finances had been severely depleted and his law practice had suffered setbacks as a result of his addiction."

"I knew no such thing."

"If it's true," Pollard said, "how did *you* find it out?"

"I was suspicious of him from the moment he asked me to stand watch on his property." That was not quite true, but what harm in a little embellishment? "Two nights ago at Dr. Axminster's, he seemed to consider me something of an incompetent buffoon for allowing Dodger Brown to escape at the Truesdale home. Why then would he choose me of all people to protect of his property? The answer is that he *wanted* a detective he considered inept to bear witness to a cleverly staged break-in. Underestimating me was his first mistake."

"Was that the only thing that made you suspicious?"

"No. Costain admitted it was unlikely that a professional housebreaker, having had a close call the previous night, would risk another crime so soon, yet he would have me believe his fear was so great he was willing to pay dearly for two operatives to stand surveillance on successive nights. An outlay of funds he could ill afford, for it was plain from his habitual drinking and the condition of his office that he had fallen on difficult times. He also made the dubious claim that he had no time to remove valuables from his home and secrete them elsewhere until Dodger Brown was apprehended, and no desire to cancel 'important engagements' in order to guard his premises himself."

Axminster asked, "So you accepted the job in order to find out what he was up to?"

"Yes." Another embellishment. He had accepted it for the money—no fool, John Quincannon. "Subsequent investigations by Mrs. Carpenter"—he bowed to Sabina—"revealed Costain's gambling addiction and a string of debts as long as a widowed mother's clothesline. He was a desperate man."

"You suspected insurance fraud, then," Holmes said, "when you asked me to join you in the surveillance."

"I did," Quincannon lied.

"Did you also suspect the manner in which the fraud would be perpetrated?"

"The use of an accomplice dressed in the same type of dark clothing as worn by Dodger Brown? Costain's arrival not more than a minute after the intruder entered the house through the rear door? Not until later. It was a devious plan that no detective could have anticipated in its entirety before the fact. In truth, a bughouse caper from start to finish."

"Bughouse caper?"

"Crazy scheme. Fool's game."

"Ah. Crook's argot, eh? More of your delightful American idiom."

Pollard said, "So the accomplice pulled a double cross, is that it? He wanted the spoils all for himself?"

"Just so," Quincannon agreed.

"Name him."

"Not just yet. Other explanations are in order first."

"Such as how Costain was murdered in a locked room? And why he was shot as well as stabbed? Can you answer those questions?"

"I can," Quincannon said, not to Pollard but to Sherlock Holmes. The alleged world's greatest detective was about to lose his mantle to a more worthy rival, and Quincannon intended to savor every moment of his triumph.

"Well, then?"

Quincannon produced his pipe and tobacco pouch, allowing suspense to build while he loaded the bowl. Holmes watched him in a rapt way, his hands busy winding a pocket Petrarch, his expression neutral except for the faintest of smiles. The others, Sabina included, were on the edges of their chairs.

When he had the pipe lit and drawing well, he said, "The answer to your first question, Mr. Pollard," he said to Holmes, "is that Andrew Costain was *not* murdered in a locked room. Nor was he stabbed *and* shot by his accomplice."

"Riddles, Quincannon?" Pollard said irritably.

"Not at all. To begin with, Andrew Costain shot himself." Quincannon paused for dramatic effect before continuing. "The report was designed to draw me into the house, the superficial wound to support what would have been his claim of a struggle with the thief. The better to bamboozle me; so he reasoned, and the better to ensure that Great Western would pay off his claim quickly and without question or suspicion."

"How did you deduce the sham?"

"Dodger Brown was known to carry a pistol in the practice of his trade, but only for purposes of intimidation—he had no history of violence. I'll wager that he carried his weapon unloaded, for it was empty when I found it yesterday in his hideout, and there were no cartridges among his possessions. The revolver that inflicted the wound was bought new that same day in a gunsmith's shop near Costain's law offices, by Costain himself. Mrs. Carpenter's investigation revealed this information and that concerning his financial troubles."

"But why the locked-room business?" Sabina asked. "Further obfuscation?"

"No. In point of fact, there was no locked-room ploy."

Pollard growled, "Dammit, Quincannon—"

"That part of the misadventure was a mix of illusion and accident, the result of circumstances, not premeditation. There was no intent to gild the lily with such theatrics. Even if there had been, there was simply not enough time for any sort of locked-room gimmick to have been perpetrated once the pistol was fired."

"Then what did transpire?"

"Costain was in the hallway outside the open door to his study, not inside the room, when he discharged the shot into his forearm. That is why the electric light was on in the hall; why the smell of burnt powder was strong there, yet all but nonexistent inside the room. The bullet penetrated the armchair because the gun was aimed in that direction when it was fired, through the open doorway into the study."

"Why didn't Costain simply fire the shot in there?"

"I suspect he met his accomplice in the hallway, perhaps to hand over the jewelry from the valuables case. That is why the light was on in the hall. The empty case was another clue that put me onto the gaff. The time factor again—there was too little time for the phantom burglar to have found his way to the study, located the case, and rifled it before Costain arrived to catch him in the act."

"And the murder, John?" Sabina asked.

"Within moments of the shot being fired, the accomplice struck. Costain was standing in the open doorway, his back to the hallway. The force of the single stab with a long, narrow blade staggered him forward into the study. The blow was not immediately fatal, however. He lived long enough to turn, confront his attacker, observe the bloody weapon in a hand still upraised—and in self-defense, to slam the door shut and twist the key already in the latch. Then he collapsed and died."

"Why didn't he shoot the accomplice instead?" Axminster said. "That is what I would have done."

"He may no longer have held the pistol. Either the suddenness of the attack caused him to drop it, or he dropped it in order to lock the door against his betrayer. In my judgment Andrew Costain was a craven coward as well as a thief. I think if pressed his wife would agree, despite her allegation to the city police that he was a brave man."

Penelope Costain's face was the shade of egg white. "I agree with nothing you've said. Nothing!"

Sherlock Holmes stirred in his chair. The grudging admiration in his eyes brought a warm glow to Quincannon. His gloat, however, was not to last long.

"Capital, Quincannon!" Holmes said. He bounced to his feet and grasped Quincannon's hand. "I congratulate you on your performance thus far. You've done a commendable job of interpreting the *res gestae*."

"*Res* what?" Pollard asked.

"The facts of the case. My learned colleague's deductions coincide almost exactly with mine."

Quincannon stiffened. "What's that? *Your* deductions?"

"Oh, yes, certainly. I reached the identical conclusions yesterday afternoon."

"Hogwash!"

"My dear fellow, you doubt my word?"

"I do, unless you can name the accomplice and explain the rest of what took place."

"I can. Naturally."

Damn his eyes! "Well? Who stabbed Costain?"

"His wife, of course. Penelope Costain."

A startled noise came from Pollard. Mrs. Costain's only reaction was to lighten another shade and draw herself up indignantly. "I?" she said with chilly bluster. "How dare you!"

Quincannon said quickly, "Dodger Brown is a small man. It was easy enough for you to pass for him in the darkness, dressed in dark man's clothing, with a cloth cap covering your hair."

"Quite so," Holmes agreed. He relit his pipe before he continued, "While joined in her husband's plan, she devised a counterplan of her own—her double cross, as you Americans call it—for two reasons. First, to attempt to defraud the Great Western Insurance Company not once but twice, by entering claims on both the allegedly stolen jewelery and on her husband's twenty-five-thousand-dollar life insurance policy, of which she is the sole beneficiary. She came to this office yesterday to enter those claims, did she not, Mr. Pollard?"

"She did."

"Her second motive," Holmes went on, "was hatred, a virulent and consuming hatred for the man to whom she was married."

"You can't possibly know that," Quincannon objected. "You're guessing."

"I do not make guesses. Mrs. Costain's hatred of her husband was apparent to me at Dr. Axminster's dinner party. My eyes have been trained to examine faces and not their trimmings—their 'public disguise,' as it were. As for proof of her true feelings, and of her guilt, I discovered the first clue shortly after we found Andrew Costain's corpse."

"What clue?"

"Face powder," Holmes said.

"Face powder?"

"When I examined the wound in Andrew Costain's back through my glass, I discovered a tiny smear of the substance on the cloth of his cheviot—the same type and shade as that worn by Mrs. Costain."

"How could that prove her guilt? They were married . . . her face powder might have gotten on his coat at any time, in a dozen different ways."

"I beg to differ. It was close and to the right of the wound, which indicated that the residue must have adhered to the edge of the murderer's hand when the fatal blow was struck. It was also caked and deeply imbedded in the fibers of the cloth. This fact, combined with the depth of the wound itself, further indicated that the blade was plunged into Costain's flesh with great force and fury. An act born of hatred as well as greed. The depth and size of the wound afforded additional proof. It had been made by a stiletto, hardly the type of weapon a professional pannyman such as Dodger Brown would carry. A stiletto, furthermore, as my researches into crime have borne out, is much more a woman's weapon than a man's."

Quincannon sought a way to refute this logic and found none. He glowered and held his tongue.

Penelope Costain once again protested outraged innocence. No one paid her any attention, least of all Quincannon and Holmes.

"Now then," Holmes continued, "we have the mystery of Mrs. Costain's actions after striking the death blow. Her evidently miraculous escape from the house, only to reappear later dressed in evening clothes. Of course you know how this bit of flummery was managed, Quincannon."

Quincannon hesitated. Hell and damn! This was the one point about which he was not absolutely certain.

"Of course," he said.

"Pray elaborate."

He drew a breath and plunged ahead authoritatively. "There is little enough mystery in what she did. She simply hid until you and I were both inside the study, then slipped out. Through one of the windows, no doubt. She could easily have prepared one in advance so that it slid up and down noiselessly, and also loosened its latch just enough to allow it to drop back into the locking slot after she climbed through and lowered the sash. The window would then appear to be unbreached."

"Ingenious."

"She may have thought so."

"I meant your interpretation," Holmes said. "Unfortunately, however, you are wrong. That is not what she did."

"The devil you say!"

"Quite wrong on all counts except that she did, in fact, hide for a length of time. She could not have foreseen that both front and rear doors would be blocked so as to impede egress; if simple escape had been the plan, she could reasonably have expected to slip out one or the other door, thus obviating use of a window. Nor could she could be certain in advance that a loosened window latch would drop back into its slot and thus go unnoticed. Nor could she be certain that we would fail to hear her raising and lowering the sash, and capture her before she could flee."

Quincannon said, "I suppose you have a better theory?"

"Not a theory—the exact truth of the matter. Her hiding place was the very same one she and her husband had decided upon as part of the original scheme. I confirmed it yesterday afternoon, when I returned to the Costain home while Mrs. Costain was here with Mr. Pollard and spent two hours in an exhaustive search of the premises."

"You illegally entered my home?" This time, Penelope Costain's outrage was not feigned. "I'll have you arrested for trespassing!"

"I think not. Under the circumstances, I'm sure even the police would consider my actions fully justified. Dr. Axminister accompanied me, incidentally, at my request. He will confirm all that I am about to reveal."

"Indeed I will," the doctor said.

Quincannon asked testily, "Then how *did* she escape from the blasted house?"

"She didn't. She never left it." Holmes paused as Quincannon had done earlier, for dramatic effect. "When you have eliminated the impossible," he said, "whatever is left must, perforce, be the truth. As applied to this case, I concluded as you did that it was impossible for Andrew Costain's slayer to have committed murder in and then escaped from the locked study; therefore, Costain could not have been slain inside the study, and the study could not have been locked when the stiletto was plunged into his body. I concluded further that it was impossible for the slayer to have escaped the locked house after commission of the crime; therefore, she did not escape from it. Penelope Costain was hidden on the premises the entire time."

"Where? We searched the house from top to bottom."

"Indeed. But consider this: Two strangers cannot possibily know every nook and cranny of a home in which they have never before set foot. The owners, on the other hand, are fully intimate with every detail of the premises."

A flush began to creep out of Quincannon's now rather tight collar. The light of knowledge had begun to dawn in the nooks and crannies of his nimble brain. He cursed himself for his failure to see what the bloody Englishman had seen much sooner.

"During my search this afternoon," Holmes continued, "I discovered a small adjunct to the kitchen pantry—a tiny room where preserves and the like are stored. The entrance to this room is concealed behind a pantry shelf. Those who knew of it could be reasonably sure that the entrance would be overlooked by strangers. The room itself is some four feet square, and while it has no ventilation, its door when cracked open permits normal breathing. Mrs. Costain had no trouble remaining hidden there for well over an hour—ample time for her to change from the dark man's clothing into evening clothes she had secreted there earlier. After the arrival of the city police, when none of the officers was in the immediate vicinity, she slipped out through the kitchen and dining room to the front hallway and pretended to have just arrived home. The first person to encounter her, Sergeant Mahoney, had no reason to doubt this."

"But you did, I suppose."

"Oh, quite. When she first entered the study I observed the remnants of cobwebs and traces of dust on the hem of her skirt, the fur of her wrap, even the ostrich plume in her hat. The pantry room contains cobwebs, dust, and dirt of the same type. I also observed that a piece had been torn from one of her fingernails, leaving a tiny wound in the cuticle. Earlier, during my studies of the carpet in the hallway, I discovered that same tiny piece, stained with a spot of fresh blood—broken off, of course, when she stabbed her husband. *Quod erat demonstrandum.*"

Penelope Costain said, "You can't prove any of this."

"Ah, but I can," Holmes told her. "After I left your home yesterday, I visited city police headquarters and spoke to Sergeant Mahoney and one of the officers who were stationed outside your home on that fateful night. Both swore an oath that no conveyance arrived and no one entered the house through either the front or rear door. The inescapable conclusion is that you were concealed inside the entire time. As for the missing jewelry and coins, and the murder weapon . . ." He produced a cloth from his coat pocket, which he proceeded to unfold on Pollard's desk. Inside was a bloodstained stiletto and the "stolen" valuables. "As you see, Mrs. Costain, they are no longer where you hid them in the pantry room."

Both her icy calm and her bluster vanished at once; she sagged in her chair, lowered her head into her hands.

The others, Quincannon excepted, gazed at Holmes with open admiration. Even Sabina seemed more impressed by his performance than that of her doting partner. Holmes placed his hand over his heart and bowed as if responding to applause—a damned theatrical gesture if ever there was one. Then he faced Quincannon again, smiling indulgently.

"Have you any other questions, my good fellow?" he asked.

Questions? Quincannon had a brace of them, as a matter of fact. One: How soon will you be leaving San Francisco? Two: Will I be able to stop myself from strangling, bludgeoning, stabbing, or shooting you before you do?

15

"The man is infuriating!" Quincannon ranted. "Insufferable, insulting, exasperating!"

"John, for heaven's sake . . ."

"Thinks he's a blasted oracle. Sees all, knows all. He's an expert on every arcane subject under the sun. He's full of—"

"John."

"—hot air. Enough to fill a balloon and carry it from here to the Sandwich Islands. Rattlepate! Braggart! Conceited popinjay!"

"Lower your voice," Sabina said warningly. "The other diners are starting to stare at us."

Quincannon subsided. She was right. The Cobweb Palace, Abe Warner's eccentric eatery on Meiggs Wharf in North Beach, was a noisily convivial place at the dinner hour, and to draw attention there required a considerable amount of bombast. The ramshackle building was packed to its creaking rafters on that evening—with customers partaking of the finest seafood fare in the city, and with the usual complement of monkeys, roaming cats and dogs, and such exotic birds as the parrot that was capable of hurling curses in four languages. Warner had a benevolent passion for all creatures large and small, including spiders; his collection of rare and sundry souvenirs, from Eskimo artifacts to a complete set of dentures that had once belonged to a sperm whale to rude paintings of nude women, were draped floor to ceiling in an undisturbed mosaic of cobwebs.

At length Sabina ventured to say, "I don't know why you carry on so about Mr. Holmes. He may be a bit full of himself, but there's no gainsaying the fact that he has a brilliant mind. Frankly, I find him charming."

"Charming! You haven't spent nearly as much time with him as I have. Today's trek through the Barbary Coast and Chinatown was interminable. He insisted on seeing every squalid nook and cranny. Opium dens, gambling hells, wine dumps, half the pestholes from Dupont Street to the waterfront . . . yes, and the Hotel Nymphomania and Belle Cora's, among other parlor houses. He even stopped half a dozen street prostitutes to ask the prices for their services, not only for comparison here but with streetwalkers in London's Limehouse. Faugh! I had half a mind to bribe Ezra Bluefield to feed him a mickey and turn him over to the shanghaiers—"

"Hush, now! That's enough."

Quincannon subsided again. He gave his attention to his abalone supper, attacking the succulent shellfish with a vengeance. Neither the attack nor his silence lasted for long, however. He laid his fork down after half a dozen bites. Gall had diminished his appetite; his stomach burned with dyspepsia. And now gloom was creeping in to dull the edge of his indignation.

He said, "That doctor friend of Holmes's in England, what's-his-name, the one who sensationalizes all of his adventures . . ."

"Watson. And I wouldn't be too sure that he's a sensationalist."

"Bah. I suppose he'll write up this bughouse caper, too. And give Holmes all the credit for solving it. Omit my name entirely."

"I rather doubt it," Sabina said. "Holmes won't want it widely known that he was sleuthing in San Francisco or anywhere else during the past three years. Dr. Watson and the world at large have been led to believe he is dead, remember."

"A pity they're not right," Quincannon muttered.

"Really, John. I don't see why you're so jealous of the man."

"Jealous? Because he managed to solve part of the Costain case? I solved most of it myself, and found and arrested Dodger Brown and recovered the swag from his burglaries unto the bargain. I am every bit Holmes's equal, if not his better."

"Just as you say." Sabina sipped from her glass of French wine. "It's not inconceivable, you know, that you'll have a biographer yourself someday."

Quincannon considered that statement. "I should have one now," he said. "By Godfrey, I should! I wonder if the gent who writes that pungent column for the *Examiner* would be interested."

"You mean Ambrose Bierce?"

"That's the lad. Maybe I'll approach him about it."

"Well, his column *is* called 'Prattle.'"

Quincannon ignored that. His gloom had begun to lift. "You're quite right, my lady, that I have no good cause to let that English pretender bother me. Sherlock Holmes—hah! He may have achieved a small measure of fame, but fame is fickle and fleeting. In a few years his exploits will be forgotten. But the name and the detections of John Quincannon . . . ah, they're bound to be writ large and indelible in the annals of crime!"

Sabina rolled her eyes and remained eloquently silent.

Reichenbach

A Professor Moriarty Story

Michael Kurland

You remember, I assume, the newspaper accounts of the accidental deaths of the consulting detective Sherlock Holmes and the eminent mathematician Professor James Moriarty at Kessel Falls at the River Reichenbach in Switzerland. Or perhaps you've read Dr. Watson's account of the confrontation at, as he called it, "Reichenbach Falls" between Holmes and the "master criminal" Moriarty. It seems that everyone in the English-speaking world has read, or at least heard, of the incident. And then, you will recall, some three years later Holmes reappeared to Watson and explained his absence and supposed death in some detail. Well, I am here to tell you that almost every word of these accounts, including Holmes's recantation, is false, and I should know. I am Professor James Moriarty.

It is not the fault of the newspapers, who published with no more than their usual disregard for the facts, nor of Dr. Watson, who believed everything told to him by his friend and companion Sherlock Holmes. There can be no greater friend than one who believes whatever he is told no matter how strongly it is belied by the evidence to the contrary. Is that not, after all, the basis of most religion?

This, then, is an account of the events that led up to the disappearance, and what transpired for a short time afterward. I was going to say a "true account," but I refrained, because memory is faulty, and there were some facts that I was not privy to that might make a difference in the truth of what happened. It is, then, an account of the events as they appeared to me at the time.

It was on the evening of Wednesday, the twenty-second of April, 1891, that Mr. Maws, my butler, ushered a man named Tippins into my study. A tall, thin, angular man wearing a black frock coat with red cuffs and pockets, and large brass buttons, he stood, top hat in hand, before my desk and peered at me through oversized gold spectacles. His nose, while not large enough to be truly grotesque, was the most prominent object on his face, possibly because of the web of red veins beneath the roseate skin. A brush mustache directly beneath the nose added character to the face, but it was not a character whose acquaintance I would have gone out of my way to make. "I have come to you from Mr. Holmes," he began. "He requires your assistance, and has asked me to direct you to the secret location where he awaits you."

I am not easily surprised. Indeed, I spend a good bit of time and effort making sure that I am not surprised. But I confess that, for a second, I was astounded. "Holmes wants to see me? Is this some sort of trick?" I demanded.

He considered. "Naw, I wouldn't think so," he said finally. "He's much too stout to indulge in that sort of tomfoolery, I should think."

"Ah!" I said. "Stout, is he? So it's Mr. *Mycroft* Holmes who desires my assistance."

"Indeed," Tippins agreed. "Isn't that what I said?"

"I thought perhaps his brother . . ."

Tippins snorted. "The consulting detective chap? What has he to do with foreign policy?"

"Foreign policy?" I inquired.

"Perhaps you'd best just go and find out for yourself," Tippins suggested.

"To the Foreign Office?"

"Naw. Mr. Holmes don't want it known that he's meeting with you, so he has arranged for my services to get you to his, so-to-speak secret location."

"Services?" I asked. "What sort of services?"

He tapped himself on the chest. "I'm a conniver," he said.

"Interesting," I allowed. "You scheme and plot for Her Majesty's government?"

"I enable people to do necessary things in unusual ways, when the more usual ways are not available." He smiled. "I occasionally perform services for Mr. Holmes, but few others in Her Majesty's government have availed themselves of my services."

"And what necessary service would you perform for me in your unorthodox fashion?" I asked him.

"Your house is being watched," Tippins said.

I nodded. I had been aware of a steady watch being kept on my house for the past few weeks. "No doubt by that very consulting detective chap you were mentioning," I said.

"Mr. Holmes did not want it known that he was to speak with you," Tippins explained, "so he sent me."

"I see," I said. "How are you going to get me there unseen?"

"I have a carriage waiting outside," Tippins said, unbuttoning his frock coat. "The driver knows where to go. You will leave here as me. I will await your return here, if you don't mind. I have brought a book." He took off the frock coat and handed it to me. "Put this on."

"It is distinctive," I said, examining the red pockets. "But I'm not sure we look alike enough, ah, facially, for the masquerade to work."

"Ah! There we have the crux of the matter," he told me. He reached for the gold frame of his glasses and carefully removed them from his face. With them came the red nose and the brush mustache. The face beneath was quite ordinary, and the nose was, if anything, rather small.

"Bless me!" I said, or perhaps it was a slightly stronger expression.

He smiled. "Simple but effective," he said. "The watchers will see what they expect to see."

I put on the glasses, with the accompanying nose and mustache, and shrugged into the coat.

"Here," Tippins said, handing me his top hat. "It will complete the illusion."

And indeed it did. Wrapped in Tippins's frock coat and wearing much of what had been his face, I thrust the journal I had been reading into the coat pocket and left my house. I clambered into the waiting carriage, a sturdy but undistinguished hack, and the jarvey spoke to the horse, and we were on our way. I waited about ten minutes before removing the facial part of the disguise. Perhaps I shouldn't have taken it off so soon, but I felt foolish enough in the coat of several colors without wearing that nose one moment longer than I had to.

I kept a careful eye out the rear window, but as far as I could tell no one was following us or taking an undue interest in our passage.

After several turns designed to force anyone following us to come into view, the jarvey took a fairly straight course to Regent's Park Road, turned off on a side street, and pulled to a stop in the middle of a block of flats. He hopped down from his perch and opened the carriage door for me. "That door there," he said, indicating a brown door much like all the other brown doors along the street. "You're expected."

It crossed my mind that this might be a trap. There are people in London who would rather see me dead than steal a million pounds, and one of them might have been inside that door instead of the rotund Mr. Holmes. But I have an instinct for such things, and this was both too elaborate and too commonplace to be anything other than what it seemed. So I pulled up the collar of my borrowed coat against the chill wind, crossed the walk, and pulled the bellpull at the indicated doorway.

No more than three seconds later the door opened, and a short woman of immense girth dressed as a maid gestured me in. Whether she was actually a maid, or some employee of the Foreign Service in masquerade, I cannot say. "This way, Professor Moriarty, sir," she said. "You're expected."

She showed me into a room that might have been the waiting room in some doctor's surgery, or for that matter the outer office of the booking agent for a music hall. There was a wide, well-worn black leather couch, several large and sturdy chairs, a heavy table of some dark wood, ill lit by three wall sconces with the gas turned low and a window with heavy, light green muslin curtains, which were drawn. A deep throbbing sound came faintly into the room; I could discern neither the location nor the function of its agent. Some sort of machinery? On the right-hand wall, leading to the back of the house, a pair of double doors were drawn closed. "Please wait," she said. "*He* will be with you shortly." The timbre of her voice changed when she said "*He*," the added resonance giving the word importance, as though I were awaiting Aristotle or Charles Darwin himself. "Please don't open the shades," she added as she left the room.

I turned the gaslight up in one of the wall sconces and settled into a chair beneath it, taking from my pocket the journal I had brought with me, *Das Astrophysische Journal der Universität Erlangen*, and immersing myself in its pages. The Austrians Joffe and Shostak have advanced the theory that the nebulosities observed through the larger telescopes are not some sort of interstellar gas, but actually vast clouds of stars much like our own Milky Way galaxy, seen at tremendous distances. If so—but I digress.

After a while I heard the door open and close, and I looked up to find Sherlock Holmes standing in the doorway. "So!" he growled, looking down his thin, crooked nose at me. "It was one of your tricks after all!" He thrust his walking stick in front of him like a child playing at dueling. "I warn you that I am prepared for any eventuality."

"How nice for you," I said, folding my journal and putting it back into my pocket.

"Mr. Holmes," said the broad maid from behind him. "Please be seated. Your brother will be down directly."

Holmes stalked over to a chair on the far side of the room and dropped lightly into it. "We'll see," he said, never taking his eyes off me. He flexed his walking stick, describing a series of shapes in the air before him, then laid it across his knees.

The door opened again, and the large shape of Mycroft Holmes loomed into the room. "Sherlock," he said, "Professor Moriarty. Good of you to come. Join me in the next room, where we can talk."

"You invited *him?*" asked Sherlock, pointing a wavering walking stick in my direction. "What were you thinking?"

"All in good time," said Mycroft. "Follow me." He stomped through the waiting room and pulled open the double doors. The chamber thus revealed had once been the dining room of the house, but was now a conference room, with an oversized highly polished mahogany table in the center, surrounded by heavy chairs of the same dark wood, upholstered in green leather. Around the periphery stood a row of filing cabinets, and a pair of small writing desks. A large chart cabinet stood against the far wall. The other walls were obscured by pinned-up maps, charts, graphs, diagrams, and documents of all sorts and sizes, and one framed oil painting of a fox hunt, which was covered with a dark patina of grime and neglect. The windows had heavy curtains over them, which were drawn closed. The room was brightly lit by three fixtures which depended from the ceiling. I observed them to be electrical lamps with great metallic filaments in evacuated bulbs. This explained the humming noise I had heard: this house had its own electrical generating plant.

Three men were waiting in the room as we entered: two seated at the table looking stern, and the third pacing about the room with his hands linked behind his back. One of the seated men, a slender, impeccably dressed, greying man with muttonchop whiskers, I recognized instantly as Lord Easthope, who holds the post of foreign minister in Her Majesty's present Tory government.

"Come, sit down," said Mycroft Holmes. "Here they are, gentlemen," he added, addressing the three men in the room. "My brother, Sherlock, and Professor James Moriarty."

The pacing man paused. "Have they agreed?" he asked.

"No, your lordship. I have not as yet explained the situation to them."

The third man peered at us over the top of his tortoiseshell glasses. "So these are the miracle men," he said.

"Come now, sir," Mycroft Holmes protested. "I never claimed that they were miracle men."

"They'd better be," the man said.

I took a seat on the right-hand side of the table. Holmes crossed over to the left side and sat where he could keep me in sight while speaking with our hosts.

Mycroft laced his hands behind his back and leaned forward. "Gentlemen," he said, addressing Holmes and me, "may I present Their Lordships, Lord Easthope and Lord Famm." (That's the way the name is pronounced. I later learned that His Lordship was Evan Fotheringham, Earl of Stomshire.) "And His Excellency, Baron van Durm."

Lord Fotheringham, the gentleman who was pacing the floor, was a tall man with an aristocratic nose and thinning hair. Baron van Durm was a great bear of a man, with heavy, black muttonchop whiskers and glowering dark eyes. He was impeccably dressed in a pearl grey morning suit, with a diamond stickpin the size of a robin's egg holding down his white silk cravat.

"I see you have recognized Lord Easthope," Mycroft said to Holmes and me, reading more from a slight widening of our eyes than most people could from the twenty-eight pages of their evening newspaper. "Lord Fotheringham is chairman of the Royal Committee for the Defense of the Realm, and Baron van Durm is general manager of the Amsterdam branch of the House of van Durm."

Although the name is not generally recognized outside of government or financial circles, the House of van Durm is one of the richest, most powerful, and most successful private banking houses in the world. With branches in every place you would imagine, and many that would not occur to you, the van Durms have supported governments in need and brought about the ruin of governments whose policies offended them.

Van Durm nodded his massive head slightly in our direction. Lord Fotheringham paused in his pacing long enough to glower at Sherlock Holmes, Lord Easthope growled a soft monosyllabic growl.

"They know who you are," Mycroft told us, "and we, collectively, have something to, ah, discuss with you of the utmost importance, delicacy, and secrecy. Before we continue, I must have your word that nothing we say here will be repeated outside this room."

I raised an eyebrow. Sherlock looked astonished. "You have my word," I said.

"You would trust that—" Holmes began, pointing a quavering finger at me. Then he paused as Mycroft glared at him, dropped the finger, and sighed deeply. "Oh, very well," he said. "You have my word also."

Mycroft sat down. Lord Fotheringham stopped pacing and stood facing us, arms behind his back. "Here is the situation, gentlemen," said his lordship. "The enemies of Britain are hatching a devilish plot, and there is danger for the safety of this realm—perhaps of the entire world—lurking in every corner of Europe. Plainly put, there is a shadow growing over the British Empire."

"What is this devilish plot?" I asked.

Lord Easthope focused his mild blue eyes on me. "There's the heart of the problem," he said, nodding approvingly, as though I'd said something clever. "We don't know."

"A shadow?" Holmes's eyes narrowed. The three noblemen might have thought that he was concentrating his attention on this growing shadow, but I—and probably his brother—knew that he was considering whether Lord Fotheringham should be forcibly restrained. I had some such notion myself.

Holmes leaned back in his chair, his fingers laced over his waistcoat, his eyes almost closed. "You don't know?"

"Perhaps I should explain," said Baron van Durm. "There are signs, subtle but distinct signs, all over Europe, that something of great import is going to happen soon, that it concerns Great Britain, and that it portends no good. Taken by themselves, each of these incidents—these signs—could be a random happening, meaning nothing, but when one looks at them all together a pattern emerges."

"We have a saying at the War Ministry," Lord Fotheringham interjected. "'Once is happenstance, twice is coincidence, three times is enemy action.'"

Sherlock Holmes leaned forward and laced his hands together beneath his chin, his elbows resting on the table. "What sort of incidents?" he asked.

Lord Easthope began: "In various centers of Socialist and Anarchist thought throughout Europe—Paris, Vienna, Prague—speakers have begun warning against British imperialism and the 'secret plans' Britain has for world domination."

"I see," I said. "'The Secret Protocols of the Elders of Downing Street,' eh? There is, I grant you, a school of thought that believes that the English are one of the Lost Tribes of Israel."

"By itself it would be amusing, and hardly sinister," Easthope said. "But if you consider these speakers to be part of a plan to pave the way for—something—then they deserve to be looked at more seriously."

"Even so," Lord Fotheringham agreed. "Most of those who listen to this nonsense now, even among the émigré Socialist communities, must realize it to be nonsense, considering that Britain is one of the few countries that allows these groups freedom of movement and association without having to worry about police spies in their midst."

"Unless, of course, they're Irish," Mycroft Holmes said bluntly, shifting his bulk forward in his chair. This was met with a complete silence, and he didn't pursue the thought.

"What else?" asked Holmes.

"Newspapers," said Lord Fotheringham.

"The editorial pages of newspapers in various European countries—France, Germany, Austria, Switzerland—are printing the occasional scurrilous editorial accusing Her Majesty's government of a secret plan of aggression against the Continental powers," Mycroft explained.

"How odd," said Sherlock.

"We know of three different men in the governments of three different countries who are preparing anti-British legislation of one sort or another," said Lord Easthope. "Preparing, you will notice, but not submitting. They are waiting for the proper moment. We must assume that they believe that there soon will *be* a proper moment. If we know of three, presumably there are more."

"Do those three men know each other?" Holmes asked.

"Apparently not," his brother told him.

"Then we must also assume there is, somewhere, a hand pulling the strings."

"We do so assume," Mycroft said.

"Is that all?" Holmes asked.

"Is that not enough?" asked Easthope.

"Actually," said Baron van Durm, "there is one other thing. The House of van Durm, as you might surmise, has agents strategically placed all over Europe. Most of these conduct the bank's business. Some merely collect information. The success of an international bank rises or falls on the quality of the information it gathers. One of these agents is highly placed in the government of, let us say, a foreign power that has not always been on the best of terms with Great Britain. In the course of his work for us he came across a document that might shed some light on these happenings. It was not addressed to him."

"Ah!" said Sherlock Holmes.

"This is a copy of it, translated into English," van Durm said, removing a sheet of paper from a folder on the table before him and passing it over to Holmes, who read it carefully twice before passing it on to me:

Thirteen—
Your concise and with information filled report was most welcome. We must continue and increase our efforts to discredit England and all things English. It is simpler to chop down a tree if you have poisoned the roots.

Sixteen has failed us. Worse, he may have betrayed us. He was seen entering the embassy on Prinz Rupert Strasse. He stayed for an hour. He will not do so again.

The day nears. The events unfold. Work and diligence carry great rewards. The Florida is now ours. Inform the brothers that the direction is up and the peak is in view. If we succeed, we will succeed together. Those who fail will fail alone. It is the time for cleverness and impudence. Stories must be told. Incidents must be arranged.

The lion sleeps peacefully. Holmes and Moriarty are watched, as are Lamphier in Paris and Ettin in Berlin. They are not alert.

Proceed to Lindau on the 16th. The company is assembling. The first place. Three white clothespins. Burn this.

One

"What do you make of that?" asked van Durm.

"It was in German originally?" I asked.

"That is so," van Durm said.

"The embassy on Prinz Rupert Strasse?"

"The British embassy in Vienna is on Prinz Rupert Strasse," Lord Easthope said.

Holmes leaned back in his chair. "Lindau is a German place name?" he asked.

"A town on the Bodensee, on the German side of the Austrian border," Easthope told him.

"Quite a distance from Florida," Holmes remarked.

"That is so," Easthope agreed. "We have not been able to come up with a plausible explanation for that line. Not even, if it comes to that, a fanciful one."

"The whole missive has something of the fanciful about it," I said. "Addressed to 'Thirteen' from 'One.' There's something of the Lewis Carroll about it."

"Why was it not burned?" asked Holmes.

"It was," van Durm told him. "At least the attempt was made. The original was found in a fireplace grate, charred and singed. But it had been folded over several times, and so it was merely the edges that suffered the damage, and the whole message was retrieved intact."

I smiled, reflecting on the image of a high government official crawling about in a fireplace.

Holmes glared at me. "I detect your hand in this," he said.

I was not amused, and I'm afraid that I allowed an ill-considered expletive to pass my lips.

"Quite so," said Lord Easthope.

"His name is on the document," Holmes insisted. "Can't you see—"

"Enough!" cried Mycroft in a deceptively quiet bellow. "Your name is also on the document. Take my word for it, Sherlock, that whatever else Moriarty may be involved in, he has no hand in these events."

Sherlock Holmes gave his brother a long glare, then assumed an attitude of sulky acquiescence from the depths of his chair.

Baron van Durm looked from one to the other of us. "I thought you said they could work together," he said to Mycroft.

"They can," Mycroft assured him. "They just need a little time to get over their mutual spitting match."

I resented that. I had done nothing to encourage Holmes in his asinine accusations. But I held my tongue.

"When we saw the references to you, we naturally checked," Lord Easthope said, "and ascertained that you were, indeed, being watched. Had you noticed?"

"I assumed that it was at the behest of the younger Mr. Holmes," I said.

"I thought Moriarty was up to more of his usual devilry," snarled Holmes.

"Well there, you see, you were both mistaken," said Easthope. He turned to Mycroft. "Are you sure these are the men we want?"

"Yes," said Mycroft.

"What of Lamphier and Ettin?" Holmes asked.

"Ah!" said van Durm.

"Would that be Alphonse Lamphier the noted French criminologist?" I asked.

"Yes, it would," van Durm affirmed.

"How can you be sure that he is the Lamphier referred to?" Holmes asked.

"Because he was murdered yesterday."

"Coincidence," said Holmes.

"He was found in the ruins of a burned-out cottage outside the village of Lindau," said Lord Easthope. "Pure accident that he was found. He—his body—could have stayed there for months. He was almost naked and had his hands tied together. He was already dead when the place was set on fire, but a section of interior wall collapsed and preserved his body from the fire."

Holmes opened his mouth to say something, but Lord Easthope continued, "He had scratched some words on his inner thigh with a pin before he died. *Ils se réunissent.* Means 'they meet,' or 'they assemble,' or 'they gather,' depending."

"I stand corrected," said Holmes. "One can stretch coincidence too far. Does anyone know precisely what he was working on when he was killed?"

"Our agents in Paris are attempting to ascertain that even now," van Durm said.

"What would you have us do?" I asked.

"As they—whoever 'they' are—are watching you," said Lord Easthope, "we infer that they have reason to fear you. Perhaps because of your known abilities, each of you in his own sphere, or perhaps because you possess some information that you might not even know you have, that would be of value."

Holmes and I pondered this for a minute. Just as I was about to disagree with this assessment, Holmes anticipated me. "I think not," he said.

Baron van Durm looked startled. "Why not?" he asked.

"In Welsh coal mines the miners take a canary down into the pits with them," Holmes said. "It is to give them early notice of bad air, as the canaries are more susceptible than the miners. We are these people's canaries."

"I fail to see the analogy," said Lord Easthope.

"Our, ah, opponents watch us because they believe that, if Her Majesty's government were to become aware of their machinations, it would send one of us to investigate. Either myself, for obvious reasons, or Professor Moriarty"—he paused for a second to glare at me, and then went on—"because of his known associations with the underworld of Europe. So much is undoubtedly so. But they no more fear us than the coal miner fears the canary." Holmes punctuated his talk with restless motions of his slender hands. "If they believe we have knowledge of their doings, they will immediately and ruthlessly eliminate us."

"How do you know this if you know nothing about them?" Lord Fotheringham asked.

"Alphonse Lamphier told me," Holmes replied.

"What? How could—oh, I see."

"Perhaps I should have said attempt to eliminate us," Holmes continued, "since others have tried, and none has yet succeeded."

I was amused at Holmes's inclusion of me in his statement, as he had so often accused me of trying to eliminate him. But I said nothing.

"So what are we to do?" asked Baron van Durm.

"Out of the myriad of possibilities," said Mycroft, "there are three that appeal more than the others."

"And they are?" asked Lord Easthope.

"One is to keep my brother and Professor Moriarty visibly at home, to reassure our antagonists, while using others to subvert their plans."

"Who?" asked Lord Easthope.

"What others?" echoed Baron van Durm.

"I have no idea," confessed Mycroft Holmes. "The second possibility is to spirit Holmes and Moriarty away without letting the watchers know."

"How?" asked Lord Fotheringham.

"Perhaps with wax dummies of the two placed in their windows and moved about to achieve a verisimilitude of life."

"Ridiculous!" said Baron van Durm.

"The third possibility," said Mycroft, "is for them to leave openly, but in such a fashion as to cause those watching them to conclude that their interests are elsewhere."

Sherlock looked at his brother. "Brilliant, Mycroft," he said. "And just how are we to achieve that?"

The possibilities of the situation appealed to me. "I'd suggest, Holmes, that you chase me to the ends of the earth, as you've so often threatened to do," I said, smiling.

Holmes glared at me.

"Perhaps," Mycroft said, "with a little modification, that is indeed what we should do." He rubbed his right forefinger along the side of his nose. "If the two of you were to kill each other, nobody who knew you would be surprised. And I think it safe to assume that the watchers would cease watching in that event."

"Kill each other?" Holmes repeated incredulously.

"How do you propose they do that?" asked Baron van Durm.

Mycroft shrugged. "Somehow and someplace where there can be no suggestion that it was a sham," he said. "Plunging over the side of a tall building together would suffice. Perhaps the Eiffel Tower."

Now this was being carried a bit too far. "And how do you propose we survive the fall?" I asked.

Mycroft sighed. "I suppose it should be somewhere less public," he said, "so you don't really have to go over the edge." He sounded honestly regretful. Which of us was he picturing leaping off a precipice, I wondered.

Baron van Durm snapped his fingers. "I know just the place!" he said. "Near the town of Meiringen in Switzerland there is a great waterfall on the Reichenbach River."

"Reichenbach?" asked Holmes.

"A tributary of the Aar," van Durm explained. "This spot has but one path leading out to it, and if you were said to have fallen, nobody would expect to find your remains. The river at that point is rapid, deep, and, er, punishing."

"Why so far from home?" asked Lord Fotheringham.

"It has several advantages," said Holmes thoughtfully. "Our trip there will give our opponents time to see that we are chasing each other rather than hunting for them, and it will leave us in Switzerland, and a lot closer to Germany and the village of Lindau."

"Even so," Mycroft agreed.

"Won't that make them suspicious, your ending up in Switzerland?" Lord Easthope asked.

I ventured a reply. "They know nothing of our interest in Lindau, and if they believe us dead, it won't matter anyway."

"That is so," Easthope agreed.

"So," said Lord Fotheringham. "Do you two gentlemen believe that you can put your personal enmity aside long enough to serve your queen?"

I was about to answer with a polite guffaw, or perhaps even a mild snicker, when to my surprise Holmes stood up and drew his shoulders back. "For queen and country," he said.

All eyes were at that instant on me. I shrugged. "I have nothing on for the next few weeks," I said.

With a slight change in the original plan, the race across Europe was to be carried out with a verisimilitude designed to convince Watson, as well as any onlookers, that it was genuine. The change was that I was to pursue Holmes rather than the other way around. Mycroft decided that would be more convincing.

Two days later the great chase began. Holmes called upon Watson to tell him that I was trying to kill him (Holmes), and he must flee to Europe. The tale was that my "gang" was about to be rounded up by the police, but until that was accomplished Holmes was in great danger. Watson agreed to accompany him in his flight, and the next day joined Holmes in "the second first-class carriage from the front" of the Continental Express at Victoria Station. Holmes was disguised as a humble elderly prelate, but Watson wore no disguise, and so the watchers had no trouble watching. They saw Holmes and Watson flee in the Express, and watched me engage a Special Train to pursue them. Holmes and Watson appeared to elude me by abandoning their luggage and getting off the Express at Canterbury. They went cross-country to Newhaven, thence by the paddle steamer *Brittany* to Dieppe.

Shaking my fist and murmuring "Curses, foiled again!," I went straight through to Paris and lingered about their luggage for several days, apparently waiting for them to come and claim it. When they didn't appear I put the word out among the European underworld that I would pay a substantial reward for information as to the whereabouts of two Englishmen who looked thus-and-so. Eventually word came to me, and I spent several days pursuing them about Europe, followed in turn by several gentlemen who did their best to stay just out of sight.

As planned, I caught up with Holmes and Watson in the village of Meiringen in Switzerland on May 6. They had gone after lunch to look at the falls, about a two-hour hike away from the inn, and I sent a boy with a note to Watson designed to lure him back to the inn to care for a mythical sick woman. Holmes was then to write a letter to Watson, put it and some article of clothing on the ledge, and disappear; leaving it to be believed that he and I had gone over the edge in a mighty battle of good and evil. Hmmph! I would then fade away from the scene and meet Holmes in Lindau in four days.

But it was not to be. Even as the lad scurried off to carry the note to Watson, I was forced to change the plan. I followed and concealed myself behind a boulder when I saw the lad and Watson hurrying back. Then I rushed forward to the ledge, where Holmes had already put the note in his silver cigarette box, placed it by his alpenstock at the side of a rock, and was enjoying one last pipe of that foul tobacco he smokes before disappearing.

"Aha!" he said, upon spying me approach. "I knew it was too good to be true! So it's to be an all-out fight to the death, is it, Professor?" He sprang to his feet and grabbed for the alpenstock.

"Don't speak nonsense, Holmes," I growled. "One of the men following us reached the inn just as I sent the lad off with the note. If I didn't come after you while he watched, he couldn't possibly be convinced that we both plunged off the cliff."

"So!" said Holmes. "It seems we must fight after all, or at least leave behind convincing marks of a scuffle and perhaps a few bits of tattered clothing."

"And then we must find some way to leave this ledge without going back the way we came. Two sets of footprints returning on the path would give the game away." I walked over to the edge and looked down. The way was sheer, and steep, and in some places the rock face appeared to be undercut, so that it would be impossible to climb down without pitons and ropes and a variety of other mountaineering gear that we had neglected to bring. "We can't go down," I said.

"Well then," Holmes said briskly, "we must go up."

I examined the cliff face behind us. "Possible," I concluded. "Difficult, but possible."

"But first we must scuff up the ground by the cliff edge in a convincing manner," said Holmes.

"Let us run through the third and fourth Baritsu katas," I suggested. I took off my inverness and put it and my owl-headed walking stick and hat on a nearby outcropping and assumed the first, or "waiting crab" Baritsu defensive position.

Holmes responded by taking off his hat and coat. "We must be careful not to kill each other by accident," he said. "I should hate to kill you by accident."

"And I, you," I assured him.

We ran through the martial exercises for about a quarter hour, getting ourselves and the ground quite scuffed up in the process. "Enough!" Holmes said finally.

"I agree," I said. "One last touch." I took my stick from the rock and gave the handle a quarter turn, releasing the eight-inch blade concealed within. "I hate to do this," I said, "but in the interest of verisimilitude . . ."

Holmes eyes me warily while I rolled up my right sleeve and carefully stabbed my arm with the sharp point of the blade. I smeared the last few inches of the blade liberally with my own blood, then threw the weapon aside as though it had been lost in combat. The shaft of the stick I left by the rock. "For queen and country," I said, wrapping my handkerchief around the cut and rolling down my sleeve.

"Left-handed, are you?" Holmes asked. "I should have guessed."

We retrieved the rest of our clothing and began climbing the almost-sheer face of the cliff above us. It was slow, tedious work, made more dangerous by the fact that it was already late afternoon, and the long shadows cast across the chasm made it difficult to see clearly.

After about twenty minutes, Holmes, who, despite a constant stream of muttered complaints, had been clambering up the cliff side with great energy, and was about two body lengths above me, cried out, "Aha! Here is a shelf big enough to hold us! Perhaps we should rest here."

I scrambled up beside him, and the two of us lay on the moss-covered rock shelf with just our heads showing over the edge as we peered down into the gathering dusk below. We were, I estimate, some two hundred feet above the ledge we had left.

I'm not sure how long we lay there, as it was too dark to read the face of my pocket watch and we dare not strike a light. But after some time we could make out somebody coming onto the ledge we had recently deserted. He was carrying a small lantern, in the light of which he proceeded to make a minute study of the earth, the surrounding rocks, and the cliff face both above and below the ledge, although he didn't cast the beam high enough to see us where we were peering down at him. After a minute he found the cigarette box that Holmes had left for Watson, and he carefully opened it, read the note inside, then closed it again and replaced it on the rock. Another minute's searching brought him to the bloodied blade, which he peered at closely, tested with his finger, then secured under his coat. Then he slowly went back the way he had come, closely examining the footprints on the path as he went.

About ten minutes later we heard voices below, and four men approached the cliff edge: two Swiss men from the inn in their green lederhosen, carrying large bright lanterns; Dr. Watson, and the man who had recently left. "No," the man was saying as they came into view, "I saw no one on the trail. I do not know what happened to your friend."

Watson wandered about the cliff, looking here and there without really knowing what he was looking at, or for. "Holmes!" he cried. "My God, Holmes, where are you?"

Holmes stirred next to me and seemed about to say something, but he refrained.

One of the Swiss men spotted the silver cigarette box. "Is that a belonging of your friend?" he asked, pointing to it.

Watson rushed over to it. "Yes!" he said. "That is Holmes's." He turned it over in his hand. "But why—" Opening the box, he pulled out the letter, tearing it halfway down the middle in the process. "Moriarty!" he said, reading the letter by the light of one of the lanterns. "Then it has happened. It is as I feared." He folded the letter, put it in his pocket, and went over to the edge of the cliff to peer down into the inky blackness below. "Good-bye, my friend," he said, his voice choked with emotion. "The best and finest man I have ever known." Then he turned to the others. "Come," he said, "we can do no good here."

As we were unable to safely climb down in the dark, Holmes and I spent the night on that rock shelf, our greatcoats offering what protection they could from the chill wind. Shortly before dawn a cold rain fell, and we were drenched and chilled before first light, when we were finally able to make our way back down to the ledge below. For the next two days we traveled overland on foot, with an occasional ride on the oxcart of a friendly farmer, until we reached Wurstheim, where we settled into the Wurstheimer Hof, bathed, slept for twelve hours, bought suitable clothing, and altered our appearances. The next morning I went down to a stationer's and procured some drafting supplies, then spent some hours in my room creating a few useful documents. Leaving Wurstheim late that afternoon were a French officer of artillery in mufti—Holmes speaks fluent French, having spent several years in Montpellier during his youth, and makes quite a dashing officer of artillery—and a German Senior Inspector of Canals and Waterworks. I have no idea whether there actually is such a position, but the papers I drew up looked quite authentic. I also crafted one more document that I thought might be useful.

"The world lost a master forger when you decided to become a, ah, professor of mathematics, Moriarty," Holmes told me, looking over the papers I had produced with a critical eye. "The watermarks would give the game away, if anyone is astute enough to examine them, but you've done a very creditable job."

"Praise from the master is praise indeed," I told him.

He looked at me suspiciously, but then folded up the *laisser-passer* I had created for him and thrust it into an inner pocket.

In the early afternoon of the fourteenth of May we arrived in Kreuzingen, a small town on the east shore of Lake Constance, or as the Germans call it, Bodensee—a great swelling in the river Rhine some forty miles long and, in places, ten miles wide. It is where Switzerland, Germany, and Austria meet, or would meet if there weren't a lake in the way. We boarded the paddle steamer *Koenig Friedrich* for the four-hour trip across to Lindau, a quiet resort town on the German side of the lake. Holmes, as *Le Commandant* Martin Vernet of the *Corps d'Artillerie*, had his hair parted in the middle and severely brushed down on both sides and sported a quite creditable brush mustache. He wore a severely tailored grey suit with the miniature ribbon of a *Chevalier* of the *Légion d'Honneur* in his buttonhole, and cultivated a slight limp. He would effect a complete lack of knowledge of either German or English, and thus stood a good chance of overhearing things he was not meant to overhear.

I became Herr Inspektor Otto Stuhl of the *Büro des Direktors der Kanäle und des Wasserversorgung*, and thus could be expected to take an interest in water and all things wet, which gave me a plausible reason to poke around in places where I had no business poking around.

We amused ourselves on the trip across by discerning the professions of our fellow passengers. The Swiss, like the Germans, make the task simpler by dressing strictly according to their class, status, and occupation. We disagreed over a pair of gentlemen with ruffled shirts and double rows of brass buttons going down their overly decorated lederhosen. I guessed them to be buskers of some sort, while Holmes thought them hotel tour guides. On overhearing their conversation, we determined them to be journeymen plumbers. Holmes glared at me as though it were somehow my fault.

We took rooms at the Hotel Athènes, carefully not knowing each other as we checked in. There would have been some advantage in taking rooms in separate hotels, but the difficulty in sharing information without being noticed would have been too great. Holmes, or rather Vernet, was to go around to the inns and spas in the area and discover which ones had public rooms where a group might gather, or more probably large private rooms for rent, and listen to the conversation of the guests. Stuhl would speak to various town officials about the very important subject of water, and partake of such gossip as they might offer. Town officials love to pass on titbits of important-sounding gossip to passing government bureaucrats; it reaffirms their authority.

"Three white clothespins," Holmes mused, staring out the window at one of the great snowcapped mountains that glowered down at the town. It was the morning of the fifteenth, and we had just come up from our separate breakfasts and were meeting in my room on the third floor of the hotel. Holmes's room was down the hall and across the way, and had a view across the town square to the police station and the lake beyond. My window overlooked only mountains.

"The last line of that letter," I remembered. " 'Proceed to Lindau on the sixteenth. The company is assembling. The first place. Three white clothespins. Burn this.' Very terse."

"The first place implies there was a second place," Holmes mused. "So it would seem they have met here before."

"More than that," I offered, "one of their leaders probably lives around here."

"Perhaps," Holmes agreed. "Consider: if the company is 'assembling,' then they are gathering in order to do whatever it is they are preparing to do. If they were merely coming together to discuss matters, or to receive instructions, then they would be meeting, not assembling. The study of language and its connotations holds great value for the serious investigator."

"Even so," I agreed.

Holmes—Vernet—went out that day and passed from inn to café to public house, and drank cassis and coffee and ate pastries. The man has an amazing ability to eat and eat without gaining weight and, conversely, to go without food for days at a time when on the track of a miscreant. I spent the morning studying a map of the town, to get a sense of where things were. After lunch I went to the town hall to see Herr Bürgermeister Pindl, a large man in many directions with a massive mustache and a smile that spread broadly across his face and radiated good cheer. We sat in his office, he poured us each a small glass of schnapps, and we discussed matters of water supply and public health. He seemed quite pleased that the great bureaucracy in far-off Berlin would even know of the existence of little Lindau.

If you would impress a man with your insight, tell him that you sense that he is worried about a relationship, about his finances, or about his health. Better, tell him that he fears—justly—that he is often misunderstood and that his work is not appreciated. If you would impress a civic official, tell him that you share his concern about the town's water supply, its sewage, or its garbage. Within the first ten minutes of our conversation, Herr Pindl and I had been friends for years. But the smiling giant was not as simple as he appeared. "Tell me," he said, holding his schnapps daintily in two chubby fingers, "what does the ministry really want to know? You're not just here to see if the water is coming out of the faucets."

I beamed at him as a professor beams at his best pupil. "You're very astute," I said, leaning toward him. "And you look like a man who can keep a secret . . ."

"Oh, I am," he assured me, his nose twitching like that of a stout bird dog on the scent of a blutwurst sausage.

Extracting my very special document from an inner pocket, I unfolded it before him. Crowded with official-looking seals and imperial eagles, the paper identified Otto Stuhl as an officer in the *Nachrichtendienst*, the Kaiser's Military Intelligence Service, holding the rank of *Oberst*, and further declared:

> *His Imperial Most-High Excellency Kaiser Wilhelm II requests and demands all loyal German subjects to give the bearer of this document whatever assistance he requires at all times.*

"Ah!" said Bürgermeister Pindl, nodding ponderously. "I have heard of such things."

Thank God, I thought, *that you've never seen one before, since I have no idea what a real one looks like.*

"Well, Herr Oberst Stuhl," Pindl asked, "what can the Bürgermeister of Lindau do for you?"

I took a sip of schnapps. It had a strong, peppery taste. "Word has come," I said, "of certain unusual activities in this area. I have been sent to investigate."

"Unusual?"

I nodded. "Out of the ordinary."

A look of panic came into his eyes. "I assure you, Herr Oberst, that we have done nothing—"

"No, no," I assured him, wondering what illicit activity he and his *Kameraden* had been indulging in. Another time it might have been interesting to find out. "We of the *Nachrichtendienst*, care not what petty offenses local officials may be indulging in—short of treason." I chuckled. "You don't indulge in treason, do you?"

We shared a good laugh together about that, although the worried look did not completely vanish from his eyes.

"No, it's strangers I'm concerned with," I told him. "Outsiders."

"Outsiders."

"Just so. We have received reports from our agents that suspicious activities have been taking place in this area."

"What sort of suspicious activities?"

"Ah!" I waggled my finger at him. "That's what I was hoping *you* would tell *me*."

He got up and went over to the window. "It must be those *verdammter Engländers*," he said, slapping his large hand against his even larger thigh.

"English?" I asked. "You are, perhaps, infested with Englishmen?"

"We have people coming from all the world," he told me. "We are a resort. We are on the Bodensee. But recently a group of *Engländers* has attracted our attention."

"How?"

"By trying not to attract our attention, if you see what I mean. First, they come separately and pretend not to know each other. But they are seen talking—whispering—together by the twos and threes."

"Ah!" I said. "Whispering. That is most interesting."

"And then they all go boating," the Bürgermeister said.

"Boating?"

"Yes. Separately, by ones and twos, they rent or borrow boats and row, paddle, or sail out onto the Bodensee. Sometimes they come home in the evening, sometimes they don't."

"Where do they go?"

"I don't know," Pindl said. "We haven't followed them."

"How long has this been going on?" I asked.

"Off and on, for about a year," he said. "They go away for a while, then they come back. Which is another reason we noticed them. The same collection of *Engländer* who don't know each other appearing at the same time every few months. Really!"

"How many of them would you say there were?" I asked.

"Perhaps two dozen," he said. "Perhaps more."

I thought this over for a minute. "Is there anything else you can tell me about them?" I asked.

He shrugged. "All ages, all sizes," he said. "All men, as far as I know. Some of them speak perfect German. Some, I've been told, speak fluent French. They all speak English."

I stood up. "Thank you," I said. "The *Nachrichtendienst* will not forget the help you have been."

I had dinner at a small waterfront restaurant, and watched the shadows grow across the lake as the sun sank behind the mountains. After dinner I returned to my room, where Holmes joined me about an hour later.

I related my experiences of the day, and he nodded thoughtfully and went "hmmm" twice. *"Engländer,"* he said. "Interesting. I think the game's afoot."

"What game are we stalking, Holmes?" I asked.

"I have seen some of your '*Engländer*,'" he told me. "In the Ludwig Hof shortly after lunch. I was enjoying a cassis and being expansively French when three men walked in and sat near me. They tried to engage me in conversation in English and German and, when I effected not to understand, bad French. We exchanged a few pleasantries, and they tipped their hats and began speaking among themselves in English, which, incidentally, is not as good as their German."

"Ah!" I said.

"They insulted me several times in English, commenting with little imagination on my appearance and my probable parentage, and when I didn't respond they became convinced that I couldn't understand and thereafter spoke freely."

"Saying?"

"Well, one thing that will interest you, is that Holmes and Moriarty are dead."

"Really? And how did they die?"

"There was this great fight at Reichenbach Falls, and they both plunged in. Their correspondent saw it happen himself. There could be no mistake."

I stared out the window at the snow covering a distant mountain peak. "Oscar Wilde says that people who are said to be dead often turn up later in San Francisco," I said. "I've never been to San Francisco."

Holmes stared intently down his long nose at me. "I don't know what to make of you," he said. "I never have."

"So, now that we're officially dead," I said, "what do we do next?"

"When the faux Englishmen left the room," Holmes continued, "I followed them. They went to the waterfront."

"I trust you were not seen," I said.

Holmes fastened a withering glare on the painting of an alpine meadow on the far wall. "When I don't wish to be seen," he stated, "I am not seen."

"Silly of me," I said. "What did you observe?"

"They entered a large warehouse next to a pier jutting into the lake. Attached to a short line by the warehouse door—"

"Three clothespins," I ventured.

"Three *white* clothespins," he corrected.

"Well," I said. "Now we know where."

"Not quite," Holmes said. "I observed several more people entering the warehouse over the next hour. And then a door opened on the water side of the building, and the men boarded a steam launch named the *Isolde*, which was tied up to the pier next to the building. It then chuffed out onto the lake and away. I investigated and discovered that there was only one man, an old caretaker, left in the warehouse."

"Ah!" I said.

"The boat returned about an hour ago. Some men got off. A few of them were the same men who had boarded earlier, but not all." He tapped his long, thin forefinger on the table. "They're doing something out there somewhere on the lake. But it's a big lake."

"That presents an interesting problem," I said. "How do we follow them over open water?"

Holmes stared out the window. "A two-pipe problem," he said, pulling out his ancient brier and stuffing it with tobacco. "Perhaps three."

Having smelled the foul mixture he prefers to smoke, I excused myself and went downstairs, where I indulged in a *kaffee mit schlag*. *Mit*, as it happens, extra *schlag*. About an hour later Holmes came downstairs, gave a slight nod in my direction, and went out the front door. After a suitable time I followed. Night had fallen, and the streetlights were sparse and dim. A chill wind was blowing in off the lake.

Holmes was standing in the shadow of an old stable a block away. I smelled the foul tobacco odor emanating from his clothing before I actually saw him.

"Commandant Vernet," I said.

"Herr Stuhl."

"Have your three pipes shown the way?"

"If we had time, we could build a large observation balloon and watch them from high aloft," Holmes said. "But we have no time. I think one of us will have to stow away on that steam launch and see where she goes."

"If nominated, I shall not run," I told him firmly, "and if elected, I shall not serve."

"What's that?"

"The American General Sherman. I am taking his excellent advice."

Holmes looked at me with distaste. "With all your faults," he said, "I didn't picture you as a coward."

"And neither am I foolhardy," I told him. "There is little point in indulging in a foredoomed course of action when it will accomplish nothing and merely succeed in getting one killed. Remember Alphonse Lamphier."

Holmes stared glumly into the dark. "I have nothing better to offer," he said. "In large parts of the ocean ships leave a phosphorescent wake that lasts for some time, I understand, but not in lakes, however large."

"What an excellent idea!" I said.

"A phosphorescent wake?"

"A wake of some sort. The craft will go wherever it is to go, and we shall follow in its wake."

"How?"

"A moment," I said, staring into space. "Why not oil? Some light oil dyed red should do it."

"Brilliant!" said Holmes. "And who shall we get to sprinkle this oil on the water as the boat progresses?"

"We, my doubting Sherlock, shall construct a mechanism to do the task," I said.

And so we did. The next morning I procured a five-gallon drum of fish oil, which seemed appropriate, and took it down to a deserted jetty Holmes had observed yesterday in his wanderings. I then went back to the main street and returned with a pair of iron exercise dumbbells, purchased from a junk shop. Holmes joined me shortly after, bringing a coil of quarter-inch marine line and a small bottle of red dye; some sort of pastry dye I believe, which we added to the oil. It seemed to mix satisfactorily, so we busied ourselves affixing some handles on the drum with metal screws. The screw holes would leak slightly, but that didn't matter.

We changed into recently purchased bathing costumes and rented a two-man rowboat, wrapping our clothing and other items we might need in oilcloth and stowing them on the bottom of the small craft. After about twenty minutes rowing along the shore we came in sight of the pier in question. The steam launch *Isolde* was tied up alongside.

There appeared to be no one on watch in the launch, so we came up as quietly as possible to the opposite side of the pier and tied our boat to a convenient hook. Slipping into the chill water, we towed the drum of oil under the pier to the starboard side of the *Isolde*. We could hear the deep chugging of the steam engine as we approached the boat, which suggested that there would shortly be another journey.

I screwed two four-inch wood screws into the hull near the stern, and fastened one end of a twelve-foot length of marine line to them. The other end Holmes fastened to the oil drum. My calculations indicated that it would take the weight of both the iron dumbbells to keep the drum submerged, so the two of them were tied firmly onto the sides of the drum. All that remained was to put a screw into the cork plugging the drum's bunghole and attach it by a short line to the pier. That way as the steam launch left the pier, the cork would be pulled and the drum would begin leaking colored oil.

As we were completing this last task, we heard footsteps above us on the pier, and the voices of the pseudo-*Engländers* as they began boarding the launch. They all spoke English, those who spoke, and their accents were slight. Yet of all the myriad of homegrown accents that pepper the British Isles, allowing one man to despise another who grew up twenty miles to his north, these were none.

After about ten minutes the boarding was completed, the chugging of the steam engine grew louder and deeper, and the *Isolde* pulled away from the pier. There was a slight but satisfying *pop* as the cork was pulled from the oil drum, and it began its journey bobbing out of sight behind the steam launch, spilling red oil as it went.

"We'd better get out of the water," said Holmes, "I'm losing sensation in my hands and feet."

"Cold baths are much overrated," I agreed, shivering uncontrollably as I threw myself back into the rowboat. I held it steady for Holmes to climb aboard, then we were both occupied for some time in toweling ourselves off and putting our garments back on.

"Let's get going," Holmes said after a few minutes. "They're getting farther ahead by the moment, and besides the exercise of rowing will warm us up."

I took up one pair of oars, and Holmes the other, and we maneuvered our small craft out onto the lake. The sun was overhead, and a slight but clearly visible red stain was slowly widening as it led off in the direction of the departing steam launch, which was already distant enough for its image to be covered by my thumb with my arm extended.

We rowed energetically after the *Isolde*, cutting easily through the gentle swells left by her wake. If she was barely visible to us, surely our small craft was no more than a speck to any of her company who should chance to be peering back toward shore. Soon she was out of sight entirely, and we followed by keeping in sight the slight red smear visible under the bright sun.

It was perhaps half an hour later when the tenuous watery red trail brought us in sight of the steam launch. She was headed back toward us, pulling away from a large black barge which had a curious superstructure, and seemed to have been outfitted with some sort of engine at the rear. At any rate, the barge was moving slowly under its own power even as the *Isolde* pulled away. The deck of the *Isolde* was crowded with men and, as it seemed probable that there were even more men inside the cabin, it looked as though the crew of the black barge were going home for the night.

We altered our course slightly to make it appear that we were headed for the opposite shore, and tried to look like two middle-aged gentlemen who were passionate about rowing, perhaps recapturing their youth. As the *Isolde* approached us we waved in a friendly but disinterested manner, and two of the men on deck replied with similar salutations. Who, I wondered, was fooling whom? I hoped it was we, them, or our story might have quite a different ending than we had intended.

"What now?" Holmes asked me, when it was clear that the steam launch was not going to turn around and investigate us more closely.

"The black barge," I said.

"Of course," Holmes told me. "I repeat, what now?"

"As it's still under power, although making slight headway, there are still men aboard," I said. "So just pulling alongside and clambering on deck is probably not a wise option."

Holmes lifted his oars out of the water and turned to glare at me. "Astute observation," he said. "I repeat, what now?"

"We could swim over to it underwater if the water weren't so cold; if we could swim that far underwater. We could come alongside and flail about, claiming to be in distress, and see whether those aboard choose to rescue us."

"Or just shoot us and toss us overboard," Holmes commented.

"Yes, there's always that possibility," I agreed.

Holmes sighed deeply. "I guess there's nothing for it then," he said, shipping the oars and lying back in his seat to stare at the cloud-filled sky. "We float about here until dark and spend our time praying for it not to rain."

Which is what we did. Our prayers were almost answered, in that a light, but extremely cold drizzle fell for a while, but then went away to be replaced by a chill wind.

One thing I must say about Holmes is that, barring his periodic fixation on me as the fount of all that is evil, he is a good companion: dependable and steadfast in adversity, intelligent and quick-thinking in a fix; a loyal ally and, as I have had occasion to discover in the past, a formidable foe. I found myself thinking about Holmes and our past history as we waited. What Holmes thought about I cannot say.

Dark fell with admirable speed that evening. By ten past eight

I couldn't read my pocket watch without striking a match—the light well shielded from view, of course. There were no lights visible from the black barge either. If lamps were lit in the cabins, the windows and portholes must have been well shielded. We waited a while longer—how long I cannot say as I didn't want to strike another match—then, dipping our oars as silently as possible, headed in the direction of the barge. The moon was a slender crescent, the light was scant, and the barge proved as difficult to find as you might imagine a black barge on an almost-moonless night would do. For a while we could hear the painfully slow throb of the barge's motor, but it was impossible to tell from just what direction it was coming. And the sound carried so well over the water that it did not seem to increase or lessen in whatever direction we rowed. And then it stopped. It wasn't until a man came on deck carrying a lantern, heading from the aft deckhouse to the forward deckhouse, that we were able to be sure of our heading. In another five minutes we were under the stern overhang of the barge, where we tied the rowboat up to the port side and paused to consider.

"Up onto the deck, find a blunt object or two to use as weapons, and get below, or at least inside, as quickly as possible," Holmes said.

"Forward or aft?" I asked.

"We are aft," Holmes said, "so let us not waste time by going forward."

I agreed. We moved the rowboat around to the side of the barge as far as we could without untying it and I felt about for a handhold. "Well!" I whispered. "Piety and good works are indeed rewarded in this life."

"What?" Holmes murmured.

"There's a ladder fixed to the side here," I told him. I took hold with both hands and started up, with Holmes right behind me. Once on deck we moved toward the rear cabin, feeling our way along the railing. I reached some impediment; a large metal object covered with a canvas and gutta-percha weather shield, and paused to feel my way around it and to determine what it was—like the blind man trying to describe an elephant. But after a few moments of grasping and groping, the outline of the elephant became clear.

"Well I'll be!" I said, or perhaps it was something stronger.

"What is it?" asked Holmes, who was right behind me.

"It is a three-inch naval gun, probably a Hoskins and Reed. It will fire a nine-pound projectile something over three miles accurately. It's the latest thing in gunnery. Royal Navy destroyers are being outfitted with them even now."

"I didn't know you were so well acquainted with naval ballistics," Holmes said. His voice sounded vaguely accusatory, but then it often does when he speaks to me.

"I am well acquainted with a wide range of things," I told him.

We continued our progress toward the aft deckhouse. I was hoping to come across a belaying pin, or a length of iron pipe, or anything that could be worked loose and used as a weapon, but nothing came to hand.

We reached the deckhouse door, and Holmes pulled it open. It was as dark inside as out. We entered. By creeping ahead silently and feeling along the wall we were able to ascertain that we were in a corridor of unknown length, with doors on each side.

Light suddenly cascaded into the corridor as a door farther down was opened. A man stood in the doorway talking to someone inside the room, but in another second he would surely come into the corridor. I tugged at Holmes's sleeve and pointed to what the light had just revealed: a stairs, or as they call anything with steps on a ship, a ladder, going up. By mounting quickly we could avoid being seen. We did so. There was a door at the head of the ladder, which I opened, and we went through. The door made a loud *click* on closing, and we paused, waiting to see whether the sound would alert those below. Holmes assumed the "standing locust" Baritsu posture to the left of the door, ready in mind and body for whoever might come through. I grabbed a spanner from a nearby shelf and stood, poised, on the right side.

There were no hurried footsteps up the ladder, no whispered voices from downstairs, so after a few moments we relaxed and looked around. An oil lamp on gimbals mounted to the ceiling cast a dull light around the room. It appeared to be the wheelhouse of a large vessel, with the forward windows covered with heavy drapes. There was an oversized ship's wheel in the center, with calling pipes, and a ship's telegraph, a chart cabinet and chart table to the rear, and various bits of nautical equipment affixed here and there throughout the room. A captain's chair was bolted to the deck on the left, excuse me, port side, and a ship's compass squatted along-side. A metal-strapped leather chest big enough to hold a fair-sized man doubled over sat on the other side of the chair.

"A wheelhouse for a barge," Holmes whispered. "How odd."

"It does have an engine," I said.

"Yes, but I doubt if it can attain a speed of greater than three or four knots. One would think that a tiller would suffice." He took the oil lamp off its mount and began a slow inspection of the room, bending, sniffing, peering, and probing at the walls, floor, and bits of apparatus scattered about. The chest was securely locked, and there seemed to be nothing else of interest in the room. After a few minutes he stood erect and put the lantern on the chart table. "This is very peculiar," he said.

"It is indeed," I agreed. "This is not the wheelhouse of a scow—this is the command bridge of a naval ship."

"Say rather a full size model of it," Holmes said. "The chart cabinet is devoid of charts, and the chart that's pinned to this table is a Royal Navy chart of the Bay of Naples."

"Perhaps," I suggested, "we have found the fabled Swiss navy."

"I think not," Holmes said. "I found this." He held out a blue cap for my perusal. It was a British Navy seaman's cap, and on the side the words "H.M.S. ROYAL EDGAR" were embroidered in gold thread.

"The *Royal Edgar* is a destroyer," I told Holmes. "Royal Henry class. Four funnels. Six torpedo tubes. Two four-inch and eight two-inch guns. Top speed a hair under thirty knots."

"How do you happen to know that?" Holmes asked, an undercurrent of suspicion creeping into his voice.

"I have recently done some work for the Admiralty," I explained. "I, of course, made it a point to learn the names and ratings of all of Her Majesty's ships currently in service."

He shook the cap in my face. "You mean they trust you to—" He paused and took a deep breath. "Never mind," he finished. He pointed across the room. "That chest may hold something of import, but the rest of the room is devoid of interest."

"Except for the hat," I said.

"Yes," he agreed. "That is very interesting."

"I didn't bring my picklocks," I said, "and if we break the chest open, we will be announcing our presence."

"Interesting conundrum," Holmes allowed.

It was one we never got the chance to resolve. There was a rumbling and a thudding and a screeching and the sound of voices from below. No—from the deck outside. Holmes closed the lantern, and we pulled one of the curtains aside to see what was happening.

The steam launch had returned and was tying up alongside. If the men embarking from it saw our rowboat tied up at the stern, life would get interesting over the next few minutes. But the rowboat had swung back around out of sight, and it would be an unlucky accident if they were to see it.

There was a barking of orders—in German, I noted—and the eight or ten men who had come aboard scurried about to do whatever they had come aboard to do. Three of them headed to the door in the aft deckhouse below us, and the two men inside had opened the door to greet them.

"If they come up here . . ." Holmes said.

"Yes," I said, remembering the layout of the darkened room. "There is no place to conceal ourselves."

"Behind these curtains is the only possibility," Holmes whispered. "And that's not a good one."

"Well," I said, hearing the tramp of boots on the ladder, "it will have to do."

We retreated to the far side of the curtains and twitched them closed scant seconds before I heard the door being opened and two—no, three—sets of footsteps entering the room.

"The lamp must have gone out," one of them said in German. "I'll light it."

"No need," another replied in the same language, the sound of authority in his voice. "All we need from here is the chest. Shine your light over there—there. Yes, there it is. You two, pick it up."

"Yes, Your Grace."

"Take it down and onto the launch right away," the imperious voice said. "This must accompany us on the train to Trieste."

"Right away, Your Grace." And, with a minor cacophony of thumps, bumps and groans, the chest was lifted and carried out the door. After a few seconds it was clear that His Grace had left with the chest, and we were once again alone in the room.

"Well," I said, stepping out from behind the curtain. "Trieste. Now if we only knew—"

Holmes held his hand up to silence me. He was peering out of the window with a concentrated fury, glaring down at our recent guests as they went on deck through the downstairs door.

"What is it?" I asked.

"One moment," he said.

For a second "His Grace" turned his head, and his profile was illuminated by the lantern carried by one of the crew. Holmes staggered backward and clapped his hand to his forehead. "I was not wrong!" he said. "I knew I recognized that voice!"

"Who, His Grace?" I asked.

"He!" he said. "It is he!"

"Who?"

"His name is Wilhelm Gottsreich Sigismond von Ormstein," Holmes told me. "Grand Duke of Cassel-Felstein and Hereditary King of Bohemia."

"Is he indeed?" I asked. "And how do you know His Grace?"

"He employed me once," Holmes said. "I will not speak of it further."

"The case had nothing to do with our current, er, problem?" I asked.

"Nothing," he assured me.

"Then I, also, shall not speak of it again." Whatever it was, it must have affected Holmes greatly, but it was not the time to pick at old wounds. "I take it he has little use for the English?" I asked.

"He has little regard for anything British," Holmes affirmed. "And I believe that he has no fondness for anyone except himself, and possibly members of his immediate family."

"Truly a prince," I said.

The last of our visitors boarded the steam launch, and it cast off and pulled away from the barge. "I wonder what prompted the midnight visit," I said.

"Nothing good," Holmes opined.

There was a crumping sound, as of a distant belching beneath the water, then another, and the barge listed toward the starboard side with a great creaking and a series of snaps.

"There's your answer," Holmes said, as we both grabbed for the nearest support in order to remain upright. "Those were explosions. They're scuttling this craft. She'll be under in ten minutes, unless she breaks apart first. Then it will be faster. Much faster."

"Perhaps we should make our exit," I suggested.

"Perhaps," he agreed.

We hurried down the ladder and onto the deck.

"*Hilfe! Hilfen sie mir, bitte!*"

The faint cry for help came from somewhere forward. "We're coming!" I called into the dark. "*Wir kommen! Wo sind Sie?*"

"*Ich weiss nicht. In einem dunklen Raum,*" came the reply.

"'In a dark place' doesn't help," Holmes groused. "It couldn't be any darker than it is out here."

The barge picked that moment to lurch and sag farther to starboard.

"*Hilfe!*"

We struggled our way to the forward deckhouse. The cry for help was coming from somewhere to the left of the door. I felt my way along the wall until I came to a porthole. "Hello!" I called inside, knocking on the glass.

"Oh, thank God," cried the man in German. "You have found me! You must, for the love of God, untie me before this wretched vessel sinks."

Holmes and I went in through the door and down a short length of corridor until we came to a left-hand turn.

"Ow!" said Holmes.

"What?"

I heard a scraping sound. "Wait a second," Holmes said. "I've just banged my head."

"Sorry," I said.

"No need," he told me. "I've just banged my head on a lantern hanging from the ceiling. Give me a second, and I'll have it lit."

He took a small waterproof case of wax matches from his pocket and in a few seconds had the lantern glowing. "Onward!" he said.

Opening the third door along the corridor revealed a short, portly man in a white shirt and dark, striped trousers and vest, tied to a large wooden chair. His exertions in trying to escape had covered his face with bands of sweat and pulled much of his shirt loose from his waistband, but his thin black tie was still properly and severely in place. "Light!" the man said. "Oh, bless you my friends, whoever you are."

We worked at untying him as quickly as possible as the barge gave a series of alarming jerks and kicks under us and tilted ever more drastically. Now, in addition to its list to the starboard, there was a decided tilt aft.

"Thank you, thank you," said the plump man, as the rope came off his legs. "They left me here to die. And for what?"

"For what, indeed?" I replied.

"It all started . . ."

"Let's wait until we're off this vessel," Holmes interjected, "or in a very few moments we'll be talking underwater."

We helped our rotund comrade up, although our feet were not much steadier than his, and with much slipping and sliding we made our way along the deck. An alarming shudder ran through the vessel as we reached the stern, and we quickly lowered our new friend into the rowboat and followed him down. Holmes and I manned the oars and energetically propelled ourselves away from the sinking barge, but we had gone no more than fifteen or twenty yards when the craft gave a mighty gurgle and descended beneath the water, creating a wave that pulled us back to the center of a great vortex, then threw us up into the air like a chip of wood in a waterfall. In a trice we were drenched, and our flimsy craft was waterlogged, but by some miracle we were still in the rowboat, and it was still afloat. Holmes began bailing with his cap, and our guest with his right shoe, while I continued the effort to propel us away from the area.

I oriented myself by the ever-dependable North Star, and headed toward the southeast. In a little while Holmes added his efforts to my own, and we were rowing across the dark waters with reasonable speed despite our craft still being half-full of water. Our plump shipmate kept bailing until he was exhausted, then spent a few minutes panting and commenced bailing again.

It was perhaps half an hour before we spied lights in the distance indicating that the shore was somewhere ahead of us. Half an hour more and we had nosed into a beach. A small, steep, rocky beach, but nonetheless a bit of dry land, and we were grateful. The three of us climbed out of the rowboat and fell as one onto the rough sand, where we lay exhausted and immobile. I must have slept, but I have no idea how long. When next I opened my eyes dawn had risen, and Holmes was up and doing exercises by the water's edge.

"Come, arise, my friend," he said—he must have been drunk with exercise to address me thus—"we must make our preparations and be on our way."

I sat up. "Where are we off to?" I asked.

"Surely it should be obvious," Holmes replied.

"Humor me," I said.

"Trieste," said Holmes. "Wherever Wilhelm Gottsreich Sigismond von Ormstein goes, there we shall go. For whatever is happening, he is the leader or one of the leaders."

"Is it your dislike of him that speaks?" I asked. "For you have often said the same of me, and seldom was it so."

"Ah, but on occasion . . ." Holmes said. "But in this case it is my knowledge of the man. He would not be a member of any organization that did not let him be its leader, or at least believe that he is the leader, for he is vain and would be easily led himself."

Our rotund friend sat up. "Is that English which you speak?" he asked in German.

"*Ja*," I said, switching to that language. "It is of no importance."

"That is what those swine that abducted me spoke when they did not want me to understand," he said, laboriously raising himself to his knees, then to his feet. "But they kept forgetting—and I understood much."

"Good!" I said. "We will all find dry clothing for ourselves, and you shall tell us all about it."

He stood up and offered me his hand. "I am Herr Paulus Hansel, and I thank you and your companion for saving my life."

"On behalf of Mr. Sherlock Holmes and myself, Professor James Moriarty, I accept your thanks," I told him, taking the offered hand and giving it a firm shake.

"I have clothing at my—oh—I don't dare go back to my hotel." Our friend's hands flew to his mouth. "Supposing they are there waiting for me?"

"Come now," Holmes said. "They believe you are dead."

"I would not disabuse them of that notion," he said.

We walked the three or so miles back to our hotel, booked a room for Herr Hansel, and set about our ablutions and a change of clothes. We gave the concierge the task of supplying suitable garb for our rotund friend, and he treated it as though guests of the Hotel Athènes returned water-soaked and bedraggled every day of the year. Perhaps they did.

It was a little after eight when we met at the hotel's restaurant for breakfast. "Now," Holmes said, spreading orange marmalade on his croissant and turning to Herr Hansel, "I have restrained my curiosity long enough, and you may well be possessed of information useful to us. Start with what you were doing on that barge, if you don't mind."

Herr Hansel drained his oversized cup of hot chocolate, put the cup down with a satisfied sigh, and wiped his mustache. "That is simple," he said, refilling the cup from the large pitcher on the table. "I was preparing to die. And were you gentlemen not on board, I most assuredly would have done so."

"What caused your companions to treat you in so unfriendly a manner?" I asked.

"They were no companions of mine," he replied. "I am the proprietor of the Hansel and Hansel Costume Company." He tapped himself on the chest. "I am the second Hansel, you understand. The first Hansel, my father, retired from the business some years ago and devotes himself to apiculture."

"Really?" asked Holmes. "I would like to meet him."

"Certainly," Hansel agreed. "I am sure he would like to thank the man who saved his son's life."

"Yes, there is that," Holmes agreed. "Go on with your story."

"Yes. I delivered yesterday a large order of costumes to a certain Count von Kramm at the Adlerhof."

"Hah!" Holmes interjected. We looked at him, but he merely leaned back in his chair with his arms crossed across his chest and murmured, "Continue!"

"Yes," said Hansel. "Well, they were naval costumes. Officers and ordinary seamen's uniforms. From shoes to caps, with insignia and ribbons and everything."

"Fascinating," I said. "British Royal Navy uniforms, no doubt."

"Why, yes," Hansel agreed. "And quite enough of them to have costumed the full cast of that Gilbert and Sullivan show—*Pinafore*."

"And the name of the ship you stitched on the caps," Holmes interjected. "Could it have been the *Royal Edgar?*"

"Indeed it was," Hansel said, looking startled. "How did you . . ."

"Much like this one?" Holmes asked, pulling the cap we had found out of his pocket and placing it on the table.

Hansel picked it up, examined it carefully, crumpled the cloth in his hands and sniffed at it. "Why, yes," he agreed, "this is one of ours."

"Go on," I said. "How did you get yourself tied up in that cabin?"

"It was when I asked about the undergarments," Hansel said. "Count von Kramm seemed to take offense."

"Undergarments?"

Hansel nodded and took a large bite of sausage. "We were asked to supply authentic undergarments, and I went to considerable trouble to comply with his request."

"Whatever for?" asked Holmes.

Hansel shrugged a wide, expressive shrug. "I did not ask," he said. "I assumed it was for whatever production he was planning to put on. I acquired the requested undergarments from the Naval Stores at Portsmouth, so their authenticity was assured."

"You thought it was for a play?" I asked. "Doesn't that sound like excessive realism?"

Another shrug. "I have heard that when Untermeyer produces a show at the Königliche Theater he puts loose change in the corners of the couches and stuffed chairs, and all the doors and windows on the set must open and close even if they are not to be used during the performance."

"Who are we to question theatrical genius?" Holmes agreed. "If Count Kramm's theatrical sailors are to wear sailors' undergarments, why then so be it."

"Indeed," said Hansel. "But why only five sets?"

Holmes carefully put down his coffee cup. "Five sets only?"

"That's right."

"And how many sets of, ah, outer garments?"

"Thirty-five complete uniforms. Twelve officers and the rest common sailors."

"How strange," I said.

Hansel nodded. "That's what I said. That's why I ended up tied up on that chair, or so I suppose."

Holmes looked at me. "Count von Kramm," he said, "or as I know him better, Wilhelm Gottsreich Sigismond von Ormstein, Grand Duke of Cassel-Felstein and Hereditary King of Bohemia, dislikes being questioned."

"I see," I said.

"Von Kramm is one of his favorite aliases."

"That man is a king?" Hansel asked, a note of alarm in his voice. "There is no place where one can hide from a king."

"Do not be alarmed," Holmes told him. "By now he has forgotten that you ever existed."

"Ah, yes," Hansel said. "There is that about kings."

Holmes stood. "I think we must go to Trieste," he said. "There is devil's work afoot."

"Yes," I agreed. "I need to send a telegram. I'll have the reply sent to Trieste."

"I, I think, must go home," said Hansel.

"Yes, of course," Holmes agreed. He took Hansel's hand. "You have earned the thanks of another royal person, and I shall see that, in the fullness of time, you are suitably rewarded."

"You are g-going to r-r-reward me?" Hansel stammered. "But Your Grace, Your Kingship, I had no idea. I mean . . ."

Holmes barked out a short laugh. "No, my good man," he said. "Not I. A gracious lady on whose shoulders rest the weight of the greatest empire in the world."

"Oh," said Hansel. "Her."

The city of Trieste rests on the Gulf of Trieste, which is the northern tip of the Adriatic Sea, and is surrounded by mountains where it isn't fronting water. The city dates back to Roman times, and its architecture is a potpourri of every period from then to the present. Although it is putatively a part of the Austrian Empire, its citizens mostly speak Italian, and are more concerned with the happenings in Rome and Venice than those in Vienna and Budapest.

The journey took us two days by the most direct route we could find. But we reconciled ourselves with the thought that von Ormstein and his band of pseudo-English sailors couldn't have arrived much ahead of us.

During the journey we discussed what we had found out and worked out a course of action. It was necessarily vague, as although we now had a pretty good idea of what von Ormstein was planning, we didn't know what resources we would find available to us to stop him from carrying out his dastardly scheme.

Before we left Lindau Holmes and I had sent a telegram to Mycroft:

SEND NAMES AND LOCATIONS OF ALL DESTROYERS OF ROYAL
HENRY CLASS REPLY GENERAL PO TRIESTE SHERLOCK

A reply awaited us when we arrived. We retired to a nearby coffeehouse and perused it over steaming glasses of espresso:

EIGHT SHIPS IN CLASS ROYAL HENRY ROYAL ELIZABETH AND
ROYAL ROBERT WITH ATLANTIC FLEET AT PORTSMOUTH ROYAL
STEPHEN IN DRY DOCK BEING REFITTED ROYAL WILLIAM IN BAY OF
BENGAL ROYAL EDWARD AND ROYAL EDGAR ON WAY TO AUS-
TRALIA ROYAL MARY DECOMMISSIONED SOLD TO URUGUAY PRE-
SUMABLY CROSSING ATLANTIC TO MONTEVIDEO WHAT NEWS
MYCROFT

I slapped my hand down on the coffee table. "Uruguay!"

Holmes looked at me.

"Uruguay is divided into nineteen departments," I told him.

"That is the sort of trivia with which I refuse to burden my mind," he said. "The study of crime and criminals provides enough intellectual . . ."

"Of which one," I interrupted, "is Florida."

He stopped, his mouth open. "Florida?"

"Just so."

"The letter . . . 'The Florida is now ours.'"

"It is common practice to name warships after counties, states, departments, or other subdivisions of a country," I said. "The British Navy has an *Essex*, a *Sussex*, a *Kent*, and several others, I believe."

Holmes thought this over. "The conclusion in inescapable," he said. "The *Florida* . . ."

"And the undergarments," I said.

Holmes nodded. "When you have eliminated the impossible," he said, "whatever remains, however improbable, stands a good chance of being the truth."

I shook my head. "And you have called me the Napoleon of crime," I said. "Compared to this . . ."

"Ah!" said Holmes. "But this isn't crime, this is politics.

International intrigue. A much rougher game. There is no honor among politicians."

We walked hurriedly to the British consulate on Avenue San Lucia and identified ourselves to the consul, a white-haired, impeccably dressed statesman named Aubrey, requesting that he send a coded message to Whitehall.

He looked at us quizzically over his wire-rim glasses. "Certainly, gentlemen," he said. "To what effect?"

"We are going to ask Her Majesty's government to supply us with a battleship," Holmes said, and paused, waiting for the reaction.

It was not what one might have expected. "There are no British battleships visiting the port right now," Aubrey said, folding his hands over his ample stomach and leaning back in his chair. "Will a cruiser do?"

Holmes leaned over the desk. "We are in earnest," he said, his intense eyes glowering over his thin, ascetic nose, "and this is not a jest. To the contrary, it is of the utmost importance and urgency."

"I have no doubt," replied Aubrey, looking up mildly. "My offer was sincere. If a cruiser will suffice, I am ready to put one at your disposal. It's all that's available. There are some four or five Royal Navy torpedo gunboats working with the Italian Navy engaged in the suppression of smugglers and pirates in the Mediterranean, but I can't predict when one of them will come to port."

"But you're prepared to put a cruiser at, er, our disposal?" I asked.

"I am," said Aubrey, nodding. "That is, I have no direct authority to do so, but the authority has been passed on to me from Whitehall. I received a cable this morning directing me to do all I could to assist you, were you to show up. I must say I've never been given an instruction like that before in eighteen years in the Foreign Service. From the P.M. himself, don't you know. Along with a screed from the Admiralty."

Holmes straightened up. "Mycroft!" he said.

"Undoubtedly," I agreed.

"Her Majesty's Ship *Agamemnon* is in port," said Aubrey, "and I have passed on the request of the Admiralty to Captain Preisner that he keep steam up and await further instructions. Now, if you could tell me what this is all about, perhaps I could be of some further assistance."

"Let us head to the docks immediately," Holmes said. "We will explain on the way."

Aubrey reached for the bellpull behind his desk. "Call up my carriage," he told the man who appeared in answer to his summons. "And fetch my greatcoat, there's a chill in the air."

Consul Aubrey gave instructions, and soon we were racing through the streets of Trieste heading toward the municipal docks, where a waiting launch would take us to the *Agamemnon*. "In case something goes wrong," Holmes told the Consul, "and there's every chance it will, you'll have to prepare."

"Prepare for what?" Aubrey asked. "In what way?"

Holmes and I took it in turns to tell him what we knew and what we surmised. "We may not have all the details correct," I said, "but if events do not unfold much as we have described, I will be greatly surprised."

"But this is incredible!" Aubrey said. "How did you figure all this out?"

"No time now," Holmes declared, as the carriage pulled to a stop. "We must hurry."

"Good luck," Aubrey said. "I shall return to the consulate and prepare for your success or failure, whichever comes from this madness."

"It must sound mad," I agreed. "But it is not our madness, but that of our antagonist."

"Come," said Holmes. "Let us board the launch."

We leapt aboard the steam launch. The boatswain saluted us as we raced past him down the gangway, then blew on his whistle twice, and we were off. The harbor was thick with shipping, and we weaved and dodged between vessels of all sorts and sizes, making our way to the great, looming bulk of the three-stack cruiser of modern design that was our destination.

When we reached the *Agamemnon* a ladder was lowered from the deck of the cruiser to receive us. The sea was calm in the harbor, but transferring from the rolling deck of the steam launch to the pitching ladder at the cruiser's side, even in those gentle swells, was more of an effort than a sedate unadventuresome man of my years found enjoyable.

Captain Preisner's flag officer met us as we stepped onto the deck and led the way to the bridge of the *Agamemnon*, where Preisner, a thin man with a bony face and a short, pointed grey beard, greeted us warily. "Mr. Holmes," he said, with a stiff nod of his head, "Professor Moriarty. Welcome, I think, to the *Agamemnon*."

"Captain," I acknowledged.

Preisner flapped a sheet of yellow paper at us. "I am requested and required by the Admiralty to give you whatever assistance you require, without asking questions. Or, at least, without demanding answers. Which, I must say are the oddest instructions I have ever received."

"This may be the oddest mission in which you will ever engage," Holmes told him.

Captain Preisner sighed. "And somehow I have the feeling that it will not bring accolades to me or my crew," he said.

"You will probably be requested not to mention it in your official report," I told him. "And, were I you, I would not enter the details in my log until I had time to think deeply on it."

"It was ever thus," Preisner said. "What am I to do?"

I pointed to the south. "Somewhere out there, not too far away, is a destroyer flying the Union Jack, or possibly the Red Ensign. We have to stop it and board it. Or, if that proves impossible, sink it."

Preisner looked at me, speechless. And then he looked at Holmes, who nodded. "Sink a British warship?" he asked incredulously.

"Ah," Holmes said, "but it isn't. And if we do not succeed in stopping it, some major outrage will be committed in the harbor of Trieste or some nearby coastal city, and it will be blamed on the British Navy."

"A ruse of war?" Preisner asked. "But we aren't at war, that I know of."

"We'd better consider it a 'ruse of peace,' then," Holmes said. "Although the ultimate purpose of the exercise might well be to provoke a state of war between Britain and several Continental powers."

"A Royal Navy destroyer," Preisner mused, "that *isn't* a Royal Navy destroyer."

"The name on her side will indicate she's the *Royal Edgar*," I told him. "In reality she is the decommissioned *Royal Mary*, which has been sold to Uruguay. The Uruguayan government, we believe, renamed her the *Florida*."

"We're going to war with Uruguay?"

"She is now in the hands of a group of rogue European, ah, gentlemen, who plan to use her to provoke animosity and, perhaps, active hostilities against Great Britain. How the transfer was made from the Uruguayan authorities to the plotters remains to be seen. It could well be that the government of Uruguay knows nothing of the supposed sale."

"My God! How did you—never mind that now!" Preisner swung around and barked out a series of orders that got the great ship under way.

While the *Agamemnon* made her way out into the Gulf of Trieste and headed down the Adriatic Sea, Captain Preisner concerned himself with the handling of his ship, but once we were in open water he turned the helm over to Lieutenant Willits, his bulldog-jawed, taciturn first officer, and called us to his side. "Now tell me what you know," he said, "and what you surmise, so that we can plan a course of action."

As rapidly as possible, but leaving out nothing of consequence, we told him our story. Holmes took the lead, and in that nasal, high-pitched voice of his outlined what we knew and how we had learned it.

Preisner rested his elbows on the ledge running around the front of the bridge, directly below the large glass windscreens, and stared out at the choppy blue-green sea. "And on these meager facts you have commandeered one of Her Majesty's battle cruisers and set out in search of a destroyer that may or may not exist, and that, if it does exist, may or may not be planning some harm to British interests? And the Lords of the Admiralty have agreed with this, ah, unlikely interpretation?" he shook his head. "I will obey orders, even if it means obeying *your* orders and racing up and down the Adriatic, but frankly, I don't see it."

"You don't agree that it is likely that this cabal has gotten possession of the *Royal Mary* and intends harm to Britain?" Holmes asked.

"Of what possible profit to them could such an action be?" Preisner asked. "I grant you your conclusion that these people were training a crew to operate a British warship, and the *Royal Mary* might well be the one. And if they were planning to come to Trieste, then they were probably picking up the ship somewhere around here. But is it not more likely that, having obtained the ship, they will take it to some distant port to commit their outrage, if indeed an outrage is planned?"

"There are several reasons to believe that, whatever sort of attack they are planning, it will be nearby and soon," I said.

"For one thing," said Holmes, "their men cannot be all that well trained in the handling of a modern destroyer."

"For another," I added, "every extra hour they spend will increase the likelihood that they will be intercepted by some ship of Her Majesty's Mediterranean Fleet. And one attempt to exchange signals would brand her as an imposter."

"For maximum effect," Holmes said, "the outrage should be conducted close to a city or large town, so that it will be observed by as many people as possible."

"That makes sense," Preisner agreed.

"And then there are the undergarments," I said.

"Yes," Holmes agreed. "That gives the whole game away."

Captain Preisner looked from one to the other of us. "It does?" he asked.

A mess steward came by with steaming mugs of tea for those on bridge, and he had thoughtfully included two for Holmes and me.

I took the tea gratefully and sipped at it. Neither Holmes nor I were dressed for the chill breeze that whipped through the open doors of the bridge. "The men in the Royal Navy uniforms are to be visible on deck during the event," I told Captain Preisner, "so that watchers on shore will believe the masquerade. But why undergarments?"

"And why only five?" Holmes added.

Preisner looked thoughtful. "A good question," he said.

"The only reasonable answer is that those five men must pass close inspection when their bodies are examined."

"Their bodies?"

"Consider," said Holmes. "The undergarments only make sense if it is expected that the men will be examined."

"Yes, I see that," Preisner agreed.

"But if they are alive when they are examined, any discrepancies will become quickly evident," said Holmes.

"As, for instance, their not speaking fluent English," I added.

"So you think they are dressing corpses in British naval uniforms?" Preisner asked.

Holmes looked away. "Perhaps," he said.

"Sail ho to the port!" a seaman outside the bridge relayed a call from the lookout on the top mast. We turned to look, but it was indeed a sail, the topsail of a three-masted barque, and not the four funnels of a British destroyer, that slowly came into sight on our port side.

We saw a variety of ships during the rest of that day, but it was dusk before we found the ship we were seeking. A four-masted destroyer appeared in the distance a few points off the starboard bow. Lieutenant Willits grabbed for the chart of identification silhouettes and ran his finger down the side while peering closely at the illustrations. "I don't believe there would be any other four-masted destroyer in the area," he said, "but it would not do to make a mistake."

Captain Preisner examined the distant ship through his binoculars and, even before Willits had confirmed the identification, turned to the duty seaman, and said quietly, "Signal all hands—battle stations."

The seaman whistled down the communications tube and relayed the command and, almost immediately, an ordered bedlam descended on the boat as the members of the crew raced to their assigned positions.

"She's flying no flags or pennants," announced Willits, who was staring at the approaching ship through his own binoculars. "But she's making no attempt to avoid us. There appears to be a small black ship of some sort to her rear."

"It would look suspicious were she to turn aside," said Preisner. "She doesn't know that we're stalking her. Hoist our own flag and the recognition code flag for today. And see if you can identify the ship to her rear."

"Aye, aye, sir." Willits relayed the command, and in a few seconds several flags were fluttering at the top of the *Agamemnon*'s forward mast.

"No response," said Willits after a minute. "Wait—she's turning to port, trying to evade us. If she completes the turn, she'll be able to show us her heels. She must have three or four knots better speed."

"Probably less with an untrained engine crew," commented Preisner. "But nonetheless—"

"I can make out her name now," said Willits, peering through his binoculars. "She's the *Royal Edgar*, right enough. Or claims she is. The other ship is keeping on her far side, but it appears to be some sort of large yacht, painted black."

"A smuggler, no doubt," said Preisner.

"I believe you're right, sir."

"Put a warning shot across her bow and run up the signal for 'Come to a complete stop,'" directed the captain. "Helmsman, turn twenty degrees to the starboard."

One of the *Agamemnon*'s four-inch guns barked once, and a fountain of water appeared off the bow of the *Royal Edgar*.

The destroyer continuing turning, ignoring the warning. The *Agamemnon* fired another shot, which plunged into the water close enough to have soaked anyone standing by the bow of the *Royal Edgar*. A few seconds later one of the *Royal Edgar*'s two-inch guns coughed a burst of flame, and an explosion sounded somewhere forward on the cruiser. A few seconds later, another burst, and a sound like the banging together of a hundred large iron pots came from amidships.

"They're firing at us!" yelled Lieutenant Willits.

"More fools they," said Captain Preisner grimly, and he gave the order to return fire.

The universe became filled with awesome roaring sounds as the eight-inch guns of the *Agamemnon* hurled their 120-pound explosive missiles into the air. In two minutes the firing from the *Royal Edgar* had stopped, and Captain Preisner gave the order for our own ship to cease fire. A total of no more than a dozen rounds had been fired by the big guns of the cruiser, but the damage done to the destroyer gave one faith in the might of modern science. She was dead in the water and already starting to list to one side. Billows of smoke were coming from amidships, and a tongue of flame was growing toward the bow.

The black yacht had pulled up alongside the *Royal Edgar*, and people were transferring over. Others were attempting to lower a lifeboat aft of the bridge.

"We should board her, Captain," Holmes said.

"Why?" asked Preisner.

"There may be documents."

"There may be wounded," added Lieutenant Willits.

"I'll have a boat lowered and ask for volunteers to row you over," Preisner told us. "But I'm not bringing the *Agamemnon* anywhere near that vessel. And I warn you, she's either going to blow up or go under quite soon, and quite suddenly."

Volunteers were found—the human race never ceases to astound me—and the captain's gig was lowered. We armed ourselves with revolvers and knives from a locker on the bridge, and we were shortly being rowed over to the *Royal Edgar*, which was not any lower in the water, although the fire was still burning. As we approached, the black yacht roared past us, headed off toward the south. A portly man in a Royal Navy officer's uniform standing rigidly in the rear of the yacht shook his fist at us as he passed.

"Would that be the king?" I asked Holmes.

"I believe it is," Holmes told me. "Yes, I believe it is."

We instructed our oarsmen to remain in the gig and to row rapidly away at the first sign that something untoward was about to happen.

"But what about yourselves, governor?" asked the bo's'n in charge of the rowing party.

"We shall dive off the ship and swim rapidly toward the *Agamemnon*," I told him.

"We'll probably be there before you are," Holmes added.

"Very good, sir," responded the bo's'n, but he was not convinced.

A couple of ropes were visible dangling over the side of the destroyer, and I grabbed one of them and pulled myself up. Holmes waited until I was on deck to follow me up the rope. There was very little damage evident on deck. Were it not for the smoke behind us and the fire ahead of us, it would look like there was nothing amiss.

"Why do you suppose they fled," Holmes asked, "instead of attempting to fight the fire?"

"Perhaps they were not trained to do so," I responded. "Perhaps they didn't have the equipment."

"Perhaps," Holmes agreed.

We had boarded amidships. By some unspoken agreement, we both turned and went forward. "If there are any useful documents," I said, "they're probably on the bridge."

"If there were any," Holmes replied, "Wilhelm Gottsreich most assuredly took them with him."

"Perhaps," I said.

We reached the ladder leading up to the bridge, and Holmes went up ahead of me. He stopped, frozen, in the doorway, and I could not get by. "What is it, Holmes," I asked, trying to peer around his shoulder.

"As I feared," he said, "but could not bring myself to believe . . ." He moved into the room, and I entered behind him.

There, lined up against the back wall, were four men in the uniforms of ordinary seamen in the Royal Navy. Their hands and feet were tied, and their mouths were covered with sticking plaster. One of them seemed to have fainted; he was slumped over, only held up by the rope around his chest, which was affixed to a metal hook in the wall. The other three were conscious: one trembling uncontrollably, one rigidly staring out the windscreen, his face frozen with shock, and the third fighting like a trapped beast against his bonds; his wrists raw, and blood streaming from his forehead.

A fifth man, his hands still tied behind him, lay prone on the floor, his face immersed in a large pan of water. He did not move. Holmes ran over to him, pulled up his head and rolled him over. After a few seconds he got up from the still body. "Too late," he said.

We used our knives to free the other men and, grabbing what papers we could find without bothering to look through them, led the men back down the ladder and out to the gig. Twenty minutes later we were aboard the *Agamemnon*, and the *Royal Edgar* was still burning but was no lower in the water, and her list seemed not to have increased.

"We can't leave her like this," Captain Preisner said, "and I can't tow her in; too many questions would be asked."

"You'll have to sink her," Holmes said.

Captain Preisner nodded. "Order the main batteries to fire ten rounds each, controlled fire, at the destroyer," he told the bridge duty officer.

About ten minutes after the last round was fired the destroyer gave a tremendous belch, and sank prow first into the sea. The entire crew of the *Agamemnon*, having been informed that it was a sister ship they were forced to sink, stood silently at attention as she went down. Captain Preisner held a salute until the onetime *Royal Mary* was out of sight beneath the waves, as did all the officers on the bridge.

Captain Preisner sighed and relaxed. "I hope I never have to do anything like that again," he said.

Later that evening Captain Preisner called us into his cabin. "I have a berth for you," he said. "We won't be back in port again until late tomorrow."

"That's fine, Captain," I said. "We still have to compose our report to send back to Whitehall."

Preisner looked at us. "Those men you brought aboard—you spoke to them?"

"We did."

"And?"

"The five suits of undergarments," Holmes said.

"But you only brought four men along."

"True," Holmes said. "Our antagonist had begun preparing for his assault. One of the men was already drowned. The others would have joined him shortly had we not come upon the ship when we did. The plan was to chase the black yacht into the Trieste harbor, getting as close to the city as possible. Then fire some shots at the fleeing craft, which would miss and hit at random in the city. Then the destroyer would, itself, flee back out to sea. A small explosion, presumably caused by the yacht firing back, would cause the five drowned men to be flung into the water, there to be found in their Royal Navy uniforms by the locals."

Captain Preisner stared at him speechless for a long moment. "And all this," he said finally, "to discredit England?" he asked. "What good would it do?"

"Major conflagrations are started by small sparks," Holmes said. "Who can say where this might have led?"

Preisner shook his head. "Madmen," he said.

"Even so," Holmes agreed. "There are an abundance of them."

Later in our cabin Holmes turned to me, and asked, "What are you planning to do after we send our report?"

I shrugged. "The world thinks I am dead," I said. "Perhaps I shall take advantage of that and remain away from public ken."

"I, also, had thought of doing something of the sort," Holmes told me. "I've always wanted to travel to Tibet, perhaps speak with the Dalai Lama."

"A very interesting man," I told him. "I'm sure you'd find such a conversation fruitful."

Holmes stared at me for a long time, then said, "Good night, Professor," and turned down the light.

"Good night, Holmes," I replied.

The Strange Case of the Voodoo Priestess

Carole Bugge

s I sit down to write this account, thunder is tearing at the skies over New Orleans, and lightning is ripping jagged steaks across a darkened horizon laced with pelting raindrops. This sudden burst of Nature's violence is entirely appropriate to the story I am about to tell.

My name is Lucien Brasseaux, and I am captain of the eighth district of the city of New Orleans. This district includes the French Quarter and its environs—in short, the most violent, crime-ridden neighborhood of a city that always attracted extremes of human behavior. There is a heady, bohemian atmosphere here, perhaps borne on the winds that blow in from the salt marshes of the bayou—but, whatever the reason, people feel a freedom in this town they seem to feel nowhere else. This Pandora's box of human appetite and impulse has created wonderful music, spicy food, and a colorful, festive social scene. But the Crescent City, as it is called, can be a blood-thirsty, lawless place—and sometimes the worst offenses are committed by our supposedly solid, taxpaying citizens.

There are those who claim New Orleans contains echoes of Paris, and they may well be right; others see in its fresco blend of cultures similarities to other European cities, such as Cannes or even Barcelona; its seamier side is perhaps reminiscent of certain

New York neighborhoods, or the outskirts of Chicago, and the Creole influence may recall Kingston or Port-au-Prince—but first and foremost, New Orleans is one of a kind. It belongs to itself.

New Orleans is a religious town, but it is even more a superstitious one. The mixture of Christianity and African voodoo clash and blend much like the waters of the Mississippi River as it rolls into the bay—churning and crosscurrents that make for treacherous tides when the spring rains have swollen the great river in its low, silty clay banks. But, like the mix of cultures in this overgrown small town, the clash of styles and speech and language and lore eventually blends, and pretty soon you can't tell where the river leaves off and the bay begins.

My family is like that. My mother was English, and my father was Cajun, which is our term for "Acadian," descendants of French folk who were expelled from Nova Scotia in the Great Expulsion of 1755 and fled all the way down to Louisiana, sliding steadily southward as though the continent was too slippery to hold them—until they ran smack out of land and ended up settling the bayou in and around the Big Easy. Why they call it that I'll never understand, but they do. So I grew up speaking French, English, and that strange mixture of both we Cajuns call "patois," and that everyone else calls Pidgin English. My parents sent me to the best schools, and while I am proud of my heritage, I like to think my English is as good as that of any Anglican.

It was with no little trepidation that I saw Madame Celeste heave her enormous bulk up the steps to the precinct house on Royal Street one warm and windy Friday afternoon in February. There was already a sense of anticipation in the air: Carnival was in its fifth week and Mardi Gras was not far away. The smell of lavender and sandalwood preceded Madame Celeste's entrance into the police station—she mixes all her own perfumes and potions, and you can usually smell her coming from half a block away.

No one is more emblematic of the marriage of religion and superstition than Madame Celeste. A quadroon Creole woman of mysterious origins, she is by all accounts the most famous and powerful Voodoo Queen in the world. A devout Catholic, she is respected and feared, it is said, by the Pope himself. By day she weaves fabric and sews beautiful dresses and scarves that she sells down at the French Market, but by night she supposedly holds midnight voodoo rituals out behind St. Louis Cathedral. No one knows how old she is, and no one can remember her ever being young. It is said that she has lived here forever, and that she is the descendant of a gypsy woman who sold her soul (and her body) to the Devil—and that Celeste was the product of this unholy union. It is said she can summon spirits in the dead of night to do her bidding, and that to be in her presence on All Hallow's Eve is to be able to peer through the thin membrane separating the living from those who have passed into the next world. In a city of ghosts, Madame Celeste holds a place all her own; some even claim she is a ghost herself, and that she never sleeps, but sits surrounded by her candles and her potions, weaving her spells deep into the night.

As I watched from the window, she took the stairs one at a time, lifting one elephantine knee to rest beside the other before assaying the next step, breathing heavily all the while. Whatever her origins, ghostly or not, Madame Celeste is a very solid corporeal presence. She must weigh close to three hundred pounds, and has a voice that suggests the union of a foghorn with a pile driver. Her appetite is as prodigious as her size—once, at Lou's Cajun Oyster Bar, she devoured four dozen oysters, followed by three dozen crayfish—before even beginning the main course.

Her prodigious bosom heaved and fell as she completed the onerous task of ascending the stairs, and sweat sprouted from her forehead like beads popping from a necklace. My sergeant, young Frank Pierce, took one look out the window and headed for the back door, claiming he was suddenly in need of a smoke. Madame Celeste inspires respect in some people and pure dread in others. Pierce was a good Catholic, and went to Mass every Sunday, but he had a healthy enough fear of the Devil that the thought of encountering one of his progeny caused him to flee like a child out the back door, leaving his newly opened pack of cigarettes in plain sight on his desk.

My own attempt to feel contempt toward his cowardice was compromised by the fit of rapid swallowing that overtook me as I heard the bell on the door commence its ting-a-ling, announcing the arrival of our august visitor. The door swung open before I could reach it, and Madame Celeste entered the room.

Her enormous figure was clothed in layers of colorful fabric—a turquoise blue vest over a sea-green linen dress, topped with a flourish of maroon and gold scarves, intertwined around her bulging neck. A tall hat of peacock feathers topped off the ensemble, worn jauntily to one side—or perhaps it had become somewhat dislodged during her journey up the stairs. Her jewelry was equally unrestrained; she wore a ring upon every finger, and a jangle of colored beads on a silver strand around her neck. Earrings dangling from each earlobe jingled with a delicate silvery tone.

She plodded to the nearest chair and sat heavily, as though the exertion she had just undergone was too much for anyone to bear, and wiped her frothing brow with a dainty little handkerchief. Her hands were surprisingly fragile, smooth and soft-looking, with delicate fingers and dimpled knuckles. Her skin was quite light, of the hue often referred to as café au lait. As a quadroon, her ancestry was likely a mixture of African and French, as well as Spanish or perhaps American Indian—as is the case of so many of our black Creoles, many of whom came here by way of Haiti.

I sat at my desk opposite her and assumed my best professional manner.

"What can I do for you, Madame Celeste?"

She gave me a sharp glance and passed the handkerchief over her forehead once again before answering me. A swirl of sandalwood perfume assaulted my nostrils, and I had to squint to keep from sneezing.

"*Tiens, c'est trop chaud,*" she said, her voice deep as the waters of mighty Mississippi. Her accent was cultivated, and her dialect was not the usual Creole patois, but a more educated French. Leaning forward, she looked me in the eye. "*Monsieur, je voudrais*—I wish to report a murder."

I leaned forward upon my desk. "A murder? When did it happen?"

She shook her head impatiently. "*Non, ce n'est pas* . . . it hasn't happened yet. But it will, no matter for dat."

I sat back in my chair, as suddenly as if I had been pushed. I did not know what to say; in all my years as policeman, I had never been presented with such a proposition. If it had come from anyone other than Madame Celeste, I would have laughed it off as a silly prank, but, superstitious or not, one did not take her word lightly. When she predicted the Mississippi would flood several years ago, some people laughed it off—after three dry summers in a row, no one thought it possible. But sure enough, that August the skies opened up and let loose a deluge, day after day, until finally the great river swelled and rolled from its banks like a fat old woman toppling out of bed. Homes were ruined, livestock was lost, crops were buried beneath an avalanche of water. And Madame Celeste sat and sewed her fabrics, and wove her cloth, and just nodded to herself. After that, everyone listened when she had something to say.

I gathered myself and looked her in the eye, to see if she was testing me in some way, but I saw only sincerity and concern. Her dark brown eyes were large and almost perfectly round, not the almond shape one sometimes sees in Creole woman. Her generous lips were puckered in a frown, and her brow was furrowed; it was clear that she was genuinely alarmed by what she was telling me.

"Whom do you believe is in danger of being murdered?" I said at last.

She shook her head impatiently. "*Alors,* dere is no belief, *monsieur*; dere is only fact! I tell you he will die, most *certainement,* as I sit here before you!"

"Very well, then," I replied as calmly as I could. "Who is going to die?"

If I had been unprepared for her first statement, the second one sent me reeling.

"Charles Latille."

I felt the blood pounding in my head, and the room spun before my eyes. Everything went black for a moment. Then I swallowed, took a deep breath, and wiped my brow.

"*Vous connais, monsieur?*"

"Yes, I know him," I responded at last. Unable to collect my thoughts, I reached absently for my coffee cup, but I seemed to have misplaced it.

Charles Latille was my best friend. My earliest childhood memories all included Charles; I couldn't remember a time when he wasn't there. We were boys together, and grew up playing in and around the bayous of Louisiana. By the time we were young men, we had become inseparable.

And less than a month before, I had become engaged to marry his sister, Evangeline.

"You are quite certain he will die?"

She nodded and then shrugged. "*Sans doubt . . . Jordi pou mwen, demen pou vou.*"

I recognized the French Creole dialect; translated, it means, "Today for me, tomorrow for you."

"May I ask you how you come by this knowledge?"

She regarded me solemnly. "I had a vision."

These words, spoken by most people, would strike any sensible person as ridiculous. But Madame Celeste was not most people.

"And in this vision—?"

"I foresaw his death."

"Did you happen to see how he was murdered? Or who the killer was?"

She shook her head. "*Je regrette a dit, mais non.* The visions are sometimes cloudy when dey come . . . dis one, a very bad feeling, but not so much information. Dis I regret."

"What are you proposing I do with about this information?"

She shook her head. "I do not know, monsieur—but it is my duty to report it to you, *n'est-ce pas?*"

There was a short silence, then she gathered up the fabric of her skirt and heaved herself to her feet, puffing a little as she adjusted her hat, which was listing even more to one side.

"Well, thank you for coming in, Madame," I said, escorting her to the door. "I will do what I can."

She turned to me. "*Faits attention, monsieur*—watch your friend, and be careful. You yourself are also in danger, I fear. *Sa ki jwé vek chyen yè trape depise yè.*"

I recognized this proverb as well; loosely translated from the French Creole, it means "He who plays with dogs catches fleas."

She laid a dimpled hand upon my arm, and I could feel the heat of her body through my uniform jacket. "Be careful," she repeated, then she was gone, the faint sound of her jewelry tinkling trailing after her as she descended the steps.

Dazed, I went back to my desk and sat, hardly aware of my surroundings. I needed to collect my thoughts, to make what I could of this extraordinary woman's disturbing advice. What could I possibly do to protect my friend—or myself, for that matter—from unknown assailants? It seemed to me I had only enough information to be deeply disturbed, yet not enough to be useful.

As I sat ruminating, Sergeant Pierce took the opportunity to show himself, creeping quietly back into the room.

"Forget something?" I inquired, indicating the pack of cigarettes still on his desk. He took one look at them and reddened from his collar to his hairline. He was fair and freckled, with copper hair the color of a new penny, and he blushed easily. I watched with smug satisfaction as he coughed nervously, sat down at his desk, and pretended to be busy.

No sooner had Pierce seated himself than the door opened again, and a man I had never set eyes on before entered the police station. He was tall and thin, well over six feet, with black hair and a long, sharp face. His eyes were so deep set that I couldn't make out their color at first, though they appeared to be grey or hazel. His features were lean and rather aristocratic, I thought—though there was an unhealthy flush to his gaunt cheeks that made me wonder if he was suffering from one of the fevers that makes it way through this swampy town from time to time. He was dressed like a gentleman, and the cut of his waistcoat was decidedly European—my first guess was British. His bearing, too, had the earmarks of a foreigner. There is a way people in this climate carry themselves, as if to spare every bit of energy they have to withstand the heat; but this man had the brisk, vigorous movements of a bird dog on a scent.

"Can I help you, sir?" I said, rising from my desk.

My visitor surveyed the office briefly before replying. There was something in his manner, and in the sweep of those deep-set eyes, that told me he missed very little. There wasn't much to see—besides my desk and the one Sergeant Pierce occupied, there were a few filing cabinets lining the wall, a bulletin board with some out-of-date notices, a map of the city on the far wall, and, of course, the inevitable ceiling fan. I glanced at my sergeant, who was fumbling with the drawers on his desk, looking for something or other, and I couldn't suppress a sigh. Apart from his fear of Madame Celeste, Pierce was a stalwart fellow, loyal and eager to please; but he was a bit of a bumbler. For some reason I found myself concerned about the impression he was making on our visitor.

"Why don't you go ahead and clear off for the day, Pierce?" I said.

"Really, sir?" Pierce said.

"Yes, yes—go ahead," I replied impatiently, anxious to be alone with the mysterious man.

"Why, th-thank you, sir," Pierce stammered, and made a hasty exit, this time remembering to take his cigarettes with him.

I addressed the tall stranger a second time. "Now, then, sir, how can I help you?"

Apparently finished with his survey of our little office, he turned his attention to me. Having those eyes fixed on me made me feel rather like a laboratory rat under a microscope—there was such intensity in his gaze, and a force of personality as I have rarely encountered.

"You are Captain Brasseaux?" he inquired, removing his hat, which was expensively made but rather worn.

"I am," I replied. "And you are—?"

"My name is Altamont. Jean Paul Altamont."

"How can I help you, Mr. Altamont?"

"I am looking for an aunt of mine who I have reason to believe is not well. I believe she lives in the French Quarter, but I am not familiar with this city, and I thought you might be able to help me locate her." His accent was decidedly English, clear and clean as the cut of his clothes.

"I perceive that you are English, sir, and yet your name, you say, is French."

My visitor regarded me sharply for a moment, then smiled. "I am of French extraction, but my family has lived in England for several generations."

"I see." I nodded. Something about this mysterious man didn't ring true; I had the feeling that he was hiding something from me.

"Your family is Acadian, then?" I said, knowing full well the answer.

He looked at me for a moment, then nodded.

"That is correct, yes."

I faced my companion and took a deep breath.

"You are plainly not who you claim to be, sir. I wonder if you would tell me the reason for your deception."

He glared at me darkly for a moment, then, to my surprise, he smiled.

"Well, I really must congratulate you, Captain. What was it that gave me away?"

"I am half-Acadian myself," I replied, "and Altamont is not one of our names. French perhaps, but not Acadian. There are a limited number of ancestral names of the families who fled Nova Scotia in the last century, and yours is not among them."

"I see," he replied evenly, giving me a look of intense scrutiny. "If I tell you who I am, you must not reveal my identity to anyone—not *anyone*, do you understand? Can you promise me that?"

"I think I can agree to that, provided, or course, that you have committed no crime."

A short, harsh laugh escaped his lips. "I can assure you that I am no criminal, though perhaps I have spent too much time in the company of that class of person."

"Very well, then," I replied, growing more curious by the moment. "Who are you, then?"

The answer, when it came, struck me like a thunderbolt.

"My name is Sherlock Holmes."

I stared at him for a moment, then sat rather heavily in the nearest chair.

He smiled. "I see you have heard of me."

"But—but I thought you were dead . . . I mean, Dr. Watson—"

I paused, unable to continue. This second shock of the day had completely unsettled me.

He sighed. "Yes, poor Watson. I allowed him to believe I was dead because I wanted certain—elements, shall we say—to believe it also. If they suspected I was still alive, I would be in considerable danger."

I blinked, unable to believe that standing before me was indeed the great detective himself, whose exploits I had so eagerly read about, endeavoring to follow his methods when I was a detective, before I was promoted to district captain.

"What brings you to New Orleans?" I asked when I had finally regained some of my composure.

"A matter of some international importance. I am acting as an emissary of my brother Mycroft. More than that I cannot say."

"Why did you come to me with the story about your aunt?" I inquired, looking around again for my mislaid coffee cup.

"Oh, that is all quite true. I do have an aunt here somewhere; my brother suggested I look her up."

"Why did you not go to the local clerk's office instead of coming here?"

"That, too, I am afraid I cannot reveal," he replied, lighting a cigarette. He offered me one, but I shook my head. I have always deplored the habit, which ruins the teeth and skin—and, even worse, destroys the taste buds.

"Well, Mr. Holmes," I said, "I am more than honored to make your acquaintance—in fact, I am quite overcome. I doubt there's a lawman in this city—or this country—who wouldn't like to meet you and shake your hand."

"Well, such is fame," he replied with a shrug. "But I thank you," he added sincerely. "I hope I shall prove worthy of your confidence."

"But you already have! I have read all of Dr. Watson's cases many times over. One of my favorites has always been the case of the Red-Headed League. I could never understand how you managed to—"

"My dear Captain," he interrupted, "Dr. Watson has a habit of romanticizing reality. I regret to say it, but you must take his recounting of our little adventures with a grain of salt."

"But the incident at Reichenbach Falls! Surely that is not—"

He shuddered in spite of the heat. "No, that is true; I did meet Moriarty and struggle with him at the precipice."

"But you lived! How on earth did you—"

He silenced me with a finger to his lips. "Why don't we leave that for Dr. Watson to tell one day?"

I nodded, wanting to ask him so many questions, but I could see it would not be advisable.

"And now," he said, "I perceive that you have troubles of your own. Perhaps you would like to tell me why the visit of that singular-looking woman upset you so?"

"How do you know I—" I began, but my voice faltered.

"From the condition of your desk, I perceive you to be an exceedingly orderly man, and yet you have paid no attention to the loose shoelace that has been flapping on your left shoe ever since I arrived. Also, you have twice laid down your cup of coffee and forgotten where you put it. You seem to be a man very much distracted by unwelcome news. I would not be surprised if it was directly linked to the woman who left just as I arrived."

My shoulders slumped, and I sank down in my chair. Outside a soft rain had begun to fall. I could hear the rattle of carriage wheels and horse hooves clattering on Royal Street, slipping slightly on the wet cobblestones as they rounded the corner onto Conti Street. The traffic was picking up, as was the sound of vendors selling their wares on street corners before heading down to the French Market for the evening. I glanced at the wall clock; it was almost six, at which time the duty watches would be switching over. My own shift would be ending, and Lieutenant Daugherty would soon arrive to take over the evening watch.

I looked up at my visitor, who stood leaning against the wooden railing that separated my desk from the sergeant's. Even standing there casually, he had a commanding presence which gave an impression of personal strength and enormous will power. I tried to imagine what kind of criminal would dare to cross him, and then I too shuddered, glad to know that Professor Moriarty was indeed at the bottom of Reichenbach Falls.

"Perhaps you would like to join me for a coffee at the Café du Monde?" I said.

"By all means," he replied.

Lieutenant Daugherty arrived at the station punctually as usual, and though he gave Holmes a curious glance, I didn't offer any explanation or introduction, but merely gave him the duty roster for the night. Except for the visit of Madame Celeste, it had been a quiet day, and it was just past six o'clock when Holmes and I slipped out into the damp February twilight, my head swimming with the giddy sensation of being in the company of the great detective. We quickly rounded the corner onto Conti Street and headed south toward the French Market.

The Mississippi River curls and twists through the city of New Orleans like a sleeping snake, as if reluctant to surrender its waters to the sea, slowly seeping into the bays and bayous of southern Louisiana, until arriving at last at its final destination, pouring inevitably into the ocean, just as we must all finally return to the place whence we came. The French Quarter lies along the part of the river where it curves and gathers around a lump of land, bunching like the back of a humpback whale.

At the far end of a series of stalls and shops, on Decatur Street, along the wide, flat banks of the Mississippi, is the Café du Monde, the jewel in the crown of the French Market. There the beignets are always fresh and hot, the coffee is rich and bitter with flavor of chicory, and the panorama of the mighty river provides a backdrop to all the forms of humanity that stream daily into the bustling port of New Orleans.

In a life of uncertainty, Café du Monde represents a certain constancy: open twenty-four hours a day ever since it was built in 1862, it is our city's central meeting place. Beggars and princes, vagabonds and counts—no matter the social standing, everyone eventually finds his way to the wide, open-air market that sits, long and low as a shipyard, nestled along the banks of the moody, muddy river that helped make this city what it is. And sooner or later everyone ends up at Café du Monde.

As Holmes and I approached through the dimly streets, I could not suppress a little gasp of delight. As many times as I had beheld the sight, the view seldom failed to stir my heart. Paddleboats and packet boats glided along the murky waters of the river as twilight settled over the city and lanterns were lit in the stalls of the vendors. It was one of those evenings when the color of the river exactly matched the sky at dusk; both were a troubled grey hue, grainy and dense as the chicory-flavored coffee our city is famous for. The murmur of buyers and sellers in the market mingled with the more lively chatter and occasional burst of laughter from the patrons sitting along the river at the outdoor tables of the café. Couples strolled along the Moonwalk, a dirt path that follows the river as it twists and curves around the French Quarter.

You could find most anything at the French Market. There were fishmongers and fruit sellers, bakers and butchers, dressmakers and tobacconists. Merchants in crisp white aprons hovered over their wares as prospective customers surveyed the row of stalls, bending over the tables and shelves of various goods. In spite of the gloom of the descending February twilight, there was a festive mood in the air. Mardi Gras was only weeks away, and you could sense the gathering anticipation among the patrons of the café.

I was not in a particularly festive mood, however; nor was my companion, from what I could tell. He viewed the scene in front of us with a detached eye, his face betraying no emotion. The wind had died down as sunset approached, and there was barely a ripple of breeze as we seated ourselves at a table near the water's edge. A harried-looking waiter appeared to take our order; I asked for coffee and beignets, while Holmes ordered only coffee. After the waiter scurried away I took a moment to observe the great detective more closely. The flush I noticed earlier on his cheeks appeared more pronounced, and sweat stood out on his forehead when he removed his hat. I did not think it was a good sign; a man as lean as he was should not feel overly exerted from our short walk, and I feared he was indeed ill. Our climate is not an especially healthful one—the hot, humid weather greatly increases the incidence of fevers and other infections.

"Mr. Holmes, are you feeling all right?" I said.

Either he did not hear my question or chose to ignore it. Instead, he turned to look at a man sitting at an adjacent table.

"You can tell so much about people from their shoes," he remarked, almost to himself. "For instance, that man over there went through a period of depression after his wife left him, but things seem to be looking up for him tonight. He was beginning to regret coming over here from Ireland, where he was more prosperous, but perhaps the affections of his new lady will change that."

I did my best to study the man closely, but from what I could observe, there was nothing singular about him or his shoes. He was of average height, with a broad Irish face and a splotch of reddish brown hair—utterly ordinary, the sort of man you might see working along the docks.

"You astonish me, Mr. Holmes," I said. "Apart from the fact that he is Irish, which you can plainly see in his face, I have no idea how you came to your conclusions."

Holmes shrugged. "You are right about his face, though I deduced he was Irish by the cut of his shoes—Dublin-made, by the look of them."

"Fair enough," I replied, "but his wife leaving him—how on earth did you reach that conclusion?"

"If you look at his shoes, you will observe that they have long gone unpolished. And yet recently—today, perhaps, an attempt has been made to restore order, and some polish has been carelessly swiped across the tops—a hasty job, but a hopeful one. The shoes have gone unpolished because keeping them up was his wife's job; but once she left he lost heart and let his shoes fall into some disrepair—you may notice that the laces are frayed as well—because he was depressed at losing her. The shoes are well made, of expensive leather, so I gather he was more prosperous in Ireland, when he was able to afford such a pair of shoes."

I shook my head. "Truly remarkable, Mr. Holmes. And the new lady friend?"

Holmes permitted himself a slight smile. "Well, there is hopefulness indicated in the new coat of polish, and also a bit of vanity, but I must admit to a bit of cheating on that score. Our friend is evidently meeting someone, because he keeps looking around anxiously every few moments to see if she has arrived. One does not look around that eagerly for a casual meeting with a friend; therefore, I deduce that he has met someone who has taken his fancy."

No sooner had Holmes spoken than he was proven right. A very attractive young lady entered the café area from the direction of the vendors' stalls, and as soon as our man saw her, he practically leapt from his chair to greet her. I turned to Holmes and shook my head.

"I congratulate you, Mr. Holmes—everything I have heard about you is true."

"I am gratified to meet your expectations, Captain," he replied, as the harried waiter brought our coffee and my plate of beignets, which were always served three at a time.

I took a bite, savoring the crispness of the crust and the soft, hot interior, fresh from the fryer. A beignet is really just a square donut—fried dough dusted with powdered sugar—but there is something about eating them in the open-air café along the river that is never disappointing.

Holmes took a sip of coffee. "This is most unusual coffee—it has a kind of charred flavor, if you don't mind my saying so."

I smiled. "You know, it's funny, Mr. Holmes—my Cajun ancestors added roasted endive root—which they called chicory—to their coffee when times were hard and coffee was scarce, to make it last longer, you know? And now the chicory coffee is one of the things folks come to New Orleans for. It's ironic, don't you think?"

"I do indeed, Captain. In fact, I have observed that whole lives can turn upon a single irony such as that." He leaned back in his chair and fixed his keen dark eyes upon me. "Now then, Captain, why don't you tell me what it is that upset you so?"

I took a deep breath and relayed to Holmes everything that happened in the station just prior to his arrival.

"I know you must think me a fool for being swayed by the words of a so-called voodoo priestess—"

"I think no such thing, Captain, I can assure you."

"You see, Charles Latille is my dearest friend, and on top of that I am engaged to be married to his sister, Evangeline."

"Evangeline," he mused. "Isn't that the name of the heroine in a very romantic tale about your Acadian ancestors?"

"Yes—Longfellow wrote a poem about it. It is the tale of a faithful Acadian girl who follows her lover, even after he has been banished."

"Yes, yes—I seem to recall coming across it at some point."

"Oh, Mr. Holmes, my Evangeline is just like the one in the legend! A more lovely creature never sat foot on Louisiana soil!" I knew it was foolish of me, but I couldn't help myself. With the beauty of the night, the river, and the exhilaration of being in the great detective's presence, I was in a rhapsodic mood. "She has the face of an angel and a temperament to match. And her eyes—they're dark brown, Mr. Holmes, so dark that in dim light they appear to be black. Such depth in them, too—you could lose yourself in those eyes."

"Well, be very sure you don't, Captain; your friend may have need of your assistance."

I grew solemn, ashamed that in my ardor I had forgotten the peril Charles was in.

"What do you think, Mr. Holmes? Who could be behind this? Who would want to harm Charles?"

"Precisely what I was going to ask you, Captain. Who indeed?"

I took a sip of coffee and stared out at the couples walking arm in arm along the banks of the river. Dusk had deepened into twilight, and the gas lamps along the Moonwalk were all lit by then, their reflected glow rippling softly upon the water.

"Well, there is heavy competition in the shipping business . . . in fact, Charles confided in me just the other day that things were not going at all well for him financially. And quite frankly, not all of his competitors are—well, lawful citizens."

"You are referring to the so-called Italian Mafia, of course."

"You know of it?"

He nodded. "I have in my own career had some interaction with members of various crimes organizations, both here and abroad. Your Italian Mafia is a rather recent import to this country, if I'm not mistaken?"

"Yes, though in Sicily it dates back to the twelfth century, when the French controlled and oppressed the inhabitants of that island. In fact, I have heard that the word comes from the first initials in the phrase, '*Morte all Francia Italia anelia*,' which is Italian for 'Death to the French is Italy's cry.'"

He cocked his head to one side. "Indeed? You seem to know rather a lot about the organization."

"With good reason. You may perhaps have heard of the events of last October?"

He nodded. "Yes. Your Police Superintendent. Hennessy was ambushed and killed in a spray of gunfire—the night of October fifteenth, I believe?"

"Yes. He had been pursuing the activities of the Italian Mafia along the docks for some time. It is widely believed they assassinated him."

"And yet the nineteen men charged with the conspiracy were never convicted, as I recall."

I snorted in disgust. "Disgracefully shoddy work on our part. Instead of going after only the men responsible, they rounded up some poor laborers—some were just off the boat and weren't even in New Orleans when Hennessy was killed!"

"There were also rumors of jury tampering."

I shrugged. "Undoubtedly. But by that time, what did it matter? Everyone in the city was in the grip of anti-Italian fervor. And the events that followed were shameful, Mr. Holmes—shameful!"

"You are referring to the murder of the defendants?"

I shuddered. "Pulled from their jail cells by an angry mob of six thousands citizens. They were murdered in cold blood, Mr. Holmes! I have never been so ashamed of my city."

"Nine were shot and two hanged, I believe?"

"Yes—and no one was ever charged in their deaths. The justice system that turns a blind eye to such a travesty is a poor affair indeed. I am still appalled by such a naked display of prejudice and vigilante vengeance. Do you know that the Italian government was so outraged that it broke off diplomatic relations with this country?"

Holmes ran a long finger around the rim of his coffee cup. "I believe I heard something to that effect."

"Rightly so, in my mind, Mr. Holmes. However, I must tell you that view is not a popular one, at least not among the non-Italian population of this city. Since that time, everyone has been more than a little on edge, and suspicions between various cultural groups have become more pronounced, the lines between them sharper."

Holmes shook his head. "That is unfortunate. But you believe that some of these more ruthless characters might be trying to intimidate your friend?"

"It's possible. What I don't understand is why they haven't threatened him directly."

"Perhaps they have, and he has yet to tell you."

"That wouldn't be like Charles. We were at school together— we have no secrets from each other."

Holmes lifted one eyebrow and put down his coffee cup. His hands were long and slender, yet, I fancied, capable of great strength.

"My dear Captain Brasseaux, it is often the people we least expect to have secrets who surprise us by keeping the darkest things hidden from us."

Holmes looked around the café as if he thought someone might be eavesdropping on our conversation. Then he turned to me and lowered his voice.

"What of this voodoo priestess, Madame Celeste—what do you know of her? Would she have any reason to wish your friend ill?"

"Not that I know of. Everyone knows who she is, but I had no idea she knew Charles."

"Perhaps it is her business to know things. In any case, I think a visit to Madame Celeste is indicated."

We finished our coffee quickly and headed off toward the heart of the French Quarter. Madame Celeste's residence was not hard to find; everyone in the neighborhood seemed to know where she lived. It was not far from Antoine's Restaurant, a favorite among both locals and the swelling tide of tourists and vacationers who streamed through our town this time of year. Though their presence was good for our economy, it made my job harder; guarding them from pickpockets, burglars, and garrotters was like trying to protect a large, placid herd of sheep from a pack of hungry wolves. You could always spot the tourists, with their stolid, passive faces, often trailing a brood of stodgy, equally dull-faced children behind them, gazing up at the elaborate wrought-iron balconies of the French Quarter. The sight of them made me wince, because they are sitting ducks for our city's ever-present criminal element—they might just as well have signs around their necks reading "PLEASE ROB ME," or "LOOK NO FURTHER—EASY MARK." Somehow, though, our rising crime rate doesn't deter them, and they keep coming, stepping out of their coaches and rail carriages like lemmings swarming from cliffs into the sea below.

Holmes and I shouldered our way through the thickening throngs of sightseers until we reached Madame Celeste's building. Her apartment was in a rather elegant rooming house on Royal Street—on the first floor, naturally, given her aversion to climbing stairs.

We soon discovered that Madame Celeste did not make appointments, nor did she keep regular hours. After knocking loudly, we tried the door, but it was locked securely, with no signs of life within. We went around to the back entrance, where there was a note taped to the door: "Out—*retourner temps à temps*," a vague enough promise that we cooled our heels in the oyster bar across the street, consoling ourselves with a few dozen blue points. Finally, after an hour of waiting, I left a note indicating that I wished to see her at her earliest convenience. When Holmes suggested we pay a call to Charles and Evangeline, I agreed immediately, and we hopped on the St. Charles Avenue trolley.

Charles and Evangeline Latille lived in one of the grand houses along St. Charles Street in the part of town known as the Garden District. The Latilles were not Acadian like my father's family, but pure French Creole, and could trace their ancestry back centuries to Provençal nobility; a branch of the family had settled in New Orleans in the mid 1700s. The Latilles who settled in the New World were a practical-minded lot, and started a shipping business that continued more or less unabated through to Charles, who took over managing the firm when his father died some years back. Though perhaps he lacked the keen business instincts of his forebears, Charles did his best to carry on and support himself and his sister.

As Holmes and I ascended the stairs to the front entrance of the house, I turned to look at him. Though he was trying to hide it, he was evidently winded, leaning on the stoop railing for support. I rang the bell.

"Are you sure you're all right, Mr. Holmes?" I said.

"Perfectly all right, thank you," he replied, unsuccessfully stifling a cough. He was obviously lying, but just then the door opened and I had no more opportunity to question him further.

We entered the house, admitted by Esthmé, the ancient octoroon who had been with the Latilles for as long as I could remember and whose family had served them for three generations. Her face was a fine network of wrinkles, like a delicate lace handkerchief that had been folded many times. Her eyes were clear, though, and her back was straight and stiff as a sapling, though she favored one leg slightly when she walked. Her hair was only just turning from black to grey, and a few wisps fluttered from the green bandana she wore in winter and summer.

"Evenun', Missah Lucien," Esthmé said, casting a dubious glance at Holmes. Esthmé did not grant her favor lightly, and even after all our years of association, I was not quite sure if she approved of me. My pedigree certainly wasn't up to that of the Latilles—and from time to time over the years, Esthmé made it quite plain that she knew this. Social status counts in New Orleans; ancestry and pedigree is important, and it wasn't uncommon for servants of grand families to look down upon anyone who did not match the social standing of their masters.

"Hello, Esthmé," I replied, handing her my hat. "How's your lumbago these days?"

"Oh, cain't say as how I kin complain. It done bother me sumpthin' terrible last month, but fo' some reason it ain't been comin' back these past weeks."

"Perhaps it's that new ointment the doctor gave you to rub on it," Holmes remarked.

Esthmé stared at him, her long jaw slack with amazement, but just then Evangeline came flying down the hallway, and I forgot all about Esthmé and her lumbago. My beloved wore a simple lemon yellow dress, devoid of frills and frippery, but my heart nearly stopped at the sight of her. Her jet-black hair, usually up in a perfect chignon, was disordered and hung around her neck in damp ringlets.

"Lucien, darling, thank heavens you've come!" Evangeline cried, wrapping her fragrant white arms around me, and I felt faint with the intoxicating mixture of love and desire. She clearly had been crying. Her pretty mouth trembled, and her dark eyelashes were heavy with tears.

"What is it, Evy darling?"

"It—it's Charles. He's not well. Thank heaven you've come!"

"What's the matter?" I said, fear seeping into my bones.

"Come see for yourself," she replied—then, with a quick glance at Holmes, she lowered her eyes. "I beg your pardon, sir; where are my manners?"

"Not at all, madam; I can plainly see you are distressed," he answered gently. "Perhaps I may even be of some assistance."

"Permit me to introduce my fiancée, Evangeline Latille. Evy, this is Mr.—" I froze. In the heat of the moment, I had forgotten Holmes's alias.

"Altamont, Jean Paul Altamont," Holmes said smoothly, barely missing a beat. I breathed what I hoped was a silent sigh of relief.

"Pleased to meet you, Mr. Altamont," said Evangeline. "I hope you'll forgive a foolish woman's rantings, but I am so terribly worried about my brother."

"Understandably so, I'm sure," Holmes replied. "Where is he?"

"This way," she said, leading us up the wide central staircase off the entrance hall. There was no sign of the redoubtable Esthmé, who had discreetly withdrawn. I had grown up in the Latille house as much as in my own, and I knew every scratch in the thick oak banister, every nick in the maple wainscoting, every knot in the floorboards. I had left pieces of my soul in the branches of the great elm tree we used to climb in the backyard, and the boy in me lingered underneath the huge magnolias that lined the front garden, seeking the shade of their broad leaves, inhaling their soft fragrance. I was no more a stranger in this house than I was in my own, and yet, when I followed Evangeline down the corridor to Charles's bedroom, another chill ran through me. It was swift and sharp, short as the flight of a swallow, but it shook me. I turned to look at Holmes to see if he felt anything; but his lips were compressed, his eyes sharp, as if he were studying everything around him. I did not like his pallor; his cheeks were unnaturally flushed, and sweat stood out on his face, though the evening was quite cool.

When we got to Charles's room, though, I was even more appalled at the sight of my friend. He lay huddled on his bed, the bedclothes up to his chin, clutching at them with whitened knuckles. As we entered the darkened room I could hear him moaning softly—he seemed only vaguely aware of our presence. I turned to Evangeline.

"How long has he been like this?"

"Since this afternoon. He took sick after lunch."

"Why didn't you fetch a doctor?" I asked impatiently. The minute the words were out of my mouth, I regretted them. Poor Evangeline dissolved into tears and was unable to answer me. I cursed myself for the unnecessary harshness in my voice, but it had been a trying day, and my nerves were on edge. To top it off, I couldn't help wondering if my friend's pitiful condition was related somehow to Madame Celeste's dire warning. I didn't want to capitulate to superstition, but when you grow up in southern Louisiana, it is difficult to banish such thoughts. Ridiculous as my logical mind told me it was, the thought struck to my brain like molasses on corn bread: *Charles Latille was the victim of a voodoo curse.*

Mr. Holmes, however, seemed to have no such predilections; he was the very soul of rationality and action. He bent over Charles and checked his pulse, then laid a hand upon his forehead. Charles looked up at him.

"Are—you—a doctor?" His voice was thin and ragged.

Holmes shook his head. "No, Mr. Latille, though I have some medical knowledge by association, you might say. Forgive my forwardness, but you look as though you could use some medical care. Your friend and your sister are quite worried about you."

"I'll be all right," Charles muttered weakly. "Probably just a spot of food poisoning." He looked up at me apologetically. "Probably one too many oysters at lunch."

It was so like Charles to be embarrassed about what he perceived as weakness. Though well over six feet tall, he was slight of build and delicate, like his sister. Gangly and spindly as an overwatered house plant, he was never very strong as a child and was the object of bullying at school. In fact, our friendship was cemented early on when I rescued him from the clutches of a big half-Cajun, half-Choctaw called Bottlenose Joe. Joe, whose nickname derived from his unusually prodigious proboscis, had Charles half-choked, half-scared to death when I showed up and suggested he pick on someone more able to defend himself. I am not especially tall, but the Brasseaux men are all built like bulls—my father came from a long line of bar brawlers. He taught me how to square off against any opponent, and I was able to give Bottlenose Joe something to think about for a while. He never came near Charles again.

That pattern of rescuing my friend from scrapes continued throughout our boyhood—there was something about him, a softness, maybe, that drew bullies to him. Whatever the reason, he was the closest thing I had to a brother, and I took it upon myself to assure his safety while we were growing up. I never regretted it—he was clever and kind and always had pretty girls after him, so I got the pick of his leftovers, as it were.

Charles had the same dark hair and pale complexion as his sister, but just then his face was stark, fish-belly white, all the color drained from his cheeks. I tried to smile, to make a pretense of not being concerned. Evangeline's tears had dried, but her face was a mask of concern. She stood at the foot of his bed, wringing her hands.

"What are your symptoms, if you don't mind my asking?" said Holmes.

"Vomiting, stomach pains, sweating, cramps—pretty much like food poisoning," he replied.

"I see. And where did you dine for lunch?"

He managed a weak smile. "Same place I always do—Antoine's."

"Ah, yes," Holmes remarked. "Quite a respectable place, from what I've heard."

"The best," said Charles. "So you're not from around here, then?"

Holmes ignored the question. "Well, you are correct in your assumption that fresh seafood does not always behave itself, no matter what the chef's credentials. At any rate, you appear to be in no immediate danger." He turned to me. "I suggest we let your friend get some rest now."

"Very well," I said.

Before we left, Evangeline fluffed up her brother's pillows and kissed him softly on the cheek. We left the door ajar behind us and tiptoed down the hall, descending the main staircase quietly. When we reached the foyer, Esthmé was coming from the direction of the kitchen, carrying a bowl of milk in her hand.

"That damn cat done gone and run off!" she muttered, heading toward the back door leading out to the garden.

"Excuse me for a moment," said Holmes. "Did you say you've lost your cat?"

Esthmé stopped and turned to face us. "It's the strangest thing, monsieur, don' ya know. Never knew that cat to refuse a bowl a' milk afore."

"How long has she been missing?" Holmes inquired.

Esthmé shrugged. "Mos' all afternoon. And usually she keeps me company whilst I chop da vegetables, so then."

Holmes nodded. "I see. Would you be kind enough to notify me when the cat reappears?"

Esthmé blinked. "It's jes a cat, sir."

That was my reaction exactly, and I told Holmes as much as we headed off to catch the St. Charles Avenue trolley. I have a cabin out on the bayou just across from the Lower Ninth Ward, and I had convinced Mr. Holmes to stay with me rather than book a hotel in town. I must confess my motive was partially selfish: the thought of playing host to the greatest detective in the world filled me with excitement. There would be time, perhaps, to pick his brain about some of his most difficult cases, and maybe even ask him about a few of my unsolved ones. Though I had risen to precinct captain, in my heart I would always be a city police detective; my happiest days were when I was out gathering evidence and chasing criminals through our grimy, gritty streets. And I was engaged in the same pursuit once more, but this time with the help of the incomparable Sherlock Holmes.

"Why were you so interested in Esthmé's cat?" I asked as the trolley car clattered along the tracks. It was late, and the car was practically empty, the conductor sitting sleepy-eyed at his wheel, his cap pulled down low over his face. "Surely the disappearance of a cat is a mere trifle."

"My dear Captain Brasseaux," he replied, "sometimes an entire case turns upon a mere trifle, as you call it."

I was silent for some time, then I turned to him. "Mr. Holmes, this may sound like a foolish question, but . . . do you believe in curses?"

"Believe in them? Well, I suppose you could say I believe in the power of suggestion—that when a man believes himself to be cursed, his life may well turn out badly."

"But do you think one person has the ability to put a spell on another?"

"There are many kinds of enchantments, Captain," he replied thoughtfully. "And many things between birth and death we do not understand. So I suppose I would have to say that I do believe it is possible for a person to fall under another's spell."

I could not know then how his words were to haunt me in the days to come.

I cooked dinner for the two of us that night, crawfish with "dirty rice," a Cajun specialty, and Holmes seemed to enjoy the meal. I persuaded him to lie on the couch while I cleared the dishes; when I had finished washing up, I returned to the living room to find him sound asleep. I draped a blanket over him, turned out the lights, and tiptoed off to my own bed, disappointed there would be no late-night discussion of past cases, but also somewhat relieved. I was exhausted. I fell asleep immediately, to a night filled with troubled dreams in which I was being pursued through the swamps and bayous by an unknown assailant wearing a mask.

Somewhere out in the night, an owl hooted.

Holmes went with me to the station early the next morning. Though it was Sergeant Pierce's job to call roll, by eight-thirty he still hadn't shown up, so I did it myself, then dismissed my men out to their regular beats. The last few days had been fairly quiet, but with Carnival in full swing, there would always be purse snatchers, pickpockets, and bar brawls—the usual pre–Mardi Gras petty crimes. We also had several undercover agents assigned to cover the growing Mafia presence on the docks.

To my great surprise, shortly after the last man had left, Madame Celeste appeared in the street outside. Her encounter with the front steps was a replay of the same heroic struggle as before, and as she entered the office, she made a grand gesture of wiping her brow as though she had just single-handedly laid down the rails for the transcontinental railway.

"*Alors, monsieur, c'est très disagreable!*" she grunted, as I motioned her to a seat.

"Thank you so much for returning to see us," I said.

Holmes stood over by my sergeant's desk; Pierce had yet to make an appearance.

"Madame Celeste, I would like you to meet my associate, Mr. Altamont."

"Jean Paul Altamont at your service, madame," Holmes said, stepping forward.

Madame Celeste looked him up and down with a critical eye. Evidently, however, he met with her approval, and she favored him with a broad smile. Her teeth were brown and even as railroad ties.

"*Alors, enchanté, monsieur,*" she said, offering him a plump hand. To my surprise, he took it and kissed the large green sapphire ring on her middle finger.

"The honor is mine. Your fame precedes you, madame," he replied gallantly.

"*Vraiment, monsieur?*" she said, giggling like a child.

"Oh, yes, most assuredly. Even where I come from they have heard of you."

"Oh, and where is dat, monsieur?" she asked with a coquettish smile.

"I'm from up north," Holmes answered vaguely, sitting across from her.

Apparently caught up in his flattery, she did not press him to be more specific.

"So, monsieur, what brings you down here?"

"Some family business, and a chance to visit my colleague here."

His words warmed me, and I blushed at the idea of being called a "colleague" by the great detective.

"Madame Celeste," I began, emboldened by the fact that she was obviously so taken with Holmes. "I wonder if we might question you further about your visit yesterday?"

She looked at me and then at Holmes, her face darkening.

"It is a bad business . . . *va!*" she added, which in this context meant something like "Shoo!" or "Begone!"

"Yes, indeed. I couldn't agree with you more," Holmes responded. "But I fear you have not told Captain Brasseaux the whole story."

Madame Celeste blinked once and opened her eyes wide.

"Mais certainement, ce n'est-ce pas vrais," she said, speaking very rapidly and entirely in French. *"C'est un couchemare, vraiment."*

Holmes nodded. "Yes, a nightmare indeed—especially if this murder you seem to fear takes place. But this information did not come to you in a vision, as you claim." He leaned in toward her. "Whom are you trying to protect?"

"Dere is no protecting, monsieur," she replied, drawing herself up indignantly and fanning her face with a lilac-scented handkerchief. "You must understand, when de people come to me, eh, dere is the same *confidance* as in the confessional—I can never betray my sacred vow!"

"But you did come to warn Captain Brasseaux that his friend was in danger."

"Yes, yes," she answered impatiently. "But more I cannot say! It is not allowed." She turned to me with pleading eyes. "Please understand me, *mon capitan*, it is not dat I wish your friend ill—but I have a vow I must keep, the sacred oath of *voudoun.*"

"She means voodoo," I explained to Holmes. "Voudoun is another word for it."

"Dis person, I have helped dem before, *oui?* Perhaps I try to heal sickness, or I weave a little fabric . . . but den dey ask me to put a *gris-gris*—a spell—and I say no I will not do that—I do not do *le Petro!*"

"*Petro* is black magic," I said to Holmes, and he nodded as she turned to me.

"So den dey go away and I come to warn you, monsieur—you can save your friend's life. You and Monsieur Altamont must watch him, no?"

The poor woman was quite agitated now, and she looked back and forth from me to Holmes with a piteous expression. He patted her hand gently.

"I understand, madame—you cannot tell us who came to ask for your services because your sacred oath prevents it."

"*Exactement, monsieur—c'est ça!*" She looked greatly relieved.

"Thank you very much for your time, madame—it is much appreciated," Holmes said, escorting her to the door. "You have been quite helpful."

"*Vraiment, monsieur?*"

"Yes, very. Please rest assured that Captain Brasseaux and I will do everything we can to keep his friend safe."

"Yes, yes—you must. *Merci, monsieur, merci.*"

"You too must be careful," Holmes replied. "Please allow me to look in on you tomorrow."

"*D'accord—merci,*" she answered, and with a flourish of her scented handkerchief, she was gone.

Holmes watched her negotiate her journey down the stairs, which took her nearly as long as coming up. "Remarkable woman," he mused. "She was very brave to come here . . . but I fear she, too, is now in danger."

I wondered at what evil person or persons could endanger not only Charles but also the famous Madame Celeste.

"Around here voodoo is considered a religion, much the same as Catholicism or any other religion," I said to Holmes.

"So I gather. She obviously takes her responsibilities very seriously."

"I personally don't see that much of a distinction," I remarked. "Sometimes I think all religion is just an excuse for indulging in socially acceptable superstition."

"Perhaps so. In any event, we are dealing with a very cunning and versatile adversary," Holmes observed, as Sergeant Pierce stumbled into the station house, looking as though he had the worst of a bout with a bottle of whiskey last night.

"'Morning," Pierce said, with a glance at Holmes; then he muttered something about it being Carnival and took a seat at his desk.

"How did you know that she was hiding something from me?" I said, but Holmes was already putting on his coat.

"I'm very sorry, but I have other business to attend to. Perhaps we could meet around noon at your friend's house? I imagine we would both like to see how he is getting on."

We agreed to a lunchtime meeting at the Latilles', and Holmes left. I devoted the rest of the morning to catching up on long-neglected paperwork; then, shortly before noon, I turned to my sergeant.

"Pierce, take over, will you? I'm going out for a while."

"Yes, sir." He cleared his throat and leaned forward over his desk. "Sir, about that gentleman . . ."

"Yes, Pierce?"

He studied his fingernails. "Well, sir, I was wondering—"

"His name is Altamont, Pierce. He's from up north."

"Oh. I see. So he's—"

"He's helping me out on one or two little matters."

"I see, sir. Very good, sir."

"I'll see you later, Pierce."

"Yes, sir."

Though Holmes seemed to feel Charles was in no immediate danger, I was concerned about my friend and anxious to see him. As I walked along Royal Street, the sound of a guitar floated out of the window of one of the older houses in the Quarter, and I stopped to listen for a moment. The Brasseaux family is rumored to have gypsy blood, and I believe it. When I hear the sound of guitar music, nothing else matters. The strum of a pick over catgut sends me into a trance, much the same way as a gator will go quiet if you stroke his head, right between the eyes. My father played the guitar, as did his father, and as far back as anyone can remember, a Brasseaux has always played the guitar.

When I arrived, Evangeline met me at the door.

"Oh, Lucien, thank heavens you've come!" she cried, throwing herself into my arms.

"What is it, Evy?" I said, stroking her black curls.

"I'm so frightened!"

"Is it Charles? Is he all right?"

"Yes, I'm fine, thank you."

I turned to see my friend, standing in the hallway, looking much improved from the day before.

"I'm glad to see you on your feet!" I said, taking him by the shoulders and studying his face. He was a bit pale, but he had regained some of his color, and his voice was much stronger.

"What is it, then?" I said, turning to Evangeline. "What's happened?"

"Come here and I'll show you," Charles answered, starting toward the parlor. Just then the front doorbell rang, and we all turned.

"Oh, that must be Mr. H—Altamont," I said, hastily covering my error.

Evy went to open the door, and sure enough, it was Holmes, looking a bit winded, as though he had had a busy morning.

"Good afternoon, Miss Latille," he said, tipping his hat as he entered.

"Hello, Mr. Altamont," she said shyly, lowering her eyes.

"It is good to see you looking so much better," Holmes said to Charles.

"Thank you—and thank you for your concern," Charles replied somewhat distractedly.

Holmes looked at him, then back at me. "What is the matter?"

"Something's happened," I said, "but I don't know what yet."

"I'm afraid we had a bit of vandalism last night," Charles told us. "Nothing much, really, probably just a prank—but Evy is rather frightened."

"What happened?" I asked.

"Someone threw a stone through our parlor window!" Evy cried.

"It's probably just a Mardi Gras prank," Charles remarked.

"Indeed," said Holmes. "Is that kind of thing common here?"

Charles shrugged. "This time of year anything can happen."

Evy tugged at his sleeve. "Tell them about the note!"

"What note?" I said.

Charles sighed and took a piece of paper from his pocket, handing it to me. "This was attached to the rock with a string. I'm sure it's just a stupid prank."

I looked at the paper—a common enough scrap of white paper,

but scribbled upon it was a crude drawing of a black hand. I turned pale and handed the paper to Holmes. The Black Hand was a symbol for a violent branch of the Italian Mafia.

"Interesting," he said, studying it. "Are you aware of what this symbol signifies?"

"Those damned dagoes!" Evy cried. "It's a warning—they're out to get Charles!"

I was used to hearing crude remarks around the police station, but I was taken aback to hear my Evy using such language.

"Hmm," Holmes mused. "Perhaps. Might I see the place where the rock landed?"

"Certainly," said Charles, with a glance at me.

"Oh, Mr. Altamont is a detective from . . . up north," I said hastily.

"Ah, I see. Well, it's right over here," Charles said, leading us into the parlor. "I'm afraid it shattered the window rather badly. Evy wanted Esthmé to clean it up, but I thought you might want to have a look. I left the rock there, too."

A pile of glass lay scattered at the bottom of one of the French windows in the front parlor. Holmes went over to the window and lifted back the curtain, studying the fabric. "This window looks out onto the street, so anyone could have come by, thrown the rock, and run away."

"Yes," said Charles. "I didn't even hear it—I was sleeping—but Evy did. It woke her up, and she came to get me."

"I was so frightened!" said Evangeline. "I thought someone had broken in."

Holmes said nothing more, but knelt to study the glass on the floor carefully, examining it under a magnifying glass he pulled from his pocket. I studied the same curtain that seemed to interest him so much, but I could see nothing unusual about it.

"Very well," Holmes said at last. "I see dark forces are at work here."

"So you think it is the Black Hand?" Charles said. He was trying to appear unconcerned, but I could tell he was frightened.

"I cannot say at present," Holmes replied, "though I have learned some very interesting facts from the crime scene. Thank you for preserving it so well."

"That's Lucien's influence," Charles answered. "Did you know he used to be a detective until he was promoted to Captain?"

"Uh, yes—Jean Paul and I go way back," I said.

"Funny," said Evy. "I've never heard you speak of him."

"Well," said Holmes, "I have an urgent call to make elsewhere, and I hope you will excuse me. I suggest you keep a low profile," he said to Charles. "Don't go into your office tomorrow, if you can avoid it."

"Very well," said Charles. "Business is not very good anyway—I doubt if anyone will miss me much. And the Comus ball is tomorrow night, so I'll just rest up for it. I suppose going to the ball presents no danger?"

"No, that will be all right," said Holmes, turning to me. "Are you free to accompany me to my next destination?"

I looked at Charles, who nodded. "We'll be fine—really."

"All right," I said. "Send for me if anything else happens."

"We will," he said, and followed us to the door.

"Where is that stalwart servant of yours?" Holmes inquired, looking around.

"Oh, Esthmé is out in the garden burying the poor cat," Charles answered.

"Dear me," said Holmes. "The same cat that was missing yesterday?"

"Yes, I'm afraid so. Poor thing just died—out of the blue, really. She hadn't even been sick, as far as I know."

"Hmm," said Holmes. "Was she an old cat?"

"No, quiet young, actually—in fact, I gave her to Evy just a year ago."

"Poor Pumpkin!" Evy said, and began crying again. "Don't let's talk about it—it's too sad!"

"Well, I'm sorry to hear it," I said. I knew the cat—a plump orange tabby, very affectionate, and devoted to Evangeline.

"I am, too," said Holmes. "The death of a pet can be such an upsetting thing."

"Will you be all right, darling?" I asked Evy, who nodded through tear-streaked eyes.

"You will come for us tomorrow to escort us to the ball?"

"I wouldn't miss it," I answered. "I think we all need some fun in the middle of these unsettling events."

Holmes and I stepped out onto the street and walked down the avenue to the streetcar stop. When we were far enough away from the house, he turned to me.

"Will you accompany me to Madame Celeste's?"

"Yes, but—"

"We must act quickly and decisively—I am afraid your friend is in great danger. I also fear for Madame Celeste's safety."

I stared at him as we climbed onto the trolley. "But you just said—"

"Never mind what I said!" he interrupted impatiently. "I had my reasons. But the death of the cat, among other things, has convinced me that he is in danger."

"What's the cat got to do with it?"

"My dear Captain Brasseaux," he replied, "don't you see? The cat was poisoned."

"Poisoned!"

"I am certain of it—and so was your friend. He was very lucky to escape . . . my guess is that the poisoner most likely used arsenic oxide. The killer was experimenting on the cat, but a lethal dose for a cat is not quite the same as for a person—fortunately for your friend."

"But—what's to stop them from trying again?" I said.

"The rock through the window indicates they are already trying other tactics," he replied. "Poisoning that fails once can look like food poisoning, but a second incident . . . well, that would look suspicious."

"What about the rock, then? What did you find in the curtain that was so interesting?"

"It is what I did *not* find that interests me," he said. "But here we are—I only hope we aren't too late!"

I followed him from the trolley down into the heart of the French Quarter, struggling to keep up with his long strides. I couldn't help think of my English counterpart, Dr. Watson, as I trailed after Holmes through the crowded streets of the Quarter. I felt a kinship to him, and I felt privileged to be walking in his shoes, as it were, if only for a short time.

When we got to Celeste's building, the windows on the first floor were all dark. However, Holmes went up to the front door and knocked loudly. Receiving no answer, he tried the door, but it was locked.

"I hope we aren't too late," he said as he hurried around to the back entrance. We found the outer door ajar, and a shiver threaded its way up my spine as Holmes pushed lightly on the door and entered. We found ourselves in the kitchen, which was dark and quiet. Bunches of dried herbs hung from the ceiling, and the aroma of sage and rosemary mixed with the smell of andouille sausage coming from a pot of stew cooling on the stove. I followed Holmes down a narrow hallway to a side parlor.

There, lying on a burgundy Oriental rug, her throat slit, was Madame Celeste. The blood around her neck was dried and caked—she had evidently been there for some time. A few fat flies circled lazily around the wound. Her open eyes stared up at a slowly revolving ceiling fan. She wore her usual layer of colorful fabrics, turquoise over sunburst yellow. A soft grey scarf lay at her side—it had not been able to protect her throat from the knife that had sliced cleanly through her jugular vein.

"Oh, no," I said softly, and bent down to close her sightless eyes.

Holmes stood staring at her silently for some time, then he hit his forehead sharply with a clenched fist and swore under his breath. He turned abruptly and left the room.

I followed after him, perplexed. "Aren't you going to examine the crime scene?"

"There is no need," he snapped. "I know perfectly well who killed her."

Try as I might, I could not get Holmes to tell me what he knew.

"But why won't you tell me?" I pleaded, as we walked toward the station house.

"I have my reasons, Captain. And I intend to bring this fiend to justice—but I must ask you to trust me." He stopped walking for a moment and faced me, his sharply etched features earnest. "I know this is difficult for you, but please believe me when I say I have a plan and that I need your cooperation. I promise you will not be in the dark for long."

My eyes met his, and I felt the full force of his personality in those grey eyes—deep-set and keen as a hawk's. I was not a man accustomed to receiving orders from others, and I did not like being kept in the dark, but, after all, this was the great Sherlock Holmes—how could I refuse him?

"Very well," I said. "Tell me what you want me to do."

"Now, as to this ball tomorrow—do you think you could procure me an invitation?"

I sighed. "It may prove difficult."

He raised an eyebrow. "Really? Perhaps you should explain."

As we walked along, I told him about the krewes of New Orleans—private clubs that each sponsored their own Mardi Gras floats. Every krewe also had its own ball, and each year they would try to outdo each other in elegance and style. The Latilles were founding members of Comus—the oldest and most prestigious of all the krewes—and Charles always managed to get me an invitation, but they were very hard to come by.

"But I'll see Charles about it right away," I concluded.

"Good—it is vital. Now, you must have a backup force of policemen at the ready—but they are not to make themselves known in any way, and are only to act upon a signal from you. Does that present any problems?"

"No. I can have them stationed outside, around the house; it will be dark, and no one will see them."

"Good, good. We need to lay a trap—but an obvious police presence would scare off our prey."

"So you feel that something will happen at the ball—that the killer will show his hand?"

"Yes, I think I can safely guarantee that."

"And will Charles or Evangeline be in any danger?"

"I would be lying to you if I said no, Captain. But I also think we must strike, and this is our best chance."

I sighed. "Very well."

I spent the rest of the afternoon following Holmes's instructions. I was able to convince Charles that procuring an invitation for "Mr. Altamont" was essential—and, in the end, we got one for Sergeant Pierce, too. I dispatched half a dozen backup men to station themselves around the exterior of the house where the ball was to be held. It was at one of the many grand houses on St. Charles Avenue, at the corner of Napoleon Street.

There were not many costumes available at this late date, but at last I was able to get something for both Holmes and Pierce, though I had to pay handsomely for them. For Holmes I found a black prelate's costume, the kind a French Catholic priest might wear. I recalled that in one of Dr. Watson's stories Holmes had occasion to dress as a clergyman, so I thought it was a fitting choice.

That evening, Holmes and I arrived at the Latilles' to escort Charles and Evangeline to the ball. When I saw Evy coming down the hall in her costume, I realized that everything I had ever felt about other women was a mere dress rehearsal for what I now experienced—utter and complete intoxication. She was dressed as a duchess, in a satin gown with white fur trim, and when she entered the foyer and those dark eyes met mine, I felt the full power of that intoxication, like a powerful drug coursing through my entire body. Charles wore a toreador outfit, and looked very dashing in his red sash, ruffled shirt, and black boots. I was dressed as a jack of clubs, and I had carefully hidden a revolver in my loose-flowing, pantaloon-style pants.

We all walked the few blocks to the party and entered the grand hallway, to find the festivities in full swing. People in elaborate costumes and masks swirled around the dance floor, and waiters circulated with heaping platters of food. Drink flowed freely, as it always did in this town. I poured Evangeline some punch from the shining silver punch bowl and escorted her to the ballroom, where a small orchestra was playing.

Following Holmes's advice, I planned to keep Charles and Evangeline in my sight the entire evening. The only other specific instruction he gave me was to be down at the lake at midnight. There was a small boating pond at the bottom of the property, and he seemed to think that whatever was going to occur would happen there. I saw him have a private word with Charles, but I have no idea what they said to each other.

As I watched Evy walk around the room greeting people, Sergeant Pierce came up to me. He looked miserable in his costume. He was dressed as a donkey—it was the best we could do at last moment's notice. His left ear drooped sadly to one side, and the costume's thick grey fabric looked uncomfortable and hot. A long, tasseled tail dragged behind him.

"Hello, sir."

"Hello, Pierce."

"Everything going according to plan, sir?"

"I hope so, Pierce, I hope so."

The evening wore on, but there was no sign of any suspicious activity, and I was beginning to wonder if Holmes for once was wrong. As midnight approached, I found myself on the other side of the ballroom from Charles and Evy, keeping an eye on them at a distance.

The partygoers swarmed about me in an ever-tightening circle of frenzy, the masks on their faces frozen into grotesque parodies of human emotion. There was something frantic about Carnival this year—it was as if if we ate, drank, and danced hard enough, we could somehow erase the stains of our sin, and wash the blood of those eleven murdered Italians from our collective conscience.

I was not far from the French doors leading out to the terrace, and I could see Holmes across the room, on the other side of the orchestra, not far from where Charles was standing, talking to some friends. Pierce was standing by the front door, looking uncomfortable in his costume, his long tail drooping, his left ear flopping over lopsidedly.

Across the room, Evangeline sat with some other women in a row of chairs along the wall, in her feathered regalia, trimmed in fur and satin. In spite of my apprehension about the evening, I couldn't help admire the whiteness of her throat, the delicacy of her wrist as she fluttered the fan in front of her masked face. I realized at that moment that I had loved her ever since I could remember, and my heart still thrilled at the sight of her. She moved to straighten the billows of laced skirts around her ankles, and I fancied I could hear the rustling of silk even over the din of music and laughter and smell the faint aroma of her perfume, dusky and hinting of wilted roses, as it rose from her downy neck.

I looked around for Holmes. He was managing to blend in, not calling too much attention to himself, in spite of the watchful attitude of his long, lanky form. His costume suited him, I thought; black as his slicked-back hair, black as the soul of the fiends who were after my friend. Holmes caught my eyes and nodded, indicating that so far, all was going according to plan. I looked at the clock—it was ten minutes to twelve. In the pit of my stomach, a cold seed of fear began to sprout, and my mouth lost all its moisture.

I tried to maintain my post as the crowd jostled me more and more—it was becoming increasingly difficult to keep both Charles and Evangeline in my sight. A plump, jolly little man dressed as a leprechaun danced in front of me, grinning madly as his fat, diminutive body spun around, his stubby legs clad in forest green leggings. His feet scampered to the beat of the music, which seemed to be getting louder. It made me quite dizzy to watch him twist and turn, the tassel on his green pointed hat bobbing up and down like a lure dangling in front of a trout. He winked at me merrily as he hopped from one foot to the other, as if we were in some sort of conspiracy together, and he was enjoying sharing our little secret. I had never seen the man before in my life, but not knowing what else to do, I winked back at him, hoping that he would go hopping off to torment some other poor soul.

But to my dismay, he stayed right in front of me, toes tapping, arms happily flailing, dancing his little jig, as if for all the world he really were one of the Little People come out of the woods to cast a spell on me. The false beard clinging to his chin began to droop and hang off in pieces as sweat poured from under his mask and down his face, loosening the glue. Still he danced and still he winked; and I felt as if I was caught in some hellish Sisyphean nightmare, doomed to forever face this demoniacal dwarf. If I moved left, he moved left; when I went right, he followed. I was beginning to wonder if the man was seriously unbalanced.

The orchestra began to play "If Ever I Cease to Love You," the song that had become the official Mardi Gras anthem some two decades ago. The music was as forgettable as the lyrics, but when the crowd heard the first strains of music, everyone cheered and began to sing along.

> If ever I cease to love
> If ever I cease to love
> May the moon be turned to green cream cheese
> If ever I cease to love

I had lost sight of Holmes and Charles entirely. The crowd had become so dense that the crush of bodies prevented anyone from moving very much. A tall, thin woman clothed entirely in white ostrich feathers slid in front of me. A preposterous plume of a hat was perched atop her head, obscuring my line of sight. Between her and the mad leprechaun, my view of both Charles and his sister was blocked. Suddenly panicked, acting out of impulse and desperation,

I began to dance. I gyrated as crazily as my green-clad tormentor, swaying from side to side as if possessed, my eyes half-closed. Somehow, I managed rather clumsily to knock the ostrich woman's hat to the floor, hopefully making it look accidental, thus opening my line of sight again. Irritated, and seeing that I was making no attempt to retrieve it, she bent to pick it up while I made remorseful gestures. By then the noise in the room was so loud that conversation was out of the question.

I peered over the stooping back of the ostrich lady as she bent to retrieve her hat—but there was no sign of Evangeline! Panic surged through me like a bolt of electricity, and I gathered my strength to push through the crowd, dense as it was—but suddenly she reappeared again, nodding and smiling, still holding a fan delicately in her fingers. But now the fan was between me and her face, and I craned my neck to watch as she bent down to say something to a passing reveler, a man dressed as an eighteenth-century cavalier.

> *May the moon be turned to green cream cheese*
> *If ever I cease to love*

Still the crowd sang, and still the leprechaun jounced, jostled, and jigged. He was breathing heavily, and by then I was convinced the man was seriously deranged. His eyes bulged like overcooked eggs from behind his mask—the mad, obsessed stare of a lunatic.

Just then the big brass clock in the foyer struck midnight, sending the revelers into an even greater frenzy. Midnight—I had to get to the garden! I somehow managed to elbow my way to the other side of the feathered lady, pushing the people on either side of me. I shoved through the press of bodies, sweating and straining to make my way out of the horrible vise of humanity. Taking a deep breath, I slipped out the French doors onto the terrace. The music and singing inside the house rose to a raucous crescendo, and the sound of drunken voices followed me out to the patio.

> *If ever I cease to love*
> *If ever I cease to love*

I closed the doors behind me, doing my best to shut out the sound. I took a gulp of fresh air and stepped out into the night.

The evening was soft and full, pregnant with promise, but my stomach was hollow with fear and anticipation as I patted the revolver at my side, glad for its reassuring bulk in the pocket of my costume. The garden was deep, bordered by hedges on either side, and a series of winding paths crisscrossed in every direction, eventually leading down to a sloping lawn, at the bottom of which was the lake. The air was heavy with the scent of bougainvilleas, and the gentle cascading of crickets blended with the sound of peeper frogs. Torches had been lit along some of the paths, but others were in darkness, their destinations a mystery. I followed one of the lighted paths, stepping carefully lest I should twist an ankle or something. Heading toward the pond, or so I thought, I turned down a dimly lighted path; half of the torches had burned out already. I thought of turning back, but it felt like the way down to the lake, so I headed forward.

I squinted and strained my eyes, trying to see farther ahead, but my line of vision was severely limited. I resolved to go back, but just then I came to a three-way fork, and was uncertain as to what was the way back. I followed what I thought was my original path, but the night suddenly seemed to close in around me. I groped and stumbled along for a few yards, straining to see, my heart pounding in my throat. The sound of peepers seemed to be getting louder—then I turned a corner and suddenly I was facing the pond. Just as suddenly, the moon emerged from behind a cloud, casting its pale blue light upon the lake, thick with lily pads, their white blossoms faint and ghostly in the moonlight. I could see the dark shapes of willow trees hanging over the water, their leaves barely brushing the shore. A small boathouse sat nestled along the willows just a few yards from me, its white-painted clapboards shining dimly in the moon's reflected light. The scene looked unreal—it had a dreamlike quality, like a landscape of the imagination. It was all too perfect, like a painting—the weeping willows, the boathouse, the stillness of the water under the cool light of the full moon.

My muscles ached from tension, and my throat was a desert, swept dry of any saliva. There was a rustle in the bushes along the side of the boathouse. I took a few steps toward it.

"*Who's there?*" I whispered fiercely.

More rustling, then a few stifled grunts.

"Who's *there?*" I whispered again, this time more loudly.

A voice came from deep within the bushes. "Is that you, sir?"

I sighed. "Yes. Come on out, Pierce."

"Coming, sir . . . it's just that—" More grunts, followed by a groan.

"What *is* it, Pierce?" I took a few more steps towards the bushes.

"Well, sir, I'm . . . I'm a bit stuck, sir."

"How on earth did you manage that?"

"If I knew, sir, I could get unstuck . . . but, well, sir, I'm afraid I need some help."

"For God's sake, Pierce, keep your voice down, or you'll ruin everything!" I said, bending over to help him. Somehow, the tail of his costume had wound itself around a yew tree shrub.

"Sorry, sir."

I tried to unwind the tail but the material had frayed and stuck to the sticky sap of the branches.

"I'm afraid you'll have to take it off, Pierce."

"Pardon me, sir?"

"The costume—take it off."

"But, sir—"

"Take it off!"

"But then I'll be naked, sir."

"Aren't you wearing something underneath?"

"Well, yes, sir, my union suit, but that's hardly—"

"Shh!" Just then I thought I heard footsteps along the path I had come from. I ducked down into the bushes next to Pierce.

"Don't say a word," I whispered, drawing my pistol from inside my pocket.

The moon dipped under a cloud and once again shadows descended over the lake. I stood up and squinted, peering out over the bushes. A movement to my right side caught the corner of my eye. At that moment the cloud slid away, and once again the lake was lighted in the moonlight. There, standing in full view at the far shore of the lake, was Charles. The red sash around his waist made him a perfect target, and I took a step toward him, but he held a hand out toward me to stop me. I started to call to him, but hesitated—what on earth was he doing here?

There was the sound of light footsteps at the entrance to one of the paths, and I looked in that direction. There, at the edge of the path, was Evangeline. Her fur-trimmed cuffs and collar shone bone white under the pale moonlight, and her vermilion satin gown had the black mottled look of dried blood. I tried to speak to warn her, but no words came—only a hoarse croak; my throat felt as thick as the bullfrogs along the banks. I rose from the bushes and started toward her, but she didn't see me; her attention was focused on Charles. She raised her right hand toward him—to warn him, perhaps. I took a breath of air and cleared my throat to speak, but just then a shot rang out.

I found my voice at the exact same moment, but the sound of gunfire drowned out my words.

"Evy! Charles! Watch out!"

But it was too late, and I watched as my friend crumpled to the ground. Evangeline turned toward me slowly, and it was then that I saw the cold hard gleam of metal in the moonlight.

At that moment my world ended.

My beloved, my dear Evangeline, held the gun that had fired at Charles, and it was now aimed at me. Still my brain refused to comprehend what my eyes told me to be true. There was a terrible silence as the frogs, the crickets, and all the creatures of the night seemed to hold their breath.

"Evy—no!" I cried, but a second shot reverberated in the stillness of the night. Instinct took over my body, and I ducked simultaneously as I lunged at her, managing somehow to grab the hand holding the gun.

"Pierce!" I yelled as I wrenched the gun away from her. Sergeant Pierce emerged from the bushes, clad only in his red union suit, and loped toward us. Evy hissed and writhed like a creature possessed, but between the two of us we subdued her.

"Hold her!" I shouted to Pierce as I dashed along the bank to where Charles lay collapsed on the ground. Bending over to examine him, I gently removed his mask. To my astonishment, it was not my friend at all under the black mask, but Sherlock Holmes! The bullet had caught him in the left shoulder—just a few inches lower, and it would have pierced his heart. He lay gasping for breath, clutching the wound, from which blood flowed freely.

He was dressed in the same toreador costume I had seen Charles wearing, complete with red sash and leather boots. I could see how at a distance and in the dark, he could easily be mistaken for Charles. Both were tall, with black hair and the same lean build, and though Holmes was wiry and more muscular, you could not discern such differences in the moonlight and at a distance of a hundred yards or more. He had pulled a switch with Charles, and both Evangeline and I had been taken in by it.

Holmes took a deep, ragged breath and attempted to speak.

"Shh," I said. "Save your strength. I turned back to my sergeant, who held the writhing Evangeline firmly, pinning her arms behind her back. "Pierce, blow your whistle, man!"

Pierce looked crestfallen. "It's—it's in my costume pocket, sir."

"Oh, for God's sake," I muttered. But it was no matter—the sound of gunfire had brought my uniformed backup squad running to our aid. A few of the partygoers also straggled down the path toward the lake, in various stages of intoxication.

"Help!" I cried. "Over here! Someone help me get him to a hospital." Though I was attempting to stanch the flow of blood, a tourniquet was impossible, and blood was seeping into the ground around us. Holmes made one more valiant effort to speak.

"Charles . . . is he safe?"

"I'm fine, thank you."

I turned to see Charles standing beside us, now dressed in Holmes's costume.

"And I have you to thank for it."

"Didn't—quite—count on . . ." Holmes muttered; and then he lost consciousness.

Sergeant Pierce and a couple of the uniformed officers lifted him gently and carried him toward the house. I could see that his injury, if properly treated, should not be life-threatening, and I was grateful for that.

I turned my attention to Evangeline, who was being held, handcuffed, between two uniformed men. I could hardly bear to look at her. I was at a loss to understand how she—of all people—could do such a thing.

"Why, Evy?" I said. I wasn't expecting an answer, but I had to ask.

Her black eyes, which I had so adored, were now hard as lumps of coal.

She looked at her brother with hatred. "All my life I've lived under his shadow," she hissed, her body rigid with rage. "Charles goes to the best school, Charles inherits the business, Charles gets the house. And why? Because I'm the second child, and a *woman!* All my life I've felt like a second-class citizen, an afterthought, living at the mercy of other people! And then I have to sit and watch as he lets the inheritance slip through his fingers because he's such a wretched businessman! That was the last straw—I couldn't take any more!"

"But—I was going to marry you! I would have supported you."

"On a policeman's salary!" She practically spit the words out, her voice dripping with contempt. "In a cabin on the bayou. What kind of life would that have been? Doing my own cooking and cleaning—no thank you! I was destined for better things!"

My voice shook as I asked the question that I knew, even then, to be ridiculous.

"So you never loved me?"

She looked at me as though sizing up a horse before deciding whether or not to buy it.

"A half-breed Cajun whose ancestors roamed the land like so many gypsies—hardly better than paupers! I'm a *Latille*—I come from an ancient, noble family! How could I ever love someone like you?"

"Take her away," I muttered, turning away, "and lock her up." Charles laid a hand on my shoulder, but I was beyond consolation—my heart was consumed with bitterness and betrayal. I walked slowly back toward the house in a fog, barely aware of my surroundings.

I have little memory of how the next few hours were passed. I remember Charles was there, and I remember sitting on the terrace drinking whatever he gave me—some sort of bourbon, I suppose. When I was able to regain some of my composure, I headed off to the hospital to see how Holmes was doing.

I found him sitting up in his bed, a white bandage wrapped around his shoulder.

"Hello, Captain," he said, as I came into his room. His voice was weak, but he appeared to be alert.

"How are you feeling?" I asked, taking a seat next to his bed.

"I expect somewhat better than you are," he remarked dryly. "I am very sorry for the shock this must have been to you."

I shook my head. "It's not really your fault, Mr. Holmes. I was misled, but not by you. One thing I don't understand, though: instead of leaving me in the dark, why didn't you tell me earlier what was going on?"

"My dear Captain Brasseaux, do you think that you would have believed me if I told you that your fiancée, the woman you adored beyond all others, was a cold-blooded murderess?"

I hesitated, as the full realization of her crimes hit me.

"No," I said at last. "In fact, I probably would have challenged you to a duel to defend her honor."

"And would you not have also warned her that I suspected her and told her of my ungallant allegations?"

"Of course."

"Then you can see the quandary I was in. Regrettable as it was, it was essential to keep you in the dark as long as possible."

I had to admit he was right. Only blunt, irrefutable proof would have ever convinced me that Evangeline—my precious angel—could wish harm on anyone, let alone her own brother. Even then, it felt like a bad dream, a nightmare from which I would soon awaken, relieved to find it was all just a dream.

"When did you first begin to suspect her?" I said.

"The odd disappearance of the family cat, at exactly the same time your friend was taken ill, indicated that poisoning was a definite possibility. In England, we think of poison as a traditionally feminine way of dispensing with people."

I nodded. "Yes, it's no different here. I just couldn't imagine Evangeline . . ."

"Then, when the cat turned up dead, I was fairly certain it *was* poison—and also that it was someone in the household. I considered Esthmé, the old servant, but a motive for her seemed unlikely. Why would she kill Charles and not his sister, for example?"

I sighed. "It all seems so logical now, but then I couldn't possibly have—"

Holmes laid a hand on my arm. "Of course you couldn't; who in your place would have?"

"So it was Evangeline who went to Madame Celeste to try to get her to put a curse on Charles?"

"And, failing that, to buy some poison from her—but poor Madame Celeste was a principled woman, and she was having none of it."

"So she came to warn me."

"Yes, and in doing so, she sealed her own fate. Somehow your fiancée learned that Celeste had been to see you, so she decided to silence her before the whole story came out."

I shook my head. "Poor Celeste. I feel responsible for her death. If only I had—"

"My dear Captain, please don't blame yourself. The past will crush you if you continue to dwell on it."

I looked at his earnest, keen face and nodded. "Very well. I'll try to do as you say, but it may take some time . . ."

"After all," he continued, "I am at fault here, too. I failed to see the lengths to which Miss Latille would go. I never thought she would murder poor Madame Celeste so ruthlessly . . . I suppose we'll never know how she managed to procure the poison," he added thoughtfully.

I snorted. "I'm sure it wasn't difficult—after all, this is New Orleans. You can get anything you want here. When did you know for certain that it was Evy?"

"When I saw the broken window."

"Yes, I remember you studied the curtain. What did you see there that interested you so much?"

"As I mentioned at the time, it was what I *didn't* see."

"And what was that?"

"Glass. A rock thrown from the street would hit the window with such force that the glass would scatter—and a few fragments would inevitably end up caught in the drapes. But there were no pieces at all stuck in the curtains—only a few scattered on the floor, as if they had been placed there. I think she broke the window from the inside, then scattered some glass around the floor to make it appear as though it had been broken from the outside. There were some fragments in the bushes outside the house, which also lent credence to my theory—had a rock actually been thrown, the amount of glass on the inside of the house would have been much greater. I knew at that moment the entire incident had been staged—and most probably by the person who 'discovered' it."

"So Evangeline planted the rock and the note to throw us off, to put suspicion onto the Mafia—the Black Hand?"

He nodded. "The ruse might have even worked had she been more careful. So I concocted that little charade at the party to entrap her—to force her hand, as it were."

"I don't know what to say, Mr. Holmes," I said finally. "I feel . . . ashamed, I suppose, that I could have been so blinded by love . . ."

"You wouldn't be the first man to be so affected by the so-called fairer sex," he replied dryly. "Do you know, for example, of the mating habits of the praying mantis?"

I had to confess that bit of arcana had thus far escaped me.

"The female initiates sex by ripping the male's head off. In fact, the male praying mantis is unable to mate while its head is attached to its body. That has always struck me as a significant parallel to the human experience."

I remained silent while he lit a cigarette, flicking the match into a wastebasket. A passing nurse—a short, stocky blond woman with a bulbous derriere—came striding up to Holmes and grabbed the cigarette from him.

"No smoking in here, sir!" she exclaimed. "*Especially* not for someone in your condition!" she added, with a dark glance at his chart.

"What did she mean by that?" I said when she had gone.

Holmes shrugged. "Oh, it seems I have a touch of fever of some sort—comes with a bit of a dry cough, apparently. No doubt it is because I am so unaccustomed to your climate. No matter—they're giving me quinine or some such thing, but . . . well, you know the medical profession." He sighed. "It does seem rather too much to bear, though, not being allowed cigarettes."

I was relieved there was a diagnosis of the symptoms I had observed earlier, though I didn't mention it to him; he seemed irritated enough about being denied his precious tobacco. However, his behavior certainly reinforced Dr. Watson's allusions to Holmes's complete indifference regarding his own health.

"I must hand it to your former fiancée," he continued. "She is a dangerous adversary—and a versatile one, who will employ any means to further her ends—poison, stabbing, shooting. She only resorted to the latter when she became truly desperate. I think she knew I was onto her." He shook his head. "In all humility, I must admit that I didn't expect her to resort to gunplay—and I certainly was not prepared for her to be such a good shot!"

"Why was she at the lake at precisely midnight, though?" I said.

"Oh, that was very simply arranged," he replied, handing me a crumpled note.

Meet me at the lake at midnight. I know your secret.

"I slipped it into the purse she carried to the ball, knowing that sooner or later she would retire to powder her nose. If she was innocent, she would have shown it to you—the fact that she hid it let me know that I was right. After that it was a simple matter to change costumes with your friend and appear at the lake so that she would mistake me for her brother, and, I was hopeful, show her hand—which she did."

"So she thought Charles wrote the note?"

"I don't think she knew who wrote the note, but she had to find out. When she saw me, thinking I was Charles, she made a bad miscalculation and tried to eliminate him once and for all—probably hoping to frame whoever wrote that note. A very resourceful woman. It's a pity she is so utterly lacking in moral sensibility."

I looked at him, a little stunned by his bluntness. "You certainly don't mince your words, Mr. Holmes."

He raised an eyebrow. "Is there any reason to? Isn't it better for you to know you what you have so narrowly escaped?"

I sighed. "I don't know that it lessens the pain right now, but I suppose someday I'll be grateful."

"I hardly expect you to feel grateful," he answered, wincing as he shifted position in the bed.

"Perhaps an injection of morphine—" I suggested, but he shook his head.

"I still have work to do. I cannot afford to be in a stupor of any kind—I need my mental facilities fully functional."

After the incidents of that night I decided to take some time off. I was tormented by a single question: how could I have failed to see Evangeline for what she really was? It was a question I would continue to ask myself again and again in the months to come. The mask she wore dazzled me, along with her beauty, and I was her doomed slave, her pawn—until the events of that terrible night unfolded, smashing my golden idol to pieces, leaving me bewildered and bereft.

Charles, too, needed a change of scenery, and took a trip to France to roam his ancestral lands in Provence. Evangeline's trial came and went; Holmes and I both testified, as did Sergeant Pierce, but the outcome was a forgone conclusion. I didn't even stay in court for the reading of the verdict but saw it in the papers the next day. Holmes stayed in New Orleans to pursue the matter he had come here about, though I didn't see much of him. I stayed mostly at my cabin, playing my guitar and staring at the bayou.

Some weeks later I read in the papers that President Harrison was awarding money as compensation to all the families of the slain prisoners in the jailhouse mob lynching that followed the Hennessy murder trial. Several days after that I received a telegram.

BUSINESS SUCCESSFULLY COMPLETED— RETURNING TO LONDON.
REGARDS TO YOU AND MR. LATILLE.

It was signed J. P. Altamont.

I had no doubt that the "public figure" Holmes had been work-ing for was none other than President Harrison himself—and that his job was to investigate the lynchings. I didn't blame the presi-dent—an objective, dispassionate inquiry by the New Orleans Po-lice Department would have been impossible—in fact, I imagined that no American police force could have done the job. Perhaps the Pinkerton men could have done it, but why involve them when you could have Sherlock Holmes at your service?

I put the telegram carefully on my dresser, to remember to show it to Charles when he returned, and went out to my porch overlook-ing the bayou. It was a soft, sweet afternoon: the crickets clicked their mysterious messages to each other, the peeper frogs peeped, the bullfrogs growled and gulped, and the myriad other creatures of the bayou began their evening serenade.

Evangeline. The name floated into my mind. Somewhere there was another Evangeline, one who was good and true—the heroic girl of the legend—but that was not my Evangeline. No, mine was a creature of pride and passion, not for love but for wealth and posi-tion and all of the worldly things she felt she deserved. And in single-mindedly going after those things, she nearly destroyed everyone who was closest to her.

But fortune and social status are will-o'-the-wisps, thin and va-porous as the swamp gas that rises and dissolves into the summer eve-ning as dusk settles over the bayou. In the end, it all vanishes like the morning mists along the river, burned up by the heat of the day. Only love endures. It alone has the power to withstand the negative, destructive forces that are brought to bear upon us all—disease, ill fortune, old age, and death. Only love can rise above the tide of time and reclaim our spirits from this temporal prison.

I wish I could have told Evangeline that—but it is not the sort of thing one person can impart to another. Life's really important lessons are learned only one way—alone and with personal suffering. They are never easy, but, once learned, they are yours forever. Evangeline was beyond knowing these things—she was caught in a prison of her own design. Though it meant leaving a part of myself behind, I had to let her go, to release her to become, someday, nothing more than a memory, like a half-forgotten tune that runs through your head one day but is gone the next, never to return.

I sat watching as the day slipped slowly into dusk, then into twilight. The air was still over the bayou, the night thick with rain that would probably fall soon, as the air grew too heavy to hold the raindrops, finally releasing them to settle softly over the city, washing away the soot and grime of the day. The rains would come, good cleansing rains, taking with them the taste of sin and sorrow, hatred and humiliation, fear and folly. And with the arrival of the morning light would come a fresh start, a new beginning for our troubled but brave city. I settled down in my chair to await the coming dawn.

The Adventure of the Missing Detective

Gary Lovisi

Here is a strange tale for you, gentle reader, one that is perhaps the most fantastic adventure of Sherlock Holmes's entire career. I have left it for posterity, secreted with my special papers at Cox & Co., to be opened in the future, and done with as my heirs deem best. Here now are the circumstances of that story as I heard them from Holmes's own lips . . .

As you know, Watson, my return to London after the happenings at the Reichenbach Falls was not in 1894 as you have written in your amusing account of the Moran case for the popular press. I will relate to you now the actual story of what occurred during those missing years when you, and the world, thought me dead.

It was during the affair at Reichenbach. Moriarty was dead, destroyed by the furious power of the Reichenbach Falls. I had seen his body dashed to the jagged rocks below. I had seen his head crushed on those very same rocks. Then I had unaccountably lost my own balance, taken by some strange sudden draft of wind, no doubt, which caused me to plummet into a mysterious vortex of whirling fog and roiling mists below. It was a cold and supercharged atmosphere that I entered, quite unlike anything I had ever experienced before. My fall seemed to descend in stages, slowly, staggered, even sluggish. I could not comprehend it at all. It was a most unnatural affair, and nothing at all in the manner of which the Professor met his timely demise barely minutes before. My descent was somewhat transcendental in nature. It may have even been miraculous, for it was unusual in the extreme and seemed to bypass what I know of our laws of physics and gravity.

That final encounter with Moriarty, and my resulting injury, caused a long convalescence. If not for the kind ministrations of an isolated hill folk couple, I surely would have passed on from a comatose state to death. As it was, I spent much time in that near-death dream state, lost in a miasma of thoughts, my mind playing tricks, nightmares wracking my brain, even as my body lay still and silent in an apparent total vegetative existence.

After some time, I came out of my coma, and as I slowly recuperated, was eventually well enough to question my Swiss rescuers. As you can well imagine, I had many questions. Hans and Gerda were a simple farm couple who had a small parcel of land below Interlaken. They told me of how Hans had found me at the bottom of a lonely ravine, apparently uninjured. Initially he thought I was merely asleep, but he soon discovered that I was in the grip of some deliberative state, and after he summoned Gerda, the couple took me into their small cabin to care for me.

Once I regained consciousness I found I had lost much weight and was extremely weak. After I had regained some strength, I listened with great interest to Hans and Gerda's story. I did not tell them about Moriarty or my tumult over the ledge near the Great Falls. That would have seemed incongruous with the fact that the few minor bruises I had sustained were much too insignificant injuries for one who had gone through such a violent fall. It did not make sense, and this was but the beginning of a series of incidents and activities that made little sense to me at the time. But by the end of this strange narrative all will be explained.

In fact, quite early on I began to believe there might be a more significant mystery here than met the eye. You see, just as Moriarty met his death from going over the falls—and I saw him with my own eyes meet his doom before I myself plunged downward—I also should have been killed by my own incredible fall. However, there was something about that mist, the wind, perhaps various air currents and updrafts? I do not know for certain, but something saved me and seemingly with great gentleness set me down upon the lush green sward of the ravine bottom where Hans later found me.

I have no explanation for it at all. I cannot explain the lack of injury or my comatose state. I am no man of science, save where the criminal element is concerned. Perhaps my friend the distinguished Professor Challenger would make something more of it. Suffice it to say that I was satisfied with the results of the situation. Moriarty was dead, and I was alive.

Before I left the area below Interlaken, I asked my kind hosts if they or those in the nearby village remembered anyone having come around looking for me. I also asked them if any tourist had gone missing, or if there were reports of anyone killed in an accident off the falls. Hans and Gerda told me they had no such knowledge, but when I told Hans to ask around the village, he returned with interesting news indeed. While I was apparently not missed at all, it appears an Englishman, perhaps on holiday at the time, had in fact died going over the falls on the very same day that I had my own descent. I was told the body had been claimed and was buried in the local cemetery by a visitor from London.

I sighed with relief. Moriarty, no doubt. I only thought it strange that you, good Watson, or my brother, Mycroft, had not yet found me.

Months later, as I took my leave from Hans and Gerda, I decided to book a small room at an inn of the lower village for a few days. It was a robust little place, one of those lively alpine respites, and I began to feel more in tune with the world I had been so long estranged from since my injury. Hans and Gerda, the souls of propriety and generosity, lived a private and lonely life in a secluded area. Now I was back in a village among people and activity and beginning to get back to my old self again. Why, I was even able to find an English newspaper to catch up with events in the world and back home. It was a copy of the London *Times*, and I began to peruse it nonchalantly.

It felt good to feel the *Times* in my hands again, to smell the newsprint, to see the well-remembered large lettering of the headlines and the many narrow columns of small and tightly packed print for the various news items from all around the world.

However, one item below the fold caught my attention as no

other has in my life. I read it with shock and dismay. The horror I felt, the alarm and confusion was something I had never experienced before. I grew dizzy, weak-kneed, my heart raced. I read it once again, very carefully. The news item was rather simple and matter-of-fact:

> The British Monarch, King Albert Christian Edward Victor, former Duke of Clarence and Avondale, and grandson of the late Queen Victoria, will bestow the honour of a knighthood upon Mr. James Moriarty. The well-known and respected professor of mathematics, formerly at one of our most prestigious universities, is the author of various noted scientific works, including, "The Dynamics of an Asteroid," which has been well-received in academic circles. He is being honoured for his invaluable service to the Crown. The ceremony is to take place upon the 24th day of April in the year of Our Lord 1892, at Buckingham Palace.

I thought this must be some bizarre type of joke or even a misprint, or perhaps suddenly I had become deranged and entirely lost my mind from my injury. Victoria, dead? Eddy, the new king! Why, was it not rumored in dark circles, that he was under suspicion in the Ripper murders? But more so, Moriarty, *alive!* It was incomprehensible! I had seen him die! His body had been buried. Now, if this news item was to be believed, he was not only alive, but to receive a knighthood of all things! It was preposterous, outrageous, and the news left me totally astonished, perplexed, and nonplussed. Yet it gave me much food for thought, and it was food that would *not* stay down.

Immediately I read that newspaper closely from front to back. It was a chilling experience. The brunt of it seemed to be that the entire world I have known all my life had gone irrevocably and incomprehensibly mad. All was upside down and *wrong!*

Here, then, is some of what I gleaned from my perusal of that one issue. Our Gracious Majesty, Queen Victoria, was, in fact, dead, as was her son, Edward. I found an article that spoke of a Court of Inquiry that had recently cleared their deaths of any but natural causes in a carriage accident, even though rumors and questions apparently abounded that it had been no accident at all! No autopsy had been performed upon the royal personages. A disturbing turn of events under the circumstances. In other areas news items leaped out at me, and they were the most incongruous with the facts that I knew. One of the most bizarre was that a military dictatorship was assuming control in the United States and that there was the threatened succession of five western states from the Union. It appeared to be civil war all over again. Russia was in turmoil, the government of France had fallen, and a united Germany had suddenly risen from the ashes of Bismarck's Prussia and appeared to be making ready for world war.

There was more, but I'll not bore you with the details of the many seemingly trivial items that in and of themselves appeared insignificant but to my trained eyes and historical knowledge were no less disturbing and fantastic by their very existence.

Something very big and far afield was happening throughout the world. Things were very wrong. I could not fathom it, but if I did not know better, I would be pressed to admit that this might be some sinister plot, set into motion by Moriarty. A fantastic thought, surely, and utterly unfounded, for he was dead. Nevertheless, while logic told me what was true, my intuition told me differently. You know I seldom listen to emotions; they are not to be trusted in my line of work. Nevertheless, one question nagged my thoughts. That newspaper said Moriarty was alive. How could that be? How could Moriarty be *alive*—and have been knighted—when I *knew* he was dead?

A chilling thought suddenly grabbed me—could it have been someone else entirely who plummeted over the falls? Someone disguised as Moriarty? Even as I considered the thought I knew it just could not be possible, nevertheless some investigation seemed warranted.

Now I knew that I must seek out that grave here in the village and determine that which was within.

The next night was cloudy and moonless, an alpine version of those evenings you may remember that shrouded the moors around Baskerville Hall so many years ago in dire gloom. It was the perfect

evening for the dark business I had that night with my nemesis—
who now seemingly dogged me in death, even as he had in life.

I enlisted the help of good Hans in my nocturnal investigation,
telling him just enough to let him know how important it was for
me to see the body in that coffin. He was somewhat concerned
about such activities, but agreed to help when I made clear it was
important to me.

Now I had to be sure that Moriarty's casket held *his* body!

It was after midnight and the village was wrapped up tightly for the
evening as Hans and I stole out of the back door of my little inn and
he led me to the small cemetery on the outskirts of the village.

We quietly walked through a carved wooden arch and entered a
small fenced-in area of burial plots topped with memorials and statues in stone and wood. Hans brought me to one such lonely grave at
an isolated spot in the end. The marker was a simple wooden cross,
its inscription Hans translated for me.

"It says, 'English Man, Died, May 1891,'" Hans whispered.

I nodded. I looked around us carefully. There was no one. All
was quiet and peaceful. Hans and I began to dig.

I cannot express to you the excitement that surged through me
as my spade cut into the hard, cold earth, and once it finally hit the
lid of the pine box that contained that which I was seeking.

Now was the moment of truth. Hans and I quickly cleared away
the last of the dirt so as to make the top of the plain wooden casket
accessible. Hans looked at me and I nodded, then he began using a
crowbar to pry open the casket.

With a loud screeching of rusted nails, the lid finally came off,
and we saw that a tall male body wrapped in shrouds lay before us. I
motioned Hans away. I quickly knelt before the corpse. Deftly, I removed the shroud cloths, until I had a full view of the face.

There had been some decay and natural parasite activity upon
the flesh of the face, but the cold climate ensured there was more
than enough left for me to make a very definite determination. I
froze with astonishment and some fear, my blood ran cold, for the
face I now looked upon was not that of Professor James Moriarty at
all. It was the face of Sherlock Holmes! It was my very own face!

Hans asked me if everything was all right. He said that I did not look well. Hans would not look closely at the face of the corpse, while I could not take my eyes away from it. You can imagine my reaction. I hardly knew what to make of this at all. At first I thought it might be some trick or joke. I was here after all, and alive, was I not?

You know my methods, and I never theorize before I obtain all the facts. I have said so over and over again, that solving cases is a matter of eliminating the impossible—and then whatever remains, however improbable, must be the truth. I felt that what I was viewing created implications that would soon test that maxim to the very limit. You see, that corpse before me bore silent witness to the truth of this strange event, and I vowed it would tell me all it knew before this dark night was over.

"Hans," I ordered. "Bring that lantern closer, I must examine the body."

Then I began what can only be described as a very methodical and detailed search of the corpse to rule out all suppositions until I could get to the truth of this matter.

What I discovered was even more bizarre and shocking than anything you could have ever put into your little accounts of my cases for the popular press. First of all, the corpse was that of an actual human being, not any statue or manikin. By all accounts the man appeared to have met his death sometime within the last year. There were severe bruises and a few broken bones from his fall that I immediately noticed. However, it was the physical characteristics that were interesting to me in the extreme. The corpse appeared to be my age, my height, my weight, wore my own clothing, and had my exact physical appearance in every category. I was shocked and dismayed. Needless to say the examination of the body was as detailed as possible under the lanternlight held so steadily by my trusty Hans. And the more I looked, the more I could only come up with one determination. It was I! There was no doubt. I even examined the sole of the right foot of the corpse. There I found the scar, an exact duplicate of which was on my own right foot. I had acquired it as a young boy. No one but Mycroft and I knew of it. I tell you, it was uncanny. The corpse was not just someone who looked like me, or was made up to look like me. It was not some copy, but an original. I was looking upon the dead body of Sherlock Holmes!

This was a discovery that set my world reeling in more ways than one. It allowed, even demanded, that my thoughts now entertain a multitude of questions that I had hitherto ignored. Surely something mysterious had befallen me at the Reichenbach. That mist, my fall, the coma, now it began to make some sense. But what indeed, did it portend? Something strange, no doubt, perhaps supernatural. The very thought surprised me greatly.

Although perplexed at this discovery and the questions it raised, I had to put them all aside. For all I knew for certain now was this: with Moriarty apparently alive, I must get home to London, immediately.

For I was sure everyone I knew there was in great danger. The world I knew did not exist any longer, and somehow I was in a new world, or a different, perhaps alternate one. Here I had died at the Reichenbach, while Moriarty had somehow lived and had been free to make his plans and schemes.

I feared for Mycroft now.

I feared for you, Watson.

I feared for England, the empire, the world.

The boat train took me into Victoria Station in London's center on schedule as always. I noticed the familiar building, but it was now draped with black sashes and bunting in mourning and remembrance of our dear deceased queen. It was a somber homecoming.

I was in disguise as an old sailor. I knew it would be best to get the lay of the land, so to speak, then decide on a course of action before I made my presence known.

Quite honestly at that moment, I was not sure what to do. For the first time in my life I was far out of my depths, but I knew there was one sure anchor in my world, or worlds, and that was you, good Watson, and our rooms at 221B. So I headed for Baker Street, an apparent elderly sailor on pension, a bit taken with drink and fallen on hard times. That latter part of my disguise was more true than I'd have cared to admit.

Baker Street came into view and appeared the same as always, but as I approached the building that housed 221B my heart sank and a great feeling of gloom overtook me. The building was closed and boarded up. It appeared a massive fire had gutted the entire structure many months back.

I ran to our lodgings and looked with disbelief at the boarded-up building, then at the people passing by on the street, desperately seeking a friendly or recognizable face. Mrs. Hudson, Billy, Wiggins, anyone!

"My good man!" I shouted to a neighbor. "Can you tell me what happened to this house and the people who lived here?"

"Aye, Pops," he replied, shaking his head sadly. "Not much to say, big fire last year, a real shame."

"What of the doctor?" I blurted.

"Oh the doctor? The doctor went off, no one knows where. The lady what owned the house I hear tell is living with a sister in Kent."

I sighed with relief. At least you, and Mrs. Hudson, were alive. But where?

"And what of Mr. Sherlock Holmes?" I asked with more trepidation than I realized I possessed.

"Aye, the detective? Dead this past year. It broke the doctor's poor 'eart, I tell you."

I nodded, feeling as if I was in a dream. Or a nightmare. This just could not be. I took one last look at the rooms we had shared for so long in happier days and went on my way.

I am afraid that I received even worse news at the Diogenes Club. After Baker Street I immediately hailed a hansom cab and made my way to Pall Mall. There I entered that venerable establishment, only allowed into the environs of the Visitors Room, where I was informed by a liveried butler that Mr. Mycroft Holmes was no longer a member of the Diogenes Club.

"Why is that?" I asked, still in my disguise as the old retired sailor.

The butler looked at me with obvious annoyance from being asked to explain such things to one of the lower classes, but then shrugged and added, "Murdered he was, last May, not soon after his famous brother died on holiday in Switzerland, I hear."

"Assassinated," I whispered. "Oh, Mycroft, now I see . . ."

"Sir?" the butler inquired.

"Nothing," I replied. "I will be leaving now."

On the street before the Diogenes Club I stood frozen, stunned, it surely seemed all was lost. Mycroft, my brother, dead? Murdered? Murdered no doubt by Moriarty's henchmen shortly after the professor returned to London from the Reichenbach. The world in turmoil, while Moriarty had since received a knighthood and was now Sir James! I balked at the effrontery of it all.

I knew now, Watson, that I must find you, and together, perhaps, we could make something of this most strange and disastrous turn of events. I tried to locate you at the usual haunts, at St. Barts Hospital, your office on St. Anne's Street, even at your old regimental stomping grounds. No one had seen you for months. Some told me a sad story of how you had fallen on hard times, that you had taken the news of my death badly, that you had fallen to drink. I was shocked. Astounded, really. It was most unlike you, old boy, to overindulge in spirits at all. To allow yourself to become so wedded to drink as I was being told was quite incomprehensible to me. At first I did not believe it at all. However the rumors I heard in my travels told me of a once proud doctor of medicine who had descended deeply into the dubious comfort afforded by the bottle.

And so it necessitated a change of tack, and I began to seek you out in those more wretched establishments frequented by denizens of our grand city who look to drown the past, and their own place in it, with drink.

I tell you, dressed as I was as a hapless old salt of the seven seas, I was able to fit in quite well with those who frequented such establishments and find out many interesting tidbits as I tracked you down. The most disturbing of which is that the common folk believe Good Queen Victoria had been murdered and the crime covered up. The people hate King Eddy, and they are restless and fearful. Many believe he seeks to restore the monarchy to its full power, and that soon now he will disband Parliament and ask for the resignation and abolishment of the office of Prime Minister. That is surely incredible, and I put these rumors to the superstitions of the common folk and less-educated classes. Yet they believe them firmly, I can tell you. A dark pall seems to have descended upon our city—a dark pall, I would wager, by the name of Moriatry.

But first things first. I had to find you, Watson, and in this most effective disguise it was but a day later that I was to stumble into the Cock & Crow, a shabby East End pub. There I saw a sight I thought I would never see in my life. There I saw a familiar figure seated at a lonely table, slumped down and obviously unconscious from too much drink.

I approached carefully and nudged you awake.

You looked up annoyed, your eyes red with drink, and barked, "Move on! Move on! Can't you see I want to be left alone in my misery!"

My heart broke to see you like that, old friend, rank and disheveled, bleary-eyed and forlorn. Nothing but a hopeless drunk. You'd have hardly fared worse had you sunk to the opium pipe.

I sat down opposite you and looked you over. You had changed significantly in my absence and for the worse. You looked terrible, but I hoped it was nothing a bath, shave, and good food would not cure.

"Barkeep! Barkeep!" I ordered. "Bring us a pot of your strongest coffee!"

"Aye, mate, coming right up," the barman replied.

Then your head rose off the tabletop and you made a valiant effort to focus your eyes across the small table to see who I was.

Of course I was in disguise, and you did not recognize me.

"Begone! Leave me alone!" you barked. Then your head dropped back to the tabletop, barely conscious.

The barman brought over a pot of steaming coffee. I poured a large cup and set it down in front of you.

"Drink," I ordered.

You looked up at me again, let out with a curse, moved to grasp the nearby whisky bottle on the table, which I promptly dashed to the floor in a dozen pieces.

"Hey! What the . . .?"

"Drink the coffee, Watson!" I said firmly. "I need you sober and keen of mind."

Well that got your attention. Your head rose off your hands, and you took a second look at the old salt in front of you. Your head swayed with the affliction of too much drink, but you steadied your gaze long enough to see through my disguise.

"Holmes?" you whispered in a low and fearful gasp. "Can it be?"

"Yes, good Watson, it is I, but keep my disguise in order, I do not want to be found out yet," I said.

"But . . . but you are dead?" you stammered.

"Not quite yet," I tried to reassure you.

"Then you must be some hallucination?"

"Watson, really!" I replied sharply.

Then your eyes grew wide as saucer plates, and a tiny smile

broke through your cracked lips. Tears streamed from your eyes.

"Holmes," you whispered, "Holmes."

"Sssshh!" I warned.

"Yes, I understand."

I had found you, my good Watson, my anchor in the world!

After half a dozen cups of the barman's strong but brutal brew, your demeanor and state of mind slowly came back to that which I know and love.

"Holmes! I cannot believe it!"

"Keep it low, my friend. It is to both our advantages that certain people continue to believe me dead. Call me . . . Sigerson."

You nodded, tried to clear your mind, and finally asked, "But you are alive. So tell me, what has happened?"

I smiled, "That is what I hoped you could tell me?"

You were quiet for a long moment, thoughtful. Then said, "Yes, much has transpired since you left. But how can this be? You are dead! What happened in Switzerland?"

"Obviously I am quite alive, Watson. Nevertheless, that is an adventure I will relate to you in its entirety some other time. Right now you have to answer me this one question."

"Anything."

"Watson, I have been gone long by some standards—but surely not long enough that such fantastic events should transpire in the world. In London."

"I take it you have been to 221B?" you said sheepishly.

"Indeed, what is left of it."

"So you saw . . ."

"I saw the results of a fire. I also know of the murder of Mycroft."

"I am sorry."

We were silent for a time.

"Now, Watson," I asked, "tell me truly. What has been going on here while I have been gone?"

You steadied your hand as you took another reassuring drink of the hot coffee. "It's terrible. The queen is dead, the new king, Eddy, is a lascivious libertine. You should hear the rumors about him; if but half are true, he is a monster."

I nodded.

Then you looked around, carefully, whispering to me, "Have a care. The king has agents everywhere. Secret police agents."

"Really?" This was news. That certainly smacked of Moriarty.

Then you whispered fearfully, "England, the world, we seem to be in the grip of some dread dilemma, and I fear where it all may lead."

"Moriarty is the source of this particular dilemma," I said in a low tone. "With my absence and supposed death, no one could stand against him or his plans. With Mycroft murdered, our enemy was left to indulge his boldest and most devious devices. He apparently has done so quite well, and on a worldwide scale."

"What do you want me to do . . . Sigerson?"

"Do you still have your revolver, Watson?"

"Of course," you replied, perking up at the prospect of action.

"Where are you living now?" I asked.

"I have a small room at the Whistle and Thump, four blocks away."

"Good, go to your room now and rest. I will meet you there tomorrow," I said. "And Watson, stay sober."

"You have no need to worry about me now, seeing you here and alive is the one true medicine for my sick and tortured spirit."

"Good old Watson, together we shall work through this conundrum."

Seeing you again, old friend, had done much to revive my own sagging spirits, but to see the state to which you had sunk with drink had not only saddened me it had surprised me as well. It also got me to thinking. It really was most unlike you.

In fact, it seemed to me now there were many events, even given Moriarty's unrestricted activity, that did not add up. Mycroft dead? Assassinated? Once I got over the shock of that, the more I thought about it, the more it seemed quite impossible. Our rooms at 221B burned and boarded up? Well that was a shock, but it was always a real possibility. What was not a possibility was that I was apparently both alive *and* dead. Then there was the queen's death, was it murder? Moriarty's knighthood, the turmoil in America and elsewhere. My body in Moriarty's coffin! All most incongruous events as far as the facts I knew in my world.

It just didn't add up. These things I have mentioned could never all have happened in the world I knew. Something was amiss, and I fear that you are a factor as well, Watson, one more piece of evidence for the thesis I have reluctantly come to put on the table as a probable explanation for these strange events. Until this moment I had been loath seriously to mention my thesis in this narrative. You see, I know you. I know there is no way that the man I know would become a hopeless drunk. Not in my world. Therefore, you are *not* the man I know. You may be Watson, but you are not *my* Watson. You are . . . *another* Watson. And therefore, with the evidence of my body in that grave, and Moriarty alive, I must be *another* Holmes!

Following this reasoning, I knew that Moriarty was not *my* Moriarty either. I also knew I must exercise extreme caution. I had much to think upon. This was certainly becoming quite the three-pipe problem.

When you and I met next morning at your room, you looked much improved, and I explained most of this to you. I told you my theory. I added, "I now believe that my falling through the mists at Reichenbach had somehow transferred me into a different world. Your world. A world that is almost identical to that which I know, but with jarring differences."

Your response, at first, was entirely expected. "It seems preposterous, Holmes, utterly, and incredibly unbelievable. I am sure it was your body I had buried."

"Not my body, but *another*. I tell you, somehow I have entered your world, which is separate from my own. If you do not believe it, Watson, at least believe that such a thing can be possible. For how do you explain that I am here before you?"

You thought this over, knowing I was serious about it. I could see that even if you did not entirely believe my fantastic tale, you *wanted* to believe it.

"Nevertheless, old friend, when you eliminate the impossible, whatever remains, however improbable, must be the truth," I said. "I put it to you, your world and my world being the same place, that is impossible. It cannot be. Therefore, these worlds exist *separately*."

"I do not know, Holmes. Truly, I have seen and heard many strange things in my service in the medical field and during my war service in Afghanistan and the Far East. This, however, is simply incredible."

"Yes it is, but mere incredibility does not negate the truth of the matter. Something strange happened at Reichenbach. Moriarty and I fought. In your world *and* mine. In mine, *he* fell and died. In yours, *I* fell and died. At the same time, in my world I fell into the mist but did not die, instead I was somehow transferred here, to your world. A parallel world, or an alternate one, Challenger would surely be able to explain it better than I. That has to be why when I exhumed the body of the Englishman who died at Reichenbach, it was not Moriarty as it *should* have been—as it *must* have been if I was in my own world. It was myself! I tell you I was quite shocked at the time, but I knew that it was a very significant fact. It was my body in the coffin! It should by all accounts and logic have been Moriarty's! That was the key that set me upon this course and raised many strange questions. Events since have only forced me to consider this thesis more seriously," I concluded.

"I hardly know what to say."

"Then don't say anything, but think about it," I continued. "However fantastic, my thesis must be true. As improbable as it sounds, it is the only one that fits all the facts. The icing on the cake was seeing you, old man. Seeing to what depths you had fallen after my 'death' alerted me to one simple but incontrovertible fact. While you are surely my good friend, John H. Watson, you can not be *the* John H. Watson I have known for so many years. Hence the corollary, that this world is *not* the world I have known for so many years either. Therefore, I am the outsider here, lost, stranded in *your* world."

"Holmes, but if what you say is true, then . . ."

"Yes, Sherlock Holmes did indeed die at the Reichenbach. It was his body I saw, it was his body you saw—and let me tell you, there can be no mistake—it was the corpse of Sherlock Holmes. *Your* Sherlock Holmes."

There was a long silence.

You nodded final acceptance, and I noticed a deep sadness creep into your features once again. Finally, you looked at me with determination and even managed a wan smile.

"You are a doppelganger of my own Watson, or I of your Holmes, if you prefer. It does not matter much now so long as we understand it and what it means. Buck up, all is not lost. Quite the contrary, in fact. For instance, I believe your descent into drink may have actually worked in our favor, for it certainly saved your life."

"How so?" you asked.

"Simply put, Moriarty held back on his revenge against you, for I am sure he reveled in your self-destruction. Such would fit his warped ego and sense of justice, and it saved you from his henchmen. So now, here we are, both alive, and none the worse for wear."

"Well, Holmes, it is good to have you back, wherever you are from," you said, managing a good-hearted smile.

"Good man, Watson. It appears the game is afoot once again. And the name of this particular game, is Moriarty. I accept the fact now that this is not my world, and I do not belong here. More than anything else I want to find a way to get back to my own world. But first, I cannot in good conscience leave this world to its own devices with Moriarty unleashed without doing something to restrain or stop him. Are you with me?"

"You know I am, Holmes."

"So now we must determine what Moriarty's game is. That is what we must ask ourselves, for only then can we thwart those plans and bring him to justice," I said.

"More crime?" you suggested.

"Not merely crime. It's rather beyond that now, if you keep up with what is being written in the popular press. I study the papers every day. It is rather amazing. The worldwide turmoil, and worse on the horizon, indicates some vast controlling factor. That can only be Moriarty. I really must say that the Moriarty of your world has far eclipsed the Moriarty of my own in his boldness and in his accomplishments."

"Well, I certainly never expected you to compliment him, Holmes."

"And why not? He has achieved much in a short time. I am afraid we have our work cut out for us."

"It certainly sounds that way." Then you gave me a determined look, and said, "I am ready to help you any way I can."

"Bravo!" Then I added, "But we must take care here. Moriarty and I seem linked in some way I cannot yet understand, but it has to do with how I came here. I must be sure that whatever I do to stop him will not interfere with my being able to get back to my own world."

"I do not understand, Holmes."

"Simple enough," I replied. "Moriarty and I are linked, simply killing him may stop his plans, but I am afraid it might strand me here forever. That will not do. I fear if I kill him, it must be in a very specific manner. Perhaps I must draw him out somehow, for one final encounter."

"Then what shall we do?"

"First, I have a little errand for you to perform," I said.

It was not soon thereafter that you were off to Scotland Yard, while I sat down and wrote a letter to a mysterious Far Eastern visitor who, the papers told me, had lately arrived in London.

It was with dire alarm that I listened to the news upon your return from Scotland Yard two hours later. You looked bleak and were reticent to speak, and I had to prompt you a bit impatiently.

"Well, come out with it! What of Lestrade and Gregson?" I said. We were seated in your small East End room. It was a pale replacement for our luxurious lodgings at 221B, but it would have to do. "Did you see them and ask them to come here?"

Well, you were evidently quite upset by what you had learned. I had a bad feeling about the entire business from the looks of you.

"Watson?" I prompted. "Are you all right?"

"Holmes," you replied, "I never saw Lestrade, nor Gregson. They were not at the Yard. When I inquired, I was told they had both been sacked."

"Sacked!" I blurted, the surprise even affected my normal level demeanor.

"Yes, the new administration, Holmes . . ."

"What *new* administration?" I began pacing the small room now, longing for my pipe, or even the cocaine needle.

"You see, I made certain inquires, very discreet, never mentioning your name or mine. It is incomprehensible! His Majesty the King has appointed a new commissioner of Scotland Yard. At first I found out that the new man was a war hero, a retired Army officer, even a big game hunter, and I thought . . ."

"Yes, well, out with it now, Watson!"

". . . but no, they told me his name was . . . Colonel Sebastian Moran."

I had to sit down. "Moran?" I whispered. "There's Moriarty's hand in that for certain."

"It gets worse. Moran has shaken up the entire Yard, he has sacked Lestrade, Gregson, and others that you have had good relations with over the years. I heard he is expanding the force of secret police agents and giving them special powers. I fear he has doomed the Yard."

"Indeed, now for certain the wolf is guarding the henhouse, and I am fearful for the good people of our fair London."

There was not much more to say. For a long moment we were quiet, thoughtful.

"What do you want me to do, Holmes?"

"I will seek out Lestrade and Gregson. Now that they are unemployed, they should be at their residences. I'll try Lestrade first," I said. Then I handed you the envelope that contained the letter I had written but an hour before. "You shall hand-deliver this message to our distinguished foreign visitor. He is in Room 600 of the Grand Hotel, and I want you to await his response."

You nodded and looked dubiously at the envelope and the strange name written upon it, saying, "*Thubten Gyatso, Ocean of Wisdom?* What does it mean, Holmes?"

"Deliver it, Watson, then meet me back here this evening."

Inspector Giles Lestrade had a small flat off Great Russell Street. I made my way there through the streets of London. I continued wearing my disguise; gray beard, stringy gray lock wig, a bulk suit that made me appear to have fifty pounds of additional weight. For all intents and purposes I was an old retired sailor who had seen better days. I walked with an unsteady gait. No one on the street approached me or paid me even the least attention, just as I wanted it. Carefully I made my way from your tiny East End room to central London and the Great Russell Street environs.

Greater London seemed not to have changed at all since I had been gone, at least on the surface. However underneath all the fine buildings and statuary, the busy crowds and traffic of hansom cabs, and the bustle of big-city life, I noticed with great trepidation those small and disturbing items that made up that dark pall I felt had enshrouded the city.

While there had not been any substantial change, there was a new meanness in the people, and I could see fear in their eyes. I had never seen such before in the good people of London. To be sure, people went about their daily business as they always have; but more than ever, they did so without paying attention to anyone else around them. Like horses with blinders on, they did not talk to strangers, they did not ever look in another's eyes. And the police and constables—well, I could see that people feared them now as they had never done so before—and even more so the plainclothes detectives of the Yard. As you said, Watson, these seemed to have been organized into some form of secret police.

I saw it all with my own eyes as I walked the streets of London. The police now take people off the streets at all hours for questioning if it is even suspected they have made some negative remark against the king. I hear tell some of them do not return. The Tower of London has been reopened and is being used for a special type of prisoner—so-called enemies of the Crown. I have been told the dungeons below the Tower are filled with malefactors who have been imprisoned for political crimes against the Crown without charges filed or any trial. Something our Good Queen Victoria would never sanction in all her years as our sovereign. Our new king seems to be seeking an expansion of the powers of the monarchy. With Moriarty an advisor behind the throne, it appears he and King Eddy are beginning a program that will strangle our nation. I fear where it will finally lead.

Another item I heard in my travels through the city today: there will be a rally in Hyde Park to seek a redress of the people's grievances with the monarchy. It seems this could be the beginning of much civil unrest in our city. I was determined to attend that rally later in the day and see for myself what the situation was in this other London I now found myself a part of.

Meanwhile, upon reaching Lestrade's rooms at Great Russell Street I was surprised to see through the front window that the former Scotland Yard inspector was already ensconced with a visitor. I smiled at my good fortune when I noticed his guest was none other than Inspector Tobias Gregson, also now formerly of the Yard. Here, indeed, was an opportunity to score two birds with one stone, so to speak.

Once more I relied upon my disguise as the old sailor, Sigerson. I could not give away my identity yet, and these men would scarcely believe my identity in any regard. To them, like this entire world I found myself in, Sherlock Holmes was dead. I would leave him dead for a while longer.

I had to keep reminding myself that, indeed, I was not *their* Sherlock Holmes, but was from another world, a different one than this, and that while my sympathies ran with the problems I had observed here, my heart yearned to be back in my true home. For in fact, this world was becoming more and more of a nightmare to me.

But now, first things first. Lestrade and Gregson were about to have a visitor.

Lestrade answered the bell, the little man looked as ferretlike as ever, his small mustache and nose crinkling up with distaste as he saw me.

"I do not accept solicitations, my good man. Now begone," he said as he made to slam the door in my face.

My foot in the breach prevented that nicely, and I responded with a powerful growl, "Lestrade, I bring word to you from an enemy of your enemy. Be you interested?"

"Here now! What?" Lestrade muttered, perplexed, but it was Gregson who, standing close behind, put his hand on his companion's shoulder saying, "I think we should hear what this man has to say."

Lestrade shrugged and moved away from the door. "Very well." Then to me he said, "You may enter, old man, and explain yourself forthwith."

I smiled and said calmly, "I serve the enemy of your enemy. My master must remain anonymous until a time in the future when it is safe for him to reveal himself."

"Sherlock Holmes is dead, old man," Lestrade said boldly.

"That, my good inspectors, has yet to be determined," I growled forcefully. "But that is not a question to be answered now. What is important now is that we confront Moriarty and his organization. He must be defeated or England and the world are doomed!"

"Moriarty?" Lestrade said. "But he is the king's man now."

"And the man behind the king's oppression of the people, and your own problem, Lestrade," I replied boldly.

Both men stood quiet for a long moment.

"Fine words, whoever you are, old man, but we have been sacked, the king has appointed Moriarty's henchman, Moran, commissioner of Scotland Yard, and we no longer have any official capacity," Gregson offered gruffly.

"Nevertheless, there are ways," I said plainly. "What I and my master want to know is this. Are you interested?"

"Aye," Lestrade barked. "I tell you at this point I care not for reinstatement to my previous position so much as I would like to wreak revenge upon those who brought this atrocity upon me. Gregson and I were discussing this very matter before you showed up, but we were at a loss what to do."

"I believe that I can remedy that situation, with a course of action," I said with a smile.

Then I told Lestrade and Gregson what I had in mind, and they promised to meet me later that evening.

On my way back to your East End room, Watson, I passed by Hyde Park. It was but a couple of blocks from our old lodgings at Baker Street, and there I saw throngs of people listening to speakers from various political parties publicly airing their grievances against the Crown and king. Such has been a custom in London and the park for generations and oftentimes it was merely the venue of fools or the unstable. But not today. Today there were thousands of citizens present from all classes and social positions who had felt the cruel yoke of oppression from this new monarch over the last year. In a rare effort, members of the Liberal and Conservative Parties had united to seek redress against the Crown. I walked over to the speaker's platform in order to hear some of the grievances and listened with intense interest to one firebrand after the other describe acts that flew in the face of our good English law. I could scarce believe what I was hearing, but then I must remember that this for all its symmetry and exactness, was not my England, not my world.

I was harshly reminded of that fact when companies of stout London bobbies, who, I noticed now, uncharacteristically carried firearms, had been brought in to break up the crowd.

"This is an unlawful assembly and you are hereby ordered to disperse immediately by order of the king," the captain of police demanded of the crowd.

Well, the speakers began to incite those assembled to taunt the police, and soon the crowd was booing and telling them to leave. To my consternation, I noticed light cavalry that could only be from the Royal Household Guard forming up at the edge of the lake. This was not a positive development.

There was alarm and concern growing now in the faces of the crowd as well. The police captain demanded once more, "You have been ordered to disperse immediately or face the consequences."

Well, this was a fine pickle I can tell you, but matters got far worse when some in the crowd went from booing the constables to throwing objects. What happened next can only go down in the history books as a day of bloody murder. For the Household Guard drew their sabers and moving upon the crowd suddenly burst into a wild charge with points down and out. The effect was dramatic and disastrous, and after ten minutes of chaos, I could see there were dozens killed and hundreds wounded.

The remnants of the crowd along with the various speakers had become a mob and its members were being herded forward and arrested. I was able to make my way to safety along the lake. Many others were not so lucky. God knows where those arrested were taken or what was done with them.

As I walked the streets of London on my way back to your room, I could not fathom the nightmare world this was. With Moriarty unchecked, it appeared that civilization itself might be doomed.

When I returned to your room you were there waiting for me.

"Holmes! My God! What has happened to you? You look like you have gone through the Battle of Waterloo!"

"Not Waterloo, Watson, the Battle of Hyde Park. I suspect you will read about the massacre at the hands of the king's troops in tomorrow's *Times*," I said, as I began to clean myself and change my clothes. "But tell me, my friend, did you see Thubten Gyatso and deliver my letter to him?"

"Yes, I did. He is a very old man and had to have the boy at his side read and translate your message to him."

"Indeed, that is most interesting." I could not help but raise my eyebrows in curiosity at that inconsistency.

"Holmes?"

"Never mind," I replied. "But tell me, what was his reply?"

"His reply was one word. 'Yes.'"

I sighed deeply, in truth I had hoped it would not be so, but knowing the facts as I knew them to be, I had to discover what part our faraway visitor played in this strange series of events.

"We must leave at once, for I believe he may be in danger. Thubten Gyatso may also be the one person in the world who can answer my questions and perhaps help me return to my own world. We must speak with him immediately."

We had to walk a number of blocks before we could acquire a growler with a driver who would deliver us across town to the Grand Hotel. The hotel was an imposing pile, one of the tallest buildings in London, with six floors. We took the new "lift," or as the Americans are calling it these days, the "elevator," to the top floor. That floor was actually taken up by an entire suite of rooms for the express use of His Holiness and his rather large retinue of monks and servants.

We were led by one monk, apparently acting as a majordomo, to wait in a small anteroom while our request for an audience with the Ocean of Wisdom, as he was reverently called, was being considered.

"Ocean of Wisdom, Holmes? Who is this strange man?"

"Not man, Watson, for he is but a boy of sixteen years. His name was Thubten Gyatso in his mortal form, but he is better known as His Holiness the Dalai Lama of Tibet. He is the thirteenth in a line of Dalai Lamas said to be reincarnated from that first of the line back in the fifteenth century."

"But what of the old man I was introduced to?"

"That old man presented to you as His Holiness was but a surrogate. He was obviously assuming the role for purposes of protection, assuming the target for any assassination attempt to save his master's life."

"I see. Rather mysterious, is it not?"

"To be sure. That sixteen-year-old boy has traveled thousands of miles here to London. That is an extremely unusual journey for one of his vaulted status and implies great danger in some manner or form. I believe he knows something about my situation here. I do not know how that can be, but I feel he may be able to help me."

"How so, Holmes?"

"The Tibetan form of Buddhism is a powerful force for peace and love, as well as the spirit of harmony and justice in the world.

They have a long history of spiritualism and knowledge in many esoteric matters, and can detect changes in the flow of worldly events," I added.

"Well, what was in your note to him? Did you ask him if he knows how you can get back to your own world?"

"No. When I read in the *Times* that His Holiness had come to London, I knew it could be no mere coincidence. After all, Moriarty and I are in London. This entire scenario of events has London as its nexus. So I asked him, was his reason for coming here because he had detected certain anomalies in the flow of worldly events? As you say, his answer to that question was 'Yes.' That is an admission I find very interesting. I also wrote that if that was his answer, then he should take precautions because his life might be in danger. That is why we are here this evening."

"What can we do, Holmes?"

"Fear not, we have allies, and I have placed them surreptitiously to unmask any danger. But hello, here is the majordomo returned and he is indicating that we are to follow him for our audience with His Holiness."

The central room of the hotel suite was large and set up as a richly appointed audience chamber in the Far Eastern style. Large and luxurious *thankya* tapestries hung from the walls bearing colorful images of the Buddha. At the end of the room was an elegant but empty throne, and off to the side standing in front of the large windows stood a young man, shaven pate, dressed in a fine yellow *namsa* silk robe. Around him buzzed a dozen Tibetan monks, in orange saffron robes, bald of pate as was their master, discussing heated issues as we approached.

Thubten Gyatso saw us and motioned his followers to silence. They quickly formed up in two long rows on either side of the Presence, as he was also known, while we walked forward to meet him.

"Your Holiness, I am Sigerson, and this is my friend, Dr. John H. Watson, who delivered to you a note earlier today," I said. We shook hands in the Western form of greeting. I had read that His Holiness was very much interested in the modern world and Western customs.

His Holiness the Dalai Lama smiled graciously, he was but a boy, but there was a depth to his face, and most notably his eyes, that made you feel you were in the presence of a much older and wiser man. He was purported to be the reincarnation of the last Dalai Lama, in a line that stretched back to the first master, and I could almost believe it true.

He surprised us by speaking English with a decided British accent, "Welcome, my friends. Yes, I speak English, Mr. Sigerson, thanks to a teacher at the monastery in my youth. I find myself fascinated by all things British and modern and so thought it best to learn the language of the modern world so as to experience it firsthand. But, to get to your question, the answer is, of course, 'Yes.' You are correct. You see, for centuries my people have observed visions of the future in the sacred Lake of Lhamo Lhatso at Chokhorgyal. It was on one such vision quest where I viewed all that has transpired and much that will transpire." The Dalai Lama suddenly stopped speaking. He turned to his retainers, motioned to them, and quickly they began to file out of the chamber. It was not long before we found ourselves alone with the Dalai Lama.

Once we were seated facing each other at the other end of the room, Thubten Gyatso looked at me intently, and said, "You are one of the two men I saw in my vision. Your actions at the exact same time in both worlds caused a breach, a doorway to open between these worlds."

Well, here seemed more verification of my theory, and even if I did not entirely believe, I knew this had to be the truth. Nevertheless I asked, "How can that be?"

"Better you might ask, how can such a thing *not* be?" His Holiness replied, answering my question with one of his own. He was silent for a moment before he continued, "Two exact events, happening simultaneously in different worlds—but with opposite outcomes—may open a doorway between those two worlds. Then, it could be possible to fall through from one world to the other. Sigerson, as you call yourself here, you see far, so much farther than most. What does your reason tell you? What do your facts tell you?"

"That what you say may be true," I replied quietly.

"*May* be true?" he prompted.

"*Must* be true," I amended.

The Dalai Lama nodded his youthful head, smiling graciously, then added, "The other I saw was your nemesis. I have seen all this and more in my visions, and fear for our world with your nemesis unchecked. My visit here, aside from a most selfish desire to see the modern world, was to see if I could alert those involved to correct this error."

"What error?" I asked.

"In your world, Sigerson, you slew your nemesis. In my world, here, he slew you. That should never have happened. The combination of his living, with your death through that encounter, has caused turmoil in my world. Which has caused his evil to exert itself to its fullest. The equilibrium has shifted. You must set it level again."

"I want to get back to my own world, Your Holiness, but if what you are saying is true, I cannot in good conscience let my enemy destroy your world. I know what he is capable of, I have seen the results of his handiwork. I agree with you, I must do something to stop him," I said.

"Then there is only one way to do that *and* for you to be able to return to your rightful world. You both are connected by the doorway. It is still open, waiting for you to return . . ."

"The Falls! That must be it!" you blurted, adding, "Sorry, Holmes."

"Correct, Doctor," the Dalai Lama continued. "Mr. Holmes, you must replay the passion of that original encounter once more, and this time you must be victorious. Seek the mist, that is your doorway."

I looked into the weary eyes of Thubten Gyatso, and there was an almost beatific smile on his face. Most incongruous, that young face, with such worldly old eyes.

"And now, Sigerson, tell me, what does that far vision of yours tell you about me?"

I was taken aback by his request, but I automatically replied, "Ocean of Wisdom seems an appropriate name, and if your youth is any indication, I see great things in store for you and your people in the coming years. You will have a long reign. You are wise. You are good. You understand evil."

The stoic look on the Dalai Lama's face never changed as he stood up, and said, "The audience is over; may you be successful in your quest, Sigerson."

As we got up to leave, His Holiness added, "Dr. Watson, please stay one moment."

Both men saw the look of surprise on my face. But I left you, Watson, and exited the room to await you in the small anteroom we had been in earlier.

The monk who was acting as majordomo came in, and said, "Your friend will be returned to you presently."

I thanked him and waited patiently. I was left wondering just what the Dalai Lama would need to speak to you about privately, out of my presence.

As I waited, I heard a ruckus in the outer hallway and suddenly Lestrade and Gregson entered the room and behind them were four brace of stout London bobbies. They held none other than Colonel Sebastian Moran in irons, as Lestrade hefted a peculiar-looking rifle in his hands. It was Moran's notorious airgun.

"Just as you said, he was across the street, aiming to get another shot off at the old man by the window." Lestrade offered, "The old man you said would be the target."

"Is the old man all right?" I asked.

"Flesh wound, but it is enough to tie Moran and his gun to alleged murder," Gregson offered with a smile.

"You cannot arrest me! I am the commissioner of Scotland Yard!" Moran demanded with substantial pomp.

"Not quite," Gregson said triumphantly. "We may not have official authority any longer, but there are still laws against murder. This is a citizen's arrest, all quite legal. You have been arrested for the attempted murder of His Holiness the Dalai Lama of Tibet. The crime may not get you gaol at the assizes because of powerful friends, but your days as commissioner of the Yard are quite over!"

"Take him away!" Lestrade ordered the constables, and soon Moran was gone.

"Things will go badly for him, and better for Lestrade and me now," Gregson said. "Who knows, perhaps there will even be a reinstatement?"

Once Lestrade and Gregson had left it was not long before you returned to me, Watson, from your private audience with the Dalai Lama.

"Well? I must admit, I am intrigued. What did he have to say?" I asked, full of curiosity.

You seemed strangely reticent, but finally you simply smiled at me, putting your hand on my shoulder in a very touching brotherly fashion. "Fear not, Holmes. His Holiness explained it all. He really does see almost as far as you do. We must find a way to make Moriarty return to the Reichenbach Falls."

I nodded. "There is something you are not telling me."

You ignored my question, and so I did not press it. Instead, my thoughts turned to the problem at hand.

I was thinking about that link between Moriarty and me. It made sense, and Thubten Gyatso's words seemed to validate the facts that I knew. However, getting Moriarty to the Reichenbach once again, and by himself without henchmen, could prove difficult, if not impossible. He was powerful now, he had a seat beside the king, and he was a brilliant criminal. My plan would be near impossible, but I would have to find a way to make it happen.

"Can it be done, Holmes?" you asked me, seemingly reading my thoughts.

"I do not know," I replied. Then I told you of the events that had transpired in the last half hour, with Gregson and Lestrade arresting Moran.

"Moran?" you said, showing evident surprise.

"Yes, Moran with his airgun, the perfect, silent, assassination weapon," I replied sharply.

"But why Moran, Holmes? Does Moran know something?"

"No. Not Moran, Watson, Moriarty. He must suspect. I wonder what it could be? Well, whatever the case, he will surely be alerted now that Moran has been taken out of the picture."

"That seems a key move," you ventured.

I looked at you, standing there, the Watson of another world and yet, so very much like my own true friend. "Indeed, you are correct. Moran being taken out of the game is a key event. A move Moriarty will not be able to accept lightly. If I know my Moriartys, and I think I do, this event will disturb him no end. Perhaps we can play on that to good effect."

"Well, Lestrade and Gregson made the pinch . . ."

"Moriarty knows Lestrade and Gregson would never be able to pull such a coup on their own. He will suspect something, see the hint of my hand in the action. He will send his agents to ask questions about the old sailor who calls himself Sigerson. That is good also. Perhaps we can nudge those suspicions a bit into fears he cannot ignore."

"How so, Holmes?"

"I feel the rumors of my demise have been greatly exaggerated and too long gone uncorrected," I said with a smile. I had an idea, one that might not only solve the problems of this world, and my own, but yours as well. You had lost your honor and taken to drink for my death. Now you shall be vindicated.

"Watson," I said, "I shall cause Moriarty to suspect through certain circles that I may, in fact, be alive. It will draw him out. He could not resist finding the truth out for himself and settling this once and for all."

"Bravo, Holmes! That will set them up in Piccadilly! But how do we do it?"

I was silent for a long moment. There was much to consider. I began to miss my pipe and the swirling clouds of helpful tobacco smoke that always offered surcease in such matters. I knew this had to be done just right. I could not overplay my hand by being too bold, nor be scant in my approach. Finally, I took out pen and paper and wrote three letters. The first two were almost identical. One each was addressed to Lestrade and Gregson at their residences. I told them that I was indeed alive, that it had been I who had directed them under disguise, as the old sailor, Sigerson. Then I explained your part, Watson, in my plan. I told them you had always been acting under my direct orders.

Next, the third and most important letter, addressed to Professor James Moriarty. The missive was short, simple and direct. It said, "If you seek the truth, then seek that which is in the grave of Sherlock Holmes." It was unsigned.

Then I gave you these three letters and asked you to deliver the first two to Lestrade and Gregson. The third letter I instructed you to leave at a West End pub in the hands of the barman, Reynolds. I knew the message would not fail to get to its intended addressee and pique his interest. Then, over your objections, I solicited a promise from you that you would stay in London and await my return.

Immediately after, I took the boat train once more, to the Continent and Interlaken, alone.

The evening of the first day I arrived at the small village below the mighty falls and took a room at the local inn. There I set my plan in motion. I contacted good Hans, and that night we stole to the cemetery, opening a grave. We moved the body within to another location and closed the grave. It was empty now, save for one small item.

The next night, from a place of concealment using my spyglass, I kept constant vigil on the grave of Sherlock Holmes.

As I expected, I spied a tall, thin figure furtively approach the cemetery with an enclosed lantern after midnight. He was alone and he carried a shovel. I watched with interest as he dug the dirt away from the grave of an "English Man, Died, May 1891." The more he dug, the faster he dug. Once he hit the wood of the simple coffin, he stopped, brought his lantern closer, and deftly cleared away the remaining dirt. Finally, he was able to open the casket lid, and after he did so, he stood motionless and silent as a statue. I could well imagine his consternation, for there was no body in the coffin. It was certainly shocking, but then, that coffin was not entirely empty either. Slowly, the tall figure brought the lantern closer to the coffin and he peered down to look at something within. Suddenly he reached down and pulled out a small envelope. It was the one I had left there the evening before. It said simply, "Moriarty," on the outside. On the inside was a small note, which he pulled out, carefully unfolded, and began to read. That, too, was short and simple. It read: "Meet me at dawn, upon the heights overlooking the Reichenbach Falls." It was signed with the initials, "S.H."

Moriarty crushed the note and envelope and in anger threw them into the empty coffin. He looked around him into the darkness, quickly extinguished his lantern, and suddenly let out a loud menacing yell of sheer animal rage. I have never heard anything quite like it in my life. It brought a grim smile to my face.

It was then far after midnight, and I gathered my things together and began my trek up to the heights overlooking the Reichenbach Falls, where I would await Moriarty, and our destiny.

Dawn at the Reichenbach is a beautiful sight, Watson, and I was surely sorry that you missed it this time. In my own world you had accompanied me to the falls, but then at the last minute had been called away upon some pretext by Moriarty, so that he and I would be alone. Now, no such subterfuge was necessary, for it would just be Moriarty and Holmes, as it was intended all along. Two primal forces engaged in the eternal struggle between good and evil.

I was out of disguise, it was no longer necessary, and I was dressed in my usual clothing, along with heavy hiking boots and jacket. It was quite chilly upon the Reichenbach, even with the sun having just come up.

I looked over at the falls below in order to discern the whereabouts of that strange mist I had encountered upon my first visit here, more than one year ago. To be sure, it was still there, a misty fog that seemed to shimmer and shift as it moved to different locations along the falls edge. I began to surmise that if the strange mist encompassed properties of movement—or at least of being able to change location—then that might be the reason why in our original encounter in my own world, Moriarty had died in his fall, while I had fallen into the mist and been transported here. The mist had to be the doorway. It seemed quite possible, and I found myself enjoying the evident logical solution to this most strange of problems once and for all when I suddenly heard a footstep behind me.

It was Moriarty! He was instantly upon me, wrapping me tightly in his arms, pinning my own arms to my sides, as he quickly dragged me to the ledge.

"Now, Mr. Holmes, I know it cannot be, but it is! You seem to plague me unto forever. Can I never be free of you? Well, I shall be free of you, Holmes. I killed you once, of that I was certain, and I'll kill you again, and this time you shall stay dead!"

"Moriarty!" I growled, shocked by what I could see of him. For this Moriarty was not the old, bent-over, bookish professor I knew from my world. This man appeared to be younger, and certainly much stronger. I was at a loss to understand why—but then why should it not be so? The Dalai Lama had told me that while this world was similar to my own, it was also different from my own world. Had I not seen so for myself?

Suddenly I realized that this Moriarty had killed the Holmes of this world in their first encounter. He could easily do so to me as well. He was bigger, stronger than the Moriarty of my own world. I felt myself being inexorably dragged to the ledge. I heard the churning, roiling waters crashing below, felt the spray from the cliff, the sun blinded my eyes, as I was pulled closer to my doom.

"You'll not escape this time, Holmes! This time you go over the cliff and die!" Moriarty growled these words into my ear.

I tried to fight him off, but he was stronger and held me tightly.

I could not free my arms from where he had them pinned to my sides. I could not break his hold over me. It was then that I realized I *was* going to die. He was going to do it again! He was going to hurl me over the ledge into the falls to my death on the rocks below.

And then I felt a heavy blow, as if from some mighty collision, and we were entirely spun around. Then, good Watson, I saw your face, and you fought with Moriarty.

"Holmes, I'm here. The Dalai Lama knew you would need my help!"

"I told you to stay in London!" I blurted as I tried to free my arms.

"Hah!" you laughed, pummeling Moriarty with blows from your fist as you tried to pull us apart.

Then I broke Moriarty's hold over me and was free. Immediately I stepped in to shield you from his blows. You hit him again, and once again, causing him to move away backward, where he seemed to hesitate, to lose his balance. Then as Moriarty slipped over the falls, I watched in horror as he suddenly grabbed your coat, and you followed him over the cliff.

"Watson!" I cried.

"Holmes, no need, I'm glad it ended this . . ." And your voice diminished as you fell down to the rocks below.

I stood at the abyss, as you and Moriarty plunged down to the falls and instant death below.

It was over. I looked down and saw that Moriarty and you lay mangled upon the stones of the falls and were soon pulled under by the furious water of the river. Both of you were gone a moment later.

"Moriarty finally dead," I whispered, shaking with sorrow, "but at what price? My good Watson, dead! What am I to do now?"

And then the words of Thubten Gyatso came back to me, "*Seek the mist, that is your doorway.*"

I looked over and saw that the mist was about twenty yards away, and I walked toward it as if in a dream. It was shimmering in a most unnatural manner, and I could well believe now that it might in fact be some form of transcendental, or supernatural, doorway between the worlds as the Dalai Lama had told me.

Moriarty in this world, and in my own world, was dead now. I had accomplished my mission. I wondered, had I been brought here for this very reason in the first place? It was a question I had no way of answering. Perhaps Thubten Gyatso knew more than he was saying?

Perhaps he had told you, Watson, and that is why, stout fellow, you had disobeyed my order to stay behind in London? Yet, your disobedience had saved my life and enabled me to accomplish that mission.

Now it was time for me to go home to my own world, where I belonged. The gate awaited me. Sadly, I was leaving behind a world where not only Moriarty and Holmes were dead, but so was your own other self. Yet now, more than ever, I yearned to be free of this nightmare world and be back home in my own London, with my own good Watson, at our own 221B, with Mycroft, Mrs. Hudson, and even dour-faced old Lestrade.

I made for the mist. Once it was stationary below me I looked carefully down upon it. I knew what I had to do. I could not live in this world. Not with my best friend dead—who had given his life to save my own. But what I was considering was incomprehensible as well. If I was wrong, I would be doing myself what Moriarty had just been unable to do. I could be killing myself, committing suicide.

I looked into the roiling mist below. I took a deep breath. The shimmering seemed to call to me. I thought of you, good friend, and home, and all the people I desired to see again, and I dove down into that doorway and my destiny.

"Are you all right, mister?" I heard a voice saying from above me.

I was coming back to consciousness slowly, breathing the chill mountain air, feeling the dirt and grass under my body, I felt my shoulders and body shaken. I opened my eyes, and there I saw good Hans.

"Are you all right? A strange place to fall asleep, no?"

"Hans?" I asked.

"Yes, that is my name. But how did you know it?" he replied carefully.

"You do not know me?"

"No, sir. Should I know you? I have never met you before this moment."

I nodded. "No, of course not, you would not know me."

On my way to London, I bought a copy of the *Times* and read it with a renewed sense of joy as I learned of the plans being set in motion for the Birthday Celebration for Queen Victoria. She was to be joined in the celebration by her son Edward, heir to the throne. I sighed with relief, the world I knew, the world I belonged in was here, and I was in my rightful place in it. I read with interest where a new American president had recently been elected, and there was nary a peep of military insurrection or succession; where the government of France was still in the usual turmoil but had not yet fallen; and where Germany and Russia were quiet. It appeared now that all was as it should be.

I also noticed a small item tucked away in the back pages about Eddy. He wasn't king here, just a minor royal. It said simply that Albert Christian Edward Victor, Duke of Clarence and Avondale, and grandson of Queen Victoria, had been hospitalized for a severe illness, previous to his sudden demise. Now it was rumored the notorious libertine had contracted syphilis and that it had been the disease that had slowly driven him mad. It appeared the disease had taken its ultimate toll on the young royal. Now there was no way he would ever become king.

I closed the paper and put it away. The train was pulling into Victoria Station. I cannot express the joy I felt. I had been gone a long time. Now I was home again. Immediately I hired a hansom cab to take me to Baker Street and our rooms at 221B.

I had a story that no one—not even you, Watson—could ever chronicle, for who would believe it? But I give it to you anyway, my old friend. You may put the narrative among your other papers in that old lockbox of yours. Perhaps someday in the future the secrets of time and space will be well enough understood so that my tale may seem credible. It seems incredible to me already, even though I lived through it so recently. And, as I said to you last week upon my return, it was good to see you after so long, my dear Watson. It was good to see you.

Cross of Gold

Michael Collins

adeusz Jan Fortunowski arrived in America in the spring of 1893, speaking no English. Three months later he was arrested for the murder of high-roller horse breeder, socialite, and one-time lieutenant governor of California, Colin "Condor" Cameron. A sensational event at the time, but in the end no more than a for-gotten incident in the turbulent history of the cities of Brooklyn and New York, and I would never have heard of the crime if Tadeusz Jan had not been my grandfather.

He was nearly twenty-one that May of 1893, born and raised by Polish parents in a small town in Lithuania, which was, at the time, part of the empire of the tsar of all the Russias. An empire where the Poles and the Lithuanians hated each other, where both hated the Russians, where all three hated the Jews, and where the Cos-sacks hated everyone, including each other. No one cared whom the Jews hated.

He died before I was born, but his widow—his second wife, not my grandmother—told me his story in the front room of the old-law tenement on Seventh Street in lower Manhattan, where she lived alone after Tadeusz's death. She told many tales of that far-off world to an eager boy who was also a Tadeusz—Daniel Tadeusz—and who had once been Fortunowski, but was now Fortune.

(A change made by my father, and old Tadeusz never spoke to his only son again.)

"It was a time of great change, Daniel. A time of industrialization where there was little for an ambitious fifteen-year-old to do in a small village in Tsarist Lithuania except plow fields behind slow horses."

Ambition was in the cities. Tadeusz went to the city to work in a foundry and send money home. But to learn, also, that he worked twelve hours a day, six days a week, to produce goods the tsar and the princes and the counts and the industrialists would sell for far more than they paid to have them made, and would therefore become rich and live good lives. To learn, in the words of the great president of the United States of America, Abraham Lincoln, that tyranny was when one man said to another, "You toil to produce the food, and I'll eat it," and that he, Tadeusz, and his fellow workers, were not among those who would eat the food.

Tadeusz read Marx and Engels, Bakunin and Blanqui, and learned that a poor man alone is powerless, strength comes from community. He learned, too, that the tsar, the princes, the counts, and the industrialists did not like those who worked for them to have such knowledge. In fact, the tsar hated that more than he hated the Poles, the Polish princes hated it more than they hated the Russians, the Lithuanian counts hated it more than they hated the Poles and the Russians, and all of them hated it even more than they hated the Jews. So they sent the Cossacks—the Cossacks still hated everyone, and it made no difference to them whose heads they broke as long as they were well paid.

Tadeusz Jan was beaten many times and thrown in jail more times. There was persecution, unemployment, prison, hunger, and little work for a militant socialist. So when his time for service in the tsar's army neared, Tadeusz decided to go to the land of the great Abraham Lincoln, where everything would be better.

Alas, by then he spoke Polish, Russian, and some German, but no English, and there was no foundry work for even a skilled man without English. The only work was unskilled piecework in a sweatshop. Except that Tadeusz had one other skill—he knew how to work with horses—and English was not needed to talk to horses, or to muck out stables. A young Russian he met on the ship found him a job at the racetrack out in the healthy sea air of Sheepshead Bay in the city of Brooklyn.

He had been at the track three months when Colin "Condor" Cameron was found dying inside a horse stall in one of the stables where Tadeusz worked. A mighty outcry arose throughout the cities of Brooklyn and New York. Cameron was a rich and honored sportsman and public servant from distant California whose early vision and toil helped build the railroad from coast to coast and thus made the country a single nation where the goods of the fertile but distant West could be sold in the populous East for the benefit of all.

It was not immediately clear how the high-roller met his end, the horse in the fatal stall having panicked and trampled on him in a hundred places. However, in the opinion of the racetrack physician the injuries from the horse were inflicted after death, especially since the horse was a stallion often ridden by Cameron, and would not have been panicked by the presence of the sportsman alone.

An autopsy had to be performed, but the members of the Coney Island Jockey Club, the socialites and industrialists with hotels in the resort and horses at the track, and the local political authorities led by police chief John J. McKane, had no need to wait. They knew the murderer—Tadeusz Jan Fortunowski.

The circumstantial evidence against Tadeusz was, for the end of the nineteenth century, strong, convincing, and alarming to both the authorities and the public. "He had come to America, your grandfather, expecting a land of Abraham Lincolns," my stepgrandmother told me in the living room of the Seventh Street tenement. "When he found only another land of tsars and princes, with the same wealth and power, and the same castles on the hills, it was a great shock. A great sadness, and a great anger. He was a man of, how do you say in English, *Integrität?*"

"Integrity, Grandma?"

"*Ja*, integrity. Tadeusz had not come to America to be silent."

Tadeusz tried to form a union among the stable hands and exercise boys. He made speeches, fought McKane's private police, was beaten and jailed. But the immigrant stable hands and exercise boys in Sheepshead Bay still dreamed of stealing their own kingdoms in this rich new land, so few responded.

Tadeusz was good at his work, and had failed in his organization attempt, so he was still employed at the racetrack when Condor

Cameron was murdered. He was a dangerous anarchist, an agitator, a criminal. He had defied the police and politicians. He had been seen arguing with Cameron inside the stable only an hour before the dying man was discovered, was there working, or hiding many said, in another stall after the murder, and was carrying a knife.

In 1893, forensic science was barely in its infancy. Foreigners, anarchists, and the defiant poor were looked upon with suspicion by the higher classes, the police who worked for them, and the native-born masses. Tadeusz was arrested on the spot, and all but convicted and sentenced. The autopsy revealed conclusively that Cameron had not been killed by the horse, and was the final proof of Tadeusz's guilt.

That the autopsy also showed the businessman and politician had not died from a knife wound, but had been shot from close range, meant nothing. A foreign agitator always had a pistol, everyone knew that. That no pistol was found was dismissed. Everyone knew that anarchists were cunning in covering their tracks. Who else could have, or would have, done it? Cameron had no known enemies, was unmarried, had retired from all public service, was liked by everyone at the track, had never failed to promptly pay a lost wager or debt, and was openly generous to all his women, employees, and servants. Even his last words, as reported by the two exercise boys who found him minutes before he died, seemed to damn Tadeusz.

"When we found him, sir," one exercise boy told Chief McKane, "he whispered something about 'our wars,' or maybe 'our laws.'"

The other chimed in eagerly, "I heard 'our straws' or maybe 'our shores,' sir."

Who else at the track that day was known to have defied the laws of the state and city? Or carried bales of straw into the stables? Or had recently arrived on our shores? That Tadeusz claimed he had been sent on an errand to another stable at the time he was "seen" arguing with Cameron, and did not return before Cameron was dead, was greeted with scorn, since everyone connected to Cameron's stable vigorously denied sending him on any errand.

"This," Tadeusz's widow told his grandson in the dim living room of the railroad flat on Seventh Street, "was when the man came to Tadeusz."

"What man, Grandma?"

"Your grandfather never knew his name. An Englishman with rapid speech and not-very-good German. The man who saved him."

"Saved Grandpa? Was he a detective?" I suppose I had already begun to think of being a policeman like my father.

"Tadeusz wondered that too, but if so, he was a very strange detective. This was all long before I met Tadeusz, but he had never forgotten the Englishman." She had a faraway expression in her eyes. "A tall man, he told me, over six feet, and so very thin he looked much taller. But it was his eyes Tadeusz remembered most. They were alight, on fire, and seemed to burn through Tadeusz like red-hot knives cutting their way to the truth. An eagle searching for prey, Tadeusz said, with his thin, hawklike nose and strong, determined chin."

The faraway expression turned sad. "Tadeusz was in the jail of the chief McKane when the Englishman came to see him. At first Tadeusz was afraid. The man was dressed as all the rich men who owned the horses at the racetrack dressed. In a high gray hat and white shirt with cravat, a long gray coat, gray trousers, and low gray boots. Like the princes and counts at home."

Without preamble or explanation, the Englishman commanded in his poor German, "Tell me everything you recall from the day of the murder, young man."

"Why?" Tadeusz retorted. "Who are you? How did you get in to see me?"

The Englishman smiled. "So, you do not grovel and beg, eh? Capital! My instincts are correct. I believe you to be innocent, young man. I have been in the stable and the stall, and there are indications, but we have little time. This man McKane, and the late Condor Cameron's cronies, want your head as soon as possible. The murder is bad for business, and you are branded a most dangerous agitator. So, it does not matter who I am, I travel incognito for the time being. As for being here, let us say I have powerful friends. Now, everything you remember, and quickly."

Tadeusz felt a sudden wave of hopelessness. "But I remember nothing."

"Nonsense! You remember, but you do not know you remember. Describe your actions that day. Everything. Leave nothing out. From the beginning."

Tadeusz, who was by nature bold and skeptical, said, "I opened my eyes, and when they were accustomed to the dark, saw that I was in my room in the tenement. I yawned, and got out of bed. I scratched, splashed water on my face, rubbed my teeth with salt water, and—"

"Is the tenement in the city of New York, or the city of Brooklyn?" the Englishman interrupted.

That was when Tadeusz realized the Englishman knew exactly what he was doing. He knew that Tadeusz was mocking him, but did not care, because every unimportant detail was precisely what he wanted.

"Brooklyn, sir," Tadeusz said, a small hope beginning inside him. "But not in Sheepshead Bay. It is too expensive. A place for the rich."

The Englishman said drily, "Yes, young man, it is. But I suggest you refrain from such comments for the time being. We do not want your accusers to become so incensed they proceed against you despite proof of your innocence. Now, continue your narration. Did anything unusual occur before you left your room?"

"No, noth—." Tadeusz blinked. "No, not before, but when I left. A man—"

"Was on the street," the Englishman interrupted again. "A man doing nothing when all others were hurrying to work."

Tadeusz was astonished. "Ye . . . yes, sir. Leaning against a wall across from the tenement. He was near the streetlamp, and I noticed him."

The tall Englishman nodded grimly. "It is as I thought. This was no spur-of-the-moment crime, but one well planned. Did you see the man's face?"

"No, sir. He had his cap pulled low and stood in shadow."

"Yes, he would have. Go on!"

Tadeusz had ridden the steam train to the racetrack by the sea. He had not seen the lurking man again. Once at the track he mucked five stalls, spread fresh straw, and rubbed down three of Condor Cameron's horses after their morning exercise. At that point Tadeusz took a short break, sitting in the sun outside the stable and breathing the sea air, when a stable hand he had never seen ran up to tell him Mr. Cameron's trainer wanted him to go to a distant stable with some tack. He was gone over an hour, and soon after he returned and resumed cleaning the stalls in his stable, the dying Cameron was found by the two exercise boys.

"Of course. That would be the way it happened," the Englishman exclaimed. He whirled toward the door at the end of the hallway. "Be of good heart, young man. I shall return soon with the key to your predicament, and to your cell."

Then he was gone.

Tadeusz waited a whole day. Alone in his cell, food shoved in from time to time without a word, he was overcome by despair. What could the Englishman do to help him? Was he not also a foreigner whom Boss McKane and the rich men would laugh at? The Englishman was mad, escaped from some asylum.

Darkness fell, and Tadeusz lay on his straw pallet, his eyes closed against the feeble light from the stone corridor outside the cell, fighting his fear. But he was young, strong of will, with the optimism of youth that had not yet been beaten down by the weight of poverty and injustice, and he soon fell asleep.

"Tadeusz!"

Tadeusz's eyes snapped open, his hand reached swiftly for his knife. Then it all flooded back. He was in jail, his knife taken, and . . . a man he had never seen before was staring down and vigorously shaking him. The man wore a cheap suit, soiled and ill-fitting, with the trousers held up by a length of rope threaded through the belt loops. His jacket torn and mud-spattered, his wrinkled shirt collarless, a rough cap jammed on his ragged hair and pulled low to his eyes. Stocky and hunched like someone who had worked all his life in the fields. A broad face and thick nose.

Tadeusz sat up, his fists clenched, and cried in German, "Stand away! What do you—?"

"Collect yourself, confound you. There is little time!"

Tadeusz stared. "*Engländer?* Englishman?"

"Come quickly, our bird may even now be on the wing!"

Tadeusz stared. Before his eyes the hunched and filthy laborer seemed to change like flowing liquid into the tall, bone-thin English gentleman with the flaming eyes that burned now like the soaring eagle who saw his prey below. Only the thick, coarse face and shabby clothing remained in grotesque contrast.

Tadeusz snatched up his jacket, flopped his hat onto his uncombed hair, and followed as the Englishman hurried to the open cell door. Only then did Tadeusz see that they were not alone. Another man waited outside the cell. A well-dressed, heavyset man with a solid gold watch chain across his broad expanse of ample belly and waistcoat, who scowled at both Tadeusz and the Englishman. Chief John J. McKane himself!

There could be only one reason McKane was there. It was all a ruse!

Tadeusz had heard of such murderous tricks perpetrated by the Cheka, the dreaded Russian secret police, to silence dissidents without anyone knowing, not even the poor wretch's family. They simply ceased to exist, disappeared. They were going to murder him!

Blindly, Tadeusz hurled himself forward to escape.

And found himself held as if by some invisible wall in the amazingly strong grip of the tall Englishman. "Calm yourself, Tadeusz. You have misunderstood, though I commend both your instincts and your speed of reaction. McKane is here only to be shown his error, much as he does not want to listen or believe."

Tadeusz could only stare at the glowering self-appointed police chief and political boss, and stammer, ". . . but . . . but . . ."

McKane growled at the Englishman, "You can show me nothing. You might fool Mr. Vanderbilt and Diamond Jim, but you don't fool me. I am a policeman, and the facts are clear. That anarchist is the murderer, and he'll swing for certain."

"Your so-called facts are as worthless as your knowledge of your own profession. The guilty no longer 'swing,' as you so colorfully put it, in the state of New York, but are executed in the new electric chair, where I confidently predict you will end your corrupt life someday. Now, step out of the way, sir, and we shall complete our business."

McKane snarled something unintelligible, but stepped aside and followed Tadeusz and the Englishman out of the jail to where ten uniformed policemen waited beside two large carriages.

McKane chose to ride on the outside driver's seat from where he could coordinate his men, and the two carriages raced through the growing light of dawn. Alone in the cab with Tadeusz, the Englishman explained that connections at home among the high-and-mighty, which included the Prince of Wales and the American daughter of the man who had been the leading figure in building the Sheepshead Bay racetrack, had forced McKane to listen to him.

"But where are we going?"

"To expose the true murderer, young man. If we are not too late." And the Englishman leaned out of the cab window. "Faster, faster!"

With the Englishman's continued exhortations, they soon arrived on a dark street in sight of the river and New York across it. Rows of shabby tenements lined the street on both sides, and the Englishman commanded the carriage to stop. Leaping out, he exclaimed to McKane, "Place three of your men front and rear, and instruct them to hold anyone who attempts to leave this building. Everyone else, follow me!"

With that, the Englishman rushed in through the unlocked front vestibule door, and, climbing as swiftly as a jungle cat, finally stopped at a door on the third floor, a long, thin finger to his lips.

"If you would have your men break down the door, Chief McKane, we will all enter. But be swift and sure, our quarry is a man of high caution, great skill with a pistol, and stout heart. He will not be surprised long, nor taken easily. I only pray he is still inside."

The four uniformed policemen formed on either side of the battering ram they had brought with them, and charged the door. It exploded in a shattering of splintered and torn wood, and they were in, the tall Englishman in the lead, his nostrils flaring and his eyes flashing like those of the lead hound who smells the fox to be near. Tadeusz came close behind, seeing his possible salvation ahead, with the policemen spreading out behind him and Chief McKane judiciously the last to enter.

Indistinct in the gloom of the early-dawn light from the single window, a shape streaked through the windowless middle rooms toward the kitchen at the rear of the narrow railroad flat. At an unexpected second door in the kitchen, the figure spun sharply and two shots ripped the air in rapid succession. A policeman cried out and clutched his right arm, his pistol falling to the floor. The tall Englishman grunted and stumbled against the kitchen table, holding to the top to keep from falling.

Two shots, two hits, and Tadeusz knew better than to hesitate a split second as he charged on into the man before he could fire again. The impact knocked the man's pistol away, but Tadeusz found himself gripped as if by some great bear and flung to the floor. In an instant, the man had the door open and was almost through when a single shot rang out. The fleeing man stumbled, slowed, and the remaining three policemen swarmed him to the floor in a narrow corridor that led to an equally narrow flight of stairs up to the roof.

"Hold him fast," the tall Englishman warned, still bracing himself on the table, his revolver in his hand. "He is clever, and a wizard with a pistol."

Tadeusz realized it was the Englishman himself who had fired the final shot that had stopped the fleeing man.

"As are you, sir," he cried, and then saw the bloodstain on the Englishman's grubby shirt a few inches above his waist. "Sir, you're hurt!"

"A mere scratch, young man. It is of no consequence."

McKane called his other men up, and while four held their pistols steady on the wounded man, the remaining five hauled him to his feet, wrestled him inside and into a kitchen chair, where he sat, his hard, clear eyes fixed only on the disguised Englishman as if he sensed who was the most dangerous adversary in the room.

"There, McKane, is the murderer of Condor Cameron."

Tadeusz blinked at the man. "But . . . he's the man who told me the trainer wanted me to carry the tack to the other stable!"

Chief McKane scowled. "What's he saying?"

The Englishman translated, and McKane swore. "Hell, that's pure bunk."

"On the contrary. You will note that, although twenty-five years older, our captive is remarkably fit, so appears far younger, and is, at a reasonable distance, nearly a double for Tadeusz. Especially if wearing identical clothes, doing the same work in the same place, and never seen before in Sheepshead Bay."

"Simple coincidence," McKane snapped.

"Coincidence is no part of this crime. Once this man arrived in Brooklyn, Condor Cameron's fate was sealed."

Oblivious to his wound, a thin smile flitted across the prisoner's granite visage, but he uttered not a word, his gaze fixed toward the wall.

"You talk in riddles," McKane sneered. "Just who is this alleged murderer, and what, pray tell, was his motive?"

"A step at a time, if you please. That is the method of science," the Englishman said calmly. "When Mr. Vanderbilt first told me of the crime and the alleged perpetrator, I had strong doubts. I decided to investigate, and learned at once that young Tadeusz spoke no English at all, and so could not have argued with a man who spoke only English. With his meager wage from the track, he could afford no more than a shared room, could barely buy food and an occasional needed article of clothing. Where, then, did he find the money to purchase a pistol? My visit to his cell confirmed my deductions. Character is important in an investigation, and I saw at once the young man had so much integrity as to be incapable of such a crime except in self-defense, and there was no evidence Cameron was armed."

The Englishman shook his head. "No, the boy was innocent. Therefore, the murderer had to be someone else at the track that day. But Cameron was barely known in New York, was well liked in racing circles, and engaged in no activity that would cause such violence. Logically then, the crime must have sprung from his past. At that point I recalled the source of his wealth—the transcontinental railroad—and realized what his dying words had been."

"An amazing feat," McKane scoffed, "since what poor Condor was telling us has never been in doubt. His killer was from foreign shores and had broken our laws, and those words pointed straight to that anarchist!"

But by then no one in the kitchen was looking at the bombastic chief, or listening to him, not even his own men. They all watched the Englishman as if mesmerized, as much by the power of his voice as by his words. All but the prisoner, who appeared to smile at some private joke.

"No, McKane. What those panicked exercise boys heard was a single word. Or, to be precise, three words of which their confused minds actually heard only the last. That word was not 'our laws,' but 'outlaws.' And the two words that preceded 'outlaws' were 'the' and 'California.' Cameron was telling us that his killer was one of the California Outlaws."

The prisoner showed no reaction, simply watched and waited with the patience of a man who knows that what he is watching for will come as inevitably as the snow of winter in the high mountains.

McKane could see the quick solution to the murder desired by his businessmen friends slipping away. "You're telling us a man like Cameron was connected to a gang of crooks in California?"

"That would depend on what your definition of 'connected' and 'crook' is," the Englishman said drily. "As it happens, I came to New York directly from California, where at present there is a furor that bears on Cameron's murder."

"What furor?" McKane demanded.

"The trial, and certain conviction, of one of the leaders of the so-called California Outlaws."

The Englishman's voice seemed to fill the tiny kitchen. "It all began with the desperation of a government that wanted a transcontinental railroad, and the bribery, venality, corruption, influence peddling, and chicanery of members of that government in conjunction with the notorious Big Four railroad barons—Collis Huntington, Leland Stanford, Mark Hopkins, and Charles Crocker. As a result of what has been fairly labeled an entirely new form of embezzlement, a monstrous octopus now holds a death grip on the state of California, and particularly the wheat farmers of the San Joaquin Valley. It is called the Southern Pacific Railroad."

Despite himself, there was enough of the true policeman in McKane to make a fact catch his attention. "That's Cameron's company!"

"Precisely," the Englishman nodded. "The Big Four are the most visible, but there are others of equal wealth and power, and one of these was Condor Cameron. His profile was kept low because, while Huntington was the idea man, Stanford the public face, Hopkins the record keeper, and Crocker the field boss, Cameron was the enforcer. The man who oversaw the ruthless coercion of entire communities into agreeing with all railroad demands, the evictions of farmers and ranchers, and the murders of anyone who tried to stand against the railroad. Hence his nickname." The Englishman glanced directly at the silent prisoner, "Is that not so, Mr. Evans?"

When it finally came, the prisoner's voice was low, and as hard as an anvil. "A condor's a scavenger. A vulture. When you see a condor, something's died."

"Quite so," the Englishman said, and said to McKane, "the basic motive was and is the Southern Pacific's ruthless ruination and murder of the small farmers, ranchers, and laborers who really conquered the West. The immediate motive was the furor in California I spoke of earlier, caused when the farmers fought back and the railroad secured a court judgment in 1878 that, the farmers charged, reeked of political corruption and bias since the governor of California was also president of the Southern Pacific—Leland Stanford."

"You're joking?" McKane's eyes widened in envy at such brazen corruption.

"You can well wonder," the Englishman said grimly. "By 1880 the valley was boiling, and at a place called Mussel Slough, a U.S. Marshal and three railroad men evicting farmers were confronted by the irate farmers. All were armed, as is the custom of your country, and someone fired the first shot. Six settlers and one railroad deputy died, and the railroad man who had killed all six of the settlers was himself gunned down later that day by 'unknown parties.' The state brought charges of 'overthrowing the government' and 'interfering with a U.S. Marshal' against seventeen settlers. Five were convicted of only the lesser charge, served five months in a local jail, where their cells were never locked, and they came and went as they pleased. When they were released and returned home, they were given a hero's welcome.

"The railroad went on evicting and ruining, the farmers went on resisting. Five years ago the Southern Pacific was the target of a series of train robberies. The California government quickly labeled the perpetrators 'The California Outlaws,' put a price on the heads of the leaders, Jon Sontag and Christopher Evans, and, with the aid of the railroad, set a manhunt in motion. Two months ago Evans and Sontag were ambushed by a large party of marshals and railroad detectives. Sontag died of tetanus from his untreated wounds. Evans lost an arm, an eye, and suffered brain damage, and is even now standing trial, which will certainly go against him. However, other members of the Outlaws were not captured, and one sits there: Mr. Andrew Evans, a cousin, I believe, of the man on trial."

In the silence, the rising summer sun slowly turning the light in the kitchen to a pale gold, the prisoner in the chair said, "They let John die, and they'll lock Chris up forever. The Outlaws are finished, but one day the Southern Pacific will go, too."

"Then why murder Cameron, Mr. Evans? Why not let time, history, and his maker punish him?"

The prisoner's eyes darkened, "Life is short, and justice is slow. For all of us they killed with their greed, I killed one of them for us."

"You're an excellent shot. Why risk getting so close, being seen with him? It was your undoing."

Now Andrew Evans looked again at the Englishman. "I wanted him to know why he was dying, and he did. He deserved what he got."

"I have some sympathy for your cause, sir, but not your methods. You would have let the boy there be punished for your crime."

"When they leave you no choice, you do what you must," Evans said quietly. "And do you really think you would have found me still in Brooklyn if I had not feared they would convict the boy? Had that happened, I would have declared myself instantly. But I've been watching your activities, too, Englishman, and when I saw you arrive with McKane and his men I knew you had guessed the truth, and there was no reason not to save myself. I only wish you had been a worse shot."

The Englishman inclined his head to Evans. "My apologies, but I could not be certain Tadeusz would be exonerated without your capture."

McKane growled, "Very pretty sentiments, I'm sure. But all Cameron did was make all the money he could for the railroad and himself, and there's not a damn thing illegal or immoral about that. It's called free enterprise, and it's why America's a great nation. This man is a cold-blooded murderer, who is going to fry since you tell me we don't swing 'em anymore."

The Englishman wrinkled his austere nose in distaste. "I believe Evans's actions to be wrong, McKane, but he's ten times the human being you are, and I will be on hand to see that he gets a fair trial. You may count on that."

McKane glared and barked at his policemen, "Take him out, damn it."

The prisoner safely in the first carriage, Tadeusz and the Englishman climbed into the second for the return trip. The carriage had barely started to roll when Tadeusz, with the rampant curiosity of youth, burst out in German, "*Mein herr,* how did you learn that Evans was the murderer?"

The Englishman laughed. "Elementary, my boy. Always cast a suspicious eye upon any solution so convenient for the authorities. An actual murderer rarely fits so neatly into the prejudices of all concerned as you did: young, poor, foreign, militant, outspoken, powerless, and essentially defenseless. Once I observed your character, confirmed that you spoke no English, and realized what Condor Cameron dying words must have been, the rest was simple."

My stepgrandmother laughed in the tenement on Seventh Street. "Your grandfather told me he nearly struck the Englishman. 'But how did any of that lead you to a man no one knew existed!?'"

"Ah, that was in itself a key. Consistent with my theory of the motive, our murderer was a stranger in Sheepshead Bay. Clearly, he was the 'stable hand' who sent you away, and who was seen arguing with Cameron. He would look like you in overall build, general coloring, and facial features, and he had to be wearing basically identical clothes. Therefore, he must have been observing the track and its employees for at least a few days to find someone with access to the stable who looked enough like him and to learn Cameron's habits."

At that point, my stepgrandmother told me, Tadeusz said he began to glimpse a hint of the Englishman's rigorous logic.

"A man from the West, wanted by the police there, and certainly of limited means, would not be found in one of the grand hotels. Discreet inquiries at the few rooming houses in the vicinity after such a man who showed great interest in the track, was out all day, and had come from the Far West, quickly turned up our Mr. Evans, who had not bothered to disguise his name, secure in the assumption that in distant New York it would mean nothing."

"Once I learned he had vacated his room the day before the murder, and knew he had been watching you that morning to know what you were wearing, it was logical to assume he had taken new lodgings near your room. A few pennies to the street urchins, who inhabit the poorer areas of all cities today with nothing to do but observe everything that happens in the area, soon turned up Evans and his new accommodations. The rest you know."

With that, Tadeusz said, the Englishman sat back and lapsed into a morose silence, as if, having told the story, the world had suddenly become a dark, empty place.

Tadeusz was given his job back by the Sheepshead Bay track, with, at the Englishman's hint of possible lawsuits, a healthy settlement for his wrongful incarceration. He used the money to move to a better room by himself and to start English lessons.

A month after that fateful morning, Brooklyn awakened to the shocking news of the daring escape of Andrew Evans. There was a great outcry against Chief McKane, with hints of his being afraid of a public trial that would reveal both his attempt to convict an innocent man and Condor Cameron's unsavory history. McKane stoutly denied such "vile slander," promptly discharged four jail officers for gross dereliction of duty, and vowed Evans would soon be recaptured.

A few days later, the tall Englishman appeared at the racetrack where Tadeusz still labored. "I doubt McKane or anyone else in law enforcement will ever see Andrew Evans again, and so with any trial now unlikely, it is time for me to depart. Ride with me to the docks and the ship that will convey me once again to Europe."

"I cannot, sir," Tadeusz said carefully in his fledgling English. "I must work."

"Tut, young man, I have spoken with your employers. There will be no problem."

Grinning, Tadeusz eagerly climbed into the Englishman's carriage, and the coachman urged the team away. The Englishman, in a curious but serviceable mixture of his bad German and Tadeusz's fledgling English, said, "How much of why Condor Cameron was murdered do you understand, Tadeusz?"

"Not *sehr* much, sir," my grandfather had to admit. "The English, it was too, ah . . . ah . . . what is it? Ah . . . quick? *Ja,* quick."

"I thought as much." The Englishman nodded, staring out the carriage window as the wealthy town houses and shabby tenements of Brooklyn rolled by in the warming summer morning. "This last year I have traveled extensively in your new country, and have seen a great struggle in progress. It is a primal contest that also exists in my own country, and in your former nation, but America is young and raw, and the struggle is naked here. It is between the forces of justice and humanity, and those of wealth and power."

The Englishman turned from the window to look at Tadeusz. "The murder of Condor Cameron was a small moment in that struggle. Do you understand that?"

"I think so," my grandfather said slowly. "Yes sir."

"Good." The strange Englishman glanced again out the window where the teeming slums of the docks had begun, the masses of people flooding along the narrow streets as the coachman cursed and forced his way through. "There is a young congressman in the state of Nebraska, where the great western plains of this nation begin, who is standing for your senate. His name is Bryan, and I envision an important future for him. When we spoke, he used an image that defines his view of this clash of contending forces—'crucifying mankind upon a cross of gold.'"

When he turned once more from the window, the Englishman looked hard at Tadeusz. "Your new nation stands at a crossroads, and I fear that in the next century it will choose the wrong road, as I now suspect my own country did in this century. A nation can be a great force for the human spirit and potential, or it can be an empire. It cannot be both."

My stepgrandmother told me that my grandfather said the Englishman again sat for the rest of the ride to his ship in a morose silence. But when they arrived, as the coachman held the carriage door open, he turned to Tadeusz, and said, "Do you know, Tadeusz, where you will stand in this struggle of which I spoke?"

"I, sir," my grandfather said, "will stand for justice."

The Englishman nodded. "That is where I have stood my whole life. Not the law, which is always created by those in power and inevitably ends favoring them and their views, or even the truth, but justice. Yet what is justice, Tadeusz? Do we know? Does anyone?"

With that, my stepgrandmother told me, the Englishman smiled at my grandfather, instructed the coachman to take him back to Sheepshead Bay, and with a final wave mounted the gangplank to follow his luggage aboard the ship.

Tadeusz Jan Fortunowski never saw him again, nor ever knew his name, but I think I know his name, and sometimes I wonder if this story of my grandfather was the first seed that set me, Dan Fortune, on my own search for justice.

God of the Naked Unicorn

Ova Hamlet

(a creation of Richard Lupoff)

I

It was a chilly winter's evening and the sound of the jingling coach bells attached to the harness of carriage horses penetrated both the swirling yellow fog of Limehouse where the Thames swerves and eddies and dark Lascar shapes flit through shaded passages, and the ancient rippled glass of the windows of my humble flat to remind even a sad lonely man that there were yet revelers at large in the city anticipating the joyous holiday of Nativity.

My mind fled back to earlier, and jollier, holiday seasons, seasons spent in my youth amidst the savage tribesmen of barbaric Afghanistan before a Jezail bullet cut short my career in Her Majesty's service, causing me to be seconded home and returned, ultimately, to civil existence. At home in London I had attempted to support my modest needs by setting up practice in Harley Street, but had been forced to accept accommodations with another person of my own class and station in order to make ends meet.

That had been the beginning of my long and happy association with the foremost consulting detective of our time—perhaps of any time. A confirmed bachelor, my associate had treated persons of the female persuasion with unstinting chivalry and kindness through all the time I had known him, yet on only one occasion had he permitted himself to entertain romantic notions concerning a member of the more gentle sex, and had, in all the years that followed the incident, refrained from ever speaking the name of the person involved.

On the occasion of each of my own marriages he had congratulated myself and my bride effusively, assisted in supervising the packers and drayers in the removal of my personal belongings from our bachelor digs, and maintained a friendly if somewhat aloof interest in my well-being until such time as the exigencies of fate dictated the termination of my marital state and my return to our lodgings in Baker Street.

That was all ended now. The great detective had disappeared from mortal ken, plunging from the parapet above the Reichenbach Falls to his presumed death—a price he seemed willing to pay in order to rid the world of the most dangerous man alive. My own latest assay upon the sea of matrimony having been brought up upon the sharp rocks of disaster, I had returned to 221B to find my old home occupied by a stranger. Upon application to the ever-faithful Mrs. Hudson I had been told, amidst the most pitiable wringing of hands and shedding of tears, that even the belongings of my associate—I should say my former associate—had been removed, lock, stock, and Persian slipper. Gone, the good woman told me tremblingly, were the famous dagger, the files of news cuttings, the phonograph and bust, the gasogene and the ill-famed needle. Donated to the Black Museum of Scotland Yard, where our old friends Gregson and Lestrade could examine them at their leisure.

Even the patriotic initials V.R. marked in bullet holes knocked in Mrs. Hudson's treasured mahogany wainscoting had been patched and varnished over so that every trace of the former occupancy was excised, and only a false and sterile pseudohominess marked the chambers my friend and I had so long occupied.

So distraught was I upon learning of this turn of affairs that I was barely able to accept Mrs. Hudson's offer of kippers and scones washed down with a tumbler of Chateau Frontenac '89 before stumbling back into the chill night.

I was disconsolate.

In a state of financial as well as emotional impoverishment, I wandered the streets of the greatest of cities, rebounding from the well-padded bodies of late shoppers and early revelers, making my way under the guidance of some ill-understood instinct through quarters imperceptibly but steadily more shabby, disreputable, and dangerous. At last I found myself standing before the facade of the building that was shortly to become my abode.

A gas lamp flickered fitfully behind me, casting weird and eerie shadows. The clop-clopping of horses' iron shoes upon cobblestones mingled with the creak of harness and the occasional distant scream that in Limehouse is best left uninvestigated, lest the self-designated Samaritan find himself sharing the misfortune of the one whom he had sought to assuage.

A yellowed pasteboard notice in a ground-floor window announced that a flat was available in the building—the condition of the pasteboard indicating that the flat had been unoccupied for some time—and by virtue of this ingenious deduction I was able shortly to bargain the ill-kempt and uncivil landlord to a price in keeping with my dangerously slim pocketbook.

Well had I learned the lessons of observation and deduction taught by my longtime associate—and now those lessons would pay me back for innumerable humiliations by the saving of considerable sterling to my endangered exchequer.

Hardly had I settled myself into my new domain when I heard the tread of a lightly placed foot upon the landing outside my chambers, then the knock of a small but determined hand upon the heavy and long-unattended door.

For an instant I permitted my fancy to imagine that the door would open to reveal smartly uniformed buttons—a street arab of the sort sometimes employed by my associate—mayhap even the homey figure of my associate himself. But I had no more than begun to rise from the cushions of a shabby but comfortable armchair when reality smote down upon my consciousness, and I realized that none of these knew the location of my new quarters. Far more likely would my caller prove to be some dark denizen of Limehouse here to test the mettle of a new tenant.

I pulled a small but powerful revolver from its place among my belongings and slipped it into the pocket of my dressing gown, then advanced cautiously toward the portal of the room and drew back the locking bar. Protesting loudly this imposition upon its seldom-exercised hinges, the door swung back and still farther back until there stood revealed in the opening to the landing the one person upon the face of the earth whom I would least have supposed to trace down my new whereabouts or to have reason of any nature ever to call upon me here.

Hardly could I credit the evidence of my own eyes. We must have stood for fully fifteen seconds in silent tableau—I with my eyes widened and my very jaw, I am certain, hanging open in astonishment. I was suddenly and uncomfortably aware of the reduced surroundings in which my caller had found me, and of the shabbiness which I fear I had permitted to come upon my personal demesne. My hair, once a rich brown in hue, had grown increasingly gray and unkempt with the passing years. My mustache was yellowed with nicotine and stained with wines and porters. My dressing gown was threadbare and marked with the souvenirs of many a solitary meal.

While my visitor was as breathtaking a figure as ever I had beheld: handsome rather than beautiful, she had borne the years since our last encounter with the grace and imperturbability that had marked her at one phase of her career as the most famous beauty of the operatic stage, and at another as the woman for whom a throne had been risked—and saved.

"May I enter?" asked The Woman.

Coloring to the very roots of my hair I stepped back and indicated that she might not merely enter, but would be the most welcome and most honored of guests. "I must apologize," I murmured, "for my boorish performance. Can you forgive me, Miss—I should say Madame—Your Highness—" I halted, uncertain of how even to address my distinguished visitor.

Yet even as I stammered and reddened, I could not keep myself from observing the appearance of The Woman.

She was as tall as I remembered her to be, a hand more so than myself and nearly of a height with my longtime associate. Her hair, piled high upon her magnificent head in the European vogue of the period, was of a raven glossiness that seemed to throw back the light of my flickering paraffin lamp with every movement of the flame. Her facial features were perfect, as perfect as I had remembered them to be on the occasion of our first meeting many years earlier, and her figure, as revealed by the closely fitted fashion of the era, which she carried with the aplomb of one long accustomed to the attentions of the finest fitters and couturiers of the Continent, was as graceful and appealing as that of a schoolgirl.

She had entered my humble chambers by then, and as I checked the landing behind her to ascertain that no footpad stood lurking in the musty darkness, The Woman ensconced herself unassisted upon the plain-backed wooden chair I was wont to utilize while wielding my pen in the pursuit of those modest exercises of literary embellishment about which my associate had so often chided me.

I turned and gazed down at my visitor, seating myself as near to her magnetic form as decorum might permit. At this closer range it was visible to me that her air of confident poise was not unstrained by some element of nervousness or even distress. I attempted to smile encouragingly at The Woman, and she responded as I hoped she would, her voice so cultured as largely to conceal the difficulty with which she maintained her equilibrium.

"May I come directly to the point, Doctor?" she inquired.

"Of course, of course, Miss-ah—"

"In private circumstances you may address me simply as Irene," she graciously responded.

I bowed my head in humble gratitude.

"You may feel some surprise in my tracking you down," the Woman said. "But I have come upon a matter of the greatest urgency. Once before I called upon you and your associate in an hour of grave crisis, and now that a problem of like proportion has arisen, I call upon you again."

"You have not heard, then—" I began.

"On the contrary," she interrupted, "the tragic news raced across the Continent like a new plague, kept to the circles of those high in rank by the most strenuous of efforts. You have my condolences, Doctor, however belatedly. It was unforgivable of me not to contact you at once when the news came to me, and indeed I tried to do so but was unable to locate you. It was only with difficulty that I was able to find you now."

I accepted her apologies with a nod. Then I inquired, "I trust that your own career has been a happier one than mine, Madame."

"Alas, such is not the case." She bent that well-formed head with the grace of a woman half her age. "The personage for whom I risked all, and whose very throne your associate saved, proved unworthy of those who risked so much in his behalf."

I offered her a handkerchief, but that noble creature bit her lip, drew a deep breath, and even managed a small, forlorn smile.

"The fates are strange," she resumed at length. "There was a time when I felt that I could never again place in any man my trust, much less my heart. But I was happily mistaken. I am now the spouse of—"

She cast her gaze carefully about the room, then leaned forward in a conspiratorial manner and whispered in my ear the name of a small but ancient and vitally important kingdom.

"I would think that I should have heard—a match such significance, Your Highness—why is it not known to one and all?"

"There are reasons of royal etiquette, Doctor, and considerations of rivalries and ambitions. My husband is regarded as the bachelor king, but in due course you may rest assured that my role and my identity will be revealed. In the meanwhile I live in comfort and in privacy, and take my greatest joy in the raising of my son: he who will someday ascend the throne of my adopted homeland when his father no longer reigns."

I shook my head in bewilderment. Never in my wildest imaginings had I envisioned such a turn of affairs. "You have my most heartfelt best wishes, Madame," I managed to intone. "But I imagine—"

At this point I rose and poured a glass of strong spirits for myself. Then I resumed, "—that you have come here on a mission that is not purely social."

She conceded that this was indeed the case. "Were your associate with us yet, I should have turned to him now as I did once before. But since that is impossible, you must assist me. Please, Doctor, I should not have come here or disturbed your solitude in any way were it not for the extreme nature of the present situation."

So saying, she leaned forward and placed her cool and ungloved fingertips softly upon the back of my wrist. As if a galvanic current had passed for her organism to my own at the very touch of her fingers, I felt myself energized and inspired. The Woman was in trouble. And The Woman had come to me in her hour of need. I could never be so mean a bounder as to turn her away—surely not now when the very mantle of my mentor seemed about to fall upon my own uncertain shoulders.

"But of course, Your High—Irene." I felt myself reddening to the very roots of my hair at the pronunciation of her given name. "Please be so kind as to wait a moment while I fetch notepaper and writing instrument so as to record the salient details of your narrative."

I rose and brought foolscap and nib, then quickly returned to my place opposite my charming visitor. For a moment I thought to offer her tea and biscuits with marmalade, but refrained at the recollection of the present condition of my larder and my pocketbook.

"Pray proceed," I said.

"Thank you. I trust that you need make no mention of the location or manner of my current domicile, Doctor," The Woman began. Upon seeing my nodded response, she said simply, "*The God of the Naked Unicorn* has been stolen."

"*The God of the Naked Unicorn*," I exclaimed.

"*The God of the Naked Unicorn*."

"No," I blurted incredulously.

"Yes," she replied coolly. "*The God of the Naked Unicorn*."

"But—how can that be? The greatest national art treasure of the nation of—"

"Shh." She silenced me with a sound and a look and a renewed pressure of fingertips to wrist. "Please. Even in more familiar and secure quarters than these it would be unwise to mention the name of my adoptive motherland."

"Of course, of course," I murmured, recovering myself rapidly. "But I do not see how *The God of the Naked Unicorn* could be stolen. Is it not—but I have here a book of artistic reproductions, let us examine a print of the statue and see."

"It is burned into my memory, Doctor. I see it before my eyes day and night. For me, there is no need to examine an artist's poor rendering, but you may search your volume to find a representation of the great sculptor Mendez-Rubirosa's masterpiece."

I crossed the room and returned with a heavy volume bound in olive linen-covered boards and opened it carefully, turning its cream-vellum leaves until I came to a steel engraving of the sculptor Mendez-Rubirosa's supreme achievement, *The God of the Naked Unicorn*. As I had recalled, the work had been cast in platinum and decorated with precious gems. The eyes of the god were rubies and those of the unicorns clustered worshipfully about the deity's feet were of sapphires and emeralds. The horns of the unicorns were of finest ivory inlaid with filigreed gold. The very base of the sculpture was a solid block of polished onyx inlaid with Peking jade.

"But *The God of the Naked Unicorn* is the national treasure of—" I caught myself barely in time. "If its theft is made public, the very crown itself would be imperiled."

"Quite so," the woman known as The Woman agreed. "And a message has been received threatening that the sculpture will be placed on public display in St. Wrycyxlwv's Square if a ransom of 80 trillion grudniks is not paid for its return. And a deadline is given of forty-eight hours hence. You can see, Doctor, how desperate my husband and I are. That is why I came to you. You alone—your distinguished colleague being no longer among us—can help."

A million thoughts swirled through my poor brain at this juncture.

"St. Wrycyxlwv's Square," I exclaimed.

"St. Wrycyxlwv's Square," she affirmed.

"But that is the national gathering place of your nation's fiercest and most implacable enemy."

"Precisely, Doctor."

I stroked my chin thoughtfully, painfully aware of the unsightly stubble of unshaved whiskers that marred my appearance.

"And 80 trillion grudniks," I repeated.

"Yes, 80 trillion grudniks," she said.

"That would be—roughly—forty crowns, nine shillings, and thruppence," I computed.

"That—or as close as to make no practical difference," my charming visitor agreed.

"Forty-eight hours," I said.

"Approximately two days," The Woman equated.

"I see," I temporized, stroking my chin once again. "And tell me, Your High—I mean, Irene—have you and your husband made response to the demand?"

"My husband has instructed his chief minister to play for time while I traveled, in the utmost secrecy you understand, of course, to seek your assistance. Yours and—" She paused briefly and cast her gaze through the mist-shrouded panes into the fog-swirled gaslight beyond "—for you see, my husband insists on holding to a forlorn hope that he might have survived his fall."

"Anything is possible," I replied. "No remains were recovered. One, perhaps even both, of the battling titans might still live. But if so—ah, if so, why have we heard of neither in the intervening years? And my associate's distinguished brother—you of course recall his distinguished brother," I averred.

"Of course."

"Rusticated," I whispered.

"Rusticated?" she echoed, clearly aghast.

"Rusticated," I repeated.

The Woman reached into her lace-trimmed sleeve with the thin, aristocratic digits of one hand and pulled from it a tiny, dainty handkerchief. She dabbed briefly at her eyes. This was the moment, some inner demon prompted me to recall, at which an unscrupulous person of the male persuasion might initiate an advance in the guise of simple sympathy. But even as I sat berating my secret weakness The Woman regained control of herself. She replaced her handkerchief and recovered her full composure.

"There is only one thing for it then, Doctor," she said firmly. "None other can help. You must come with me. You must give us your assistance."

I rose and without a word slipped into mackintosh, mackinaw, and cape, cap, and galoshes, and extended my arm to the grateful and trembling Irene.

The game, I mumbled grimly to myself at a level of vocalization well below the audible, *is afoot.*

Leaving my humble chambers, I paused to set up the deadfall, intruder trap, burglar interdictor, automatic daguerreotype machine, and the bucket of water on top of the door. Then I drew the latch string and, turning to my charming companion, said "I am at your service, Madame."

We made our way down the stairs, checking at each landing for the presence of footpads or traitors, and emerged safely into the Limehouse night. A fine mist had begun to fall, wetting the soot-blackened remnants of a previous snowfall into a gray and slippery slush. My companion and I made our way through shadowy, echo-filled by-lanes until we emerged upon the West India Dock Road, site of so many infamous deeds and unexplained atrocities.

A shudder ran unrepressed through my form as we crossed a cobblestone-floored square. For a moment I imagined it St. Wrycyxlwv's Square, and before my mind's eye there arose the silvery gray and jewel-sparked shape of *The God of the Naked Unicorn*—the national art treasure of The Woman's adoptive homeland and the potential cause of revolution and anarchy in that ancient landlocked kingdom.

Somewhere a scream rent the Limehouse night—whether that

of a tramp beating her cautious way up the fog-shrouded Thames or of some poor unfortunate victim of the crime rampant in the streets of the ill-starred district, it was not for me to know.

A cab wheeled by, its curtains drawn, driver in muffled obscurity on the box, dark horses' accoutrements jingling and creaking with the movement of the steaming beasts.

My companion and I walked nervously through the impenetrable murk until, drawn by the lights of a lower-class establishment where the very scum of Limehouse roistered out their pitiful nights, we had the good fortune to see a cab roll up and discharge its passengers, a couple of debauched-looking mariners obviously somewhat the worse for wear and seeking a place in which to squander what poor remnants of their seamen's wage they retained after being gouged and cheated by parsimonious owners and dishonest pursers on their ship.

I was about to call the cabby when my companion stopped me with an urgent hiss and a pressure upon the arm.

A second cab pulled up before the tavern and as its load of unsavory occupants made their way from the conveyance we climbed into the cab and Irene softly delivered her instructions to the cabby, who peered inquisitively through the trap into the passenger compartment.

The first cab had departed and my companion leaned toward me saying, "I should have thought by now, Doctor, that you would know better than to engage the first cab you encounter."

"But it had only just arrived," I protested. "There could have been no way for a malefactor to know we would be seeking transportation just at this place in time to send a cab for us."

At that point our conversation was interrupted by a flash of light and a loud report from a point directly ahead of our cab. The other vehicle had exploded in a gout of flame, and tongues of orange licked upward among clouds of black, oily smoke.

"Incredible." I gasped in amazement. "How did you—?"

The Woman smiled inscrutably as our driver carefully picked his way around the first cab, now violently ablaze and all but blocking the intersection where the West India Dock Road was met by a winding thoroughfare that made its way upward from the Thames and into a safer and more reputable quarter than Limehouse.

We passed through numerous thoroughfares, some of them

bustling and lighted as if it were noonday, others eerie and shrouded, until I felt that there was no way I could ever retrace our passage, much less deduce the location of the moment, when at last the cab drew up at a kiosk whence individuals dressed in every manner and description entered and emerged into the street.

I chivalrously went halfies with Irene as to the cost of the cab, despite the embarrassing deficit of my financial situation, and we climbed from the cab onto the wet cobblestones of yet another London square surrounded by shops and restaurants, all closed at this hour of the night. Without a word my companion led me carefully toward the kiosk and drew me with her down a flight of darkened and ill-kept stairs until we reached a platform illuminated by a form of lighting totally unfamiliar to me. The flames seemed to be wholly enclosed in miniature glass globes and to burn with a peculiar regularity and stability that permitted neither flickering nor movement. How they obtained the air to sustain combustion was a puzzle beyond my comprehension, but my companion refused to remain still long enough for me to make inquiry.

She led me past a large painted notice board marking the area of Ladbroke Grove, and depositing tickets in a turnstile device we made our way across the platform to wait for—I knew not what. There were railroad tracks before us, and my induction that this was a station of some sort was borne out in a few minutes when a train of a type and model unfamiliar to me approached. The train halted and we climbed aboard a coach, took seats, and rode in a strange and uncomfortable silence until my companion indicated that it was time for us to exit the odd conveyance.

II

We made our way back to the surface of the earth and I discovered that we were standing on the edge of a broad, level area as large as a cricket field and then some, but whose surface, rather than being of grass, was composed of a hard, gritty stuff that exhibited none of the usual give and responsiveness of a natural substance.

My companion led me by the hand across the hardened surface until we stood beside the strangest contraption it has ever been to my wonderment to behold.

The thing was as long as a coach and rested on wheels, two rather largish ones at one end and a small one at the other. Its main substance seemed to be devoted to a ridged cylinder some rod or so in length and covered with a stressed fabric glistening wetly in the night's drizzle.

Two open seats were located on the upper side of the thing, with curved shields of celluloid or isinglass before each and a set of bewildering dials and knobs in one of them. Stubby projections extended from the sides and rear of the machine, and a large wooden device not dissimilar to a marine screw was attached to one end, mounted to a black and powerful-looking contrivance resembling one that I sometimes saw being used in small experimental marine craft.

Oddest of all, four free-swinging vanes projected from a pole mounted on top of the machine, their ends drooping of their own unsupported weight and their entirety creaking and swaying slightly with each variation in the icy, drenching wind.

My companion reached into the closer seat and pulled from it a headgear for herself and one for me, demonstrating wordlessly the manner in which they were to be worn. Each was made of soft leather and wholly enclosed the wearer's cranial projection. A strap caught beneath the wearer's chin, thereby ensuring a snug and secure fit to the headgear, and a pair of goggles fitted with transparent lenses could be slipped into place to protect the eyes from wind or moisture or raised onto the forehead to facilitate an unencumbered view in time of eased conditions.

My companion placed one shapely foot upon the stubby projection that stood away from the side of the machine and climbed gracefully into the seat. By means of silent gestures she communicated her desire that I emulate her actions, and not wishing to distress this lovely and courageous woman I acceded, climbing upon the projection and thence into the second seat. There I found myself seated upon a not uncomfortable leather cushion.

My companion turned in her place and indicated by gestures that I was to secure my seating by clamping a webbed belt across my lap. Again I acceded, watched over my companion's shoulder as she belted herself into position, and gasped in amazement to see a grease-covered mechanician clad in canvas coveralls suddenly appear from a nearby outbuilding, race across the open area to our machine, grasp the wooden member which I could not help dubbing (in my mind) an aerial screw in his hands, and whirl it.

My companion, having acknowledged the arrival of the mechanician with a one-handed thumbs-up gesture, adjusted some of the controls before her, whereupon the self-contained engine at the front of the strange little craft coughed and sputtered its way into life. After warming the engine for some minutes my companion again gestured to the mechanician, who pulled a set of inconspicuous chocks from before the wheels of the vehicle, and we rolled forward at an astonishing rate of speed, the wind whipping past us making me grateful for the helmet and goggles provided by my companion.

Before I had time even to wonder at the destination of this unusual mechanically propelled journey I was distracted by the sound of a strange *whoop-whoop-whoop* coming from directly overhead and obviously keeping perfect pace with our own progress. I cast my gaze above in hopes of detecting the source of the peculiar sounds and discovered that they were coming from the four vanes mounted on the low tower above the cockpit where I sat.

The vanes were revolving so rapidly that I could barely follow them with my eye, and startlement was piled upon startlement when I felt the odd craft into which I was helplessly strapped actually rise from the field it had been crossing and move unsupported through the thin air.

I must have shouted my astonishment, for my companion turned toward me with a grin of such total confidence and surety of self that I laughed aloud at my momentary panic and vowed inwardly that I should permit nothing to interfere with my enjoyment of this unprecedented experience. *The God of the Naked Unicorn* might be missing, the great detective might be lost to the world, but all was well with myself, and I would take the pleasure that was offered to me and worry later about my problems.

We flew—yes, I use the word advisedly and with full awareness of the gravity of its employment—in a great circle over the edges of London, watching the sun rise over the distant Channel to the east, passing over the very sites where my lost companion and I had striven to face down perils and to unravel puzzles, then swung in a northerly direction, passing over dark green woodlands and lighter meadows, leaving behind us England, Wales, Scotland, and the Orkney Islands.

No word was spoken—none could have been heard over the steady droning of the engine that turned the aerial screw that gave us our forward headway through the sky and dragged the windmilling vanes of our overhead rotors through their vital revolutions—but I was amazed, from time to time, to see my companion half climb from her cockpit and reach down toward the stubby projections from the sides of the craft and retrieve small teardrop-shaped containers of fuel, which she emptied into a nozzle mounted on the body of the craft in front of her own celluloid shield.

The sun had risen fully, the sky was a sparkling northern blue with only spotty clouds of pure white dotting its cerulean regularity, and neither land nor handiwork of man was visible on the sparkling aquatic surface beneath us. I know not how long we flew nor how far north we had proceeded, save to make note that the air around us was growing increasingly frigid and I increasingly grateful for the foresight that caused me to dress warmly before leaving my Limehouse chambers, when there appeared below us and in the far distance a glimmer of blinding white.

My companion reached for the last remaining fuel container mounted on the vehicle and emptied its contents into the nozzle she had used before her shield. Glancing over her shoulder toward me she pointed ahead of us and shouted a series of words that were lost to me in the drone of the engine and the rush of the air past my leather-covered ears.

But I soon came to understand the significance if not the actual content of her speech as, under careful guidance, our little craft nosed downward and began a long, steady approach toward what I came now to recognize as nothing less than the great ice pack of the north polar regions of the planet. Lower and lower our little craft made progress, as the dark waters beneath our extended wheels gave way to jagged white icebergs, pack ice, and finally great glaciers.

The mountainous formation of the ice slipped beneath our droning craft as we sped through the lower reaches of the atmosphere, in due course to be replaced by a flat and level area of glistening white. We crossed this new expanse and at length my companion swung the craft into a pattern of tight circles, spiraling slowly downward before a formation I had initially taken to be an icy projection of unusual beauty and regularity, and only after many moments recognized for an artifact created by human efforts.

There—in the northernmost wastes of the polar ice fields—was the handiwork of man. I nearly wept at the audacity and beauty of the construction and was distracted from this train of thought only by the landing of the craft in which I rode. The vehicle rolled across the hard-packed snow and came to a halt near the entrance of the gorgeous building.

A gale sped across the gleaming ice cap and flung a playful spray of snow against the exposed lower half of my face. I ran my tongue around my lips, tasting the clear purity of the melting crystals. No sign of life or activity emerged from the glittering spires that confronted us. Neither greeter nor guard debouched from the arched entry of the edifice.

Before we even reached its portals I said, "Irene—what place is this? I thought that we were going to your capital. Instead we have reached the northern polar cap of the planet, a region always believed uninhabited save for polar bears, seals, and gulls. Yet we find this magnificent structure."

Blinking my eyes in wonder, I cried out, "I beseech you to elucidate."

She turned upon me the dazzling smile that had melted the hearts and won the applause of audiences the world around and that had brought her to the side of one of the crowned heads of Europe in as brilliant, if secret, a marriage as the century has seen. "Pray exercise patience for a few more minutes, Doctor. All will be made clear to you once we are inside the Fortress."

"The Fortress?" I echoed helplessly.

"The Fortress of Solitude. The structure, which appears to be part of the ice floe upon which it stands, is actually constructed of marble, pure white marble quarried from a secret deposit and transported here in utmost concealment. Within it are—those who have summoned you. Those whose willing agent it is my honor to be."

We strode beneath towering portals and through echoing corridors until at last we entered a chamber occupied by a single bronzed giant seated in a posture of intense meditation. As we entered the room he seemed momentarily to be stationary, but in a few seconds I realized that he was engaged in a series of the most amazing solitary exercises.

Before my very eyes he made his muscles work against each other, straining until a fine film of perspiration covered his mighty frame. He vocalized softly, and I realized that he was juggling a number of a dozen figures in his head, multiplying, dividing, extracting square and cube roots. He turned to an apparatus that made sound waves of frequencies that disappeared beyond the limits of audibility for me, but which he could, from the expression on his face, detect.

At the end of the series he looked up at my companion and myself. In a voice that commanded confidence and obedience he spoke. "Hello, Patricia," he said informally. "I see he came with you. I knew of course that he would."

He rose from his seat and crossed the room toward us, embracing the woman known as The Woman in two mightily muscled arms of bronze. Yet, for all the affection that was visible in that embrace, it was clearly one of brotherly—or perhaps cousinly—fondness, nothing more.

Patricia, I pondered. He had called her *Patricia.* But was her name not *Irene?* No time was available for consideration of this conundrum, for the bronze giant released her and turned toward me.

"And you, sir," the bronze giant said, extending a mighty hand in manly greeting, "you are none other than John H. Watson, M.D., are you not?"

I gave him my hand in as strong a grip as I could muster, and will confess that I felt pleased to receive it back in one piece, the bones not crushed farther than they were, in the viselike grip of the man of bronze. "I am indeed. And may I have the honor of your own credentials, sir?"

He smiled most disarmingly, and said, "Of course, of course. My name is Clark Savage, Jr. I hold a few degrees myself, picked up here and there over the years. Most of my friends just call me Doc. I'd be honored if you would do the same."

For some reason I felt more flattered than offended by the offhandedness and informality of the man, and agreed to call him by the name he preferred. *Doc* it would be. "I suppose," I said in reply "that we might avoid some certain degree of confusion were you to call me what my dearest friend, now lost these several years, always did. That was, simply, *Watson.*"

"I'll be happy to do just that," the bronze giant said.

"But did I not hear you address our female companion as Patricia?" This, I had decided, was my opportunity to unravel a puzzle all my own.

Doc Savage nodded his bushy, copper-colored poll in agreement. "My cousin, you see."

Perturbed, I said, "But is she not—" I turned to The Woman and addressed her directly. "But are you not the former Irene Adler, now, Her Royal Highness—"

"Please," the charming young woman interrupted. "To Doc I am known as his cousin, Patricia Savage. To you and your associate, I am known in another persona. Let us leave it at that, I pray you."

Her words puzzled me no end, but I felt that I had no choice under the circumstances in which I found myself than to accede.

"You must forgive me, Watson," the bronze giant said. "My cousin has helped me in a minor deception that was necessary to get you here to my polar Fortress of Solitude. If word had become current in the capitals of the world of the meeting to which you have been secretly summoned, an outbreak of crime unprecedented in the entire history of human civilization would be bound to take place."

"You mean—" I stuttered dumbfoundedly, "—you mean that *The God of the Naked Unicorn* has not been stolen? It is not being ransomed for a sum of 80 trillion grudniks? It is not going to be displayed in St. Wrycyxlwv's Square if the ransom is not paid? This entire proceeding has been some sort of hoax?"

"Oh, the robbery is real enough, Dr. Watson," The Woman stated. "*The God of the Naked Unicorn* is missing, and everything that I described to you will happen if it is not recovered. But this is merely one tiny part of a worldwide threat."

"Exactly," Doc Savage said. "I have only myself returned from a trek across the earth, escaping the clutches of a fiend unparalleled in the annals of crime. What is taking place here today is nothing less than a council of war, a council of war against one who menaces the orderly structure and just proceedings of the entire world order. Someone whose very identity, no less his base of operations, is a mystery wrapped in a puzzle locked inside an enigma."

"Well said," I applauded. "But is it just we three who stand between the forces of order and civilization and this fiend?"

"Not we three, Doctor," said The Woman. "I must leave you now. My role has been played, my exit speech spoken. It is time for me to leave the stage of this drama and return to the side of my husband and the supervision of my child, there to watch and pray for those into whose hands the very fate of the world may have been given."

Once more she exchanged a chaste contact with the man of bronze, then shook my own hand heartily and disappeared from the room. In a moment I heard the sound of her machine as it coughed into life again, then began its steady droning and the *whoop-whoop-whoop* that meant its rotors were spinning, lifting its fabric-covered body into the chilly air above the arctic reaches. Then it faded slowly from audibility.

I stood, alone in the room, with the bronze giant Doc Savage.

"Please come with me, Watson," he said at last. I felt that I had no choice but to obey. Savage strode powerfully to a doorway, adjusted some device that I took to be an automatic guard of a type infinitely more advanced than those I had set in my Limehouse flat, and stood aside as I walked into the next room.

Here I found myself in a chamber that would have done proud the finest men's club of London, Chicago, or the European *bund* of exotic Shanghai.

Wood-paneled walls rose to a magnificently carved high ceiling from which hung old wrought-iron chandeliers. Candles guttered atmospherically while skillfully concealed lights of an artificial nature provided supplementary illumination. The walls were lined with row upon row of books in matched sets of the finest buckram and morocco binding; hand-stamped titles in finest gilt gave back the light of the room.

Across a deep-piled Oriental carpet of infinite richness and exquisite workmanship, a small portion of the luxuriant flagstone flooring was exposed before the great ornate fireplace, where there roared a jolly bonfire of the greatest beauty and the most subtle yet pleasing fragrance.

Overstuffed chairs of rich leather and masterfully carven dark woods stood about the room, and each, save for two conspicuously left vacant, was occupied by a man of imposing mien if slightly eccentric dress.

In one chair sat a muscular figure all in gray. Gray hair, gray complexion, gray tunic and trousers. As I stood, aghast, in the entranceway of the room, he turned dead, cold eyes toward me, taking me in from my sturdy British boots to my own faded crop of hair. He nodded curtly, but did not speak.

In the chair beside him sat a man all in black, black clothing swathing him from head to foot save here and there where the scarlet flashing of his clothes was exposed. His collar was turned up about his face, and the brim of a black slouch hat was pulled down. Only his brilliant eyes and hawklike nose protruded between brim and collar. With one hand he played with a strange girasol ring that he wore upon a finger of the other.

Next to him was a man with a contrastingly open, boyish expression about his face, blond wavy hair, and sparkling blue eyes. He wore a tight-fitting jersey, tight trousers with a broad stripe running down their sides, and high, polished boots. He somehow impressed me as an American—as, strangely, did most of these men. But this one carried a further, distinctive feeling of being a great college athlete—a product of Yale or Harvard, I guessed.

Beyond him lazed another young, open-faced individual, this one wearing a red zip-suit that matched his curly red hair. And beyond him two more persons of muscular and athletic build—one nearly naked, clad only in jingling harness and jouncing weapons, the other wearing ordinary clothing that looked by far the worse for wear, while he himself seemed strong and competent.

There remained only two others. One was another figure in dark cloak and slouch hat, a figure strangely resembling the hawk-nosed man, save that in this latter case there was no red flashing to relieve the gloomy hues of the clothing he wore, but instead a network of silvery threads that covered his clothing, giving one the uncanny feeling of a gigantic spider's web.

The other was a young man of pleasant mien albeit with a touch of the indolent attitude of the very wealthy. He looked at me with an open, friendly expression, and I was therefore all the more startled to make note of his reversed collar and the monotonous coloration of his rather ordinary-looking suit—of mild jade green.

III

"Gentlemen," I heard Doc Savage say from behind me, "may I present our final member—Dr. John H. Watson, late of 221B Baker Street, London, England.

"Dr. Watson," the bronze giant continued, "won't you walk in and make yourself at home. This is our library. The thousands of volumes that you see lining the walls of this room represent the biographies, published and secret, of the men gathered in our presence. Even a few of your own works concerning your former associate have found their way into our archives—as has your associate himself on more occasion than one."

"Holmes—here?" I gasped. "Why, he never told me—he never so much as hinted—"

"No, Watson?" the bronze giant responded. "Well, perhaps someday when he knows you better."

"Perhaps," I agreed, my eyes downcast. "Perhaps—"

"Don't be harsh on yourself, Watson. Now that the time has come for you to be of service, here you are at the Fortress of Solitude, and this is your chance to do a favor for the world—and for certain individuals within this world. But first, let me introduce our other members."

He took me by the elbow and I made my way around the circle of easy chairs, shaking hands in turn with each of the men I had previously observed. As I approached each he introduced himself to me:

"Richard Benson—the Avenger," said the man in gray.

"Kent Allard—the Shadow," the hawk-nosed man chuckled grimly.

"Gordon, Yale '34—my friends call me Flash."

"Curtis Newton, sir, sometimes known as Captain Future."

"John Carter, former captain, Confederate cavalry."

"David Innes of Connecticut and the Empire of Pellucidar."

"Richard Wentworth," said the second of the black-clad men, "known to some as the Spider." Even as he shook my hand I detected a look of suspicion and jealousy pass between him and the man who had identified himself as the Shadow.

And finally, the man in the green clergy suit. "*Om*," he intoned, making the Oriental sign of greeting with pressed hands before extending one to me in Western fashion. "Jethro Dumont of Park Avenue, New York. Also known as Dr. Charles Pali and—the Green Lama."

"I am honored," I managed to stammer, "I had never dreamed that any of you were real persons. I always thought you the figments of fevered imaginations."

"As indeed that same charge has been hurled against your good friend and associate of Baker Street, wouldn't you say, Watson?" It was the bronze giant, Clark Savage.

I acknowledged that such was indeed the case. "I am assailed from both sides," I said. "On the one side there are those who maintain that my good friend and associate whose cases I have chronicled to the best of my mean ability for many years, is merely a creature of my own fevered imaginings and has no being in the real world at all."

I gazed around the brilliant assemblage, then continued. "While on the other hand the gentleman who serves as my own literary agent, Dr. Arthur Conan Doyle, has himself been accused of writing the very narratives that I furnish to him and which he in turn peddles to the magazines on my behalf."

A chuckle of sympathetic agreement made its way around the circle of men in the room. I thought again of the volumes that covered the walls of this library—not one of my companions but whose exploits had merited the efforts of some chronicler like mine own self, however humble his talents.

"And this band, this assemblage of adventurers—do I see before me the entirety of their sort?" I asked the personages at large as I assumed the rich and comfortable chair offered me by Doc Savage.

Again there was a buzz of low-pitched discussion as the colorfully garbed figures exchanged comments upon my question. Then one of them—I believe it was the Yale man, Gordon—replied in the role of tacitly designated spokesman for them all.

"We hardy few are just the present representatives of a movement whose number is legion. From the days of our founder, whose portrait hangs above the fireplace, to this moment, there have been hundreds of us. Their names are inscribed upon the scroll of honor, which stands beside the window over there."

He gestured, first toward the painting to which he had referred, then to a tall, narrow window through the thermally opaqued panes of which the long arctic night was beginning to descend. I strode first to stand before the roaring fire and gazed upward at the gracefully executed and richly framed depiction above it. The painter had done his work in rich colors of deep brown, rust, and maroon. The face that gazed back at mine showed strength, intelligence, and a fine tincture of insouciant wit. The costume was that of a French chevalier of a previous century. The small engraved plaque beneath the canvas bore but a single word in simple script: *D'Artagnan*.

Paying momentary silent homage to the subject of the portrait, I strode across the rich carpet to the scroll previously indicated by the American, Gordon. Its heading was a simple phrase the initial characters of which cleverly formed a word of but a single syllable, the relevance of which, I fear I must admit, quite escaped me. The head of the scroll read PERSONAGES UNITED IN LEAGUE AS PROTECTORS. The names subtended therefore were indeed numerous, including not only all of those in the room (myself excepted, of course) but also many others of which a random selection included such familiar and unfamiliar appellations as Jules de Grandon, Anthony Rogers, Sir Dennis Nayland Smith, Jimmy Dale, Arsene Lupin, Kimball Kinnison, Nicholas Carter, Stephen Costigan, and entire columns more.

"A splendid company," I could not help exclaiming when I had completed my perusal of the gilded scroll. "But if I may make so bold as to ask, how is this establishment maintained? By whose efforts are these facilities operated? Who builds the fire, prepares comestibles, serves libations?"

"Oh, we have flunkies aplenty, Dr. Watson," the young man in the red zip-suit supplied. I identified him at once as Curtis Newton. "Each of us contributes his own staff of assistants to the general service of the League. My own aides include Otho the android, Grag the robot, and Simon Wright the living brain."

"And mine," the Shadow stated with a sinister chuckle, "are the playboy Lamont Cranston, my chauffeur Moe Shrevnitz, the communications wizard Burbank, and the near suicide Harry Vincent."

In turn each of them named a group of bizarre assistants, each as peculiar and eccentric as his employer.

"Every one of these," Doc Savage concluded, "serves his time in the kitchen, the armory, or elsewhere in the Fortress and the other far-flung outposts of our League between assignments in personal service to his respective employer."

"I comprehend," I stated, sipping idly at the beverage that had appeared, all unnoticed, beside my easy chair. I stopped and sniffed, surprised, at the contents of my glass. Sarsaparilla.

"And yet I am puzzled by one matter," I said, addressing myself once more to my hosts at large. In response they looked at me to a man, with expressions of inquisitive anticipation. "Why," I brought myself at last to ask, "have you summoned me to this redoubt? You are clearly a band of the most capable and dashing of heroes. I know not what puzzle confronts you, other than the matter of the purloined *God of the Naked Unicorn*. Surely you do not require my own humble talents in the solution of this, which must pale before your eyes to the pettiest of puzzles."

Once more the chairmanship of the assemblage was assumed by Clark Savage, Jr. He strode to and fro, stationing himself at last before the crackling fire so that the flames, as they writhed and danced behind his heroic figure, cast monstrous shadows across the ornate library of the League. With his feet spread wide, his hands clasped behind his back, his magnificent chest thrown out, and his proud head held high, his entire form backlighted and semisilhouetted against the dancing flames, he made as glorious a picture of masculine power and grace as ever I had beheld.

"John Watson," he intoned impressively, "what I am about to tell you is a piece of information of the most sensitive and yet earthshaking nature. I place you upon your honor as a junior associate of the Personages United as Protectors to reveal it to no one until such time as the case has been brought to a triumphant conclusion. Have I your solemn word, John Watson?"

"You have it, sir," I whispered. There was a lump in my throat, and my eyes were oddly watery at that moment.

"Very well." Doc Savage continued, "I must inform you that there is at large an archvillain whose malefic machinations utterly overshadow those of the most infamous evildoers in the entire annals of the League."

"Blacker than Cardinal Richelieu," a voice cried out.

"More sinister than the insidious Dr. Fu Manchu," added another.

"More brilliant than the revolutionist Ay-Artz of the planet Lemnis."

"More treacherous than Hooja the Sly One."

"More dangerous than Blacky Duquesne."

"More ruthless than the master mind Ras Thavas."

"More threatening than the very Napoleon of Crime himself," exclaimed Doc Savage, bringing the list to a crashing conclusion.

"The Napoleon of Crime?" I repeated incredulously. "You

mean—you mean the warped genius Professor James Moriarty? But he has been unheard of since he plunged with my great associate into the Reichenbach Falls. Are you telling me that he survived?"

"Perhaps he was killed, John Watson—then again, perhaps he escaped, as did his rival and opponent in the epic struggle that had its culmination there in Switzerland. Many a man has seen fit to disappear, and what better hiding place than the grave, eh, Watson?"

Savage was now striding back and forth before the great fireplace, his titanic shadow swaying across the wooden beams and metal chandeliers above our heads. The other men in the room sat silently, expectantly, observing the exchange between their leader and myself. I vowed silently not to fail my absent associate in the upholding of his honor.

"In raising the name of the Napoleon of Crime," I said with some heat, "in making that reference, Doc Savage, you bring by implication the charge that my own associate has somehow failed to rid the earth of this menace."

"Quite so," Doc Savage stated. "Your associate—Sherlock Holmes—is in the hands of a fiend before whom Professor Moriarty and these other petty peculators pale to a paltry puniness."

He strode forward and stood over me, towering fully six feet and more into the air. "I am here only because a timely bit of aid by my cousin Patricia caused me to escape the clutches of this archfiend. I slipped through his net, but two companions with whom I was pursuing the missing *God of the Naked Unicorn* were less fortunate than I, and are at this time held in durance vile by the mad genius whose efforts may yet bring the entire fragile structure of civilization crashing to destruction."

"Two companions?" I echoed dumbly. "*Two?* But who can they be?"

He crouched low, bringing his metallic-flecked eyes glimmeringly close to my own and pointed his finger at me significantly. "At this very moment there rest in the clutches of this brilliant maniac both Sherlock Holmes and Sir John Clayton, Lord Greystoke, the man known to the world at large as—Tarzan of the Apes."

"Holmes and Greystoke? At one time? And very nearly yourself as well, Doc Savage?" I exclaimed. "Who can this devil be, and how can I assist in retrieving your associates from his clutches?"

"Wentworth, you are our supreme intellectual," snapped Doc

Savage to the personage in the spiderwebbed cloak. "Enlighten Dr. Watson as to our strategy, will you please, while I retire briefly to extract a few square and cube roots?"

Doc Savage retreated to his own seat, and the Spider began to speak in a low, insinuating voice that seemed almost to hypnotize the listener.

"This archfiend is unquestionably the most brilliant and most resourceful opponent any of us has ever faced," he averred. "Yet, Watson, as all who fight crime and anarchy know in the innermost recesses of their being, there has never lived an evildoer whose warped brain has not caused him to commit one fatal mistake that in time led to his being brought before the bar of justice and punished. Sooner or later, Watson evildoers pay the price of their misdeeds."

"The abduction of Tarzan, Holmes, and Doc Savage was to have taken place at the brilliant Exposition of European Progress where *The God of the Naked Unicorn* was on display."

This was Richard Henry Benson, the Avenger, speaking. He fingered an odd dagger and an even odder-looking pistol as he spoke. "A brilliant replica of *The God of the Naked Unicorn* was substituted, a substitution that would escape the practiced eye of the most discerning lapidarist, and yet was discovered by a mere woman."

"Yes, a mere woman." Captain John Carter took up the narration. "A woman of protean nature whose admirers have identified her variously as the Princess Dejah Thoris of Helium—as Joan Randall, daughter of the commissioner of the interplanetary police authority—as Margo Lane, faithful friend and companion of the Shadow—as Jane Porter Clayton, Lady Greystoke—and as Miss Evangl Stewart of New York City's bohemian quarter, Greenwich Village, among others."

"This woman," Jethro Dumont intervened suavely, "*The* Woman, if you will, detected the clever substitution and sought to notify Sherlock Holmes, Lord Greystoke, and Doc Savage. She had alerted both Greystoke and Holmes and was speaking with Doc Savage when the first two members of the League, unaware of the presence of Doc, moved to uncover the fraud and fell into the trap of the archfiend."

"I moved to their rescue," Savage concluded the tale, "but the evildoer was prepared. He used *The God of the Naked Unicorn* to trap

Holmes and Tarzan, and using them as bait nearly netted me as well. I escaped with my life and nothing more, and Holmes and Tarzan were spirited away, along with *The God of the Naked Unicorn*."

"Then the threat of which Her High—The Woman spoke," I stammered, "the threat to display *The God of the Naked Unicorn* in St. Wrycyxlwv's Square—was merely a device? A hoax?"

"No, Dr. Watson," the Shadow interposed, "that threat is real, it is all too real. But a far greater threat to the order and security of the world is posed by the madman who holds Sherlock Holmes and Tarzan of the Apes in his clutches at this moment."

"I see, I see," I mumbled in stunned semicoherency. "But then— then what role have you chosen for me to play in this drama? What can a humble physician and sometimes biographer of the great do in this exigency?"

"You," said Doc Savage commandingly, "must solve the crime, rescue the victims, and save the order of world civilization, Dr. Watson."

IV

I fumbled in my lounging robe for my pipe, shoved aside the futile revolver with which I had foolishly menaced The Woman as she entered my Limehouse flat so seemingly long ago, and began to pace to and fro myself. My mind raced. My thoughts whirled about like bits of flotsam caught in a maelstrom. *What would Holmes do?* was all I could think at that moment. *What would Holmes do, what would Holmes do?*

At last I halted before Doc Savage, and asked, "Did the villain leave behind any clue—any scrap of evidence, however trivial or meaningless it might seem to you?"

Furrows of puzzlement and concentration cut deep grooves into the brow of the man of bronze. At last he said, "There may be one thing, Watson, but it seemed so inconsequential at the time that I hardly took note of it, and hesitate to mention it to you now."

"Permit me to be the judge of that, please," I snapped in as Holmes-like a manner as I could muster. To my gratification the man of bronze responded as ever had witnesses under the questioning of Sherlock Holmes.

"The fiend had apparently developed a superscientific device of some sort that reduced the stature of his victims to that of pygmies, and he strode away with poor Holmes under one arm and Greystoke under the other."

"Yes," I said encouragingly, "pray continue."

"Well, Dr. Watson," Savage resumed, "as the fiend left the Exposition of European Progress he seemed to be mumbling something to himself. I could barely make out what it was he was saying. But it seemed to be something like Angkor Wat, Angkor Wat. But would could that possibly mean, Watson?"

I smiled condescendingly and turned to the assemblage, who sat in awed silence at the confrontation between Savage and myself. By a tacit gesture I indicated that I would accept information from any of them.

"Is it an exotic drug?" one asked.

"The name of the fiend himself?" another attempted.

"A secret formula of some sort?" queried a third.

"Some religious talisman?"

"A Princeton lineman?"

"The greatest scientist of ancient Neptune?"

"An obsolete nautical term?"

"The seat of an obsolete monarchy?"

"That's it," I cried encouragingly. "I knew the knowledge lay somewhere among you. Angkor Wat is a city lost in the jungles of heathen Asia. We must seek this fiend and his victims in Angkor Wat.

"Quickly," I exclaimed, turning toward Doc Savage, "have transportation made ready at once. We depart for Angkor Wat this night."

"Can I come along?" the Shadow asked, twisting the girasol ring on his finger.

"No, no, take me," the Avenger put in.

"Me," cried Gordon of Yale.

"Me," shouted David Innes. "I know Tarzan personally."

Soon they were all jumping from their seats, jostling one another to approach closest to me and squabbling as to which among them should have the honor of accompanying me on my mission to rescue Sherlock Holmes and John Clayton, Lord Greystoke.

"This is a task for Doc Savage and myself alone," I told them as kindly but definitely as I could. "The remainder of you are to remain here and hold yourselves in readiness should there be a call for your services. Now, Savage," I addressed myself to the man of bronze, "have some of those well-known flunkies of your establishment make ready a vehicle suitable for transporting us to the lost city of Angkor Wat in the jungles of the faraway Orient."

"Yes, sir," he acceded.

Firmness, I vowed, would be the salient feature of my *modus operandi* henceforward onward.

Within minutes a crew of grotesque creatures had prepared one of the strange flying machines, which Doc Savage informed me were known as autogyros, with a plentiful supply of reserve fuel, a wicked-looking advance-design Gatling gun, and belts of ammunition. Almost before there was time to shake hands heartily with each member of the League we were leaving behind, Savage and I were airborne over the arctic wastes.

Before many hours passed, our remarkable autogyro was *whoop-whoop-whooping* its way across the great Eurasian world-island, passing, at one moment, over the very St. Wrycyxlwv's Square, where *The God of the Naked Unicorn* was to be displayed to the distress of The Woman and the disordering of the stability of European civilization, in what was now little more than twenty-four hours, should Doc Savage and I fail in our mission.

We passed over the Germanic and Austro-Hungarian Empires, the semibarbarous Slavic states to their east, fluttered dangerously through frigid snowcapped passes in the sinister Ural Mountains and into Asia. Nothing stopped us, nothing slowed us. Savage's flunkies had equipped the autogyro with numerous auxiliary tanks of fuel and had thoughtfully provided for Savage and myself a huge wicker basket filled with delicate viands.

We passed over teeming Bombay, curved northward tossing clean-picked bones of squab onto the nomad-haunted sands of the Gobi Desert, hovered high above teeming hordes of heathen Chinese as we completed a repast of cold lobster in mayonnaise (dropping the empty carapaces of the aquatic arachnoidea into the hands of awed Orientals) and moved at last across the Gulf of Tonkin, waving greetings to tramp steamers as they plied their routes, until we came once more over land, and I saw far beneath the wheels of the autogyro the green lushness of the ancient jungle.

Shortly my companion and pilot pointed downward toward an opening in the jungle. Through the widely spaced palms I could see the pyramids and temples, colonnades and pagodas of an antique metropolis, one lost for thousands of years and only late rediscovered, to the awe and wonderment of even European scholars.

Doc Savage worked the controls of the autogyro, and we dropped, dropped, dropped through the steaming tropical air, until the rubber-clad wheels of the aerial vehicle rolled to a rest atop the tallest pyramid in Angkor Wat.

We climbed from the autogyro and stood overlooking the ancient city. It was dawn in this quarter of the globe, and somewhere a wild creature screamed its greeting to the sun while great cats padded silently homeward from their nocturnal prowls and birds with feathers like brilliant jewels soared into the air in search of tropical fruits upon which to gorge themselves.

"There's only one place in a city like this where a maniac like our foe would make his headquarters," Doc Savage growled. "That's in the high temple of the sun, and that's why I landed us where I did."

Through the eerie stillness of the jungle metropolis we made our way down the giant granite steps of the pyramidal edifice, pausing now to gasp in awed admiration of the handicraft of some long-forgotten Asiatic artisan, now to kill a poisonous serpent, now to pot a brilliant-plumaged denizen of the airy reaches for the sheer fun and sport of it.

At last we reached the earth, and making our way to a grand colonnade that gave onto the great chamber of the temple, we found the prison chamber of the archfiend—but our prey had flown the coop. Savage and I stood at the torture device of the maniac, chilled not so much by its massiveness—for it was smaller than an ordinary kit bag—as by the malignant potentialities in its complex controls.

Clearly the fiend and his victims had been here shortly before us, and the villain had fled in haste, abandoning his infernal device as he made good his escape. And yet, the very carelessness exhibited by the malefactor suggested that he owned as bad or worse and was keeping them somewhere other, to which place he had repaired, victims in tow.

Savage and I sprinted back to the autogyro, pausing only to ferret out such clues as were required to determine the destination of the fleeing fiend and his captives.

Thus pursued we them from Angkor Wat to bustling, modern Tokio, thence to mystery-shrouded Easter Island, where we wandered among the strange monolithic sculptures in bafflement until Doc Savage summoned the talents of the Green Lama by remote communication. That luminary induced one of the weird statues to reveal to Savage and myself that it had observed the fiend and his two captives only minutes earlier than our arrival, departing on a course dead set for the American settlement of Peoria in the province of Illinois.

We pounded our way across the Pacific, the autogyro's rotors *whoop-whoop-whooping* as we fled from day back into night.

We passed above the gleaming lights of San Francisco harbor, rose to the frigid heights as we passed over the Rocky Mountains, dropped low again to wave to a cowpoke here, a sourdough there, and we saw the sun rise once again before we reached Peoria.

Less than a day left to us. My horrified mind's eye pictured the scene at St. Wrycyxlwv's Square and the inevitable disintegration of world order that must follow—especially in the absence of those two saviors of the sane and the normal, Holmes and Greystoke.

Each outpost of the fiend, as we uncovered it, revealed him to have abandoned a similar but more hideously advanced model of his infernal torture device, its case glistening, its control panel studded with keys and levers, each marked with some arcane abbreviation of alphabetical or cabalistic significance known only to the torturer and—I inferred with a shudder—to Sherlock Holmes and John Clayton.

From Illinois the trail led to an abandoned warehouse located on New York City's lower Seventh Avenue. There Savage and I found more and different devices of the fiend's trade, and heard a distant door slam at the far end of the building even as our boots pounded angrily after the fleeing maniac.

We pursued him down a long tunnel that seemed to dip and curve away beneath the very bedrock of the island of Manhattan, then there was a rumble—a flash—an uncanny sensation of twisting and wrenching, and Savage and I found ourselves standing side by side outside the very London kiosk where The Woman had brought me at the outset of my weird odyssey.

"Where now?" Savage gasped frantically, consulting a chronometer that he wore conveniently strapped to the wrist of one mighty bronze limb.

I thought for a moment, wondering where in the great metropolis the maniac would go. Suddenly I was seized by a stroke of inspiration. I grasped the bronzed giant by one elbow and with him raced to the nearest hack stand, where we engaged the second carriage in line. I stammered my instructions to the cabby and he set off at a rapid clip, the hooves of the horses clop-copping over the London cobblestones to my great comfort and relief until we drew up before a familiar old building where I had spent many happy years in the past.

I tossed a coin to the cabby, and Savage and I raced up the stairs, hammered frantically at the doorway of the ground-story flat, and urged its occupant, the owner and resident manager of the establishment, to join us in our mission above and to bring her pass key with her as she did so.

As that good woman turned her key in the lock to the upper flat Savage burst open the door with a single thrust of his mighty bronze shoulder and I stepped past him, revolver in hand, and surveyed the scene within.

There I beheld the fiend seated at his infernal machine, operating its keys and levers with maniacal rapidity while upon the table beside him I saw the pitifully shrunken figures of Sherlock Holmes and John Clayton, dancing and twirling with each strike of the keys of the maniac's machine. To one side of the machine stood a huge stack of pages covered with typed writings. To the other stood an even taller stack of blank pages waiting to be covered with words.

A single sheet was in the fiend's machine, and each time he struck a key a new letter appeared upon the page, and with each word I could see the pain upon the faces of the two heroes growing greater as their stature grew less.

"Halt, fiend!" I shouted.

The maniac turned in his seat and leered maniacally up at Savage and myself. His hair was white, his face satanically handsome, yet marked with the signs of long debauchery and limitless self-indulgence.

"So, Savage"—he lipped grimly—"and Watson. You have found me, have you. Well, small good that will do you. No man can stand in the way of Albert Payson Agricola. You have played into my hand. You see—there are your two compatriots. All of the rest in your moronic League will follow. And I alone shall possess *The God of the Naked Unicorn.*" And with that he gestured grandly toward a table on the opposite side of the room.

There, on the very mahogany where my gasogene had stood for so many years between Holmes's violin case and his hypodermic apparatus, there now reposed the silvery and begemmed majesty of Mendez-Rubirosa's masterpiece, *The God of the Naked Unicorn.*

"And now," Agricola hissed triumphantly, "I shall add two more trophies to my collection of puppets and husks."

He bent to the keyboard of his infernal device and struck this lever, then that. With each strike I either felt a jolt of galvanic dynamism scream through my own organism or saw poor Savage writhe in bronzed agony.

"Stop it," I managed to howl at the fiend. "Stop it or—"

He struck still another key. SUDDENLY I FELT HUGELY MAGNIFIED AND EMPOWERED. I JERKED THE TRIGGER OF MY REVOLVER AND ALBERT PAYSON AGRICOLA FLUNG HIS ARMS OUTWARD. HIS ELBOW STRuck a lever on the machine, and I returned to normal. I saw Doc Savage at my side massaging his painfully twisted limbs. I saw Sherlock Holmes and Tarzan of the Apes beginning with infinite slowness and yet by perceptible degrees to regain their proper form and stature.

Albert Payson Agricola fell to the carpet, a hole neatly drilled between his eyes.

From the wound there seemed to flow neither blood nor spattered brains but shred after shred of dry, yellow, smearily imprinted wood pulp paper.

About the Authors

Michael Mallory ("The Beast of Guangming Peak") A freelance entertainment journalist working out of Los Angeles, Michael Mallory has published more than 250 magazine and newspaper articles. He is also the author of some seventy short stories, including "Curiosity Kills," which won the Derringer Award from the Short Mystery Fiction Society for Best "Flash" Mystery Story of 1997, and has had short fiction in publications ranging from *Discovery Magazine*, the inflight publication of Hong Kong Airlines, to *Fox Kids Magazine*. His Amelia Watson stories have appeared in various publications, and twelve of them are collected in the book, *The Adventures of the Second Mrs. Watson*. The first Amelia Watson novel, *Murder in the Bath*, is in bookstores now.

Carolyn Wheat ("Water from the Moon") Students at the University of California at San Diego are fortunate to have Carolyn Wheat as a writing instructor, as anyone who has taken any of her writing workshops around the country can testify. She is a winner of the Agatha, Macavity, Anthony, and Shamus awards for her short stories, and her book *How to Write Killer Fiction* has been described by *Booklist* as an indispensable guide for writers of mystery and suspense.

Peter Beagle ("Mr. Sigerson") Peter Beagle has a way with words. And imagery. And characterization. As can be seen in over a dozen novels and short story collections, including *A Fine and Private Place*, *The Last Unicorn*, and *I See by My Outfit*. He also writes short stories, screenplays, teleplays, and the occasional libretto, and conducts writing workshops, along with giving readings, lectures, and concerts. The concerts? Beagle is a folk singer of some note and four languages—English, French, German, and Yiddish—who has played at various venues around California and a few other states. As he has said, "Singing and dishwashing are the only other things I've done for money."

Linda Robertson ("The Mystery of Dr. Thorvald Sigerson") Linda Robertson practices criminal law with a San Francisco–based nonprofit law firm. She has published nonfiction in the *San Francisco Chronicle*, the online magazine *Salon,* and the *CACJ (California Attorneys for Criminal Justice) Forum*, and is the coauthor of *The Complete Idiot's Guide to Unsolved Mysteries,* which covers topics ranging from UFOs and Bigfoot to who really wrote Shakespeare's plays.

This is Robertson's second foray into the world of Sherlock Holmes, the first, "Mrs. Hudson Reminisces," appeared in *My Sherlock Holmes*.

Rhys Bowen ("The Case of the Lugubrious Manservant") The author of the extremely readable Constable Evans novels, set in her maternal homeland of Wales, Rhys Bowen grew up in Bath, England, and went to school in England, Austria, and Germany. After having her first play, *Dandelion Hours,* produced by the BBC in London, Rhys fled to Sydney, Australia, and went to work for Australian broadcasting. In 1966 she and her husband settled in San Francisco, where she has been ever since, entertaining the English-speaking world with award-winning children's books, young adult books, historical romances, and mysteries. Her latest series, the Molly Murphy mysteries, traces the adventures of a young Irish immigrant girl in the New York City of a century ago. Molly is brash, bright, liberated, and, as they said in New York a century ago, has plenty of moxie.

Bill Pronzini ("The Bughouse Caper") Versatile, prolific, imaginative, and one of the finest prose stylists in the known universe, Bill Pronzini is the author of sixty novels, including three in collaboration with his wife, novelist Marcia Muller, and twenty-nine in his popular "Nameless Detective" series. He has written four nonfiction books, ten collections of short stories, and scores of uncollected stories, articles, essays, book reviews, and napkin doodles, and he has edited or coedited numerous anthologies. His work has been translated into eighteen languages and published in nearly thirty countries. He has received three Shamus awards, two for Best Novel, and the Lifetime Achievement Award from the Private Eye Writers of America, as well as six nominations for the Mystery Writers of America Edgar award.

Michael Kurland ("Reichenbach") The author of over thirty novels and a melange of short stories, articles, and other stuff, Michael Kurland gave up his career in the theater and took up writing when the horse died. His stories are set in epochs and locations from ancient Rome to the far future; anyplace the reader won't spot anachronisms too easily. His works have been nominated for two Edgars and an American Book award, and have appeared in many languages, sometimes three or four on the same page. They are believed to be fragments of one great opus, a study of the *untermensch*. Kurland has written four novels and a cluster of short stories about Professor James Moriarty. More can be learned at his Web site: michaelkurland.com.

Carole Bugge ("The Strange Case of the Voodoo Priestess") Playwright, author, and teacher, Carole Bugge has enriched us with the variety of her accomplishments. Her plays have been performed at The Players Club, The Van Dam Street Playhouse, Manhattan Punchline, and Playwrights Horizons in New York City. And, as everyone knows, if you can make it there, you can make it anywhere. Her mystery novels include *The Star of India* and *The Haunting of Torre Abbey*.

Gary Lovisi ("The Adventure of the Missing Detective") A recognized Holmes aficionado and knowledgeable person, Gary Lovisi has written several previous Holmes pastiches, including "The Loss of the British Bark Sophy Anderson," and "Mycroft's Great Game." He is the author of the reference bibliography *Sherlock Holmes: The Great Detective in Paperback*, and the editor of *Paperback Parade*, the leading publication on collectible paperbacks in the world. As a publisher this many-faceted gentleman has published Holmes pastiches by several authors, as well as a variety of nonfiction Sherlockiana.

Lovisi will welcome, or at least tolerate, comments addressed to him at his Web site: www.gryphonbooks.com.

Michael Collins (Dennis Lynds) ("Cross of Gold") In 1967 Dennis Lynds wrote the first Dan Fortune detective novel using the *nom de machine à écrire* of Michael Collins. At the time he was also Mark Sadler, John Crowe, William Arden, and Carl Dekker. There are now twenty Dan Fortune books, the latest being *Fortune's World*, a short-story collection. He has won many awards, including an Edgar and two Edgar nominations, and collected many honors, including Private Eye Writers of America's Lifetime Achievement Award and a Special Commendation from the West German *Arbeitsgemeinschaft Kriminalliteratur*.

Richard Lupoff ("God of the Naked Unicorn") This final story is set in the world of Richard Lupoff's alter ego, Ova Hamlet. For, as the French put it so well, *Ova Hamlet est un pseudonyme de Richard Lupoff*. Ova is the master of parody as "God of the Naked Unicorn" proves beyond any possible probable shadow of doubt.

Lupoff has dwelt in the world of Sherlock Holmes before, in such stories as "The Case of the Doctor Who Had No Business," "The Adventure of the Boulevard Assassin," and "The Adventure of the Ghooric Sign." Lupoff's story "The Incident of the Impecunious Chevalier," which appeared in a previous Holmsian anthology, *My Sherlock Holmes*, was selected for reprint in the *Best American Mystery Stories 2004*. And we are all proud of him.